MW01154703

A Rational Attachment

LAUREN GILBERT

WITH ALL BEST WISHES,

Lauren Gilbert

authorHOUSE

AuthorHouse™
1663 Liberty Drive
Bloomington, IN 47403
www.authorhouse.com
Phone: 1 (800) 839-8640

©2019 Lauren Gilbert. All rights reserved.

Cover art by Brenda Brunello, Logan, UT Copyright (c) Lauren Gilbert 2019

No part of this book may be reproduced, stored in a retrieval system, or
transmitted by any means without the written permission of the author.

Published by AuthorHouse 12/23/2019

ISBN: 978-1-7283-3802-6 (sc)
ISBN: 978-1-7283-3800-2 (hc)
ISBN: 978-1-7283-3801-9 (e)

Library of Congress Control Number: 2019919337

Print information available on the last page.

This book is printed on acid-free paper.

Because of the dynamic nature of the Internet, any web addresses or links contained in
this book may have changed since publication and may no longer be valid. The views
expressed in this work are solely those of the author and do not necessarily reflect the
views of the publisher, and the publisher hereby disclaims any responsibility for them.

This is a work of fiction. All of the characters, names, incidents, organizations, and dialogue
in this novel are either the products of the author's imagination or are used fictitiously.

Dedication

To four women who encouraged me, influenced me and guided me: the assistant director of the public library, my two favourite English teachers and, most of all, my mother. My love and gratitude to you.

Special thanks to Brenda, Beth, Mimi and Deb for their advice and encouragement.

Chapter 1

M r Walter Emmons sat at his desk and stared at his clasped hands resting in front of him. Anne was his youngest child and the pride of his heart, but he could not deny she had an odd kick to her gallop. (He had recently purchased a horse to run in the York Races, so tended to think in equine terms at present.) He looked around his library and hoped to gain inspiration, but saw nothing but his grandfather's portrait over the fireplace. Anne bewildered Walter.

Anne's mother, Walter's beloved Caroline, died when Anne was very small, which circumstance left Walter to manage her as best he could. Anne was nine years old when her father decided to send her away to school. After thorough consideration, Mr. Emmons chose a most exclusive young ladies' seminary in Bath for little Anne, and made sure she had all of the extras: dancing and languages, as well as special masters for the pianoforte and the harp and drawing.

He deliberately selected a school with students drawn from some of the finest families in England with a view for Anne's future friendships. In spite of her shyness and isolation at school, Anne made one friend, Frances Mary Catherine Kidwell. Fanny was a lively girl, a few years older than Anne. The only child of a baronet situated in Kent, she and Anne were friends at first glance. The two girls became inseparable, sharing lessons and free time. That summer, Fanny invited Anne to visit her home for a month. Mr

Emmons and Miss Crawford in the post chaise escorted Anne to Fanny's home near Sittingbourne, in Kent.

A few years later, the two girls, with Anne just entering her teens and Fanny fast becoming a young lady, walked out with Miss Crawford whilst their fathers sat in Mr Emmons' comfortable, book-lined library as they congratulated each other on successful business ventures. Lord Kidwell had said, "I can make certain Anne gets an introduction to society, if you like. My wife plans to bring Fanny out in soon, when she is eighteen. Anne will still be too young, but I am sure there will be opportunities to introduce her about, let her see something of Society with Fanny there to lend support." Mr Emmons thanked Lord Kidwell but thought little more about the matter.

As he looked back over their long friendship, Mr Emmons sighed heavily. He had hoped Anne would settle long before now. At almost twenty-three years of age, she had long participated in the social seasons at home in York, and in London. Lord and Lady Kidwell had done their best by Anne, put her in the way of meeting eligible young men, even arranging for her presentation. Somehow Anne had just never "taken." Even at home in York, acting as his hostess, she had entertained numerous young men, ranging from young fashionables in town for the races to successful young merchants and bankers. She had never indicated the slightest *tendre* for any of the young men. Well, he would have to take a hand, distasteful as he found it.

Unaware of her father's concerns, Anne sighed and picked up the letter from Fanny again. She read it for the second time, concerned by the urgent tone. She moved to the sitting room window and looked out at the sunlit garden. "Poor Fanny. Who could have imagined matters would develop as they did?" Glancing at the last paragraph, she read again, *"Pray, let me come to you in York. I cannot be in Kent when he arrives. I will not see him. If this time is not convenient for me to visit there, could you and Miss Crawford accompany me for a holiday? We could visit the Highlands or the Lake Country, possibly go abroad. I must be otherwhere before the end of the month. Please, Anne, do not fail me.*" Anne's thoughts drifted back over the history of their friendship and of Fanny's current dilemma.

As girls, Anne and Fanny continued their studies at the seminary in Bath until just before Fanny's eighteenth birthday. Fanny's mother decided Fanny needed to come home to learn how to conduct herself in Society before her presentation. "No daughter of mine will be pushed into Society straight from the schoolroom," she declared. "You can always identify the ill-prepared little wretches by their titters and giggles, their pertness, and their complete lack of rational conversation." That May, Lord Kidwell took a house in York for the York Races and Lady Kidwell planned a series of small dinners and entertainments to introduce Fanny to adult social activities. Mr Emmons was invited to these events, as was Anne invited to those suitable to her age.

After the Kidwell family returned to Kent, Anne begged her father not to send her back to the academy. "I cannot bear it without Fanny and I can continue my studies at home with Miss Crawford. Besides, Papa, if I am to keep house for you, I must learn what must be done, and *that* is not taught at school!" Unwilling to admit how much he had missed her and how glad he would be to have her at home, Mr Emmons held out for a little time before he conceded.

Delighted to be at home, Anne applied herself diligently to home management with Mrs Hubbard, the housekeeper, and picked up the threads of her friendships, especially with Jenny Chamberlayne. Miss Crawford continued to guide her reading and encouraged an interest in the Grey Coat School for girls in York. That winter, Anne journeyed to London with Fanny and her mother to watch whilst Fanny became one of the Season's belles. Their friendship was warm as ever.

Tall, slender, with silvery blonde curls, and unusually dark grey eyes, Fanny looked like a fairy princess in the whites and pastels favoured for debutantes. Anne's glossy dark, almost black, hair, and violet blue eyes made a striking contrast, but her lack of height and sturdier frame meant the ethereal styles so becoming to Fanny did not flatter her at all. Anne consoled herself with the thought that her complexion was almost as fair as Fanny's. She imagined the two of them would be a dazzling pair in a few years, when she was old enough to make her own debut. She stayed with the Kidwells for two months, vicariously enjoying Fanny's season enormously, before Miss Crawford escorted her home to York.

Frequent letters flew back and forth between London or Kent and York, keeping Anne abreast of Fanny's affairs. When Fanny became engaged, she begged Anne to come to London to take part in the Season with her and to be present for the betrothal dinner. Mr Emmons was dubious: Anne, at almost seventeen, was younger than some young ladies making their debut and Fanny would be preoccupied. Anne cajoled and pleaded until she convinced him to send her with Miss Crawford.

"Well," Mr Emmons conceded, "you'll have your way. Mind, you listen to Lady Kidwell and Miss Crawford, my girl. They will put you in the way of things and Lady Kidwell will make sure you meet the right people." Right after Christmas, Anne and Miss Crawford were packed into the comfortable chaise with their trunks, bandboxes and bundles, and set off for London.

The next few weeks were a whirl of shopping trips. Fanny and Anne, under the watchful eye of Miss Crawford, enjoyed excursions to Millard's where they purchased fabrics, trimmings, silk stockings and such goods for less than the cost at the more fashionable *modistes'* wares. Miss Crawford lectured on the concepts of prudence and practicality, even as they purchased the components of a frivolous costume. She also encouraged Anne to look for the clear colours that suited her dark hair and fair, creamy complexion and emphasised the unusual violet blue of her eyes. After several long and agonising sessions at the *modiste*'s shop (Anne was sure half the pins were permanently embedded in her sides), the new clothes both girls had commissioned were delivered. Suitably gowned, Anne was ready to make her first appearance in Society. Unfortunately, it seemed likely to be her last....

Fanny had entered Society at Almack's and encouraged her mother to consider a smaller, private affair for Anne. "She is so shy, Mother, and the Patronesses can be very intimidating. Would it not be better for Anne to meet a few people, to form some acquaintance first?" Lady Kidwell considered the matter and was forced to concur with her daughter. She remembered an invitation. "Fanny, run down to the drawing room and gather the invitation cards on the table near the window." Upon Fanny's return, the two ladies leafed through them. At the bottom of the pile, Lady Kidwell espied what she sought.

"Just the thing!" she exclaimed. "My dear friend, Mrs Julia Eastland, is holding a rout party to introduce her niece next week! You surely remember her, my dear. She and I were friends as girls. I understand the young lady is near your age and I am certain Mrs Eastland will be delighted to include Anne amongst the guests. We should call on her tomorrow. It seems ideal – with all of the attention focused on the niece, Anne will have the opportunity to meet people and be seen in public without strain." Fanny applauded her mother's idea.

The next day, Lady Kidwell, accompanied by Fanny and Anne, called on Mrs Eastland. Mrs Eastland was delighted to extend an invitation to the rout party to Anne. "I regret my niece is from home this afternoon. Another tiresome fitting, I am afraid. Louisa will be so sorry to have missed you." Anne blushed and thanked Mrs Eastland in an almost inaudible voice. Fanny noticed her friend's discomfiture and added her thanks as well. "We look forward to your party, Mrs Eastland. It will be Anne's first social event and I am delighted to be able to introduce my dear friend to such unexceptionable company." Mrs Eastland inclined her head graciously. "Yes, my dear, I flatter myself that it will be a small but select group. I will be honoured to have you all present." After more compliments, Lady Kidwell rose. "Thank you for your kindness, my dear Julia. We must take our leave as Fanny and Anne have fittings themselves. Pray, call on us soon with your niece. We are eager to know her."

As they walked down the steps to the barouche, Lady Kidwell said with satisfaction, "It could not be better, girls. My dear Anne, you will be charmed – a small, select gathering of young people. Just what is needed to introduce you gradually to society." She glanced at Anne and added kindly, "I hope you will work to overcome your shyness, my love. I am aware that London society is new to you but you have attended social gatherings at home. Your manners are above reproach and you need not hide in a corner. We have made certain you are properly gowned well before the party. You will see, you need take second place to no one." The door of the carriage closed behind them and they bowled on to the *modiste*'s shop for a final fitting.

Chapter 2

A week later, Anne found herself back in the carriage, accompanied by Fannie and Lady Kidwell, on their way to the rout party. Fanny looked most becoming in filmy white, embroidered with silver motifs, whilst Lady Kidwell was resplendent in rich blue silk, lavishly trimmed with golden braid and fringe. Anne privately considered herself almost unrecognisable, dark hair twisted up in a knot and soft curls falling about her face, gowned in soft lilac muslin trimmed with delicate lace, wearing her late mother's amethyst earbobs and a matching hair ornament. Her blue-violet eyes, enhanced by the colour of her gown, rivalled the deep purple glow of the amethysts. For the first time, she saw herself as grown up, equal to Fanny.

Although she was still nervous about meeting sophisticated strangers, Anne took comfort from the thought that she looked well and her best friend was with her. Anne was startled when she met the hostile eyes of Mrs Eastland's niece, Louisa Dixon, in the receiving line. However, as she made her way down the line, her pleasure was restored by the warmth of Mrs Eastland's greeting. She followed Lady Kidwell and Fanny to a room set aside for the ladies to leave their wraps and on to the drawing room. Lady Kidwell headed for a group of her oldest friends near the fire where they discussed a new novel. Conversation halted briefly as she introduced Anne. The ladies acknowledged Anne kindly and returned to their chatter.

Fanny whisked Anne over to two of her own friends, as they

looked over some music at the pianoforte in the corner. "Eleanor, Mary, I want to make you known to my dearest friend, Anne Emmons. She is visiting from York, come for my engagement ball. Anne, my dear, these are two of my closest friends in town, Eleanor Wentworth and Mary Jamison." Both girls offered their hands to Anne and they fell to discussing their musical preferences. Anne listened as Fanny and her friends cheerfully debated their musical choices, content to look around her.

As more young people joined them round the pianoforte, it was only a matter of time before someone would begin to play. Her head in a whirl of new names and faces, Anne looked for a discreet seat from which she could listen and watch. Before she could make her escape, Fanny took her arm and whispered, "Oh, no, do not think it! I know you too well and will not allow you to hide in a corner all the evening! Never fear, I will not abandon you. Just stay with me." As Eleanor began to play a popular ballad, the crowded drawing room was filled to capacity and beyond. The music and the heat swirled through the room and ladies flicked open their fans. The women by the drawing room fire gave up their seats and retired to the library for cards, where several tables had been made ready for whist and piquet.

During a break in the music, Louisa made her presence felt. Unbecomingly flushed from the heat, her curls starting to droop, Louisa did not look her best. Her high-pitched voice penetrated the chatter as she said to someone near her, "The veriest nobody, my dear! A friend of my aunt asked that we take pity on the poor thing. I believe her father is in trade or some such thing." Anne froze as Louisa and her friend moved away, not daring to look up from the sheet music in her hand. Fanny paled in outrage, and held Anne's other hand tightly. She pulled her friend to the pianoforte and pushed her gently to the seat. "My dear friend Anne will play for me," she announced gaily to the crowd.

Anne blindly began to play an air that she and Fanny had often enjoyed, a gay ballad popular a few years before. Fanny began to sing, and her sweet soprano recaptured the attention that had been distracted by Louisa's malicious remarks. As she played, Anne began to recover her shattered poise, winking back tears. Surely Louisa had been talking about herself, Anne thought. "Why is she so unkind? We haven't spoken a word to each other, beyond a courtesy in passing." After the ballad was finished, the group around the pianoforte clamoured for Mary Jamison to play. Fanny and Anne unobtrusively melted away from the group, finding an abandoned window seat where they sat down to catch their breath.

"Anne, take no notice of her," urged Fanny. "We cannot be certain she even spoke of you." "Who else could it be?" asked Anne, miserably. "I seem to be the only stranger here tonight. Why would she say such unkind things, Fanny? I have done nothing to her." Fanny glanced across the room at Louisa. Tall, almost painfully thin, lank brown hair crimped into curls already becoming limp and dishevelled, Louisa was laughing with a group of her own particular friends. Fanny had no doubt that jealousy prompted Louisa's verbal attack.

The contrast between Louisa and Anne was almost painful. When added to the fact that Louisa's portion was respectable at best, Fanny had every reason to consider Louisa's comments the opening salvo in a concerted attempt to create difficulties for Anne. "Obviously, she is displeased at having another young lady introduced to society at her party, my dear. I fancy she is jealous of you. It should be fairly easy to avoid her – this is such a squeeze!" replied Fanny.

Just then, the butler announced that supper was served in the dining room. Fanny and Anne joined Lady Kidwell in the hall and the three made their way to the dining room. Anne was dismayed when they were separated almost immediately. Anne lost Fanny and Lady Kidwell in the throng, but found a place at a table where Fanny's friends Mary and Eleanor were seated.

Eleanor kindly included Anne in the conversation and one of the gentlemen brought Anne a plate of refreshments. Gratefully,

Anne thanked him. As she listened to Mary describe a visit to the Lake Country with her family, Anne managed to eat a few bites of her supper. She gradually relaxed and began to enjoy herself again as she responded to Eleanor's question about her friendship with Fanny. "We were at school together in Bath, and have visited back and forth. Our fathers have become great friends," replied Anne. The conversation became more general as the others began to reminisce about school days, governesses and tutors. A great deal of laughter ensued as each recalled pranks and mischief.

Anne retired to the background again, enjoying the opportunity to listen to the conversation. Eleanor and Mary were the only persons at the table to whom she had been introduced, and Eleanor belatedly rectified the situation. "Anne, my dear, I am so sorry! I have been remiss. Let me introduce you." She went around the table and introduced Anne to each young lady and gentleman. Anne responded correctly to each, feeling flustered and conspicuous, forgetting each name as the next was produced. Supper ended and they rose to return to the drawing room.

As Anne surveyed the room, looking for Fanny or her mother, someone touched her arm. "I am certain you don't recall my name," she smiled. "I am Emily DeWitt. Are you making your come-out this year, too?" Emily was the same height as Anne, with glossy auburn curls and green eyes. Deep dimples in both cheeks made her smile infectious. Involuntarily, Anne smiled back and replied, "I am pleased to make your acquaintance. Yes, I will be presented this year."

As they made their way back to the drawing room, Emily said, "I am delighted to meet another new face. I felt like the only unknown here!" Innocently, Anne asked, "I understand this party is held in honour of Mrs Eastland's niece, Miss Louisa Dixon. Is she not making her debut this year as well?"

Emily shook her head, "No, this is Louisa's second season. Mrs Eastland is determined, this year, Louisa will be a Success. Are you staying with Fanny and her family?" "Yes, indeed I am. They are so kind. They have invited me to spend the next few months with them, to share in Fanny's engagement parties and celebrations."

"My sister knows Fanny well. We will come to call on you and you must come to us as well. You will like my sister. Kate is the dearest thing in nature! She could not be here tonight because of an epidemic cold or I could introduce you at once," rejoined Emily.

Near by, two older gentlemen stood near a window watched the company, unmistakeably bored, and continued a conversation. Because of the music and chatter, they raised their voices to be heard. "Miss Dixon assures me the entire family is *déclassé*. Provincial merchants at best. Apparently, Kidwell became entangled with them in York and cannot avoid the acquaintance." The other man snorted, "Well, that is no excuse to inflict them on Society!"

Condescendingly, the first man observed, "Well, nothing wrong with the girl's appearance, at any rate. Pretty enough, conducts herself well. I have heard there is a huge dowry; that could make a difference, you know. Plenty of good families are cash-poor these days." The second man retorted, "Still smells of the shop, old man! No, no, I would not welcome such a mushroom into *my* family." They moved away as Anne froze into silence.

Emily looked at Anne in concern. "What is wrong, Miss Emmons? Are you ill?" Anne flushed and then paled, not even hearing Emily's questions as she turned over what had been said in her mind. Miss Dixon … Louisa! She was continuing to spread her unkind gossip. She raised her head and caught Emily's eye. She flushed deeply and stammered, "I – I am sorry, Miss DeWitt, I did not hear you. Did you say something?"

Emily glanced toward the two retreating men, and back to Anne. "Miss Emmons, Anne, I cannot pretend I did not hear the conversation between those two gentlemen. I do not know what their remarks mean to you. However, I must tell you Louisa Dixon is widely recognised for her malicious tongue. Please do not pay attention to her."

Anne smiled gratefully, but could not be sanguine. "You are most kind. I ... I have the headache a bit. I believe I will look for Lady Kidwell to see if I could go home. I hope we meet again." Emily squeezed her hand and asserted, "I can assure you we will. Will you be at home tomorrow?" "Yes, I will," Anne replied, and instantly resolved to stay in. "I will call on you, then, with my sister Kate if she is recovered."

Anne rose and made her way to the library, where she found Lady Kidwell rising to take her leave. Gracefully, Anne made her curtsey to her hostess, put on her wraps and waited in the hall for Lady Kidwell to find Fanny and take her leave as well. Fanny and her mother chattered happily about the evening, whilst Anne's face flushed deeply. She was mortified as she recalled all she had overheard, and was determined not to put herself in position to be so humiliated again.

Chapter 3

The next day, Fanny asked Anne bluntly about the previous evening. "Did you not enjoy it, Anne? I am sorry we did not sit together at supper. I did look for you..." Carefully, Anne replied, "Your friend Eleanor was most kind. I sat at her table and she introduced me to a great many people. Are you acquainted Emily DeWitt?" "Yes, I am. Her sister Kate and I have long been friends. She will be my other attendant," Fanny answered.

"Your 'other' attendant? I didn't realise your plans were so far advanced!" cried Anne. "Who else will attend you?" "Who else indeed, silly, but you, of course! We shan't have a large wedding party but it wouldn't be complete without you and Kate. I know you will like each other. Emily is your age, and a sweet girl. I am glad you are making friends." Distracted by talk of Fanny's wedding, the two girls did not refer to Mrs Eastland's rout again.

Lady Kidwell brought the party up again at breakfast to Anne's discomfiture. "What a nice evening! Julia's suppers are always so well chosen and she makes such careful arrangements for her guests. I must say, I was rather shocked by her niece. She has become so thin and sharp-tongued." Anne paled as Fanny said, "I have never known her well but she does seem to be rather ... *acidic* this year, Mama. She was most unpleasant about Anne."

Sharply, Lady Kidwell turned to Anne. "Louisa, unpleasant, my dear? What did she say?" Miserable, Anne hung her head and repeated Louisa's remarks and then told of the two men she had overheard. Fanny and her mother looked at each other, appalled. "Anne, my dear, I must apologise," said Fanny's mother. "I would not have you subjected to such an ordeal for worlds."

Anne lifted her chin. "What did she say that was untrue, ma'am? My father's family did earn their fortune through trade. My father has active business and banking interests. I am not ashamed of him. However, I didn't consider that, in London, society might view our family through such a narrow lens. In York, society is less rigid, less unforgiving. My first two years at school taught me that I am a nobody in society, but I had forgotten. Now I am only afraid I might be an embarrassment to you and to Fanny. Do you not think I should go home to York...?" Fanny broke in hotly before Anne could continue. "What? Run back to York? Indeed, you shan't! You could never be an embarrassment; you are my dearest friend! Do you think I am so shallow?"

Lady Kidwell raised her hand. "Girls, we must discuss this calmly. Mr Emmons' connexion to trade is certainly a consideration. It's important to note that he has been successful, and owns a great deal of land as well. As well, his birth is by no means a disgrace, and he is a well-educated, well-spoken man whom my husband is proud to consider a friend." She looked at Anne kindly. "Your mother's family was entirely respectable. We've always been happy to welcome you as Fanny's friend. You mustn't let the malice of an ignorant young woman overset you." Mollified, Anne allowed herself to be convinced to remain in London. Still, she held to her resolve to stay in whilst Fanny and Lady Kidwell paid calls this day.

Anne sat in the drawing room attended by Miss Crawford that afternoon. Each lady was occupied with needlework. Anne gave Miss Crawford an unvarnished account of the previous evening, and the discussion with Fanny and her mother that morning. Miss Crawford said nothing whilst Anne talked, and sat for a few minutes after Anne finished. "What do you think, Miss Crawford? Am I right to stay? If I do stay, how will I face those people? I was ready to sink, I was so mortified!" Miss Crawford took up her needlework again. "Frankly, my dear, this is an issue you must face eventually. You are an heiress, whose father's money comes from trade. Whilst your great-grandfather built the family fortunes as a merchant, your family includes many of respectable birth as well."

Anne reflected. Her mother was connected to a most distinguished Yorkshire family and her father's mother's family was imminently respectable. Miss Crawford continued, "Miss Dixon is unlikely to be significantly better born than you are. Your father received a gentleman's education and owns several large properties that generate a significant portion of his income in addition to his activities in banking and trade. He educated your brothers and you as thoroughly as children at the highest level of society. Many prominent families have shored up their fortunes by alliances with those having much less to recommend them. You will, of course, have to decide how you really feel about your father's situation, and your own value."

Anne considered Miss Crawford's words. *Value...* She suddenly realised she had felt unworthy, somehow lacking. Miss Crawford looked down her nose. "Besides it is a well-known fact that heiresses have their own advantages. Rank and money are all very well, and only a foolish person pretends they are not. None the less, the contents of an individual's brain and heart must also be considered. Better unwed than tied to a person who is an ignorant fool or someone with no kindness at heart." Anne raised her head. "Thank you, ma'am. You have given me much to consider. You are very wise."

The next few weeks passed in a blur of activity. Emily and Kate came to call, a call happily returned by Fanny and Anne. Lord and Lady Kidwell hosted a formal dinner and elegant ball at which the climax was the announcement of Fanny's betrothal to an imminently suitable young man, Mr Carleton Thomas, with whom she was completely in love. Subsequently, both girls were plunged into a maelstrom of gaiety: breakfasts, card parties, shopping, and more rout parties. Louisa remained a sore spot in the back of Anne's mind like a bruise, painful only when touched. Finally, their activities culminated in Anne's first visit to Almack's.

To Lady Kidwell's surprise, Lady Jersey, with whom she was only slightly acquainted, provided Anne's vouchers. Fanny and Lady Kidwell, with Anne, made a party with Emily, Kate and their mother. Fanny's *fiancé,* Carleton Thomas, met them there. Anne thought them the perfect couple, Carleton whose tall, dark good looks complemented the fair and slender Fanny. Lady Jersey produced a partner for Anne for the first set, and she danced almost every dance for the rest of the evening, except for an occasional pause to rest.

Anne and Emily kept each other company at these moments, sitting in chairs near the floor, as they watched Fanny and Kate swirl by. As they chatted, Anne looked up and met the gaze of a man whose face looked vaguely familiar. He was one of the two men at Mrs Eastland's rout party! She flushed slightly, put up her chin and looked back at him, then let her gaze wander away, as if uninterested.

The dance ended. Fanny and Kate returned to chatter with them, and, under the cover of laughter, Anne asked Fanny, "Fanny, who is that gentleman over there?" Fanny glanced casually over her shoulder. "Propping up the wall? He is Mr Hopecroft. I had not noticed him here. Everyone is aware that he is all to pieces. It's a shame; his family is an old and distinguished one. He has searched for an heiress for his son for this age. Why do you ask?" Anne murmured something noncommittal. The rest of the evening passed in a whirl of gaiety.

Looking back, Anne could hardly believe she had been in town for several weeks already. Lady Kidwell had arranged for Anne's presentation at a Drawing Room, in which Fanny was also included, and all three ladies had ordered elaborate toilettes for the occasion. Anne was drilled mercilessly in the management of her hoops and feathers, the curtsey, and the all-important technique of backing away without tripping over the obligatory train. Her gown of creamy white silk, delicately embroidered and sewn with pearls, did not flatter her small, sturdy frame, although the colour set off her eyes and glossy dark curls. Standing next to Fanny, she moaned, "I appear almost as wide as I am tall, like a box! *Why* must I wear hoops? They're so old-fashioned!"

Fanny, who looked as though she had stepped out of a portrait from the last century, sympathised with her. "The hoops are awkward, but the Court fashions have never kept up with the current mode. The embroidery and lace are lovely and your pearls are perfect. At least, you look better than most!" Fanny wore her favourite white silk with a lace overdress, diamond drops in her ears, and a diamond hair ornament to hold her plumes in place. "It is unfair," complained Anne. "You look like a fairy princess out of an old story book, whilst I look...."

"Not another word!" exclaimed Lady Kidwell. "You both look prodigiously elegant, and I am proud of you." Fanny's mother looked positively regal in plum satin, silver lace, and a diamond parure. Anne turned back to the mirror. She wore her mother's double strand of pearls and pearl drops in her ears. Another strand of pearls was woven through her hair, dressed high on her head with the required feathers. A few curls fell around her forehead and her ears, with delicate curling wisps at her temples and the nape of her neck. "*It could be worse,*" she thought gloomily.

Anne directed all of her attention at the management of her hoops and train as she followed Lady Kidwell and Fanny. She was so preoccupied with managing the weight of her *ensemble* that she started when Fanny touched her arm and hissed, "Come, Anne, pay attention! We are called." Suddenly she was curtseying low to the Queen and one of the princesses. Lady Kidwell uttered a few dignified words of introduction, whilst Fanny and Anne stood quietly, eyes respectfully lowered.

Anne was in a fog of anxiety. The three ladies stood back,

curtseyed deeply again and backed away, Anne in agony about her train. Lady Jersey was present; she nodded and smiled as they moved away. The rest of the evening passed in a blur. Anne finally relaxed with a sigh when they were back in the carriage. Fanny and her mother congratulated themselves on the success of the evening. "Her Highness was all graciousness," exclaimed Lady Kidwell. "She and the princess commented most kindly on your deportment, girls."

Fanny and Anne exchanged glances. Guiltily, Anne replied, "I did not hear, ma'am. I was so afraid I was going to trip, I noticed very little...." Fanny giggled. "I know you so well; I could tell you were completely preoccupied! It was all I could do not to give you a pinch!" Both girls laughed. "Well, you did extremely well in spite of your worries, my dear. Fanny, of course, knew what to expect. Just think, dear girl, you have been presented to Her Majesty! You should have no qualms now about attending social events. Not everyone can claim such an honour."

Later that night, after she retired, Anne pondered Miss Crawford's words, as well as Lady Kidwell's comments. "...your own value." "Not everyone can claim such an honour." She considered her father, his kindness, his unobtrusive willingness to help others, his wide-ranging interests, and realised he was more of a "gentleman" than many of the men she had met who claimed that title. Anne regretted that she had never known her mother and grandparents more now than ever.

Idly thinking back over the evening, Anne remembered Lady Jersey's smile, as she backed away from the queen. She snuggled sleepily into her pillow. "So kind. I wonder why she furnished my vouchers." It did not occur to her to wonder how Lady Kidwell had arranged for her presentation to the Queen.

A few days later, whilst shopping with Fanny, Anne again encountered Lady Jersey. She and Fanny were in Hatchards Bookstore looking for new books. They separated, each to indulge her own taste. Fanny enjoyed poetry whilst Anne preferred novels, and pamphlets on history. Anne was browsing through a novel titled *Castle Rackrent* which looked most enjoyable, when she sensed someone waiting to pass by. Looking up, she bobbed a curtsey, and murmured shyly, "I beg your pardon, my lady; I didn't mean to block the aisle."

Lady Jersey smiled and replied, "Certainly, my dear, I do understand what it is to be caught up." She paused as she started to pass Anne. "We met briefly at the Drawing Room, did we not? I think your name is Anne Emmons?" Lady Jersey said questioningly. Anne blushed furiously and answered, "Yes, we did, Lady Jersey. I fear I was thinking about my train...." Lady Jersey laughed and responded, "A frightful business, I know. You are staying with Lady Kidwell and her family, as I recall. I hope you are enjoying the Season, Miss Emmons." "Yes, indeed, my lady," murmured Anne hesitantly.

Lady Jersey looked at her for a moment and raised her brows. "Try not to take it too much to heart, my dear. One's first Season is always the most difficult." She smiled again and swept by, leaving Anne no opportunity to do more than bob a hasty curtsey. Anne hurried to find Fanny, peering down several aisles before running her to earth.

"Fanny!" cried Anne, as she clutched her arm. "Oh, Anne, only see what I have found! The most beautiful edition of *The Lay of the Last Minstrel*! I must have it!" Anne shook her arm gently. "Fanny, do listen! Lady Jersey was here! She remembered me, and she spoke to me!" Fanny replied, "Truly, Anne? How did she seem? Was she friendly, or did she seem distant?" Anne said, "Oh, Fanny, she was most kind. She remembered my name and that I was staying with you. I hardly remember being introduced! I didn't look for such attention, I assure you." Fanny hugged her. "My dear, if Lady Jersey approves you, your Season is made! She is such a high stickler. You will be included on every invitation list. We must tell Mama as soon as we return home."

Chapter 4

The knowledge that she had the approval of one of the powerful Patronesses gave Anne more confidence as the days passed by. The acquisition of a few friends, including Kate and Emily, also bolstered her spirits. Although she determinedly refused to accompany Fanny and her mother to another rout party at Mrs Eastland's home, she attended a card party at the home of the DeWitts which she enjoyed very much. Both of Fanny's parents attended, being friends with Emily's and Kate's parents, and the atmosphere was relaxed. Anne and Fanny were becomingly gowned in muslins, Fanny's of palest blue and Anne's of a soft yellow, and were ready to be pleased.

The evening passed quickly, with tables set up for whist and piquet in the library and other games in the drawing room where the younger guests gathered. Speculation, jackstraws and other childish games quickly replaced silver loo, and soon reduced them to gales of laughter. The evening ended with a delightful supper and Anne and Fanny returned home, completely satisfied with the party.

The high point of their Season was, of course, the magnificent set ball given by the Kidwells. Preparations began days before the event, with the ballroom opened, aired, and thoroughly cleaned. The parquet floor was polished until it shone like glass. The great chandelier was lowered and each crystal polished until it sparkled like a diamond. The musicians were to sit on a small dais at the far end of the room, and gilt chairs were arranged against the walls in small groupings separated by large arrangements of flowers, which gave the effect of bowers. Lady Kidwell planned to have a muslin tent erected over the musicians' dais. Ivy would twine around the poles holding the tent to accent the garden theme. At the front of the house, long glass windows opened onto a small balcony where more flowers were to be massed.

"I flatter myself that it will be beautiful when the chandelier and sconces are lit," declared her ladyship complacently. "And if it gets too hot, we can open the glass windows for air. The banked flowers will prevent too many people from wandering out there." Fanny and Anne were both delighted with their gowns. Fanny's was in her usual white, a silk underdress with a delicate gauze overdress. The gown was delicately embroidered with small golden motifs that glinted through the gauze. Golden ribbons tied the high waist. Wearing her betrothal gift for the first time that night, Fanny wanted nothing to detract from it. An unusual family heirloom, the large oval sapphire, circled by pearls, was set in heavy gold on an intricate chain. She intended to wear only her mother's pearl and sapphire earrings as her other ornaments.

Anne's gown was of amethyst silk with sleeves, bodice and a band around the hem embroidered with little flowers in shades of pale blue, lavender and deepest violet. Tiny pearl and amethyst beads clustered in the heart of each flower which shimmered when she moved. Delicate silver lace edged the short puffed sleeves and scooped neck. Her mother's amethysts again, this time with the matching necklace and bracelet, would complete her *ensemble*. The colour of her gown and her jewels deepened her eyes to a clear violet. Her silk slippers, tied with amethyst ribbons, and her reticule of matching amethyst silk set off her *ensemble* to a nicety. Her evening gloves in a delicate pale lilac hue complemented her gown perfectly. Anne knew she would be in her best looks.

The night of the ball was clear and cool, perfect for such an event.

Lady Kidwell seated thirty persons for dinner, including Carleton's parents and grandparents, Kate and Emily DeWitt (who were staying with them for the next few days), and other friends of Lord and Lady Kidwell. Conversation flourished throughout the evening, even though each diner was confined to conversing with the person to his or her right or left, as etiquette demanded such formality. Finally, Lady Kidwell rose, and the women retired. Fanny and her friends went upstairs to make sure their hair and complexions were perfect for the evening's festivities, whilst her mother and the other women retired to the drawing room for coffee.

The receiving line began to form as Fanny, Anne and the other young ladies descended. Anne, Emily and Kate were shooed to the ballroom, and Fanny was engulfed in family. Anne glanced over her shoulder in time to see Fanny look up into Carleton's eyes, a glow of happiness on her face, whilst he smiled down at her, their hands locked together. The evening flew. Fanny and Carleton disregarded custom to open the ball with a waltz. They were shortly followed to the floor by both sets of their parents and other couples.

Anne had never learnt to waltz so, *per force*, she sat in one of the gilt chairs along the wall and watched the couples swirl past. Emily sat with her and they chattered eagerly, admiring gowns, graceful dancing and the delightful music. Mrs Eastland approached and spoke. "Mr Deschevaux, may I present Miss Emmons who is visiting with us from York, and Miss Emily DeWitt? Anne, Emily, I must introduce Mr Charles Deschevaux. He is one of our neighbours in Kent and is known to Fanny's parents." The young man bowed and murmured politely.

Anne surveyed him curiously. Of medium height and slender build, he was not nearly as impressive a figure as Fanny's betrothed. Still, he had a charming smile, and attractive dark hair and dark eyes as well. Discreetly dressed in evening garb, he was clearly not a dandy but his calm, assured manner showed that he was accustomed to such social events. "Pray, be seated, Mr Deschevaux, and give us your opinion of the music." He sat next to Anne and commented, "Choosing a waltz for the opening set was quite daring. The musicians played it beautifully, I thought. Fortunately, Miss Kidwell, her betrothed and their parents are excellent performers of that dance. It's a beautiful scene to watch."

Anne and Emily exchanged glances; neither could think of anything to add. An awkward little silence grew between the threesome. A little desperately, Anne asked, "Are you in London for the Season, Mr Deschevaux?" "Alas, no, Miss Emmons. I am in town on business. I wanted to consult with Lord Kidwell and came up to town yesterday. I had forgot how occupied he would be with the Season.... Mrs Eastland obtained an invitation for me to attend this evening." Anne and Emily glanced at each other again. Just then, the waltz ended; the couples bowed and curtsied before leaving the floor. Seeing his chance to speak with Fanny's father, Mr Deschevaux rose, bowed hastily, murmured his pleasure at meeting the young ladies, and strode away.

Anne and Emily, startled at his abrupt departure, giggled behind their fans. Fanny and Carleton approached, joined by Kate and her partner, and animated conversation broke out. To Anne's secret relief, Mr Franklin, a friend of Carleton's came up, was introduced, and asked Anne to partner him in the next set, a country-dance just striking up. Anne dropped a curtsey and they took to the floor. Subsequently, Anne's evening was filled. The next few hours flew by, a colourful whirl of music, dancing and happy chatter.

A large group of young people, including Fanny and Carleton, Anne, Emily and Kate and their partners in the supper dance, shared a table for supper. Anne spotted Mrs Eastland and her niece Louisa, seated at a small table off to the side with Mr Eastland and Mr Deschevaux. Louisa chattered vivaciously. The low neckline of her jonquil silk gown revealed an unattractive amount of protruding collarbone, whilst her hair began to straggle. Mr Deschevaux sat quietly, until Louisa stopped to draw breath. Anne saw him rise, ask a question, bow, and head for the buffet table. "Poor man!" she thought, as she turned back to the conversation. After the diners had finished the appetising refreshments, Lord and Lady Kidwell led their guests back to the ballroom to resume the festivities. The remainder of the evening flew by on waves of music and the scent of flowers....

Chapter 5

The next day, Fanny and Anne relaxed in Fanny's room, Fanny reclining against her pillows, whilst Anne rested comfortably on the *chaise longue* near the window. "The ball was beautiful, was it not, Anne?" sighed Fanny. "Everything was utterly perfect." "You made a most unusual choice to open with a waltz," said Anne. "People talked about propriety. I thought it was lovely, though. You and Carleton seemed to float."

"I knew there would be a fuss, but I wanted it so. It *was* a private ball, after all, and most of the guests were family or close friends. Mama danced with Mr Thomas and Papa with Mrs Thomas, and they were guests of honour. Besides, the rest of the evening proceeded according to the usual considerations; the last dance was even a *Boulanger.* I fell in love with Carleton during a waltz, when the musicians played the same composition, and I was determined to have it."

After a sip of chocolate, Fanny continued, "I am delighted Mr and Mrs Thomas enjoyed the ball. They spend most of their time in the country, and do not visit town often. Mr Thomas and Father tend to talk estate matters, and things of that nature." Anne asked, "Where is their home?" "They have a large country home in Essex. I have not yet seen it. I believe Mr Thomas inherited some kind of property or interest in one of the colonies, Barbados or Bahama or somewhere, which generates income. Carleton spoke of it once. He has suggested that we visit their properties after our wedding."

Fanny changed the subject. "You sat out the waltz with Emily. Was not the young man who joined you Charles Deschevaux?" "Yes, I believe his name was Deschevaux. Mrs Eastland introduced him. He seemed pleasant." "He is one of our neighbours in Kent. His estate is not far distant from ours, nearer to Faversham. A distinguished family, they came over with the Conqueror if you can believe it. I think they are connected to the Eastlands. He is a bit older, and I never knew him well. He was always away, somehow. His older brother was the heir, but he and their father died a few years ago." "How sad!" exclaimed Anne. "He seemed anxious to speak with your father; a matter of business, he said..." "Probably something to do with estate matters," Fanny shrugged, losing interest. "Did you notice Louisa Dixon? My dear, that gown!"

Anne smiled, but countered, "The colour was becoming, I thought. I had no conversation with her, I am thankful to say. Lady Kidwell graciously excused me from receiving." A maid arrived with a breakfast tray, and conversation languished. Anne was happy to find a letter from her father on the tray. In response to her own letter describing her presentation, he replied, *I am delighted to know your presentation was successful. Please convey my thanks to Lady Kidwell for her efforts on your behalf. I hope you take advantage of your opportunities to further your acquaintance."* Anne thought fleetingly of Louisa Dixon, then of Mr Deschevaux.

Later in the afternoon, Anne and Miss Crawford departed to shop. They stopped at Madame Francine's shop to look for a new hat, and walked on to Grantham's where Anne happened upon a new pair of evening gloves. They then turned their steps to Hookham's Library, where Miss Crawford wished to search for a new biography. The two women separated, to permit Anne to browse the histories and the novels. Much to her surprise, she came upon a pamphlet about the Roman ruins in York. Anne glanced through it with interest, determined to purchase it, if possible.

As she turned to move to the section with the current novels, she ran headlong into a man lost in perusal of a journal. "Pray, pardon me, sir! I am so sorry. I didn't see you...," she gasped. To her surprise, the gentleman was Mr Deschevaux. He smiled and bowed, and murmured, "Think nothing of it, Miss Emmons. I did not pay attention either." They looked at one another, and an awkward pause ensued. Anne fought for composure and curtsied hastily, and said, "Forgive me, Mr Deschevaux, I must join my companion. Again, please pardon my clumsiness."

She fled around the corner, where she found Miss Crawford. "Oh, Miss Crawford, I am so mortified," she whispered. "Pray, let us leave immediately!" "What is amiss, my dear?" "I just ran into Mr Deschevaux, almost knocked him down. I wasn't looking, and there he was! I was so embarrassed!" Since she had found what she wanted, Miss Crawford assented, and the two ladies made their way to the clerk. As they walked home, Anne talked to Miss Crawford about Mr Deschevaux.

"I met him briefly at Fanny's betrothal dance. He was difficult to converse with, I thought. He is so... downright, and leaves no room for comment after his remarks. After I collided with him, I apologised. When he responded, it was as if he...he closed a door in my face! I could think of nothing more to say. So very awkward! All I could do excuse myself, and escape as soon as may be. He must think I am so *gauche*."

Kindly, Miss Crawford replied, "Well, my dear Miss Emmons, we must trust he will put it down to your youth, and the fact this is your first season. That is, if he thinks of it at all. These things do happen." Anne flushed with embarrassment mixed with annoyance. "My youth? I am nearly eighteen years old, as you well know, Miss Crawford. I can hardly be considered some...schoolroom miss!"

Amused, Miss Crawford responded, "Indeed, I meant no such

thing. Merely, Mr Deschevaux is older in years, and is in town on estate matters. He will hardly be concerned with two such brief encounters, as you have described. If he thinks of you at all, I daresay it will be as a young girl he met briefly in town. That is all." Anne remained silent, unaccountably piqued by Miss Crawford's prosaic remarks; after all, she suddenly recalled, he *did* remember her name.

After they arrived home, Anne took her pamphlet to her room and read with great interest. One paragraph caught her attention, as it described a bit of a mosaic, now in the British Museum. Surely, it was similar to one in a glass case in her little sitting room! The face of a girl, broken out of a pavement or wall decoration, it showed her large dark eyes and dark hair, and just the hint of a smile... Not much bigger than her father's hand, it had turned up in the garden, when the gardeners were digging the site of a new succession house, and he had had it cleaned and brought to her. Anne resolved to visit the museum this very week.

A few days later, Anne, with her pamphlet in her reticule, was in a hackney, accompanied by Miss Crawford, on her way to the British Museum. Miss Crawford read from her copy of *THE PICTURE OF LONDON* as they drove along. "My dear Miss Anne, we will have an opportunity to see Sir William Hamilton's collection of Greek vases!" Anne's eyes twinkled. "A high treat for you, surely, Miss Crawford. I am more curious about the Roman artefacts. Father will be most interested in whatever we discover about the mosaics."

They presented themselves for admission, and were escorted by an under librarian through the collections. Anne bore with the printed books and the manuscript collections with patience. Neither lady was enthralled with the nature specimens, although both were surprised at how much they enjoyed the modern curiosities. At last, they came to the rooms with the antiquities exhibits.

Anne drew her pamphlet from her reticule, as they browsed the cases. Finally, they found the mosaic described. Summoning the under librarian, Anne began to ask questions about the section of mosaic enshrined there. The under librarian conceded, "My apologies, madam, but I am far from expert on Roman mosaics. Do you care to wait, whilst I see if one of the librarians is available? Mayhap one of them could answer your questions." After their assent, the attendant left Anne and Miss Crawford alone. "Miss Crawford, is this not similar to the bit I have in my sitting room? The style is so like."

Miss Crawford leaned forward and studied the remnant closely. "You may be right, Miss Anne. The one at home seems in much better condition and more detailed." Just then, the under librarian returned, accompanied by an elderly man. "You are interested in Roman mosaics, ladies? A most unusual interest." Anne showed him the pamphlet and explained about the mosaic fragment, found in the back garden. She was surprised when he pelted her with questions about when and how it was found, whether anything else was uncovered, and whether anything similar was found in other locations near her home.

Anne replied she knew little about it, other than the piece in question had been brought to her father, who gave it to her. At this point, the gentleman asked for her father's name and direction, bowed hastily, and vanished! The under librarian, looking somewhat embarrassed, apologised. "I ask your pardon, ladies. Mr Smith gets... enthusiastic, shall we say? Now, in this *next* exhibit, you will see some exquisite vases...." Frustrated, Anne had no choice but to follow Miss Crawford and the attendant to the next exhibit.

The next several weeks passed in a blur of parties and entertainments, interspersed with visits to see the sights of London, and back to the museum. Miss Crawford insisted on serious reading for an hour every day. "Just to balance out all of the frivolity," she suggested drily. Anne and Miss Crawford also discussed materials to order for the Grey Coat School. Always practical, Miss Crawford suggested books on cookery, household management or embroidery designs. "The girls are being fitted to go into service, you know, and these will be useful to them." Privately, Anne wondered if there was a girl there interested in further study than that designed to equip her for a position as a household servant.

"What if one of the girls aspires to be a governess or teacher? Should we not provide something to encourage such an interest?" asked Anne. Miss Crawford pondered the issue. "I think you should discuss such an issue with the subscribers before you make such a purchase. We do not know if they are equipped to encourage such an enterprise." Anne conceded the point, and resolved to visit the ladies in question upon her return to York.

Fanny and her mother were increasingly busy with wedding plans, and Anne was aware the month of May and the York races approached rapidly. She was sitting with Lady Kidwell, who exclaimed distractedly, "Thank goodness the wedding will be at home in Kent in the autumn! I could not tolerate the summer in town, especially with Fanny in the state she is now! It will be good for her to get out into the countryside." Anne concurred, "She has been so busy, ma'am, and there have been so many parties and celebrations from which she cannot excuse herself. I dare swear she will be relieved to be away. When do you go?"

Lady Kidwell patted Anne's hand and replied, "Not for some weeks yet. We have much shopping yet to do, for Fanny's wedding clothes and various necessities. Please, accompany us, my dear. Your common sense and calm nature are so good for Fanny." Anne blushed and smiled. "Thank you, ma'am, but I fear I must return to York. I must be there to help prepare for my father's guests. The York Races, you know..." "Ah, yes. Lord Kidwell looks forward to Race Week so much. Unfortunately, Fanny and I will be too much occupied this year." "I do understand, ma'am. Mayhap next year, you and Lord Kidwell can come, and bring Fanny and Carleton with you."

In her room, Anne sat in the comfortable chair near the fireplace to read. A short time later, Miss Crawford entered the room. "Miss Anne, I must visit Grantham House to match some silk. Have you any commissions for me?" Anne looked up with a smile. "No, I thank you, I need nothing. Do you want me to accompany you? I would enjoy getting out for a bit." Miss Crawford assented, and the two donned their bonnets and other outdoor wear.

Although still quite cool, it was a lovely, clear day. Unfurling their sunshades, the two decided to walk for a bit before they hailed a hackney. Miss Crawford asked, "Have you decided when you wish to return to York, my dear?" Anne replied, "I have received no word from my father as yet, but I hope to depart in early April. Jane has written to me of some of the parties and celebrations planned. We had discussed attending the Spring Gala at Burlington Assembly Rooms before I came to London. I want to allow time for the journey, and to review Mrs Hubbard's preparations for Race Week."

She laughed deprecatingly. "Mrs Hubbard allows me to consult with her and to approve the arrangements she makes every year. I have been adding my own notes to my mother's household book. I realise Mrs Hubbard truly does not need me for the planning, but I have some suggestions to make. After my experiences in town this season, I want to add some new dishes, and I have a few additional guests to invite." Miss Crawford nodded approvingly. "I am glad to see you take an active interest in household management, my dear. I was concerned it was a passing fancy, an excuse to leave school, but you have been most faithful. I have observed your letters to Mrs Hubbard, and hers to you. The fact that you are adding to your mother's book is most useful. This is excellent preparation for the day you will have your own household to manage."

Just then, a hackney approached and stopped at their hail. Miss Crawford gave the driver the direction, and the two ladies fell to discussing possible purchases as they rode away. A few hours later, Anne and Miss Crawford returned to the Kidwell house to find ...chaos.

Chapter 6

Anne heard Fanny sobbing upstairs. She and Miss Crawford looked at each other in consternation. Just then, Lord Kidwell came out of his study, accompanied by his man of business. "See if you can get on with someone at the Admiralty. Mayhap they can find some answers." The man bowed and left hastily, leaving Lord Kidwell in the hall. He caught sight of Anne and said, "Anne, my dear, please come to my study. We received disturbing news..." Unobtrusively, Miss Crawford followed Anne and took a seat near the window, whilst Anne seated herself next to the fire. "Pray, sir, tell me what has happened and how I can help," she responded quietly.

Too agitated to sit, Lord Kidwell paced by the hearth. He sighed heavily and said, "Young Carleton has disappeared. Vanished! He dropped out of sight with a few of his cronies, for some sport. Of course, he did not tell Fanny the details-females do not understand these things. They were supposed to return a couple of nights ago. Well, I thought little about it-a group of young bloods, celebrating as they were, easy enough to overdo, stay longer than planned."

Sighing again, he paced further. "Well, it appears they didn't leave London, after all, just wanted to go their own way without a need to make excuses. Carleton and young Franklin were returning to their lodgings. You remember young Franklin?" Anne nodded as she recognised the name of the young man with whom she had danced first at the engagement ball. "Well, he has finally surfaced.

All he can tell anyone is Carleton was gone when he came to himself. They made a pretty batch of it, drinking and gambling. Franklin lost heavily, and has been playing least in sight." Anne gasped, "How dreadful, sir!"

"Carleton's family was notified immediately, of course, and they sent a messenger here. Fanny is beside herself, of course. She will need your support, my dear." Anne put out a timid hand, and replied, "Never doubt, sir, I will do all I can for her. But Carleton... is there any clue?"

"Little information has been found so far. They were in an ... unsavoury neighbourhood, near the docks. If anyone heard a disturbance, no one admits to it. Young Franklin seems to think they were down on the docks, watching a merchant ship getting ready to sail. He has a vague idea Carleton has gone aboard. I suppose it is possible, but it seems so unlikely."

Anne gasped in horror. "But why?" Lord Kidwell paused, and then acknowledged slowly, "I cannot really imagine it. Carleton never showed the slightest interest in ships or sailing. Something else might have happened to Carleton, and Franklin simply has no recollection." He snorted in disgust. "Drunk as he was, anything could have happened and he would not have noticed or been of any use. In any case, this is idle speculation. Mr Thomas and I called at Bow Street and spoke to Mr Ford. I also put my man of business onto finding someone at the Admiralty who might know aught of ships trafficking on the Thames these last few days." Anne offered, "I will write to my father, sir. He must have connexions who could help." "Thank you, my dear. Now, if you please, go up to Fanny."

Anne left the study, followed discreetly by Miss Crawford. "My dear Miss Anne," said Miss Crawford, "do you go directly to Lady Kidwell, whilst I write to your father immediately. I cannot help but perceive Mr Emmons would be of great benefit here." "Thank you, Miss Crawford," replied Anne gratefully. She passed on down the hall to Lady Kidwell's sitting room, and quietly opened the door. Peeking in, Anne saw Lady Kidwell where she sat by the fire, exhausted. "Oh, my dear girl," she said, "I am so glad you are come home. We have been so distracted..." "I have seen Lord Kidwell, dear ma'am, and he gave me the dreadful news. Should I go to Fanny now, ma'am?" asked Anne.

"No, my dear, she is sleeping. I gave her a few drops of laudanum, before she could become ill with crying. Poor Mrs Thomas, too. She was here earlier, when Mr Thomas conferred with Lord Kidwell. She and Fanny wept together. My dear, I hope I am not hard hearted, but I was so relieved when Mr Thomas took her home. She kept repeating, 'He's dead, my poor son is dead!' which, of course, is of no help at all."

Lady Kidwell held Anne's hand tightly as she said, with tears in her eyes, "We must contrive to keep our spirits up and be brave for poor Fanny." Anne clasped her hand warmly and replied, "My lord told me he and Mr Thomas have conferred with Bow Street, and his man of business is already looking for other avenues to pursue. Miss Crawford writes to my father as we speak. Surely, we will soon receive word! We must hope for the best, dear ma'am."

Although Anne wanted to be of service to her friend, she was surprised at how little opportunity she had to see Fanny. Indeed, Fanny was seldom at home. Fanny rose early in the next morning and assumed an almost adamantine calm, rejecting any form of comfort or soothing. "Of course, he's all right, Anne," asserted Fanny calmly. "I'm certain Carleton will be returned to us soon." After breakfast, Fanny dressed and went to the Thomas household, where she remained for the day. Anne offered to accompany her, but Fanny indicated Anne's presence was unnecessary. "Truly, my dear, poor Mrs Thomas cannot receive any company at this present."

Taken aback, Anne replied, "Fanny, I only want to be of service...." Fanny replied more kindly, "I know you do, dear friend, but I do not require assistance just now, and am so taken up with Mrs Thomas that I have little time to spare." Lady Kidwell, busy with household concerns and her own friends, also had little time to spare for Anne. "Really, Miss Crawford, I feel completely in the way," admitted Anne wretchedly. "My father has written he will come for me in a few weeks, after he gets replies to his inquiries. He is so busy I do not want to disarrange his plans, but I cannot be comfortable, staying here like this."

Before Miss Crawford could reply, a maid came to the door and bobbed a curtsey. "You have a caller, Miss Emmons," she said, and handed her a card. "Lady Jersey," said Anne in surprise, reading the card. The maid curtseyed again. "The lady is waiting in the drawing room, Miss. What shall I tell her?" Anne rose and answered, "I'll join her immediately. Please bring tea to the drawing room."

Pausing before the mirror to check the smoothness of her hair, Anne hurried down the stairs. She entered the drawing room, where Lady Jersey stood before the fire. She swooped upon Anne, already chattering in her light voice, "How too dreadful, my dear! Have they found out any information about the poor young man? And poor Miss Kidwell-how does she hold up? My dear, the stories are almost too wild. And what of you, my dear?" Anne curtseyed, and did not attempt to answer. "Pray, be seated, Lady Jersey." Thankfully, the footman came in with a tray. "Do you care for tea, my lady?" Anne poured a cup and extended it to Lady Jersey without waiting for an answer.

Lady Jersey took the cup and, as her eyes met Anne's, she smiled kindly. "How are you, my dear?" she asked. Anne drew a shaky breath, and replied, "I am well enough, my lady. We all hope for the best." Anne took a sip. Lady Jersey continued to regard Anne. "I am sure you are a support to your friends, my dear." Anne looked up and replied bluntly, to her own surprise, "Not really, my lady. Fanny has made it plain she has no need of my support, and spends virtually all of her days with her *fiancé*'s mother. Lady Kidwell is occupied with her household and her own affairs. Indeed, my lady, I feel quite in the way."

Lady Jersey leaned back in her chair, and returned, "Ah? May I make a suggestion, then? I came to invite you, and your companion, of course, to spend a few days at Osterley Park. My husband is away, and I have business there. The estate is only a few miles out of town, and I think you will find it well worth a visit. The library and the gardens will give you much to see." Taken aback, Anne replied, "Why, Lady Jersey, I did not intend...."

Amused, Lady Jersey responded, "My dear, I didn't think you were cadging for an invitation, if that is your concern. Merely, I should enjoy a little of your company whilst I attend to some business, and, it transpires, you could remove yourself from an awkward situation for a few days." Anne blushed in embarrassment as she said, "Indeed, Lady Jersey, I thank you for your kind invitation. I *would* like to remove for a few days, and would greatly enjoy bearing you company."

Lady Jersey rose. "Thank you, my dear. I'll take you up Friday after breakfast. We will be there in time for dinner." Anne curtseyed deeply, as Lady Jersey took her departure. Anne approached Lady Kidwell, who was resting in her *boudoir*. She told Lady Kidwell of Lady Jersey's invitation. "If I thought I could be of use here, ma'am, of course, I would have declined the invitation. However, we both know Fanny has no need of my presence, and I think I should be out from under your feet for a few days."

Lady Kidwell embraced Anne warmly. "My dear, I know how difficult this has been for you. I didn't anticipate that Fanny would become such a pillar of fortitude, or that she would want to be so much with Mrs Thomas. The Thomas's are such a large and close-knit family. Fanny and Mrs Thomas had scarcely a thought in common! I vow, I do not know how this will end... I'm delighted you accepted this invitation. We will, of course, expect you to return before your father reaches us. I believe Lord Kidwell eagerly anticipates Mr Emmons' arrival; he so hopes your father will be able to shed light on this sad business." Anne and Miss Crawford had little to do but to make ready for the visit to Osterley. Sadly, Anne thought, "Fanny will not even notice I am gone."

It was a bright, beautiful afternoon, a perfect day to travel, when Anne and Miss Crawford found themselves in Lady Jersey's chaise. Graciously offering her hand to Miss Crawford, Lady Jersey said, "Thank you so much for accompanying Miss Emmons and me, Miss Crawford. I hope you will enjoy your visit to Osterley Park." Miss Crawford inclined her head and replied, "I'm grateful to be included in the invitation, my lady. I seldom have the opportunity to visit the country." Conversation was desultory as they drove along and finally entered the parkland surrounding the house itself.

"Ah, there it is," said Lady Jersey. The huge house dominated the view. "It was originally Elizabethan, and Robert Adam did a great deal of work on it for my grandfather." As they left the chaise, and made their way into the grand entrance, Anne stopped and stared at the grand entrance hall. Awed, she gazed around the impressive room. "Henry will show you to your rooms, and I will have Mrs Hall, the housekeeper, take you on a tour after you have had a chance to rest," said Lady Jersey. "Pray excuse me for the moment." She vanished down a hall before either Anne or Miss Crawford could respond.

Following the steward up the stairs, they were shown to an elegant suite of rooms, which included Anne's bedchamber, a sitting room, a dressing room and a smaller room made comfortable for Miss Crawford's use. Henry bowed and said, "Miss Emmons, Miss Crawford, your luggage will be brought up and unpacked shortly. Some refreshment is waiting in your sitting room. If you care to repose yourselves for a short time, I'll let Mrs Hall know you are settled." Indicating the bell pull next to the fireplace, he added, "Please ring when you are ready." Henry closed the door silently behind him and departed.

After they took seats near the fire, Miss Crawford poured coffee. As she passed a cup to Anne, Miss Crawford said, "My dear, I am relieved they housed me so near you. I had no idea this was such a vast place." "I, too, am glad we are together," responded Anne, gazing round-eyed around the room. "These rooms are incredibly luxurious, are they not?"

Both women having finished their coffee, Anne crossed over and tugged the bell pull. It seemed no time at all before the door opened silently, and an elderly woman gowned in black silk with an elegant lace cap entered the room. "Miss Emmons, Miss Crawford, I'm Mrs Hall, the housekeeper. Is everything to your liking?" Resisting the urge to curtsey, Anne replied, "The rooms are lovely, Mrs Hall. Lady Jersey indicated you would show us around the house. Are you available now?" "Yes, ma'am. My lady specifically bade me to hold myself ready at your convenience," answered Mrs Hall. The three women set off.

Anne lost track of time as they walked through the various halls, galleries, the state apartments, and so forth. Hopelessly confused, she followed quietly as Miss Crawford and Mrs Hall discussed the original Elizabethan house and the changes effected by Mr Adam. A few particular rooms stayed with her: the tapestry room, glowing with colour, the magnificent panelled library, and a beautiful gallery with its walls setting off a magnificent collection of paintings. They were in a large room with high arched windows that overlooked a lovely garden, when she saw a small domed building with similar arched windows.

"That's the garden house, Miss Emmons," replied the housekeeper to her question. They continued on their way, up a different flight of stairs and, somehow, ended up back at their rooms. "There you are, Miss Emmons, Miss Crawford. Dinner will be served in two hours' time. You've time to rest and change." Mrs Hall added, with a smile, "Please ring when you are ready to come down. A footman will come to show you the way to the drawing room." Anne thanked Mrs Hall, and proceeded to her own room. A *chaise longue* near the fire tempted her to rest. Finding her trunk unpacked and her brushes on the dressing table, Anne reclined on the *chaise* and soon nodded off.

Anne was glad she had brought one of her favourite gowns, a soft pale rose silk. She wore with it her pearls, and a cream silk shawl. Miss Crawford, handsomely attired in silver grey, accompanied her downstairs behind the footman. Although they were dining in the enormous formal dining room, Lady Jersey thoughtfully had dinner served at a small table in an alcove. "So difficult to converse when one must shout down the length of the table, is it not? Besides, I do not care to stand upon ceremony when I am here alone."

Curious, Anne was emboldened to ask, "Do you not live here, Lady Jersey? Such a magnificent estate so close to town..." "No, my dear. In fact, I'm seldom here. My husband prefers his family's estate, and we spend little time here. Our home is Middleton Park, in Oxfordshire. The boys usually stay there when we come to London. When George is away, whilst I am in town, I do occasionally like to come here for a few days to be sure all is well." Surprised, Anne responded, "He does not care for it? Surely, this is his home...." "In fact, Miss Emmons," Lady Jersey replied with a slight smile, "Osterley Park is mine. I've always suspected Lord Jersey was never comfortable here because it reminds him of my situation."

Although she did not wish to seem inquisitive, Anne looked enquiringly at her hostess. Lady Jersey continued. "Osterley Park came to me through my mother's family. Everyone knows she eloped with my father, the Earl of Westmorland, and my grandfather did not approve. I inherited as a child and, when I came of age, it all came to my control. Many in society prefer not to think of my grandfather." "Who was your grandfather, ma'am?" asked Anne. "Why, he was Robert Child, of Child and Company, the bank." Thunderstruck, Anne looked at Lady Jersey. "Child's Bank?" she said blankly.

Eyes twinkling, Lady Jersey inclined her head. "Indeed, my dear, and now you see why Lord Jersey prefers to be otherwhere. He disregards much of what I do, including the fact I am the senior partner in the bank. I beg you will not discuss this in society, my dear. You must see how unfit this is for a woman of my position." She laughed aloud.

"Now I understand why you have been so kind to me, my lady!" said Anne. Sobering, Lady Jersey acknowledged, "I do comprehend your feelings, my dear. I well remember my own first season. Even though I was an earl's daughter, there were those few who let me know clearly that my father's rank and bloodline were not... quite sufficient to balance out my mother's background, wealth notwithstanding. Then, when I married my lord, I was another Lady Jersey; many people assumed I would go the same way as his mother, who had created frightful scandals. I chose to walk a very narrow road, and I was determined to walk it successfully. I am aware I am not always well liked, but I have achieved a certain standing in society. I knew of you from my correspondence with your father. I had observed you when you were in town with Lord and Lady Kidwell. In your case, I decided to ... shall we say, even some of the odds? Whatever you may choose to do, my dear, don't let yourself be limited by small-minded people."

"You mentioned your boys, my lady. How many sons have you?" Anne asked. Lady Jersey smiled. "I have three boys, lively rascals." She rose from the table and nodded to Anne and Miss Crawford. "I regret I will be able to spend little time with you over these next few days. I will be involved with personal affairs, as I mentioned before. However, please make yourselves at home. The library and the music room are at your disposal, and tomorrow you must see the park and the gardens." Anne and Miss Crawford both curtseyed. "Good night, Lady Jersey. Thank you for everything."

The next few days passed in a blur. Lady Jersey always appeared at breakfast, inquiring as to their plans for the day and ready with suggestions. "Unfortunately, some rather tiresome business has become necessary, so I won't be able to show you my favourite places." They spent hours in the gardens and explored the pinery.

Anne played the pianoforte in the music room, and both ladies read and wrote in the library, or sketched in the gallery to occupy more of their time. Mrs Hall came to them one evening after dinner, as they sat by the drawing room fire, and announced, "My lady's apologies, Miss Emmons, but she has had such a press of business that she will be unable to accompany you back to town tomorrow. She sends her regrets, and hopes you have had a pleasant stay. She will look for you when she returns to London."

Guiltily, Anne inclined her head, and answered, "Pray beg her ladyship not to think of it. I will write her all that is proper. At what time do we leave tomorrow?" "The chaise will be ready directly after breakfast, ma'am." "Thank you, Mrs Hall. We shall be prepared to depart." Somewhat taken aback, Anne looked at Miss Crawford. "I was unaware of the passage of time. How strange we saw so little of Lady Jersey." Miss Crawford asserted, "No, I think not, my dear. I suspect she simply followed up on her original impulse, to give you a breathing space before you returned to York. She seems a more sympathetic person than she is credited for being. You will want to write her a note before you retire this evening, of course."

Chapter 7

Back in London, Anne was grieved to learn there was still no news of Carleton. Mrs Thomas had been persuaded to return to their country home with her daughters. Fanny was making the social rounds with new acquaintances, as she showed a cool, poised face to the world. Anne was chilled to realise Fanny had scarcely noticed her absence. "I hope you had a pleasant time, Anne. Lady Jersey invites few people to her country home," said Fanny. "Indeed, yes," replied Anne. However, before Anne could elaborate, Fanny passed on quietly to her room.

Lady Kidwell caught Anne's hand. "Do not follow her, dear Anne. She will not welcome your attention. She sits alone by the fire until time to retire. She only wants her maid's help in changing. We see her at breakfast and briefly in the evening. She won't talk to us at all." Anne saw the tears in Lady Kidwell's eyes. "Is there nothing we can do, ma'am?" asked Anne sadly. "She has pushed me away, and I don't understand."

"I, too, regret this separation very much. We have always been so close, and now she will tell me nothing. She looks at me with those cool grey eyes, and I see nothing of my daughter! I even spoke to a doctor, and he told me this was just her way of being strong for Carleton and his family, and to leave her be. I simply do not know what is best." With that, Lady Kidwell broke into tears. Anne held her hand and cried with her. After a few moments, Lady Kidwell collected herself, and wiped her eyes. "This helps nothing," she stated firmly. "We must continue to hope for Carleton's safe return." "Oh, yes, Lady Kidwell," replied Anne fervently.

The next day, Mr Deschevaux called. Anne was the only one available to receive him. As they shook hands, he said, "Miss Emmons, I was never so shocked in my life. Has there been any word about Mr Thomas? May I be of assistance?" "Thank you, Mr Deschevaux, but Lord Kidwell and Mr Thomas's father have undertaken what can be done here, and my father will do his possible. Now all we can do is wait." Anne gestured for her guest to sit down as she took her favourite chair. "The weather has been so lovely and mild, sir. I trust you are enjoying it?"

"Very much, Miss Emmons. The weather is indeed delightful, and I had a pleasant ride in the park this morning." Mr Deschevaux looked at Anne, his dark eyes full of concern. "Must we speak of pleasant nothings, or may I ask how you are, ma'am? I cannot help but be aware of the strain everyone must be suffering at this difficult time." To her horror, Anne's throat tightened, and tears stung her eyes. She paused and willed herself not to show her distress.

"Certainly, sir, it's been painful for Fanny and her family. She is a pillar of strength for Mr Thomas's mother, whilst Lord and Lady Kidwell do all they can to support her. Having to wait for knowledge like this chafes everyone's emotions so dreadfully." She glanced up and saw his warm gaze on her, as he commented, "I'm sure they are grateful for your presence. Miss Kidwell and her mother must value your concern and support in this dreadful situation."

Anne coloured, and lowered her eyes. "As to that, sir, I do my best to be of service, but cannot help feeling an intruder." He did not argue with her but pondered her words and replied kindly, "Indeed, I can understand your sentiments. The position of a visitor must be uncomfortable in these circumstances. Yet, you're too valued a friend to be regarded as anything but a welcome member of the household." He rose and bowed.

"I must not stay. Pray extend my greetings to Lord and Lady Kidwell, and Miss Kidwell. Do not hesitate to send word if I may be of service. Lord Kidwell has my direction." Anne rose and accompanied him to the door. "Thank you so much for calling, Mr Deschevaux. I'll relay your messages."

A few days later, Mr Emmons arrived. He closeted himself with Lord Kidwell and Mr Thomas. His banking and shipping interests had, as yet, turned up little information. Several merchant ships had sailed the same evening and night of Carleton's disappearance, bound for various ports of call. Until the ships put into ports somewhere, there was no way to know if Carleton was taken aboard any of them. Mr Emmons had already sent letters to several of his agents with requests that they advise him as information became available.

"At this present, there is nothing more we can do," said Mr Emmons heavily, "unless he's been kidnapped and is held for ransom, in which case it is surprising that no demand has been received." Mr Thomas sighed, and replied, "We have received no word of any kind. The Runners turned up no witnesses or, more accurately, no one willing to admit to any knowledge. No one has any idea where else to search. We are hanging all of our hopes on these ships..."

Kate and Emily came to call the next day. When Anne entered the drawing room, Emily ran to her and hugged her gently. "My dear Anne, what a difficult time for you all! Has there been any word?" "None, Emily, I'm afraid," replied Anne. Kate asked, "What of Fanny, Anne? I have not seen her nor heard from her these several days, though I have written to her." Just then, Fanny entered the room. Anne looked at her, surprised.

Clad in soft grey, Fanny had evolved from the storybook princess of Anne's presentation to an ice maiden. Pale and more slender than ever, Fanny's grey eyes showed the glitter of polished steel, hard and cold, instead of their former silvery glow. Calm and glacial, she shook hands with Emily and submitted to Kate's hug, then sat down in a chair. "Kate and Emily. How kind of you to call. I'm pleased to see you, to thank you for your notes," said Fanny quietly.

Anne silently took a seat next to Emily on the settee near the fire. The conversation limped along, as Fanny asked questions about various acquaintances, whilst Kate struggled to bring the conversation back to Fanny. In desperation, Kate finally implored, "Oh, Fanny, dearest friend, I am so concerned for you. Tell me, what can I do?" Fanny looked at Kate, her eyes reflecting no emotion at all.

"My dear Kate, I'm perfectly well. There is nothing to be done. Your concern for me is needless. At this moment, we must focus our thoughts on finding Carleton, and restoring him to his family and friends." Rising, Fanny moved toward the door. She smiled slightly, with no show of warmth, and curtsied. "Thank you so much for calling. Your civility is greatly appreciated." The door closed silently behind her as she disappeared from view.

Kate burst into tears, and Emily turned to Anne. "Anne, what has happened to Fanny? She is grown so cold...." Anne's voice quivered. "Since the morning after we learned of Carleton's disappearance, Fanny has been as you saw her. She's been an unfailing support to Carleton's family. Yet she has been so distant from her parents and her old friends. You're the first callers for whom she has emerged, though she does attend social gatherings with new acquaintances. I hardly see her myself, and, when we speak, I feel that I speak to a stranger. Lady Kidwell is most upset. My father will take me home in a few days, and I don't believe Fanny will even notice I have gone. She seems to prefer the company of strangers or persons she knows only slightly, to her own family and friends."

Emily hugged Anne again. "You must not mind, dear Anne. Fanny is coping as best she might. Time will restore her to us, I am certain of it. Before your return to York, you must come to us. We're having a small party tomorrow night. A few friends for music and games; just a chattery evening, you know. I sent a card, but you probably have not noticed it. I count on you to join us." Anne agreed to look in, if only for an hour or two. Kate regained her composure, and the two sisters took their leave of Anne. Anne continued to sit next to the fire and shivered with cold in spite of its warmth.

Lady Kidwell joined her there, and said, "I thought Kate and Emily were here." "They just took their leave, ma'am, and left all manner of kind messages for you. They were so sorry not to see you," Anne replied. "Did...Fanny come down?" Lady Kidwell asked, hesitantly. "Did she speak to Kate and Emily?" Bitterly, Anne responded, "Certainly, Fanny came in for a few moments. She spoke as coldly as if she were conversing with importunate strangers, then she left the room. Kate was most upset." She looked at Lady Kidwell.

"At least, I know it isn't myself alone whom Fanny cannot bear to see. Fanny rejects any help or comfort. I've seen how different she is with you and Lord Kidwell, too. She seems... frozen inside, and we can do nothing to reach her." Lady Kidwell sighed heavily. There was nothing more to say.

Several days crawled by before the first responses to Mr Emmons' letters came. At first, there was only disappointment. Then came the first glimmer of light. A young dockworker remembered two young men, well-dressed and extremely drunk, hanging about. "He wasn't watching them in particular, as he was busy working. However, at some point, he noticed that there was only one, leaning against a post. He didn't see where the other man went, and is adamant there was no fight or disturbance. The ship weighed anchor without any incident. Sometime during the melee of departure, the dockhand noticed the drunken man was no longer there.

"At last we have somewhere to start," exclaimed Mr Thomas. Mr Emmons, Lord Kidwell and Mr Thomas departed to meet with the dockhand, to see if more information could be gleaned. They hoped to discover at least the destination of the ship.

Anne walked quietly to her room, to start the business of sorting her belongings to be packed. She looked forward more each day for her return to York, and knew her father planned to depart soon now.

Anne wanted nothing more than to wake up in her own bedroom, with her own things around her, with her brothers and old friends from childhood near at hand. All at once, she was overwhelmed and exhausted by the strain of always being at one's best, always considering the most advantageous position, and, most of all, by the recent emotional storm caused by Carleton's disappearance and Fanny's response to it.

Seated at her dressing table whilst she sorted ribbons and silk flowers, Anne looked at herself in the mirror, and acknowledged to herself just how much of an interloper she felt now that Fanny no longer needed or desired her companionship. Miss Crawford tapped at the door, and then entered. "Good afternoon, my dear Miss Anne. I understand there may be a clue in young Mr Thomas' disappearance." Anne roused herself, "Yes, Miss Crawford. Lord Kidwell, Mr Thomas and my father are looking into the situation."

"Excellent! At least they will have something to do. Nothing makes one feel more hopeless than being unable to *do* something. And what of you, my dear? What are your plans this evening?"

"I have no plans, ma'am. I decided to look out my things to decide what to have packed for my return to York, and what I want to give to the maid. She has been so kind and obliging, and Fanny has told me her own maid always appreciates finery Fanny no longer wears. I also have some writing I wish to complete."

"A good plan, my dear. I know Mr Emmons has it in mind to return to York very soon. You may also wish to sort through your books and music…" "No, my dear Amelia, I'm afraid all of those must go back to York with me," said Anne decidedly. A gleam of humour lit her violet eyes. "I could part with *all* of my ball gowns more easily than I could decide which book to leave behind!" Miss Crawford laughed sympathetically. "I, too, have that difficulty. Books are my only extravagance. I am deeply grateful we return with Mr Emmons. I really do not know if I could afford to pay to send them on!"

Anne smiled, and asked, "Have you any idea when we go? I hope to make one more visit to Hatchards." Miss Crawford replied, "No, for he did mention a few business matters to which he has yet to attend. This sad business of Mr Thomas has pushed several things to one side. He mentioned a meeting with a Mr Deschevaux...." "Charles Deschevaux?" interrupted Anne. "How comes my father to have business with him?" Miss Crawford looked at her with surprise, brows raised. "My dear Miss Anne, how you do take me up! Your father doesn't confide his business details to me, and it would be most unbecoming of me to question him." Embarrassed, Anne asked her pardon.

Mollified, Miss Crawford continued, "I believe Lord Kidwell may have arranged it; I understand the meeting is to be at his lordship's club. Mr Emmons merely mentioned it with a few other matters to which he plans to attend before the end of the week. He wanted to know when you will be ready to depart, and I ventured to assure him you would be ready at his convenience." "Thank you, Amelia," Anne responded, with a sigh. "I will be very happy to go back to York. It will be good to be at home again. Suddenly, I need to ... retreat for a space, so I can turn things over in my mind." "A time to pause and reflect is always beneficial," agreed Miss Crawford. "Be sure you write to take your leave of Lady Jersey, as well as the Misses DeWitt."

So saying, Miss Crawford retired to her own room. Left to herself again, Anne seated herself at her writing table. She penned a graceful note of thanks and farewell to Lady Jersey, in which she expressed her gratitude for her ladyship's kindness and understanding. She also wrote a quick note to Emily and Kate, to advise them of her impending departure and to enquire if it would be convenient for her to call tomorrow afternoon. She asked a passing maid to take them downstairs for the post, then returned to her writing desk and sat down with a sigh.

Home... Suddenly, she looked forward eagerly to preparing for guests in for the Spring Meeting of the York Races, attending the remaining assemblies at Burlington's Assembly Rooms, walking along the New Walk by the River Ouse. "It seems so long since I have been there," she thought nostalgically. "It will be such a relief to be home again!" She set aside the pile of finery for her maid and took pen and paper to make one last list for shopping. Several of these items, she decided, would be shipped directly to York. A good history of England and a few novels, she wrote, some lengths of silver lace for an overdress, a gift for Mrs Hubbard – maybe a visit to Fortnum & Mason's. She also added cookery books to her list for the Grey Coat School.

"Maybe they can be prizes for excellence for the older students, something to take with them when they finish," Anne thought, and made a note to write to the ladies managing the school for an appointment when she returned home. Finishing her list, Anne pulled out several sheets, closely written with numerous corrections. Taking a fresh sheet, she wrote busily for some time, then put down her pen to close the inkwell with a sigh. She rose and went over her wardrobe. A few of the gowns she had brought with her were already *démodé*, and not needed in York, such as the blue twilled sarcenet walking dress....

Chapter 8

Later that evening, Anne sat with her father in the drawing room. Mr Emmons roused from a brown study to give her a summary of what the men had discovered from the dockhand. "But what of Carleton, sir? What has this to do with him?" enquired Anne, bewildered. "As best we can determine, Mr Carleton Thomas boarded the ship. I cannot imagine how he could have taken ship if he did not identify himself. Perhaps he was mistaken for a tardy passenger. If no one looked closely, in a bustle of activity, it is barely possible."

Anne was aghast. "To what port is the ship bound?" Mr. Emmons sighed heavily. "Bahama. The voyage is expected to last four weeks, possibly six, if the good weather holds. If that happened, it may be two to three months before we know for certain, unless young Thomas gets a letter off. I have written to my agent there; my man of business will find the fastest means of getting it to him. At this point, there is naught to be done but wait."

Having done all possible, Lord and Lady Kidwell sat down to dinner with Anne and her father. The whole party behaved with a kind of determined gaiety. Anne and Lady Kidwell discussed Anne's plan for one last shopping excursion before she took leave of London. "I perfectly understand, my dear. York has delightful shops, but one cannot deny London has so many more of them!" Lady Kidwell frankly avowed no interest in a trip to Hatchards, but entered into her plans for Fortnum and Mason's and the *modistes'* shops with enthusiasm. Privately, Anne determined to ask Miss Crawford to accompany her to the bookstore and, if time allowed, one last visit to the British Museum the same afternoon.

The last days flew by for Anne, between supervising her packing, and paying last calls on the friends and acquaintances of whom she wished to take leave. Anne saw little of Fanny during this time. The time since Carleton's disappearance, almost a month, had taken its toll. With nothing to do but wait for word, Fanny's social activities were decreasing. Fanny was spending more of her time alone, in her own suite. She had lost considerable weight, now more wraith than sprite, but her grey eyes had lost their icy hardness, as if her frozen spirit were melting at last.

The last shopping expedition had been most successful. To Anne's and Lady Kidwell's surprise, Fanny joined them. It was too much to say that Fanny was her old self, but she roused herself to smile and chat, and to show interest in Anne's errands. In Fortnum and Mason's, Anne settled on exotic teas and preserved fruits for Mrs Hubbard, and later selected a Wedgewood teapot to go with them. At Madame Francine's shop, Anne selected gloves in various colours for friends at home and a pair for herself, and a beautiful silk shawl, woven in soft shades of blue and violet with a hint of silver.

The ladies decided to visit Grantham House, where Anne found the panels of silver lace for the desired overdress, and Fanny unexpectedly selected a dress length of beautiful gauze, glinting with small silver spots, and matching silver ribbons. As they were leaving, a soft dark blue silk that would be perfect under the silver lace caught Anne's eye.

"My dear Anne, I vow those beautiful blue gloves you found at Madame Francine's inspired you! They are a lighter shade than the silk, and will be the perfect touch to the *ensemble*," enthused Fanny. Anne and Lady Kidwell looked at her with surprise and dawning pleasure. "Indeed they will," smiled Anne, "and your silver and white gauze will make a lovely gown for summer parties, as well. You already have silver slippers." At last, the ladies returned home for tea, satisfied with their successful outing.

The next day, Miss Crawford and Anne made their final visits to the British Museum and to Hatchards. "I do want to see those mosaics again, and look more closely at the other Roman items," declared Anne. "It is so interesting to imagine the Romans in England!" At Hatchards, Anne said firmly, "I want a good history of England, one that discusses the Roman presence here." In surprise, Miss Crawford reminded her, "My dear Miss Emmons, recollect, at home, your father's library has all four volumes of Mr Goldsmith's *History of England*." "I am aware but some consider Mr Goldsmith's work to be full of errors and odd theories. I want something more solid, more informative."

After considering the choices for several moments, Anne threw herself on the mercy of the clerk who recommended David Hume's work, *A History of England from the Invasion of Julius Caesar to the Revolution in 1688*. "Mr Hume was a tutor, and a historian of some note, ma'am. He had rather unorthodox views, but his *History* is highly thought of." Anne took all six volumes, and added (in spite of her doubts regarding Mr Goldsmith's scholarship) Goldsmith's *History of Rome*.

Miss Crawford picked up a copy of *A Vindication of the Rights of Woman* by Mary Wollstonecraft, saying, "I have long wanted a copy of this. The author has an unfortunate reputation, but I believe many of her ideas are sound." Both women selected a few novels as well. Six cookery books were selected as well; enough, Miss Crawford decreed, until they knew how best the school could make use of them. The resulting package was large and heavy; Anne was relieved when the clerk courteously indicated it would not be difficult to ship their books directly to York. She kept volume one of Hume's works by her, to read on the journey.

That night, as Anne prepared for bed, a soft tap at her door startled her. As she started toward it, the door opened and Fanny peeked around. "I must speak with you, Anne. These last days have flown by so quickly, and I have much to say." Anne gestured for Fanny to take the chair by the fire, whilst she curled up on the *chaise longue*. Fanny gazed into the fire saying nothing for several long moments, whilst Anne waited. Finally, she signed deeply.

"Anne, my dearest friend, I'm so sorry for these last weeks. I truly did not mean to ignore you or shut you out. I was so...stunned by Carleton's disappearance, and his mother's immediate conviction of his death. I couldn't feel anything but horror." She swallowed with difficulty. "It was much easier to be with people I did not know well."

A fleeting glance up, then Fanny looked back at the fire, and continued. "There is now hope we will find Carleton, and I feel as if I'm awakening from a nightmare. I hope you can forgive me." Anne extended her hand.

"There's nothing to forgive, my dear. I cannot say I fully understand but I had faith you would remember our friendship. I'm just glad we've had this chance to talk before I returned home." The two friends embraced heartily then, Fanny sitting next to Anne on the *chaise* as they continued their conversation.

Earlier in the day, Fanny had been to call on Kate, and the two friends had mingled their tears of relief and reconciliation. "Kate was so upset. She could not understand your emotions, and felt so keenly your shutting yourself off from us," said Anne. "I am aware," replied Fanny remorsefully. "I could see how much I wounded my friends and my parents; I just couldn't help myself. I was numb, and felt nothing. Now there is anticipation for information concerning Carleton, I'm myself again. Kate was gracious enough to forgive me, and to stand my friend, just as you have. I'll not go back to that awful state even if our hopes are dashed." Anne replied, consolingly, "I trust that word will come soon. We must just have patience."

The conversation turned to more cheerful topics, and Anne asked Fanny to consider a visit to York, if not for the spring Race Week, then for the August races. Fanny agreed to consider it, and insisted that Anne plan to make her usual summer sojourn in Kent. "There are no memories of Carleton in either place," said Fanny with relief. "Our courtship took place in town and in Bath; Carleton and his family were to come to us after the engagement was announced. Now all is at a stand, and I am almost happy we were not together in other places." "We can simply enjoy the peaceful countryside and, I hope, the lovely weather," said Anne, with a mischievous twinkle. The two friends talked long into the night before Fanny finally returned to her own rooms.

It seemed like no time at all before it was time to say farewell and get into the coach. Realising it would require at least a week, Mr Emmons carefully planned the journey to York, with changes of horses along the route. He also wrote ahead to arrange overnight stays at comfortable posting houses where he was known and could expect good meals and clean beds. The goodbyes were spoken, tears shed, and the coach rolled away. Anne and Miss Crawford wiled away many hours with reading, when the road permitted. Sometimes Anne read aloud whilst Miss Crawford knitted; sometimes each lady tended to her own book. Mr Emmons occupied himself with business papers, and occasionally challenged Miss Crawford to a game of chess on the travelling chessboard.

The weather remained pleasant, which allowed the journey to be as comfortable as possible. The travellers were met at each stop with refreshments when the horses were changed, or with a good dinner and warm bed when they stayed the night. Still, it was with great relief the party descended at the door of the Emmons' home in York. Although clear, the air was considerably cooler than it had been further south. Anne was glad to go inside and run up to her room to remove her pelisse and bonnet, and to wash her face and hands.

In no time at all, the bandboxes, portmanteaus and other baggage were brought in and unpacked, and the three weary travellers were settled. Within a few days, it was almost as if they had never been away. Anne found the large parcel of books waiting for her in her sitting room. Taking Miss Crawford's volumes to her room, she returned to arrange Hume's *History of England* and Goldsmith's *History of Rome* with her cherished pamphlet on a special bookshelf she requested a servant to place near the mosaic in its glass case. She also had her writing table moved nearer to that part of the room. She was well into the first volume of Hume, and looking forward to reading through the other books as well.

Anne decided to look out the Goldsmith *History of England,* and see if there were other useful volumes in her father's library. "It makes more sense to have them together in one place, so I may use them more easily." She put the novels in the case in her bedroom, near the fireplace, where she kept volumes of poetry, novels and periodicals such as Ackerman's *Repository, La Belle Assemblee,* and *The Ladies' Fashionable Repository.* Anne had been a week at home, when the letter from Fanny came. Carleton was indeed in Bahama, having boarded the ship that night so many weeks ago. The shocking fact was he had actually planned the journey, and did not intend to return immediately.

"He knew his plan would be discouraged, so kept it to himself. Even Mr Franklin was not aware. It seems he wrote to me and to his mother the evening he departed; the letters were left to be posted at an inn but were forgotten. Carleton believes that his wish to visit Bahama to look into business for his father and to plan for our honeymoon journey are sufficient reasons for his abrupt departure and decision to stay. Apparently, he has made some acquaintance on the voyage and has accepted certain engagements. He has decided his presence is not necessary to plan the wedding, and he can return in the autumn in time to wed.

Anne, I do not know what to think. Whilst we have been so anxious, so distressed, he enjoyed the voyage, made new friends, and conceives nothing amiss with extending his stay! He planned this to the point that baggage was waiting for him on board, and he gave no hint to anyone! It seems I never knew him, Anne. I have his direction, but hardly know what to say to him, how to respond."

Chapter 9

Anne sighed, and returned to Fanny's present letter. Carleton's mad voyage had been over five years ago, and he only now decided to return to England. So much had happened during those years, so many changes had occurred. She wondered to whom he had written, and what he said about his return. She knew Fanny only received one other letter from him, in the late summer after that fateful voyage, in which Carleton apologised for his long silence and his absence, and then informed her he had decided to stay in Bahama. He found the differences intriguing, the climate salubrious, and his new acquaintance more stimulating than his friends in England. He had visited his father's properties, and enjoyed the business activities. With a show of remorse, he told Fanny to keep the heirloom sapphire he had given her. That was all.

A few weeks after receiving this letter, Fanny quietly returned the jewel to Carleton's parents. *"You could scarcely imagine a more humiliating and uncomfortable meeting,"* she wrote to Anne afterwards. *"I don't know whether I or his parents were more distressed. It was a relief to bid them farewell, and depart. Fortunately, neither of them tried to embrace me. I would have disgraced myself, I'm certain."* For Carleton, or his family, to expect Fanny to meet him now, as a casual acquaintance (if nothing more), seemed the height of insensitivity.

Anne gazed out of the window towards the pinery. So much had changed here as well. The man from the British Museum, Mr Smith, had come to York himself, after several months of correspondence with her father. He was in the area to study Roman remains and to see what other discoveries might be made. Her own studies and writing engrossed Anne. She completely redesigned her sitting room to accommodate the built-in bookcases needed to accommodate her volumes of history, art and antiquities.

The small glass case originally which originally the mosaic of the girl had been expanded to include a few coins, a beautifully sculptured hand (broken off a statue, she thought), and a lovely cup of carved alabaster set in silver, among other pieces. Her writing table and chair were by the window. The only other furniture pieces were two comfortable chairs in front of the fireplace and a tea table pushed to one side. Instead of a woman's sitting room, she had achieved more the affect of a lady's library, heightened by the matching blue leather bindings on many of her books. (The blue bindings were her father's idea. When he finally demanded the return of his volumes of Goldsmith's *History of England,* Mr Cave's *Antiquities of York,* and other works Anne had appropriated, he ordered copies for her as a surprise, and ordered them bound to match in blue leather with the titles and her initials tooled in gold.)

The scribbled pages begun in London had become a finished article, in which she discussed the Roman presence in York. Anne continued her writing, having an idea for a novel. The Grey Coat School was still an interest, and Anne donated books for class work and prizes. After a meeting with the subscribers, she had set up a scholarship for girls interested in continuing their studies to attend a reputable seminary in Leeds.

Anne continued to spend a month or so of the Season with Fanny and her family in London, but enjoyed it less each year. Whilst her friendship with Fanny was as warm as ever, she could not deny that the two friends had developed widely different tastes and interests. After the awkward season following her broken engagement, Fanny enjoyed the social whirl of balls, parties and cards as much as ever. Anne, who cared little for cards, enjoyed other games and especially enjoyed dancing, but was interested in more serious forms of entertainment.

She and Miss Crawford spent considerable time visiting the museums and exhibitions, attending lectures at the Royal Society, and browsing the bookstores and libraries. Whilst Anne and Fanny both had stopped going to Almack's two years before, she did accompany Fanny to some of the balls and rout parties, preferring those where she knew the hosts and felt comfortable. Anne maintained her cordial acquaintance with Lady Jersey, and they exchanged calls.

Anne had even received a few offers of marriage, all of which she refused. One was from a pleasant young man whom she had met only a few times before he made his offer. Another, to her shock, was from Mr Hopecroft's son. She had spoken to him only in passing at various social events, and did not hesitate to refuse his offer. When Mr Hopecroft himself called to press his son's suit, Anne showed none of her distaste for the man but courteously declined to discuss the matter further. She could not deny a certain satisfaction at *that* turn of events! None of the young men in question had touched Anne's heart, or seemed to have an idea in common with her, and she did not regret at her refusals.

Anne also spent a few weeks at the Kidwell estate in Kent each summer, where she relished the quiet of the countryside. Not a rider, she enjoyed long walks with Lady Kidwell in the lanes and the shrubbery, and the occasional visits to Canterbury and other places of interest. To her own surprise, she had struck up a friendship with Mr Deschevaux, as he appeared both in London and at the Kidwell's estate with unexpected frequency. She had met him in York, at the races, in the last few years, which was not remarkable since he raised racehorses and hunters on his property not far from Lord Kidwell's estate, with a certain amount of success. Mr Deschevaux and Mr

Emmons developed a cordial relationship, discussing business and other interests in common.

Anne seated herself at her desk and wrote to Fanny. *"My dear Fanny, Of course you must come to us, for a few weeks at least. I cannot travel right now, as I have several engagements and commitments, which I cannot put off, besides preparations for the last races and entertainments of the summer. You know you will be included in any you care to attend, and you have acquaintance here after all these years. You are always welcome."* She continued the letter with general news of her father and Miss Crawford, a few wardrobe suggestions as the late summer breezes blew cooler in York, and an affectionate closing. She sealed and directed the letter, then put it downstairs for the Mail.

On her way back to her sitting room, Anne stopped by Mrs Hubbard's room to advise her of Fanny's imminent arrival and to suggest the blue and silver room which overlooked the garden, be readied for her. "From her letter we may expect to see her within the next two weeks or so," speculated Anne. "Well, Miss Anne, we shall be ready for her at her convenience," replied Mrs Hubbard, comfortably.

Anne retired to her dressing room, to look over a new treasure. As he browsed in a small shop, Mr Emmons had come across a weathered, battered object that intrigued him. The shopkeeper could not tell him anything about the small, square object except it had been unearthed locally and, in its dilapidated condition, he was willing to part with it for a few shillings. Mr Emmons took it to a jeweller of his acquaintance who specialised in rare and antique items, to see what he could do with it. Once it was cleaned, polished and restored, Mr Emmons could barely recognise the piece.

"Well, sir, this appears to be a reliquary made of gold, quite old, perhaps two or three hundred years old. As you see, the piece is hinged and has an eye for a ring to hang on a chain. There is an interesting design etched on the back and around the edges of the front. Inside, it could only have held something small, such as a fragment of wood or fabric. I found it intriguing that the border on the front appears to surround an initial, 'A'."

Mr Emmons found it most unusual and attractive; when hung on a chain, it appeared to be diamond-shaped, and the overall appearance was simple and elegant. He had a miniature of Anne's mother, which he instructed the jeweller to fix in place, and selected a chain for it. Mr Emmons had presented the necklace to Anne as a gift just yesterday.

"Two or three hundred years old, Papa? A reliquary... Who could have lost such an object?" Amused, Mr Emmons refused to speculate. "It could be of the fifteenth century...it might be Richard III's time, might it not? An 'A'-mayhap for Anne Neville?" mused Anne. "How very interesting! The miniature is lovely, Papa. Can you bear to part with it?" I always intended it for you, daughter. I had just not found a locket or frame that appealed to me. It somehow seemed right with this piece."

Anne seated herself before her mirror, and then clasped the gold chain around her neck. The locket, as it now was, looked perfect and accented the simple neckline of her soft green day dress. She touched the golden diamond-shaped object with her finger and mused about Anne Neville wearing the reliquary with a piece of the true Cross, a shred of the Holy Mother's robe, or a similar object, and her distress over its loss. With a wry smile for her own absurdity, she rose and returned to her study.

The next morning, Anne was pleased to find two letters beside her plate at the breakfast table, both written in hands she knew well. She opened and read the message from Lady Kidwell with great interest. Lady Kidwell advised Anne that she and Lord Kidwell would follow Fanny to York. *"Fear not, dear Anne. We will not descend on you* en masse. *My lord and I will stay with our friends, the Langleys. Ostensibly, we plan to attend the last Races, for a change. However, we just wanted to be near Fanny. The news is too true; Mr Carleton*

Thomas has returned to his family. We were in London last month, and he had the effrontery to leave his card at the house just before we returned to Kent. That is what has Fanny in such a fever to be gone.

The on dit is that his wife died in childbed, with the baby, leaving him a widower with a young child. He sold the property and business interests in Bahama for his father, and has brought the child to England. Understandable enough, I am sure. But to call at our house is outside of enough! A polite nod in passing is more than he is entitled to expect. Did he imagine we would receive him? As if that were not sufficient, I received a letter from Mrs Thomas enquiring affectionately after Fanny. I had not heard from her in years. This situation is too peculiar and uncomfortable for words."

Shocked, Anne folded the letter, and sipped her breakfast coffee. "What brazen presumption, after that hideous scandal years ago! I never suspected Carleton of such a lack of breeding, such arrogance. He cannot have given Fanny's sentiments a moment's consideration at any time."

Opening the other letter, Anne found a note from her friend Jane Chamberlayne to remind her of a meeting of the "York Bluestocking Society" that afternoon. She smiled and excused herself from the table. She ran upstairs to look over the materials she wanted to take to the meeting. She had formed close friendships with two other young women of similar interests and tastes. Because they enjoyed more scholarly literature and pursuits than many of the other young females of their acquaintance, they had taken to meeting weekly when at home and jokingly used the name "York Bluestocking Society" among themselves, in honour of an earlier group of ladies of scholarly tastes. Miss Crawford frequently accompanied her, and was a welcome contributor.

Anne changed her slippers for brown kid half-boots, put on her gloves, bonnet and spencer, then made her way downstairs. She walked the short distance to Farleigh House, where she joined her friends. Diana Farleigh, a connexion of the current owner, had been invited to reside with the family at Farleigh House several years ago, and she had formed an immediate friendship with Anne. Jane Chamberlayne, whose father was the well-to-do owner of a local bookshop, was the third member of the group. She and Anne had been friends since childhood, but only in the last few years discovered their more literary interests in common. She was engaged to Hugh Heron, a worthy young man. The three discussed a wide range of interests, from literature to science, and enjoyed themselves immensely.

Anne showed them her locket, explaining what the jeweller had told her father. "A reliquary? I'm amazed such a fragile object should survive," commented practical Jane. Diana was inclined to scoff at Anne's romantic notion of the reliquary having belonged to Anne Neville, Richard III's sad queen. "It is more likely to have belonged to an Anne Farleigh, I fancy. I believe there was a daughter of the family at that time named Anne, who died young. Anne was a highly favoured name in the family," suggested Diana. "Another idea is that it might have housed a relic of St. Anne. There have been Armitages and Armstrongs in the area forever. There are many possibilities, after all."

Anne laughed. "I prefer my own theory, and shall hold to it until evidence forces me to change my opinion." The conversation then turned to the books each young woman was presently reading. Jane brought a new pamphlet on rare plants to discuss. Anne read her finished article. "Well done, Anne!" exclaimed Diana. "Very well-written, and interesting material," added Jane, critically. "Have you considered publishing it, Anne?" Anne was surprised. "I hadn't thought of it. Do you think I might?" "Talk to my father," Jane suggested. "He constantly does business with publishers, and might be able to assist you." "Will he not think it odd?' asked Anne. "No, indeed. He is very glad to help." Thoughtfully, Anne nodded. "I will certainly consider that."

Chapter 10

Anne was in her sitting room, reading, when Miss Crawford entered. She looked up and smiled, as Miss Crawford said, "Good morning, my dear. Mr Emmons required me to tell you Mr Deschevaux will dine with us this evening." Anne was surprised. "How curious, Amelia. What brings him to York at this present, I wonder?" "I understand he will attend the last races, and brought his horses up early to rest and train," replied Miss Crawford. "I remember now. Well, he and Papa have a topic for conversation. I will instruct Mrs Hubbard to increase the covers."

Miss Crawford said, "And do not forget to speak to Mr Somers about the wines and so forth. He keeps a close eye on gentlemen's preferences, and will know what to serve." Anne smiled and thanked Miss Crawford for the reminder. "Indeed, he is an excellent butler." The two ladies descended the stairs together, and turned toward the housekeeper's room.

That evening, as dinner progressed, Mr Deschevaux engaged Anne in conversation. "Do you enjoy the races, Miss Emmons?" he enquired diffidently. "I enjoy the spectacle, Mr Deschevaux. The racing colours, the beautiful beasts, even the excitement of the crowds. Still, I do not care for the wagering, and I sometimes wonder what happens to the jockeys and the horses who do not win."

"As with any game of chance, it has its serious side," he agreed. "Many people can to enjoy a wager and still know when to draw line.

Unfortunately, there are those who do not. As for the losers, much depends on the reason for the loss, whether a lack of skill by the rider, poor training of the horse, or the horse simply being unsuited for racing. Additional training may remedy the first two, you know."

"Tell me about your home, Mr Deschevaux. I have visited Fanny and her parents many times, but know little of Kent." Mr Deschevaux paused. "I'm very attached to my home, I must confess. Besides maintaining my stables, I've become something of an agriculturist, almost by default. There are large fields of hops, which keep my tenants busy. We also grow barley. There is a small cherry orchard. My mother had a fondness for plums, so my father had several trees planted for her. The flowerbeds are also very lovely. My grandmother loved roses and herbs, and designed her garden to incorporate the flowers and herbs together. During the summer, the scent is intoxicating, and I never changed the basic design."

He smiled. "It is ironic; I did not expect to come into the estate, and it means much to me. My father and older brother viewed it as a backwater and continually tried to be otherwhere, as they each preferred the life of a fashionable gentleman." Anne exclaimed, "There must be several gardeners then, to manage such a variety of plantings, sir."

"Well, I have a gardener with a few men under him to manage the flowers and kitchen garden. However, my tenants maintain the grain fields and orchard. My bailiff supervises, and brings suggestions, problems or concerns to my attention. I am fortunate in my bailiff, as he usually offers suggestions to solve the difficulties. One thing I do require is that any unusual finds must be brought directly to me."

"Unusual finds? What do you mean, sir?" Mr Deschevaux replied, "You may not be aware of this, but Kent has a fascinating history. Because it has a salubrious climate, and excellent conditions for agriculture, many different groups emigrated to the area over the centuries. Its proximity to Faversham makes it an excellent location for transport by water. There is a navigable creek, which allows sea access, which was expanded by a canal. The Romans settled in the area...." Anne exclaimed, "The Romans were also established in York! Have you found any Roman artefacts?"

"As it happens, I have," asserted Mr Deschevaux, in surprise. "I have a small collection. A few coins, a small figure of a horse, and bits of broken items. I also found a few items that do not seem to fit with the Roman pieces. These include a silver brooch with an odd geometric pattern, and a small amber glass vessel. Are you interested in such things, Miss Emmons?"

The question was all that was needed to set Anne off. Brimming with enthusiasm, she told him of her mosaic, the pamphlet she had found in Hatchards, and her visits to the British Museum. "You may wish to consider visiting there when next you are in London, sir. They may possess answers to your questions regarding the brooch and the amber glass." He looked at her warmly and with a new awareness.

"This seems an unusual interest for a young lady, Miss Emmons. May I say how refreshing it is to discuss matters of this nature with a member of your sex?" He hastily added, "Forgive me if I seem patronising. Most young ladies with whom I have had occasion to chat seem to be more interested in social activities than with subjects of this nature." Cheeks flushed, Anne laughed, and confessed, "I hope I will not seem a traitor to my sex if I confess I, too, enjoy this type of conversation much more. I am afraid I have no talent for society chat, and often sit mum chance in such settings. Social conversation is not one of my gifts. I find it more and more difficult to pretend an interest in a subject I find inconsequential or dull."

They smiled at each other, and Anne noticed how his dark eyes seemed to light up when he smiled. Before they could continue, Mr Emmons interrupted their conversation with a comment which required a response from Mr Deschevaux. After a brief exchange, conversation waned.

Miss Crawford commented on the beautiful weather and

speculated whether it would hold for the races. Anne then took the opportunity to enquire again of Mr Deschevaux's home. "How did you leave matters in Kent? It must be lovely now. The spring seems to come earlier there, and the summer to last longer." He smiled his unexpectedly charming smile and responded, "So beautiful it was difficult to leave. My gardens are at their most luxurious now. Many of the roses will be finished within a few weeks, but when I left, they were magnificent. The meadows are green and lush. When we turn them out, the horses behave almost as children sent out to play."

Involuntarily, Anne smiled back. "I see. A great deal of frisking and head tossing, I dare say?" "Assuredly," agreed Mr Deschevaux. "I had the honour of speaking with Lord Kidwell just before departing. He indicated Lady Kidwell and Miss Fanny are both well. I know they are planning to come to York very soon. I was a bit surprised, as they are usually fixed at home for the summer and autumn." Anne replied only that she was expecting them, and looking forward to their visit. She thought he looked at her enquiringly, but drew her father into the conversation with a question about entertainments planned after the last race.

The rest of the evening passed comfortably, as Miss Crawford and Anne conversed by the drawing room fire, whilst Mr Emmons and Mr Deschevaux enjoyed a hand of piquet. Anne and Miss Crawford retired before the game ended. As they mounted the stairs, Anne said, "Mr Deschevaux does not seem aware of Fanny's plan to come ahead of her parents."

"He is unlikely to know that Mr Thomas has distressed Miss Fanny by making an approach. You were wise to respond to him as you did, my dear. The less said about the circumstance the better," returned Miss Crawford. Uncomfortably, Anne murmured, "Poor Fanny! What can Mr Thomas be thinking, Amelia?" Austerely, Miss Crawford replied, "Certainly, not about anyone's comfort but his own. Had he the smallest elegance of mind, he would not have announced his return in such fashion."

The next day, Anne decided to visit her brother Robert at the Cathedral. She dispatched a note to see if he could spare her some time in the afternoon. Upon receipt of his invitation to call at his home, near the Minster, she set off in a hackney. Soon seated at the tea table facing Robert, she beamed at him fondly as she enquired as to his health. "I am never ill; you know, Anne," he exclaimed with a laugh. "I am delighted to see you. We seem to spend so much time in our own pursuits. What is your news?" Anne told him of the most recent meeting with her friends and the planned entertainments for the last of the summer races. Then, she told him about Fanny's projected visit and the reason for it.

"She may be here at any moment, Robert. Her letter showed such distress, almost panic. She told me little of Carleton's letter, only that she refused to meet him. After all these years, I do not know what to credit!" Robert said soberly, "Well, my dear sister, until Fanny arrives and tells you what she wishes you to know, all is merely speculation. Whatever has happened, Fanny clearly needs a sanctuary, and you have offered it by welcoming her. There is really nothing else to consider at this point."

Robert rose to ring for the servant to clear. "I will be glad to see Fanny again. It has been several years since I last met her." Anne looked at him with surprise. "Why, Robert, you always said you were unable to attend social gatherings due to your work and other commitments...." Quietly, Robert replied, "And such has always been the case. I have seen to it." She looked at her brother closely and saw a shadow in his deep blue eyes, so like her own. "Robert, are you saying you care for Fanny?"

Unexpectedly he laughed. "My dear sister, any male with blood in his veins would care for Fanny! As lovely as she is, with such a delightful spirit, your friend is quite the paragon. I realised years ago I was forming an unwise attachment. Lord and Lady Kidwell may look as high as they choose for Fanny, after all. A clerical secretary, no matter how well off, is hardly a brilliant match for their daughter.

Then there was Mr Thomas. No, Anne, I had a young man's dream. I put it aside long ago. I will be happy to meet her again as a family friend, nothing more."

He smiled. "You must know, I have enjoyed making the acquaintance of your friend, Miss Diana Farleigh. She is charming and a very interesting young lady with whom to converse." He firmly turned the conversation to family matters and asked if she had heard from their brother Matthew in Leeds. "Not from Matthew. However, I received a letter from our sister-in-law, dear Lydia. She was so kind as to invite me to stay with them for the next several weeks. You know she is increasing again. Had she not mentioned how ill she is, and how troublesome little Walter was, I might have regretted that I must decline. As it was, I was delighted to have legitimate reasons to stay at home. Matthew enjoys his customary rude good health, much to Lydia's annoyance!"

Robert and Anne both laughed. Then Anne said with a little remorse, "I should not make fun at her expense. Lydia has always been most kind to me. However, I have never had such a letter of invitation; she implored my attendance yet gave me so many reasons *not* to want to be there! She mentioned that her mama will be there within a week or so, so she will receive all of the cosseting she could desire."

Robert chuckled involuntarily. "And Matthew will wish himself otherwhere within two days! We may yet see him for the races, or mayhap he will recall an important meeting with my father. I will have a room prepared for him, in the event he appears." Brother and sister laughed again, and then Anne rose to take her leave.

Unbeknownst to Anne, Mr Emmons had entertained an unexpected caller. He had been working in his library, reviewing letters from various agents, when Somers brought a visitor's card to him. Brows lifted, he instructed the butler, "Bring Mr Hopecroft here." He rose as Mr Hopecroft entered. "Good afternoon, sir," he said urbanely. "How may I serve you?" Disconcerted, Mr Hopecroft paused. "You *are* Mr Walter Emmons?"

With a slight smile, Mr Emmons inclined his head. "I am, undeniably," he replied. "To what do I owe the honour of your call?" He indicated a chair to his visitor and resumed his seat. Mr Hopecroft leaned forward, and responded earnestly, "My son, Mr Emmons, has made your daughter an offer of marriage, which she refused. It occurred to me afterwards she might have considered it improper to accept an offer that did not come through you. I am here to formally present the offer on my son's behalf to you as her father, so you may present the matter to her correctly."

Mr Emmons leaned back in his chair as he considered his visitor dispassionately. "As I am sure you are aware, Anne is of full age, and needs neither my permission to entertain an offer, nor my consent to accept. She mentioned young Mr Hopecroft's offer to me, and told me of her refusal. I was a bit surprised neither you nor your son had approached me, but the event was already in the past. I fear any reiteration of your son's proposal would not elicit a different response." Mr Emmons remembered what Miss Crawford had told him of the circumstances of Anne's acquaintance with Mr Hopecroft, and thought sardonically, "And I would discourage any thought to change that response!"

Mr Hopecroft pressed his case. He outlined the advantages of the match, spoke of the depth of his heir's sincere affection for Miss Anne, and mentioned how delighted he himself would be to call her his daughter. Mr Emmons repressed a sigh. "And what of her dowry, sir? What settlements are you prepared to make, and what provisions do you require?"

Nonplussed, Mr Hopecroft sat back in his chair. "You are extremely blunt, sir!" Drily, Mr Emmons responded, "I am always direct in matters of business, and business is a major concern in arranging any marriage. My daughter indicated only the slightest acquaintance with your son. In point of fact, she has never mentioned his first name, and I cannot understand when he has had an opportunity to form the deep attachment to which you refer. When I set the tender emotions aside, the matter is then reduced to the business aspect of the proposal. What have you to say, Mr Hopecroft?" Mr Hopecroft's eyes dropped as he smoothed the sleeve of his coat.

After waiting a few moments, Mr Emmons added softly, "Does it make it easier if I say I am quite aware of your financial... circumstances?" Flushed with anger, Mr Hopecroft raised his head and replied through clenched teeth, "My *circumstances*, as you call them, are not at issue. My one thought is to further my son's cause...."

Mr Emmons responded in disgust, "Don't talk fustian, sir. Do you imagine me a fool? Or one to be so impressed by your lineage that I might disregard the facts? In plain words, sir, you are in debt. Vast debt incurred, in large part, by your *penchant* for gambling. I know, for example, the Master of Ceremonies here in York welcomes you to the Round Room only as a spectator, not permitted to play. Your illustrious ancestry will not ensure my daughter a home and security, when your property is taken, and you are incarcerated in debtor's prison!"

Mr Hopecroft rose, and paced hastily to the fireplace and back. "It will not come to that, sir! Our family is ancient and respected. I am taking steps...." Mr Emmons interjected, "And your son's marriage to an heiress, in control of her own funds, would be a significant step indeed. Let me relieve your curiosity, sir. Anne's funds are in trust, and cannot be accessed for expenses such as we are discussing. Further, I myself would not undertake to part with a farthing piece to clear debts of this nature. Given these circumstances, do you still wish to discuss the advantages of the match?"

Mr Hopecroft stood before the desk, his face dark red with choler, and replied in a voice choked with rage, "You go too far, sir! You, a mere tradesman, to address me in this fashion!" Mr Emmons laughed. "I am a tradesman, sir, but not an ignorant one. My daughter does not need your ancient family name to secure a place amongst intelligent persons of real stature." He rose and rang to summon the footman. "Mr Hopecroft, I thank you for the 'honour' you have bestowed on my daughter by making this offer. I fear her refusal must be considered as final. I bid you good day." The door opened to disclose a young footman.

"Pray, show Mr Hopecroft out." Mr Hopecroft stood for a moment, his glare meeting Mr Emmons' cool, contemptuous gaze. Through clenched teeth, he returned, "You will regret this day's work, sir. You have not heard the last of this." Mr. Hopecroft nodded curtly and followed the footman from the room. Mr Emmons shook his head as he resumed his seat at his desk and continued contemplation of his letters.

As Anne mounted the front steps to the entrance of her home, Mr Hopecroft rushed out the door. She paused and looked up at him with some surprise. He looked back at her with hatred. "Too good for my son, are you, madam? When I am finished, you will be most fortunate if any respectable family considers you a worthy prospect!" He stormed past her, almost jostling her on the step. Bewildered, Anne entered the house and walked straight to her father's library.

"Papa, I just had the most uncomfortable encounter with Mr Hopecroft, at our door. He was so enraged. Whatever has occurred?" Mr Emmons outlined the purpose of Mr Hopecroft's call, and said only Mr Hopecroft had renewed his son's offer unsuccessfully. (He saw no reason to give the details of the discussion; it would merely serve to increase Anne's distress.) His brief description increased Anne's bewilderment. "Why is he so angry now? When I first refused young Mr Hopecroft's offer, he and his father were disappointed, but nothing like so irate. What he said to me on the steps was almost a threat!"

In concern, Mr Emmons asked Anne what had transpired. When Anne told him, he shook his head. "He is angry, my dear, but there is little he can do. He may be unpleasant, but he can hardly hope to affect your situation in any way that matters. It is in every way unfortunate that you met him at that particular moment. Do not consider it further, sweetheart."

Chapter 11

The sounds and bustle of an arrival in the hallway disturbed them. Anne turned back to see who was there. Mr Emmons stood for a moment, and then returned to his library. He seated himself at his desk and thought of Anne's words, "almost a threat." Almost, indeed! He pulled out a sheet of paper and a pen and wrote.

"Sir. My daughter informed me of your parting words to her. I take this opportunity to advise you that, if any unpleasantness concerning my daughter is traced back to you or to a connexion of yours, I will be forced to take a serious interest in your affairs. I do not respond well to threats in business affairs, or to my family. You will find I possess a certain reputation for concluding matters as expeditiously as possible, once my attention is fixed. I thank you for your attention."

Mr Emmons signed his name, leaned back in his chair and drew a long breath and deliberately relaxed his clenched fingers. Only the tautness of his jaw, and the tight muscles in his neck revealed his ire. He sat for a moment, and then began another letter, this time to an associate in London, in which he requested certain information. Meanwhile, Anne hurried toward the door, and found Fanny just entering the hall with her maid. The two friends flew into each other's arms and hugged each other.

"Fanny, I'm so glad you are come at last!" cried Anne. Standing back from each other, the young women smiled. "We shall have such fun!" responded Fanny. "Let me show you to your room at once, so you can put off your hat and rest," Anne suggested. "I have put you in the blue room, near my own. It has just been redecorated, and I am sure you will be comfortable there." The two friends climbed the stairs, chattering all the way.

The next several days flew by, with race meetings, card assemblies on Monday nights for those who enjoyed play, dinners and banquets, and plenty of dancing. Anne and Fanny had their pick of invitations. Just last night, they had attended a large ball at Farleigh House. Anne lay back against her pillows and reviewed the evening with mixed emotions. Her father had accompanied her and Fanny to the ball in the carriage. Both young women looked their best: Fanny wore a silver tissue over white satin with diamonds, and Anne was clad a soft violet silk with her favourite pearls. They arrived early, to find the entry already crowded. Patiently, they stood in the receiving line to greet their host, and his guests, Lord and Lady Jersey.

Anne recalled with pleasure the kindness of Lady Jersey's smile and greeting. As she took a sip of chocolate, her pleasure faded a trifle. Lord and Lady Kidwell were there ahead of her and Fanny, accompanied by Mr Deschevaux. Her friends, Diana Farleigh and Jane Chamberlayne, were also there. The ballroom, decorated by masses of flowers and lit by hundreds of candles in chandeliers and sconces, was almost too warm. Anne's brother Robert, dressed in immaculate evening clothes, joined them. Introductions were made, and dances claimed.

In the opening set, all was according to protocol. Subsequently, Mr Emmons led out Lady Kidwell, Mr Deschevaux Miss Farleigh, and Lord Kidwell claimed Anne. As they stepped and bowed through the country dance, Anne glimpsed Fanny, who performed with grace as Robert's partner. A fleeting thought of surprise was lost in the enjoyment of the dance. It was after the second set when Anne glanced about her and realised that Mr Deschevaux had yet not solicited her to dance. To her own surprise, she was somewhat chagrined by his apparent neglect. Mentally, she shook herself and set herself to enjoy the next pair of dances, this time with Lord Jersey. The evening passed quickly.

For the supper dance, Anne danced with Robert. Content without conversation, the brother and sister glided easily through the set. Turning, they saw Fanny with Mr Deschevaux, his dark head bent to her fair one. The next movement of the dance swept them away. "Fanny and Mr Deschevaux?" thought Anne with incredulity. She remembered Fanny's few comments about him, and would have sworn Fanny indifferent to him. After supper, she sat out with Lady Kidwell and Lady Jersey.

In the midst of their enjoyable conversation, her eye was caught when Fanny swirled by, this time in a waltz, again with Charles Deschevaux. They made a striking couple, her silvery locks and grey eyes contrasting with his dark colouring, but Anne took little pleasure in the sight. She turned her gaze aside in time to see Robert dance by with Diana Farleigh, his dark head bent over her soft brown curls. With an effort, she forced her attention back to the conversation. The rest of the evening passed slowly for Anne. At one point, Mr Deschevaux smiled, bowed and spoke to her, but did not linger.

Late in the evening Mr. Deschevaux approached her for the last set. Anne smiled, dropped a quick curtsey, and they took to the floor. The couple exchanged a few remarks, touching on the splendid music, the excellent supper and the delightful evening, and then fell silent. *"Why did he ask me to dance now?"* thought Anne. As if in answer to her thoughts, Mr Deschevaux broke the silence. "I enjoy dancing with you, Miss Emmons. You don't strain to converse through the set." Anne smiled, and murmured a response, surprised at her own annoyance.

As they drove home, Anne yearned to ask Fanny what she thought of Mr Deschevaux, to know if the old neighbourly indifference had changed. Somehow, the words stuck in her throat, and she confined herself to inane pleasantries about the delights of the evening. The friends rode home with Mr Emmons, chatting in an unsatisfactory, superficial way that left Anne confused about her own emotions.

The next morning, as she lay back against her pillows, Anne pondered, "Why do I even care that Fanny danced with Charles? They are neighbours; it may mean nothing. If they have become fond of each other, it is a most suitable arrangement. Their properties are similar, they are acquainted since childhood, and they are well matched by birth. If anything, I should be glad to see Fanny move forward with her life." Reason and logic did not make the memory of those two heads so nearly touching any more pleasant. She did not even notice that she thought of Mr Deschevaux as "Charles".

With a sigh, Anne set her cup down, threw back her quilts and rose. She rang the bell for Ellen and began the process of getting ready for the day. There was much to do before the evening's entertainment. She glanced out the window, and smiled with involuntary pleasure at the lovely late summer day, with the sun shining and the trees gently swaying with the breeze. She selected one of her favourite day dresses from the wardrobe, rose-striped muslin, with a deeper rose spencer in sarcenet. She wore no jewellery except small pearl earbobs. Satisfied with her appearance, she ran down the stairs, and headed for the housekeeper's room to confer over the day's meals.

After writing a few letters in the morning room, she proceeded to the breakfast room. Anne seated herself at the table and greeted her father and Amelia Crawford affectionately, and enquired for Fanny. Miss Crawford replied, "Miss Fanny went out earlier. It seems she had a message from her mother requesting her to join them for breakfast." Rather relieved, Anne enjoyed her light repast more than she had expected.

She was sitting in the garden when Fanny returned. Anne looked up from her book as Fanny sat down next to her on the garden bench. "How were Lord and Lady Kidwell this morning?" Flushed, Fanny answered, "Both well, I thank you. Mama wanted to talk to me before anyone else could." Fanny sat for a moment, obviously irritated. "It seems Mr Thomas is here in York. A friend of Father's saw him at the races yesterday." Concerned, Anne closed her book.

"Oh, Fanny, now what's to do?" Fanny rose and strode over to the rose bed. She turned, looked Anne squarely in the eye.

"Why, nothing, dear Anne, nothing at all. It no longer matters where he is, who he sees or what he does. I am not sure why or when it happened, but he is no longer a object of concern." She returned to the bench and sat down again. "My mother was upset and worried for me. I only regret that the situation has distressed her." Anne looked at her with surprise and solicitude. "Are you so certain, Fanny? His appearance in London worried you to the point that you left Town."

"I know, and I am annoyed that I allowed him to overset me in such a way." She glanced at Anne. "It has been a short time, and I have not yet seen him since that day in London. However, since I have been here with you, I have gained a new perspective. All of the hurt and humiliation is finally behind me."

Anne clasped her hand and said, "Fanny, I am so glad for you." Fanny smiled. "I thank you, dear friend. It is past time I moved forward with my life. In truth, my mother has been saying words to that effect anytime these last five years!" She laughed. "I am glad to look *ahead*, instead of continually remembering that painful time. It simply no longer matters."

Fanny paused, thoughtfully. "Come to that, nothing did happen; we had no quarrel. Carleton was the one who caused the uproar and the scandal. I have been very foolish, have I not?" Both young women laughed, and Anne replied, "Well, goose, your mother and your friends tell you that regularly, so I must agree with you!"

After a companionable silence, Anne steeled herself to ask casually, "What brought you to this realisation, Fanny? Did something happen? Is there someone...?" Fanny shook her head. "I really cannot say. Nothing in particular has occurred," she chuckled, "and there is certainly no man in my eye at this present. I only know these last days have shown me it is possible, and long past time, for me to ponder the future. Whether I fall in love again, marry, or not, I believe I can have a good life and it is simply time to do so." She paused again, and looked at Anne.

"I've watched you here in your home, as you manage the household, pursue your own interests, and meet with your friends. That has encouraged me to see that I could do more than attend parties and go shopping. I have lately become so *bored*, but never tried to do anything about it. I am not yet certain what direction I will take, as the studying and writing that so engage you will not do for me, but I have some ideas in mind. When we return home, I plan to have a long talk with Mama." Fanny blushed faintly and mentioned casually, "Your brother Robert has also made suggestions." Relieved, Anne hugged her friend.

"I am so happy to hear this from you, my dear. In the last few years, I have been so concerned for you. I knew you received little pleasure from many of the social engagements you pursued, but did not know what to suggest." They rose from the bench and strolled toward the pinery.

"Let's see if there is any ripe fruit." Anne continued, "I was so relieved when we decided not to attend the assemblies at Almack's." She grimaced. "That last time, two children in their first season referred to us as 'old things' and I felt miserably out of place." Fanny laughed and agreed. "I heard them as well, and had great pleasure in teaching one little minx some manners. Such a set-down as I gave the child! I find the Marriage Mart holds little interest for me now." Anne agreed. "It is too cold, too calculating. When I was younger, I saw the glamour, the *cachet* of receiving a voucher. I did not really understand the intense business negotiations behind the match-making."

Anne looked at Fanny soberly. "Do not misunderstand me. I understand the importance of marriage and accept the business aspect is significant. I simply want to be more than a piece of merchandise. Mayhap I have been too sensitive, but I have always known that my father's fortune is my redeeming feature to Society. At Almack's, I was too uncomfortable, too uncertain of my welcome in society, to enjoy the game of courtship as played there."

Fanny nodded. "I, too, could not help but be aware. Now I am older, especially after the disastrous end of my engagement, I am aware that my 'value' as a marriage prize has deteriorated. However, my dear, we must be of good heart! We are not quite old tabbies yet! Women with our advantages make good matches every day." Anne concurred, and continued, "We must also remember that women with our advantages do not *have* to marry. We are fortunate neither of us will have to worry about being destitute if we do not marry. Yet I do not want to become an encumbrance, a weight around the neck of either of my brothers."

With flushed cheeks, Anne carried on, "I would also like children, I think, and it is difficult to consider a family without a husband and father." Fanny looked at Anne with a mischievous expression on her face, and said, "Well-nigh impossible, I would hope!" They looked at each other and giggled irrepressibly. Anne entered the pinery, took the basket with two plump, golden specimens from the gardener, and then both young women strolled back to the house, chatting about the evening's plans.

Chapter 12

The days flew by, and September approached. The last races were held (Mr Emmons' horse placed third in his race, whilst one of Mr Deschevaux's horses actually won) and the last parties enjoyed. Lord and Lady Jersey had already left for their engagement further north, and other visitors departed. As Anne glanced over the London papers, an article caught her eye. "Papa, whatever do you think? The *TIMES* says Mr Hopecroft is bankrupt! It seems there was an execution served, and his property seized to recover debts! How shocking and sad it is."

"Sad, indeed, daughter, that a man of such distinguished family wasted his fortune so." Something in his voice made Anne look at him curiously. Before she could question him, Mr Emmons excused himself and rose, murmuring that he had letters to write. He left the room for his library, and Fanny looked at her friend. "A lucky escape for you, Anne." Startled, Anne replied, "Whatever do you mean, Fanny?" Fanny answered, "I believe he was seen leaving this house, and you told me yourself his son offered for you. Did not Mr Hopecroft seek to engage you to his son?" Anne blushed. "Yes, but there was no chance of his success. I was scarcely acquainted with his son when he approached me, and I have never forgotten my first encounter with Mr Hopecroft, all those years ago." Fanny looked thoughtful. "Yet Kate mentioned a rumour in her last letter...."

At that moment, Somers entered the room and announced, "Miss

Emmons, there is a caller for Miss Kidwell." Anne asked, "Did he give you a card or a name?" He bowed and said, "He is a Mr Thomas, Miss Emmons. What shall I say, ma'am?" Wide-eyed, Anne and Fanny looked at each other. Before Anne could ask Fanny her preference, Fanny instructed, "Show Mr Thomas into the drawing room. Miss Emmons and I will see him there."

After Somers left, Anne asked, "What are you about, Fanny? You do not have to receive him." "I know, my dear. I wish to end this pointless pursuit, and meeting him seems the only way to do it. Please come with me; I want no one else to witness this sad occasion and I refuse to see him alone!" Anne saw the force of her arguments and acquiesced. Each young woman finished her tea and then rose.

Carleton stood by the long glass window, staring out at the garden. To Anne's eye, he looked sallow and thinner, somehow diminished. Anne stayed just inside the drawing room door, whilst Fanny glided to the centre of the room. "Mr Thomas," she said. "I won't pretend this is a pleasure. I was told that you wish to speak with me. Well, pray do so, and let us have done with this." Awkwardly, Carleton bowed. "Please, Fanny, Miss Kidwell, can we not be seated and discuss matters like rational beings?" He looked at Anne, and added, "Miss Emmons, I make my apologies for the intrusion of my personal matters into your home." His lifted brow and glance toward the door invited her to be gone.

Nettled, Anne replied, "Sir, I am here at Miss Kidwell's request." He shook his head, turned back to Fanny and looked a question. Fanny sat down next to the fireplace. Anne selected an armchair near the door, trying to be as inconspicuous as possible, and wished she were anywhere else.

"Fanny," Carleton said earnestly, "I don't expect you to understand or to forgive me. I must explain what occurred; try to make peace with you." He paused. "It's so difficult to know where to start..." She rose from her chair. "The time is long past for this conversation, Mr Thomas. We meet as virtual strangers now, and I prefer to let us remain so." He looked up at that. "Ah, Fanny, don't hate me!" he pleaded sadly. She stood rigidly, "Sir, you lost the right to address me so personally when you broke our engagement. As for 'hate,' that is far too strong a word. Pity and revulsion come nearer the mark." He winced.

"I have earned that. Only let me tell you the whole." As she looked at the mantle clock, Fanny said, "Sir, I will give you five more minutes. Use them well." She remained standing. Carleton sighed. "Do you remember the ball, the night we announced our betrothal? It was so beautiful. However, that evening was the beginning of my disquietude. The obligation, the commitment, became real that night and, the more congratulations I received, the more doubtful I became. The wedding, even though it was weeks away, had an immediacy that was appalled me.

When we made our social rounds, when I visited my clubs, where ever I went, I received felicitations on our engagement that brought me no pleasure. I became more and more confused. I told myself I needed to get away for a space, to take time to think. When I hit upon the idea of visiting Bahama, I convinced myself it was reasonable. I could take care of some business for my father and look about for suitable honeymoon accommodation for you and me. On impulse, I found a ship, paid my passage, and had my luggage placed aboard. I told myself there was no need to discuss it with anyone, no sense to upset my mother, when I would leave letters to explain all, and would soon return in any case."

Carleton continued, "Franklin did not have a notion of my plans. He had no idea, that last night, it was a farewell party. We made our rounds, had a bang-up evening; I drank too much. At the last, when we were down by the docks, I saw the ship and, in my stupor, it seemed to beckon to me." He paused and groped for words. Unconsciously, Fanny sank back into a chair, as mixed emotions roiled within her, whilst Anne focused her gaze on her clasped hands in an agony of embarrassment.

"Somehow, I got on board and stumbled around the deck. I am ashamed to admit I was so drunk I was barely able to stand. A seaman found me wandering, and escorted me to my cabin, thrust me in and shut the door behind me. I was only able to find a place to lie down, to recover myself. I threw myself onto a berth and fell asleep." Carleton looked at her squarely. "I believe I slept, or was unconscious, for two days. When I awoke, I had no idea where I was immediately. I was horrified to find myself on a ship headed out to sea, knowing I had not the courage to discuss my actions with anyone beforehand. I was fortunate in that I had won heavily that last night; at least, I was in funds." He sighed.

"I was relieved when I discovered my luggage." He looked away from Fanny. "I nerved myself to approach the captain and explain my situation. He was gracious enough to accept my apologies for my awkward boarding and my condition. I wrote to my mother, to inform her that I was safely aboard. I also wrote to you." Fanny looked away, feeling a confused blend of sympathy and contempt. "Fanny, that letter..."

Fanny interjected, "You must know that we did not receive the letters you had left behind you. Are you surprised, sir, to learn that I did not receive another letter, until you wrote to break our engagement? Your mother received no other communication either. Can you imagine how your mother felt, sir? We will not even discuss my own emotions. We imagined all manner of horrors." He drew a breath. "I did not know for some time, until my mother wrote in answer to my later letters. At any rate, such as they were, I entrusted my letters to the captain with no guarantee that they would be sent."

With difficulty, Carleton continued, "I won't bore you with a description of the voyage. After I wrote those letters, a weight dropped away from my spirits. I formed friendships, which continued when we reached land. I moved into lodgings and investigated my father's holdings and business there. To my own surprise, I became interested and involved in the work and managing the property. I started a social life." At this point, he swallowed.

"I did not realise how much more strictly propriety is observed in the colonies than in London. So many things I did not realise.... When I discovered how deeply I was involved with a young lady, through my own ignorance and careless behaviour, I wrote you to break our engagement. I could not tell you how compromised I was. It seemed better to let you assume I was a shuffling rogue without knowing the full circumstance than to reveal what an utter swine I had behaved to you and to Lucy."

Carleton raised his head and looked Fanny squarely in the eyes. "We were married within a few weeks. Neither she nor her father ever learnt of my engagement to you. Her mother knew; she received a letter from a friend in London. However, Lucy and I had already married, so her mother did not tell her." Carleton smiled wryly. "She did not care overmuch for me before then; after she received that letter, she could hardly bear to be in the same room with me. As we neither of us were desirous of hurting Lucy, she managed to be civil when we met. Lucy and I were... comfortable together. We developed a fondness for each other. When we had our son, our life together was warm and pleasant. Our daughter was born three years ago. Then, the fever struck."

He walked to the window. Gazing out, Carleton continued. "Lucy and our daughter both died, followed by her father. I hated the distance from my own family and England. My mother-in-law made no secret of the fact she blamed me for Lucy's death. Finally, I broached the possibility of selling our interests in Bahama, and my father agreed. My son lives at our country home where my mother is happily engaged in spoiling him." Anne looked at Fanny, who glanced back at her. There was a long silence.

Finally, Fanny asked, "This has been most interesting, sir, and I am sorry for your losses; they are heavy indeed. Still, I fail to see what this has to do with me." Carleton returned to his chair, and asserted, "Fanny, Miss Kidwell, I owe it to you and to my poor Lucy to explain how it happened, and to ask your forgiveness. I hoped...." Fanny rose again.

"If forgiveness is what you wish, you have it, Mr Thomas. It took time, but I have recovered from the pain I experienced during that period. I must tell you now that there can be nothing more between us. You cannot expect me to stand your friend. My family and yours have had no intimacy of any kind since our engagement ended, and I am convinced we would all be more comfortable to leave the situation as it is." She glanced at Anne, who also rose, and back to Carleton.

"I thank you for calling. I am certain you meant it kindly, but must ask you not to call on me again." She and Anne both curtsied briefly, and Fanny led the way out of the room. Anne paused only to instruct a footman to show Mr Thomas out, and hurried after her.

Limp with relief, the two young women sank into chairs in Anne's sitting room. Fanny sighed, "Thank God that is over! Anne, I cannot thank you enough for staying by me during that hideous interview. I shouldn't have asked it of you, and can only thank you again and again." Anne replied, "Fanny, I was never so mortified in my life. Yet you could not receive him alone, and it is done." Anne rang, and asked the maid who answered to bring tea. "Or would you prefer something else, Fanny?" she asked.

"Frankly, my dear, I think sherry would be delightful." "Sherry, then," said Anne, and the maid departed. Fanny and Anne sat in silence, and watched the fire. After they had each taken a sip of sherry, Anne roused herself to speak. "What do you think brought Mr Thomas here today, Fanny? He might have written to you any time these last few years." Fanny shook her head.

"In truth, my dear Anne, I don't believe he even thought of me until after he returned to England. Although his parents and intimate friends welcomed him gladly, others are not as willing to greet his return as if nothing had happened. There is some awkwardness in

London society as a result of his behaviour those years ago. Kate mentioned in a letter that her mother said he had been cut in public more than once, and was left off various invitation lists. I am certain his sudden eagerness for forgiveness has more to do with smoothing out his social difficulties."

Anne pondered Fanny's words. "I understand, yet he seemed so sincere. I wonder what he hoped." Fanny asked, "What do you mean?" "At the last, before you ended the call, he said, 'I hoped...' I just wonder what he meant to say." Fanny responded crisply, "I did not want to know what he hoped; that is why I ended it so abruptly. I was ill mannered, but I did not want to hear any more of Carleton's experiences, his concerns or his hopes. His sole interest was his own welfare. Did you not observe how he completely ignored the fact that his mother and I had been so worried about him? I don't understand how I failed to notice Carleton's lack of concern for other people! He is not the man I thought him."

Anne replied, "Well, at least his parents will enjoy their grandson." Fanny gave a most unladylike snort, and commented, "I'm certain they will. His mother will be delighted to spoil another generation of Thomas boys." After they finished their sherry, Anne and Fanny decided to change and go to the New Walk to walk by the river. "Nothing like fresh air to clear the mind!"

As they strolled in the shade of the elms, Anne and Fanny were each preoccupied by their own thoughts, content to make idle observations on the beauty of the day. They rested on a bench from time to time, and watched the river traffic and other passers-by. Anne took the opportunity of one such pause to tell Fanny about her article. "Should I consider publication, Fanny? I hadn't seriously thought of such a thing, I confess," said Anne.

"You never told me what you were writing, Anne. I have not read it, so I find it difficult to advise you. However, I know you to be meticulous in all of your projects. It cannot hurt to enquire for information about publishing." She hugged her friend. "A famous authoress! It is a wonderful idea." Anne flushed. "Not famous, Fanny. If I publish, it must be anonymously, or under another name. What if it isn't well received? I could not embarrass my family and friends so." Finally, as the afternoon passed, they returned to the house to prepare for the evening.

Chapter 13

A few days later, Anne sat at her desk, attending to her correspondence. She reread a letter from Emily. *"Kate is not yet recovered from losing the baby a few weeks ago. She is low in spirits, and is still feverish. Thank heavens, her husband won't allow the doctor to bleed her further. He and Mama took her to their country home for a space, which I fancy will help her enormously. The house is located in a beautiful area, and her husband has established excellent succession houses. Kate will be assured of good air and succulent fruit to tempt her appetite."*

Emily went on to discuss her father's preoccupation with politics and her own doings. *"My aunt has proposed carrying me off to Bath or another watering place for a few weeks. She is great fun so I expect to be well entertained..."* Anne gazed absently out the window as she pondered her reply. Engrossed in her letter, she did not hear the soft tap at the door and started, dropping her pen, as Fanny burst in impetuously.

"It is so exciting, Anne! You must read the note from my mother immediately. We are invited to Littlebrook House!" Fanny held out three notes to Anne. "A grand ball is planned, and we are invited to spend a few days at the estate." Anne took her letters and looked over them, and recognised Lady Kidwell's hand as well as that of Lady Jersey. The third missive was directed in an unfamiliar script. Somewhat bewildered, she looked up at Fanny, as Fanny continued,

"I have already spoken to Mama, and read the invitation. Pray, Anne, are you not thrilled?" Anne smiled in sympathy.

"My dear Fanny, I don't yet know what to think. I quite thought that you and your parents had made other plans. By your leave, I want to read my letters before I burst into raptures." Anne glanced through Lady Kidwell's note and saw that Fanny was correct; the two young ladies were invited to accompany Lord and Lady Kidwell to Littlebrook House for a few days, to attend the ball. She turned her attention to the unfamiliar hand, and admired the elegant card of invitation from Lady FitzMaynard. Bewildered, she looked up at Fanny.

"Are your parents acquainted with Lord and Lady FitzMaynard? I confess I visited Littlebrook House on a Public Day, several years ago, but never had the slightest contact with either of them. I wonder..." Impatient, Fanny interrupted, "Papa has acquaintance with Lord FitzMaynard through business in London. Anne, what says Lady Jersey? You have not yet read her note." Anne laughed at Fanny's eagerness, broke the seal and spread open Lady Jersey's missive.

"Fanny, Lady Jersey is responsible for the invitation. She writes that she and Lord Jersey will break their journey at Littlebrook House for a space. She ventured to suggest that you and I would be unexceptionable companions for Lady FitzMaynard's cousin, who is visiting them. It seems Lady FitzMaynard recalled an introduction to your mother, and was pleased to agree to include us in the invitation to your parents." Fanny sank into the chair facing Anne.

Anne continued slowly, "I know little of Lord and Lady FitzMaynard. The Farleigh family, of course, knows them. The late Lord FitzMaynard was a powerful and influential politician. They were seldom in Yorkshire and even less often in York, mostly for the races in May. The estate is near Kinhurst, some thirty miles away. I understand the current Lord FitzMaynard still attends the York Races occasionally; his father had a famous racing stable many years ago, which the current lord has maintained. They do not attend the Assemblies or visit York with any frequency, of late."

Anne and Fanny looked at one another and Fanny declared, "We must call on my mother this minute! She will put us in the way of things. Littlebrook House! A great treat, my friend!" She ran out of the room to don her hat, spencer and gloves. Anne moved with reluctance, uneasy about the invitation. As she tied her bonnet strings, she met her own eyes in the mirror, registering the doubt. Although the FitzMaynards were not as influential as in by-gone days, the society in which Lord and Lady FitzMaynard moved was quite elevated and very political.

An active Member of Parliament, Lord FitzMaynard was on good terms with an inner circle which included Lord Castlereagh. Anne wasn't at all sure she wanted to accept this invitation, in spite of Fanny's enthusiasm. Anne picked up her shawl, gloves and reticule, and walked slowly out the door and down the stairs, where she caught up with her impatient friend.

A short time later, they were sitting with Lady Kidwell in the Langley's tasteful drawing room and Anne voiced her doubts to Fanny and her mother. "I'm uncomfortable with this invitation. I have never met Lord or Lady FitzMaynard and know nothing of politics. It seems presumptuous to accept." "My dear Anne," said Lady Kidwell. "You are too modest. You have been out in society, visited Lady Jersey's home, been presented to the queen herself. Why is this invitation different to any other? Lord and Lady Jersey will be there. In fact, Lady Jersey herself paved the way for your presence. This is, after all, just a social engagement."

Fanny chimed in, "Imagine, Anne, what an opportunity this presents for us to expand our acquaintance! Besides, Lady FitzMaynard expects us to be company for her cousin." Lady Kidwell continued gravely, "I fear you'll disappoint Lady FitzMaynard if you refuse and of course, Fanny and I will miss you. Lady Jersey may even be offended; you do owe this invitation to her efforts. She can be capricious." "I am still considering the matter," conceded Anne, "but I can't deny I am hesitant. May I ponder it until tomorrow?" Graciously, Lady Kidwell replied, "It will be entirely correct to respond tomorrow. I do hope, my dear, that your answer will be an acceptance. We are so looking forward to your accompanying us."

Grateful to escape, Anne returned home alone. She found her father in his library, showed him the letters and invitation, and confided her misgivings. To her secret dismay, she discovered her father ranged with Lady Kidwell and Fanny. "This is exactly the kind of invitation I want for you, Anne, an opportunity to meet people of stature," Mr Emmons acknowledged. Anne looked at him in surprise. "Do you want me to go to this ball, Father? Are you acquainted with Lord FitzMaynard?"

"I have met his lordship several times, and we have shared business interests upon occasion. I have not met him socially, of course. In spite of that, I see no reason for you to hesitate to accept this invitation. It would be an excellent thing for you, my dear." He looked at her calmly.

"It is no secret that I hope to see my children established at a higher level of society than that which I have enjoyed. Your brother Matthew has done well for himself, and Robert has his opportunities. I want you to benefit from the advantages that come your way. I do not require that you marry solely for advancement. However, if you could form an attachment to a gentleman of rank, it would be no bad thing. Occasions such as this give you the chance to meet such individuals. Especially since you have not expressed a particular interest so far..."

The image of Charles Deschevaux rose before Anne. She didn't mention the gentleman's name aloud, but his face was in her mind's eye as she rose and walked to the window. "As you say, Father, I have not shown an interest in a gentleman; of course, no gentleman has approached you with evidence of a sincere attachment for me. It wouldn't be seemly of me to evince emotions in this situation, even if I felt them." As she gazed out at the flowerbeds, she continued, "I'm not comfortable with the idea of spending several days in the home of strangers. I am not known to Lord and Lady FitzMaynard. Other than Lady Jersey and the Kidwells, it is improbable that I'll have personal acquaintance there, and Lady Kidwell has only a slight acquaintance with Lady FitzMaynard." She paused.

"You are aware, Father, I have interests other than dancing and flirtations, and I'm not socially ambitious. I gather that Lord FitzMaynard is involved in government in some capacity, and I expect many of the guests will be persons of political importance. I am afraid I will be absurdly tongue-tied, or bored, and end up sitting mumpish in a corner somewhere." Mr Emmons smiled with sympathy.

"I know you are rather shy, my dear. However, consider this an opportunity for you to learn about matters to which you have not been exposed, and to meet new people. An interested listener also makes an important contribution to a conversation. Please remember, my dear, you are as well educated as any young lady and you have interests of your own. You'll spend most of your time in social activities with Fanny and other young ladies, music, dancing and the like, and you will certainly be able to hold your own there. It is, of course, your choice, Anne, but I prefer that you accept this invitation."

"Do you already have someone in mind for me, Father? If you do, please be open with me," she said rather acerbically. He lifted an eyebrow and replied, with a slight edge in his voice, "My dear, I merely consider the possibilities." Anne sighed, and walked toward the door. "I shall, of course, do as you wish, Father. I'll write to Lady FitzMaynard to accept her kind invitation, and to Lady Kidwell and Lady Jersey to thank them as well." As she left the room, she consoled herself with the thought that, since Lord FitzMaynard knew her father, there could be no misunderstanding of her own connexions. With Fanny and Lady Kidwell at her back, and her friendship with Lady Jersey to lend encouragement, there was reason to hope for a pleasant visit.

Chapter 14

Their party arrived in the afternoon after an uneventful journey. Anne and Fanny were introduced to Lady FitzMaynard, a lovely woman some years older than Fanny, and her cousin, Miss Grace Worthington. After a bit of refreshment and a brief conversation, Lady FitzMaynard had the housekeeper show Lord and Lady Kidwell to their rooms. She then bade Grace do the same for Fanny and Anne. Grace was a small, pale young woman who appeared to be of an age with Anne and Fanny, who blushed at her cousin's request.

"Your rooms are next to each other, near Lord and Lady Kidwell's suite, and that of Lord and Lady Jersey. I hope you will be comfortable," said Grace, as they mounted the stairs. "I am sure we will be,' replied Fanny. "What a magnificent staircase!" "Yes," Grace replied, "the staircase and the ceilings are famous. The gardens, too, are lovely. Perhaps, when you have recovered from the journey, you will allow me to show you a few of my favourite spots." Anne responded, "I would love to walk in the gardens later. Just what is needed after sitting in the carriage for a few hours!"

Grace smiled shyly. Fanny's room came first, and then Grace escorted Anne to her door. Anne's eyes widened in appreciation as she took in the large, comfortable space assigned to her. Her things had already been brought up, and her maid Ellen was unpacking. Anne turned to Grace and said impulsively, "Thank you for your kindness! I look forward to our walk later." Grace smiled. "It is my pleasure, Miss Emmons. I have anticipated meeting you and Miss Kidwell. We'll meet downstairs in an hour or so, after you have had a chance to rest. A footman will come for you."

An unexpected twinkle appeared as Grace added, "We won't risk losing you to the corridors. The house is a bit confusing at first!" Anne smiled appreciatively. After Grace left her, Anne took in the satiny wallpaper of a rich cream with a delicate rose pattern. The soft, glowing colour of the flowers was repeated in the bed curtains and quilt, and the velvet that upholstered the chair near the fireplace. Draperies of the same rose colour framed long windows that looked out over the gardens. Anne noticed that Grace's enthusiasm was not misplaced. She turned back to the room, she asked her maid to press out a fresh gown, and unbuttoned her pelisse.

The afternoon fled. A quick walk around the gardens with Grace melted into refreshments on the terrace with the present company. Then everyone scattered to change for the evening. As everyone gathered in the large drawing room, Fanny and Lady Kidwell were absorbed into a group, which left Grace and Anne to become further acquainted. However, at dinner, the formality of the dining room was maintained, and Anne perforce conversed only with the person to her right or left. Much to her surprise, and secret pleasure, the gentleman to her right was Mr Deschevaux!

"Good evening, Miss Emmons." He greeted her with a smile. "Are you enjoying your stay at Littlebrook?" "How delightful to see you, Mr Deschevaux," she responded. "Littlebrook House is all a great house in the country should be, is it not? A most imposing estate and the rooms are sumptuous, yet comfortable. The gardens are perfection. Miss Grace Worthington was kind enough to take me on a quick tour, and I so look forward to a walk in the gardens again tomorrow. And you, sir? I dare say you have at least visited the stables." Mr Deschevaux laughed, and Anne suddenly noticed the dancing golden lights in his dark eyes.

"I have, indeed, Miss Emmons. In fact, I owe my presence here to the stables and their occupants. I am here at Lord FitzMaynard's invitation to view them. The stables are excellently planned and I have acquired ideas for alterations at home that I may carry out. I have not yet visited the gardens, however. May I escort you around them tomorrow afternoon? We can explore them together perhaps." Anne hedged, "Perhaps. I'm not sure..." Before she could say more, he leaned closer to her and asked, in a lowered tone, "You have not mentioned the company, Miss Emmons. I trust you are enjoying that, as well as the house." Anne's cheeks flamed.

"Definitely, Mr Deschevaux, everyone has been all that is polite and kind." He smiled. "I apologise if I've embarrassed you, ma'am. I would not overset you for the world." He looked around and continued, "It is indeed an interesting mixture of interests, is it not? It should make for lively conversation." Anne made no reply, uncertain how to respond. To her relief, the gentleman on her left chose that moment to interject a comment. She turned to him and made a suitable rejoinder. It was several moments before she turned back to Mr Deschevaux, and she was not dismayed to see him in conversation with the lady on his right. She was relieved to be able to concentrate on the delicious dinner for a moment.

The first course had been cleared, and they were well into the second before Mr Deschevaux turned back to her. "Shall you take part in the dance this evening, Miss Emmons?" he enquired. "I am not sure," she answered. "With the ball tomorrow evening, I had not thought to dance tonight. Cards and other amusements are planned for those who do not. And you, sir?" He smiled wryly. "I will be dancing. Her ladyship has added the *Lanciers* to tomorrow night's ball, and thought it wise to give those not familiar with it a chance to try it before the event. Do you know it?"

"I've never seen it danced," confessed Anne, "and will be glad to have the opportunity to acquaint myself with the steps. Do you know the dance, sir?" "I've danced it once or twice. I attended a ball in Dublin a year or so ago and first saw it there. Acquaintances had morning balls where it was practised, and I was able to learn the steps. However, it doesn't seem to be widely popular. Have you danced the quadrille?"

"Yes, I enjoy the quadrille very much." He nodded. "Then you should pick up the *Lanciers* easily enough. Mayhap you and I could help each other through a set or two this evening?" Anne laughed. "I don't understand how I can aid you, sir, but will be glad of your guidance." He also laughed. "You will be of the greatest help. I am sadly out of practice. You would stand my friend, Miss Emmons, by allowing me to partner you, so we may learn together." He looked at her earnestly. "And we are friends, are we not?" Caught by his direct gaze, Anne blushed again. "Indeed, sir, my father values your acquaintance, as do Lord and Lady Kidwell...."

"And you, Miss Emmons?" he asked in a low yet compelling voice, "Do you consider me a friend?" Before she was able to reply, the gentleman on her left offered to serve her some damson tart. She accepted with gratitude and waited, relieved for the break in her disconcerting conversation with Mr Deschevaux. She tasted he damson tart, and regained her poise. She turned back to Mr Deschevaux, and was unaccountably annoyed by his smile. Clearly, he enjoyed her discomfiture. Anne lifted her chin.

"Mr Deschevaux, we have been acquainted for several years. However, I am not forward enough to claim *friendship* with you, and cannot find this a proper conversation at dinner." She paused to glance around the table. "Tell me more about the *Lanciers,* sir. You indicated it was related to the quadrille, I believe?"

After dinner, the guests who were to dance met in the large drawing room. Miss Grace Worthington sat at the pianoforte, while Lady FitzMaynard stood nearby and turned over the sheets of music. Anne was relieved to find Fanny standing with a group of young women and hurried over to join her. Fanny was delighted to meet her friend Eleanor, and Anne espied an acquaintance or two from her London seasons. There were several gentlemen gathered in conversation, as well. Anne was relieved to observe a number of the guests were persons she recognised by sight from previous encounters in London. She did not see Mr Deschevaux enter the room.

Lady FitzMaynard took command at once, and Miss Worthington readied herself to play. Lady FitzMaynard had four couples who knew the dance form a square, and they walked through the steps slowly. Then Miss Worthington began a lively quadrille tune, and the four couples stepped and twirled through the elegant yet sprightly dance. Anne found many of the steps were similar to those she already knew; only the intricacies of the "Cage" confused her. The gentlemen asked the ladies to dance, and Anne was not surprised when Mr Deschevaux appeared at her side. They formed sets, and the couples walked through the steps, guided by the experienced performers. Miss Worthington played again, marking the time emphatically.

At the end, her cheeks flushed with exertion, Anne spoke to Mr Deschevaux as she curtsied. "Sir, I apologise for treading on your toes. I fear I stepped on you more than once...." He smiled and bowed. "I did not notice, Miss Emmons. You did uncommonly well for a first effort. I hope you will save the *Lanciers* and at least one waltz for me tomorrow night." She laughed. "Thank you for the compliment, but it is undeserved. The best I can say for myself is I did not fall on my face. However, you deceived me, sir. You seemed very comfortable with the steps. If you are prepared to brave it, I would be happy to save the *Lanciers* for you. The waltz will be delightful as well."

Lady FitzMaynard had the couples change squares, and the music began again. Laughter filled the air as the novice dancers stepped and occasionally stumbled through the unfamiliar patterns. After two hours of changing partners and practising the steps, Lady FitzMaynard dismissed the exhausted dancers with a smile, and they resumed their conversations. Anne spoke to Grace. "How beautifully you played! You must be tired." Grace thanked her with a smile. "I enjoyed it very much. Frankly, I prefer to play rather than to dance. The *Lanciers* in particular is quite exhausting. I must confess that I prefer the cotillion or the waltz." Anne laughed.

"The dance *is* vigorous, indeed. I find it delightful. It was wonderful of Lady FitzMaynard to provide this opportunity for us to acquaint ourselves with the steps before the ball tomorrow night." The two young ladies found seats near the fire, and accepted glasses of ratafia to refresh themselves. Anne saw Fanny across the room with a strange young man, heads together in conversation. As she watched, Fanny smiled, blushed and fanned herself gently. Anne glanced around the room and idly noted that Mr Deschevaux was nowhere to be seen. She and Grace continued their conversation about music and dance.

The next morning, Anne woke early and blinked as sunlight streamed through the windows. On the table next to the bed sat a steaming cup of chocolate, its tantalising fragrance wafting toward her. She sat up and sipped the chocolate, as she remembered the previous evening. She smiled as she thought about the dancing lesson. Mr Deschevaux had made it easy for her to learn as he guided her firmly through the pattern. As she recalled their conversation at dinner, her smile faded. His question about friendship... The whole conversation seemed vaguely improper, and somehow unlike him. Although they had been acquainted for several years now, only recently had she felt at ease with him.

Anne rose and gazed out of the window of her room, admiring the lovely gardens. Her new gown reposed in the wardrobe, ready for the ball, and she was confident she would look her best. The lavender blue silk undergown, with its short puffed sleeves, shimmered through a diaphanous overdress of sheerest silver net daintily embroidered with sparkling beads. The brief bodice and sleeves were decorated with fragile antique lace, with the lace at the sleeves falling gracefully almost to the edges of her evening gloves. With it, she would wear her mother's diamond drop earbobs, and a silver fillet set with sparkling diamonds would hold her dark curls in place. A silver spangled scarf, palest lavender evening gloves, and a delicate antique painted fan completed her *ensemble*. She crossed the room to sit by the fireplace. So far, the visit proved to be much more enjoyable than she had anticipated.

Anne recalled her discomfort when she saw Mr. Deschevaux dance with Fanny, and her relief when Fanny disclaimed any attachment. She was embarrassed that she thought of him as Charles instead of Mr Deschevaux. Had he developed a *tendre* for herself? Resolutely, she put the thought from her. He had shown no signs of such a thing; it was probably because they were both in an unfamiliar setting and he was relieved to see a familiar face. Then she remembered how well acquainted he seemed to be with other members of the company. She dismissed the entire train of thought from her mind, and rose to dress.

Descending the stairs in her dark green jaconet walking dress and half boots, Anne joined several others at breakfast. Glad to see Grace just beginning to break her fast, Anne took the empty seat next to her. "Good morning, Miss Worthington," smiled Anne. "It is a delightful day." Grace put down her cup.

"Yes, indeed, Miss Emmons, and I hope that you still plan to view the gardens with me. To my mind, they are at their best in the morning." Both young women enjoyed a light breakfast of coffee and rolls with butter, then ascended the stairs to their rooms to get their outdoor things.

As Anne and Grace strolled through the gardens, conversation was awkward at first. Surprised to find Grace was even shyer than she was herself, Anne made an effort to draw Grace out. The two young women were pleased to discover similar tastes in music and novels, and enjoyed a discussion of their respective favourites. As they followed the gravelled path, they left the shrubbery and paused at a graceful footbridge. Before them spread a small meadow, dotted with large trees. "What are those flowers?" asked Anne, as she gazed at the drifts of pale lavender blossoms.

"They are a wild flower called meadow saffron," replied Grace. "They always look like spring to me, yet they bloom in the autumn. They are early this year. The trees are Cedars of Lebanon, planted by his lordship's grandfather." "This is beautiful," said Anne softly, as her gaze followed the stream that flowed beneath the footbridge meander its way through the meadow.

"This path is my cousin's favourite in the summer. She loves the walk down into the meadow. You cannot see it from here, but there is a bench built under the large cedar. A delightful spot to sit with a book. The scent of the cedar is so fresh and the boughs shelter one from the sun. My cousin and I have enjoyed it this summer. Do you prefer to walk further, or to visit one of the other gardens?"

"I want to explore the meadow, but also hope to see the other gardens. Lady FitzMaynard mentioned the dahlias; she told me they are beautiful pink flowers, and I am not familiar with them."

Grace nodded, and they turned back to continue on the gravel path. "They are indeed lovely," said Grace. "I have never seen them anywhere else. I believe that his lordship's father convinced Lady Holland to give him a plant, and his gardener managed to keep it alive. I gather he and the gardener were very proud of that accomplishment, as the plants were considered quite difficult to maintain. You will see them in beds near the conservatory." After a lengthy tour of the garden, Anne and Grace returned to the house. Anne was surprised to see Fanny taking a turn on the terrace in the company of a young man. Idly, she asked Grace, "Who is that young man with Fanny?" Grace glanced over.

"He is Mr Martin Burrell. He is involved in politics, in Kent, I understand." "Burrell?" mused Anne. "I wonder if he is connected to Mrs Drummond-Burrell." "I am not sure, but my cousin hints he may be a distant relation off Mr Drummond-Burrell," said Grace.

Anne glanced at the couple again. Mr Burrell was speaking earnestly to Fanny. Anne noticed he was barely taller than Fanny, stocky and well built, with light brown hair. Not handsome, no, but somehow attractive. Anne and Grace continued on their way to the house.

Chapter 15

Later in the afternoon, Anne was in the library, writing a letter to Miss Crawford. Her pen idle, she absently admired the late-blooming roses seen through the window as she pondered her visit to Littlebrook House so far. To her own surprise, she was enjoying herself. Although she had seen almost nothing of Fanny since their arrival, she was comfortable with her acquaintance with Grace. Lady Kidwell and Lady Jersey had both spoken to her kindly when they came upon her. Although she had not been much in his company, it was obvious Lord FitzMaynard was as kind a host as his wife was a hostess. She had described the *Lanciers*, and the garden, but did not know what else to say.

Miss Crawford would want to hear who was present, and what she thought of them. However, Anne felt too shy to mention Mr Deschevaux, and knew too little about Mr Burrell to discuss him. She contented herself with a brief mention of Grace and their similar taste in novels. After she folded and sealed her letter, Anne took it downstairs for the post. She decided to look for Fanny, and peeped into the drawing room. There was no sight of Fanny but, as she started to turn away, a very young lady, whose face was vaguely familiar, called her name.

"Miss Emmons!" she called. "Pray join us for a moment." Hesitantly, Anne approached the small group. "I am sorry but your name escapes me," she apologised. "Were we introduced?" "How remiss of me," gushed the young lady. "I was not out last season, but a connexion of mine pointed you out to me, and spoke much of you so I felt as if we were already acquainted. You may recall Miss Louisa Dixon. I am her younger sister, Maria." Nonplussed, Anne hesitated. *Louisa Dixon?* Now she understood why this girl looked vaguely familiar. Coolly, she replied, "Indeed I do recall Miss Dixon. I hope she is well?"

"Oh, yes. She is married these two years or more and settled. I am just out this year." "How delightful," Anne said, at something of a loss. Before she managed to excuse herself, Miss Maria went on, "We were discussing the sad situation with Mr Hopecroft's bankruptcy. Louisa seemed to think you were acquainted with the son rather... intimately before the scandal broke." Miss Maria and the two girls with her looked at Anne with a kind of avid expectancy. Anne looked at the three with distaste. With an air of reserve, Anne replied, "I am afraid your sister is mistaken."

"Oh, but surely... Louisa gave me to understand that Mr Hopecroft was on the point of announcing an engagement between you and his son before he lost everything. They must have been more than mere acquaintances of yours. Of course, there is also a rumour Mr. Hopecroft himself was rather dismayed with your family's connexions." The three girls tittered.

"Your sister is kind to take an interest in me; I can only assure you no engagement was contemplated. It has been delightful to meet you. I do hope you will remember me to Louisa when next you write. Pray excuse me, ladies." Anne inclined her head slightly, swept out of the room and up the stairs, her eyes shooting sparks of temper.

As she approached her door, Fanny's door opened. "There you are!" exclaimed Fanny. "I have hardly seen you these two days! What have you been doing?" Seeing the expression on Anne's face, she continued, "Whatever is the matter, Anne? You look ready to scratch someone's eyes out!" "I am, Fanny. Are you aware who is here? Miss

Maria Dixon, the odious Louisa's sister." "Maria Dixon? I was not aware she was even out yet," frowned Fanny. "But what matter?"

"It seems Louisa still busies herself in my affairs, and has Maria whispering that I was on the point of announcing an engagement to Mr Hopecroft's son and broke it off when the bankruptcy scandal broke." Fanny, surprised, began to laugh.

"I never heard of anything so ridiculous! If it were known that you even considered an engagement to young Hopecroft, there would have been no bankruptcy, at least not at the time! The mere possibility of an alliance to an heiress would have certainly bought the family an extension. And how does Maria think Louisa might be in a position to be aware?" Fanny lost her smile. "I am sorry, Anne, that you experienced this unpleasantness."

"It *is* unpleasant, Fanny, not least because I do not wish the reputation of a jilt or an heiress on the hunt for a socially advantageous marriage partner." Anne sighed and walked to the fireplace. "I feel smirched, Fanny. Sadly, Maria is as unpleasant as her sister." She sat down in a chair, and Fanny seated herself on the *chaise* opposite. Fanny said, "The situation is most annoying but I am glad to see, this time, you are angry instead of hurt!"

Anne sighed again and smiled. "You are right, my dear. The people I care about here know the truth; what matters the rest? I doubt anyone would take it seriously." She looked at Fanny. "What of you, Fanny? I saw you on the terrace with a young man I have not yet met." With heightened colour, Fanny responded, "That must have been Mr Burrell. I asked him to explain a political issue." Anne's brows rose.

"A *political* question? Fanny, you have never concerned yourself with political matters in your life." Nettled, Fanny retorted, "That is true, but it is not too late to expand my interests. Mr Burrell is working for the member from the borough of Faversham on tax issues that affect our country directly. It was most interesting." Anne looked at her quizzically, "And *he* appeared to be rather intriguing, as well." Fanny caught her eye, and laughed. "Well, he *is* enthusiastic and explains things so clearly." She smiled mischievously.

"He is also charming, and an excellent dancer. We danced the last *Lanciers* together. It was delightful. He has already asked me for the first set tonight. What of you, Anne?" Anne looked conscious as she said, "Mr Deschevaux asked me to save the *Lanciers* and a waltz for him." "Mr Deschevaux?" asked Fanny. Anne blushed slightly and said defensively, "Why not? He was my partner last night, and we did fairly well together." Fanny looked at her friend consideringly.

"Mr Deschevaux..." she repeated slowly. "I see!" "You see nothing of the kind, Fanny!" snapped Anne. "Pray do not get any ideas." Fanny only shook her head and smiled. "My dear Anne, what ideas could I have?" Exasperated, Anne caught Fanny's eye. Fanny's eyes twinkled with mischief, and Anne was unable to prevent a smile.

In the afternoon, after a nuncheon, Mr Deschevaux and Anne strolled through the gardens. "The roses are exquisite," he said, as he gazed around with appreciation. "The yew hedges give them enough shelter to protect them from the cooler temperatures." Anne agreed, and told him about the meadow. When they reached the footbridge, they paused as he surveyed the view, admiring the lush green grass, the drifts of lavender meadow saffron and the majestic Cedars of Lebanon. "Delightful, indeed!" he exclaimed. As they stood there, Anne realised it was unwise to go further, and suggested that Mr Deschevaux might enjoy a sight of the dahlias.

"They are lovely, sir, with their pointed petals and beautiful colour against the wall of the conservatory. There is a taller plant behind them with which I am unfamiliar, which gives a delightful scent." "Well, Miss Emmons, let us return that way," he replied, looking at her with a smile. As they strolled, they encountered Fanny and Mr Burrell, who bowed as they passed. They also passed Miss Maria Dixon and her friends, who whispered and giggled behind their hands. Annoyed, Mr Deschevaux glanced after them. "She becomes more like her sister every day," he said. Anne, who had barely acknowledged the little group, looked at him enquiringly. "Her sister? Do you mean Miss Louisa Dixon that was? I am afraid I never learnt her married name."

"The same. They are distantly connected to my family, and I have had occasion to see both more frequently than I prefer. Miss Louisa, as she was then, was not unintelligent; yet, she could not control a tendency to giggle and languish. I found it most disturbing that she continually found cruel and untrue things to say about others, as she was jealous of other young ladies' advantages or successes. It was a relief when she finally achieved her desire and married. I am sorry to see Miss Maria engage in the same poor behaviour."

Anne made a noncommittal reply, and commented on the beautiful late-blooming white hydrangeas as they passed. Inside, she felt guilty about the pleasure his words gave her. As they strolled past the dahlias, she asked about his victorious horse. "Dare I confess?" he asked whimsically. "After his victory, a buyer approached me. Not only did he purchase the horse, I convinced him to hire the jockey. I am acquainted with the gentleman. He maintains excellent stables and treats his people well. I believe it to be an excellent situation for both the horse and his rider, and a most advantageous transaction for me."

"I congratulate you, sir! A fortunate arrangement, when all involved are so well satisfied. What of your other horses?" "Thank you. I left them happily settled at the stables. After the races end, I prefer to let them rest a few days. My steward will see that the tack and the horses are prepared to travel back to Kent in easy stages." They continued a desultory conversation as they approached the house, there to part and go their separate ways until the evening. Mr Deschevaux took her hand. "I remind you, ma'am, we are engaged for the *Lanciers* and a waltz. May I dare to ask for the first waltz?" Anne smiled and replied, "It will be my pleasure, sir."

"Until this evening, then, Miss Emmons." With that, he bowed and kissed her hand. She followed him with her eyes as he strode away, unconsciously touching the hand he had kissed with her other hand. Anne was crossing the hall toward the stairs, when she decided to stop in the library for a moment, to take a closer look at the books collected there.

Half-way through the door, she noticed three women, seated near the window, deep in conversation. Immediately self-conscious, she dipped a quick curtsey. "I am sorry to intrude. Pray excuse me...." The women looked up, and she saw Lady Jersey and Lady FitzMaynard both smiling at her. The third woman turned her head enquiringly, and Anne identified Lady Sefton.

"Pray join us, Miss Emmons," invited Lady Jersey pleasantly. "There is no intrusion, my dear." Flustered, Anne walked forward and took a seat near them. Lady FitzMaynard smiled again, and said, "I hope you are enjoying yourself, Miss Emmons. My cousin has mentioned how kind you are."

"Indeed, the kindness has been Miss Worthington's, ma'am. She has been a most thoughtful guide. The gardens are so beautiful, and we had a delightful walk," replied Anne.

Lady FitzMaynard said, "We were just commiserating with Lady Sefton; she had an extremely uncomfortable journey, replete with bad weather and breakdowns. She and Lord Sefton have only just arrived." After a few moments of conversation, Lady FitzMaynard and Lady Sefton departed, leaving Lady Jersey and Anne together.

"I am so glad to see you, Lady Jersey. Fanny and I are most grateful for your kind intervention with Lady FitzMaynard on our behalf," Anne began. Lady Jersey stopped her with a gesture. "It was my pleasure, my dear. Young Grace needed companionship, and I consider you and Miss Kidwell unexceptionable. I am delighted all falls together so well." Suddenly, the library door flew open, and Miss Maria Dixon burst in. "A servant told me I could find you in this room, Miss Emmons. Tell me; are Lord and Lady FitzMaynard aware that your father is in trade?" Maria began. She stopped short when Lady Jersey turned her head.

"Lady Jersey!" gasped Maria. "I had no idea...." "That is obvious," said Lady Jersey, her voice dripping icicles. She raised her glass to her eye and surveyed Maria from the top of her head to her heels. "We have not been introduced, young woman. I am occupied with my friend, Miss Emmons. I suggest you withdraw. I also suggest you make an opportunity to study *The Mirror of Graces*; your conduct is sadly wanting." Lady Jersey turned back to Anne. "Now where were we, my dear?" Scarlet with humiliation, Maria turned and left the room, shutting the door silently behind her. Tongue-tied, Anne sat still.

"I have yearned to give that young woman a set down since she arrived. One can only hope she is still young enough to benefit. Otherwise, it will take her even longer to settle than did her unpleasant sister." Lady Jersey looked at Anne enquiringly. "Well, my dear?" Anne flushed, unable to think of a response. She had never witnessed such a crushing snub, and could not help but pity Maria. She had heard Lady Jersey could be excruciatingly rude, but had not believed it. Anne pulled herself together.

"Why, ma'am, I'm afraid my thoughts had wandered. I was thinking of the ball this evening and hoping the weather would continue as fine." To her relief, Lady Jersey laughed. "By all means, let us turn the subject to something pleasant..." The rest of the conversation continued cheerfully, until Lady Jersey finally noticed the time, and took her leave. A bit shaken, Anne sat for a bit before she departed for her own room, book forgotten.

That evening, Anne and Fanny joined Lord and Lady Kidwell at the top of the stairs, as they prepared to descend for dinner. Fanny wore palest grey silk that shimmered through a delicate gauze overdress. The subtle colour turned her eyes to glowing silver as well. Fanny provided a striking contrast to Anne, whose lavender blue silk was every bit as becoming as she had hoped. Lady Kidwell was the height of elegance in her lustrous bronze satin trimmed with blonde lace. Lord Kidwell accompanied the three ladies proudly to the drawing room, where the company gathered.

After a sumptuous banquet (Anne lost track of the various dishes and their removes), the company adjourned to the ballroom. Anne stopped short at the entrance. Two enormous crystal chandeliers glowed with candles. The floor was chalked in white, with a huge silver crescent moon in the centre and silvery stars scattered over the floor. Overhead, deep blue gauze draped the ceiling, accented with glittering crystal stars that dangled singly and in clusters, that gave the illusion of a starry night sky. Large silver urns filled with white flowers stood on pedestals at intervals, and scented the air. Ivy twisted with white, gold and silver ribbons twined up the pillars. Branched candleholders stood in pairs on the twin fireplace mantles, and girandole sconces reflected the candlelight. The orchestra sat on a dais in a corner of the room.

"Oh," breathed Anne, "we will dance amongst the stars tonight! How lovely!" "Exquisite!" exclaimed Fanny. More prosaically, Lady Kidwell commented, "I have not seen a chalked floor in an age. Mind your trains are securely pinned up all the evening, girls. Chalk can be ruinous."

When she looked back, Anne regarded that evening as nothing short of magical. She danced every dance, enjoying each step and bow. One young man called her "Twilight personified," saying her gown was the colour of the sky at early dusk, and her eyes put the stars to shame. Charles Deschevaux claimed her for the *Lanciers*, and she danced confidently and with joy. The dancers scuffed the silver stars on the floor into sparkling swirls that made her feel as if she were dancing on the clouds that remained after the stars had set.

The waltz Charles claimed was the supper dance. As they moved gracefully around the floor, she was conscious of the warmth of his hand at her back, as he guided her confidently. She looked up at him, and, as he gazed into her eyes, her heart pounded. Just as she almost forgot they were in company, the music ended, and it was time to go in to supper. Charles steered her to a table where Fanny and Mr Burrell had already claimed seats. As Charles and Mr Burrell advanced to survey the buffet table, Fanny and Anne shared a few hurried confidences.

"Oh, Anne," whispered Fanny. "I have never met anyone like him. Mr Burrell talks to me like a *person*, whose intelligence he respects, not just a female. He knows what he wants to accomplish. He can enjoy all this, yet not lose sight of his purpose. And what of you, Anne?" Anne blushed, and smiled. "I, too, am having a wonderful time. Indeed, there has never been such an evening. I have danced every dance, but dancing with Mr Deschevaux has been delightful. He often seems so preoccupied with his horses or his estate, yet on the dance floor tonight...." She sighed. She and Fanny caught each other's eye, and laughed aloud together. Anne gasped through their giggles, "My goodness, we sound like a pair of school girls, Fanny!"

Just then, the two young men returned, with loaded plates. The laughter continued as the conversation turned general. After enjoying the delectable supper, the company returned to the ballroom, and the magic continued unabated. In the wee hours of the morning, after Anne was comfortable in her dressing gown, she brushed her hair before the fire while she reviewed the evening dreamily.

Although propriety forbade that she dance another set with Charles Deschevaux, she was conscious of him the rest of the evening, aware that, when she glanced his way, he gazed back at her. As she left the ballroom, he grasped her hand and invited her to walk in the garden with him after breakfast. She gazed up at him, her violet blue eyes glowing, and agreed. She gazed into the fire, as she remembered the ball with the faintest smile playing about her lips... She had danced with him many times in the past; why was tonight so very different?

Chapter 16

Anne awoke earlier than she expected and experienced a surge of anticipation that bewildered her for a moment. Next to the bed, a cup of chocolate steamed invitingly. She rose, put on her rose velvet dressing gown, and took the cup to the window. She sipped it leisurely as she gazed out upon the new day, absently admiring the clear sky flushed with the early morning sun. She rang the bell for the maid before she turned to the wardrobe to select a walking dress for her garden walk with Charles Deschevaux. Lemon yellow muslin paired with a soft green sarcenet spencer just suited her sunny mood. A green bonnet trimmed with curled yellow ostrich feathers and matching yellow ribbons and her sturdy green half-boots made the ensemble complete.

As Anne descended the stairs, the young man who had likened her to Twilight the previous evening now hailed her as a yellow rose, which caused her to blush profusely as she made her way to breakfast. Only Grace Worthington was seated at the dining room table, and she smiled welcomingly at Anne. "Good morning, Miss Emmons. I am delighted to have your company this morning. I hope you enjoyed the ball." Anne replied enthusiastically, "It was a wonderful evening. The ballroom was so beautiful. I had never seen a chalked floor before. It was a most elegant touch, and it made dancing so much easier. I did not fear to slip." Grace nodded.

"I am afraid it has gone out of fashion, but my cousin wanted something unusual and we designed the floor to harmonise with the night sky effect on the ceiling." Anne nodded her thanks as the servant set coffee and a roll before her. The two young women sipped their coffee and enjoyed their breakfast in silence for a few moments. "Have you plans this morning, my dear?" enquired Grace. Anne nodded. "I am supposed to meet a friend for a stroll in the gardens. This is a lovely morning for it."

Grace concurred, and suggested, "Mayhap after your walk, you would join me in the library. A few of us plan to discuss books we enjoy, and I understand you are a great reader." "I would love to share in that discussion! I will be delighted to join you," responded Anne with pleasure. Rising from the table, she bade Grace a friendly good morning, and left the room to put on her bonnet and gloves and find her sunshade.

Anne and Mr Deschevaux strolled across the terrace to the steps that led to the garden in silence. Anne suffered unaccountable shyness, and could think of nothing to say other than "Good morning" and an inane comment on the beauty of the day. When asked her preference, meadow or garden, she elected the garden with an eye to propriety. Several other members of the house party were also in the garden, enjoying the sunshine. Mr Deschevaux acquiesced and offered his arm. The two wandered silently down the path to the rose beds. Just as the silence became awkward, Mr Deschevaux said, "I hope you enjoyed the ball last night, Miss Emmons."

"Indeed, I did, Mr Deschevaux. The room was decorated so beautifully, and the musicians were excellent. It was a delightful evening." "I found it delightful as well," he replied with a smile. "I thought the *Lanciers* passed exceptionally well." Anne laughed. "It was fun, was it not? Such a lively dance! Our set seemed well matched; no one stumbled, even in The Cage."

Once again, he was the comfortable acquaintance he had been previously, and they compared notes on favourite dishes at the banquet, their personal favourite melodies performed by the musicians, and the excellence of the supper refreshments. As they laughed and chatted, Anne stopped to admire a bush covered in deep red roses in full bloom that shed their perfume for yards around it. "How heavenly!" she exclaimed. "The scent is exquisite. Would one could bottle that heavenly aroma."

Mr. Deschevaux took out his pen knife and cut a glowing half-opened bud and stripped it of its thorns. He bowed slightly in mock formality and presented it to her. "A memento of a beautiful morning," he said, and looked into her eyes. She blushed becomingly as she accepted the flower and murmured her thanks. They continued on, conversing sporadically. As they circled the garden, Mr Deschevaux suggested they go past the dahlias again.

"I have never seen flowers quite like that, and I have it in mind to beg Lord FitzMaynard to allow me to take a cutting to try in Kent. If they can be nurtured along to flourish here in Yorkshire, I judge they will do as well, or even better, in the gentler climate of Kent."

Anne glanced over her shoulder and caught a glimpse of Fanny and Mr Burrell, deep in conversation on another path. She smiled to herself as she lifted the rosebud and inhaled its perfume. When Mr Deschevaux paused, she asked, "Do your roses have such perfume, Mr Deschevaux? You mentioned the roses were in bloom when you came away to York." The conversation led from roses to other flowers and plants. Both agreed that roses were a garden essential, but Mr Deschevaux was obstinate in his preference for the mingled scents of lilies of the valley and mint to the heavier perfume of roses. The dahlia bed was before them, and Anne suddenly realised, although the voices of others enjoying the garden carried, she and Mr Deschevaux were, to all intents and purposes, alone.

She looked up at Mr Deschevaux and caught his intent gaze upon her. Flushing, she said, "Sir, we should rejoin...." "Miss Emmons, I must speak to you," he interrupted. Apprehensive, Anne lowered her eyes and tried to edge away. "I don't think..." she started, and found her hand crushed in an iron grip. Startled, she looked up and his eyes blazed into hers.

"I see I have surprised you," he said with what seemed to be disappointment. "I have yearned for you for months and you didn't even notice. Has it never occurred to you that I might care for you?" Anne looked at the ground and shook her head slightly. "I thought you were kind to me as Fanny's friend," she said, apologetically. "I knew you were an old friend of her family. I never dreamt you thought of me in that way. You always seemed so formal until recently."

"Formal..." he echoed. "Indeed I was, had to be. He dropped her hand and turned away. "You're aware my father and brother were killed. They left the estate deeply encumbered, close to bankruptcy. Until I was clear of debt, I could not in honour approach any woman, especially you. But all of that has been long since resolved." Surreptitiously Anne rubbed the hand he had gripped as she queried, "'...especially me'. What do you mean, sir?"

"I am surprised your father has never mentioned it. Several years ago, before I met you, I was desperately trying to sort out my family's affairs. I considered giving it up, letting go of the family estate in Kent. At last, I swallowed my pride and consulted with Lord Kidwell. He immediately referred me to Mr Emmons. Your father directed me to a man of business to help me clear up the estate accounts, and a steward skilled in agricultural matters to work with me and my bailiff to maximise the income. He also discovered the owners of successful racing stud, so I was able to meet with them, to determine if my late brother's stables might be made into a profitable enterprise. He loaned me money to pay some of the most pressing debts, against the estate in Kent and property I inherited in Devon. He even bought a race horse from me. When I was finally in funds, he guided me in some investments." He laughed suddenly. "He was quite relieved when I bought back the horse, I will say."

Anne stood stock still in surprise, and Mr Deschevaux swung around to face her. "I owe him everything, you see. You and Fanny were still at school when this all began; I didn't meet you until that ball. I knew even then you were special somehow. In honour, all I could do was contrive to stay in the background until I could see my way. Now, however, I am at liberty to speak." He lifted his head proudly.

"The debts are paid in full four years since. The estate brings in a steady income, and the racing stable is doing well. In fact, I have received a very advantageous offer for the entire stable. With your father's help, I have managed to restore much of what my father and brother squandered. Do you now understand why I had to consider you so especially? How was I to offer your father's daughter less than the comfort and the elegancies of life she has a right to expect? My fortune is, of course, not nearly so extensive as that your father possesses, but I finally possess the means to support a wife in the comfort and the style she deserves. At last, I can speak my mind, and my heart."

Anne looked at him with incredulity. She had just begun to consider him more, perhaps, than a friend. It was as if she had taken a step on a familiar path, only to find herself in an unexplored country. "Sir, I had no idea of your feelings. Truly, I believed that, if you thought of me at all, it was as a connexion of Fanny's family. You have always been kind, but I saw no sign of ... partiality. Why, we only recently discussed matters that were other than superficial. I do not know what to say to you. I am unprepared..." To her exasperation, he interrupted again.

"Unprepared, I understand. What I must know is...are you unwilling? Will you allow me to hope?" This time, Anne pulled herself together, and answered him. "Sir, there is always hope. You are a gentleman I have come to respect and esteem. Of late, we have discovered interests in common. Who can say what may happen?" She smiled slightly. "I can see my impression of you as a cautious man wrapped up in his stable is not completely accurate. You may find your impressions of me equally faulty. For example, although my father holds country properties, I have always lived in a town. I do not ride. Your life is centred in the country, and horses are important to you." She took a step toward the path back to the house, then swung back to face him.

"I must ask, sir, did you discuss this matter with my father? Is he aware of your interest?" Tensely, she awaited his response. He flushed slightly, and said, "You may consider it wrong of me to speak to you first, but I confess I did not, in so many words." He looked at her directly. "I did mention that the man who captured your affections would be most fortunate. Your father made it clear that the choice is ultimately yours." Anne relaxed and smiled.

"You need not concern yourself, sir. My father is very acute. Had he any objection, I assure you that he would have made them known." She turned back to the path. "We must return to the house, sir. I am engaged with some ladies to discuss our favourite literature this afternoon." They walked in silence, at a much faster pace than before. She stole a glance at his face. Curiously blank, his jaw was clenched and his gaze was fixed ahead. She hurried to keep up with him, determined not to ask him to slow down or otherwise break the silence between them. Half annoyed and half flattered, she mulled over what he had said, and her own recent thoughts of him. Suddenly, he came to a halt.

With a jolt, she realised they were already at the foot of the terrace steps. "I will leave you here, ma'am. I can only hope that my importunities have not made you late for your engagement," he said in an expressionless voice. Anne blinked; it was as if he had slapped her. This show of indifference after his unexpected (and improper) declaration threw her off balance again. About to send him off coolly, she looked up into his eyes. Her curt dismissal died on her lips as his dark eyes could not conceal his uncertainty. She extended her hand.

"I thank you for the lovely walk. I look forward to seeing you later in the evening, sir." She smiled tentatively. He took her hand gently, and looked at their clasped hands for a moment. "I will look forward to that," he said as he raised her hand to his lips. He released her to step back, and then bowed. As she curtsied slightly, he turned away and walked swiftly down the path toward the meadow. Still feeling the warmth of his lips on her hand through her glove, she walked slowly into the house and up to her room to take off her outdoor things.

Anne removed her bonnet and gloves as she entered her room. She intended to tidy herself, but the sight of two letters lying on the little writing table near the window distracted her. She opened the top letter, knowing it was from Emily. She sat in the chair to read. *"My aunt and I are having a lovely time in Bath. I do not drink the waters-too nasty, my dear! She chokes down a glass each morning. After that, she and her friends talk about how wonderfully well they are. Of course, we have shopped. Milsom Street has charming shops, and I found the most beautiful lace in a little shop in the Orange Grove, near Meyler's Library."* Anne smiled as she pictured Emily's enthusiasm, and continued to read.

Emily wrote of Kate's improved health, and her plans to return home soon. She absently setting the letter aside, to be answered later, then went to stand by the window to gaze out at the garden as she pondered Charles Deschevaux's shocking confession of attachment. "Am I really that blind? Is it possible that he had such feelings for me and I was so completely unaware?" She moved back to the writing table and sat in the chair again, still pondering. "It seems so unlikely. He was polite, cordial, sympathetic when called for, but I'll swear there was nothing more until recently. Unless he has iron self control, there would have been a gesture, some hint..." She carefully folded the rose he had cut for her in paper, and pressed it between the pages of a book.

Anne caught a glimpse of the clock on the mantle, picked up the novels she had set aside earlier and hurried from the room, forgetting her second letter. Anne entered the library a few minutes late, to find the conversation brisk and lively. Several young ladies were present, as were (much to Anne's surprise) Lady Jersey and Lady Kidwell. Anne slipped into the window seat and listened. As she had expected, each participant had her own favourite author, and defended her choice eagerly. She listened to the points each raised with interest and made mental notes of books to borrow from the circulating library. During a lull in the voices, Grace asked, "Anne, what do you have to say? Have you a favourite novel?" Anne smiled shyly.

"Indeed, I am fond of novels and my favourite changes so often, I feel almost capricious. At this present, I am reading a novel, titled *Persuasion,* which I'm enjoying exceedingly." "Has anyone else read this work?" asked Grace, as she glanced around the circle. Another young woman said, "I have read it. This book is written by the author of *Pride and Prejudice,* yet is quite different to that book. I must confess that I preferred *Pride and Prejudice.*" Anne demurred.

"I, too, found *Pride and Prejudice* delightful, but there is something most appealing about *Persuasion*-the idea that one could have a second chance for happiness after all hope was gone..." She gathered her composure. "I also was taken by the portrayal of a young woman who learned to trust her own judgement and sentiments."

Someone mentioned that the author, who had unfortunately died before publication of *Persuasion,* was a woman named Jane Austen. This led to a spirited discussion of women writers, to which Anne listened with trepidation. One young woman maintained that it was a shame that her name had been revealed at all. "Imagine the notoriety!" she shuddered.

Another proposed that, as her family had revealed the author's identity after her death, the public notice was a family's tribute to a loved one. "After all," she said sensibly, "there will be no more novels; the public will forget quickly enough." Unfortunately, opinion regarding a woman who wrote for publication as a profession was very low.

"She might equally as well become a shop girl. A lady of taste has no business to go into a trade; who knows how her contacts with publishers might contaminate her?" sniffed Miss Dixon. Pushed by her own convictions, Anne asked, "But what if she has talent and wants to write? Should her work simply lie in a box, to be exposed only to her family and friends? And if her work is good, why should she not be paid for it? I do not perceive that being appropriately rewarded for her ability makes her less of a lady." She flushed as Miss Dixon nudged her neighbour and whispered.

Grace said thoughtfully, "You raise a valid point. No one thinks less of a gentleman if he invests in trade or other activity, to maintain his family fortunes. Madame d'Arblay is received, and she has published novels which have been much admired." There was a buzz of excited conversation as the debate continued.

Chapter 17

A few hours later, Anne was back in her room changing when she espied the second letter, which she had forgotten in her musings. She recognised her father's hand, picked it up and broke the seal. As she unfolded it, another folded page fell out. She ignored that for the moment whilst she read her father's letter.

"My dearest daughter," he wrote. *"The coach will take you up Sunday morning, so you will be home in time for dinner. Miss Crawford and your maid will accompany you home. In your absence, we have had much excitement, and cannot do without you any longer. Although I disapprove of Sunday travel, your presence is essential. I am delighted to announce the engagement of your brother Robert to Miss Diana Farleigh. I feel certain of your pleasure in this event, as I know Miss Farleigh to be your good friend.*

In addition to this happy event, Matthew and Lydia have become parents for the second time, to a baby girl whom they propose to name Anne Isabel, for you and for Lydia's mother. Needless to say, her arrival was earlier than expected. Matthew and Lydia want you to be her godmother. Robert has obtained special permission to christen the child and we must depart for Leeds as soon as may be. Pray forgive this abrupt demand, and make my sincerest apologies to Lord and Lady FitzMaynard and Lord and Lady Kidwell. I enclose a note from Miss Farleigh. Your affectionate Father, etc."

Stunned, Anne sank into a chair. So much had happened in such a scant few days! Her packing! She remembered the note that had dropped to the floor, picked it up and unfolded it.

"My dear Anne," wrote Diana. *"I am sure you have read your father's letter. I realise he has advised you of my engagement to your brother. I hope you are pleased. I know that I have been less than frank with you on this matter; indeed, I never mentioned anything about it. In all honesty, I did not expect to receive an offer from your brother and could not bear to discuss my feelings for him. I was completely surprised when he told me he had spoken to Mr Farleigh, and asked me to do him the honour of becoming his wife. It was like a dream.*

Please know that I am the happiest woman alive, and will do all in my power to make your beloved brother a good wife. To have such a dear friend for a sister is an added blessing. Robert has asked me to accompany you and your father to Leeds. I look forward to seeing you, and hope you can forgive me for my apparent secrecy. Pray believe there was no intent to deceive. Ever your friend, Diana"

Anne recalled Robert's mention of her charming friend during their conversation such a short time ago. Apparently he had already made up his mind... She picked up her father's letter and rang for her maid.

When Ellen presented herself, Anne instructed her to begin packing, and to leave out only her night garb and her gown for that evening's dinner. "Pray, do not touch my writing materials. I will attend to those myself." She hastily tidied herself, rushed out of the room, and knocked on Fanny's door. "Fanny, where is your mother? I must speak with her immediately," she gasped.

"Good heavens, Anne, whatever is the matter?" Anne showed her the letter from Mr Emmons. Brows raised, Fanny looked at Anne after she perused the missive. "My goodness, they *have* been busy. You haven't been gone a week." Anne shook her friend slightly.

"Fanny, this is no time for a joke. This letter came this morning, and I must speak to your mother and to Lady FitzMaynard as soon as may be. What will they think of me, if I rush off like this?" Fanny replied soothingly, "My dear, your family needs you. Thank goodness, these are happy events. We were to leave within a few days in any event. I will remain until my parents depart; you will return to York tomorrow. I am certain that your father has arranged for everything. I last saw my mother in the conservatory with Lady FitzMaynard. With luck, we will catch them both together." The two young ladies hurried to the conservatory where, to Anne's relief, they found Lady Kidwell deep in conversation with Lady FitzMaynard. As they approached, the two older ladies saw them and smiled welcomingly.

"I made sure you were resting before it was time to change, my dears," said Lady Kidwell. "Is something amiss?" Anne stepped forward to hold out her father's letter. "I am so sorry, Lady Kidwell, Lady FitzMaynard. My father writes that I must return home tomorrow, because of family matters..." Calmly, Lady Kidwell took the letter and read it, while Lady FitzMaynard gestured for Anne and Fanny to be seated. "Lady FitzMaynard, I am grateful for your invitation and have vastly enjoyed my stay. I deeply regret that I must leave so abruptly." Lady Kidwell handed the letter to Lady FitzMaynard.

"Well, I must say that Mr Emmons is certainly decisive. Obviously, he has arranged everything down to the last detail. My dear, I do understand your situation." Lady FitzMaynard handed the letter back to Anne and said kindly, "My dear Miss Emmons, while we are sorry to lose your company, we must honour your father's wishes. What can we do to assist you?" Anne blushed deeply.

"My packing is under way. I do not wish to disturb your ladyship or the household. When my father says 'in the morning', he usually means early, around nine o'clock. I will be ready-it will just be a matter of someone to bring down my things." Lady Kidwell patted Anne's hand.

"I must congratulate you on your new niece. You will be a fine godmother, my dear. And your brother Robert is engaged! I remember Miss Farleigh-a delightful young woman. Your father must be beside himself with joy. That explains his haste." Anne smiled tremulously. "Indeed, I know you are right, although he is also anxious as the baby is early. My father always worries..."

Lady FitzMaynard added her congratulations and said, "Please be sure to talk to Grace this evening. She has come to regard you as a friend, and would be sorry not to make her *adieux*. I am sure that we will meet again, Miss Emmons. I look forward to continuing our acquaintance." In what seemed the blink of an eye, Anne found herself at dinner. She was at once pleased and dismayed to find Mr Deschevaux seated beside her yet again. Memories of their walk in the garden that morning left her aflutter with confusion.

"Good evening, Mr Deschevaux." She strove for cool politeness. "I hope you had a pleasant afternoon." "Indeed I did. And how was the discussion in the library?" he responded with an amused smile. "Quite stimulating." She found his amusement annoying. "How did you entertain yourself, sir?"

"Lord FitzMaynard took Lord Jersey, Lord Sefton and myself on a ride to his racing stud farm. His hunting and riding stables have some useful innovations, but his racing stud farm is an education in itself," he answered, suddenly serious. "I consider myself privileged to be included, and I believe that my own stables may benefit from some of those innovations if I decide not to sell." He looked up with a smile.

"I will not bore you by describing these matters." In spite of herself, she smiled back and replied, "I thank you for your consideration, sir. I fear I could not respond suitably, as I know nothing about such affairs." Dinner progressed pleasantly. Conversation was general and light hearted, and Anne found herself able to respond easily to Mr Deschevaux and to the gentleman on her other hand. Over fruit and nuts at the end of the meal, Mr Deschevaux claimed her attention.

"There will be dancing later this evening. Dare I presume to ask for a waltz?"

Anne looked at him, suddenly stricken with disappointment. "I am so sorry, but I fear I must decline. The maid has already begun to pack my things as I must leave early in the morning." Concerned, Mr Deschevaux asked, "I hope there is nothing wrong. Was it something I...?" Before he could finish, Anne rushed on, "Indeed, sir, you have nothing with which to reproach yourself. I have had news from my father. My oldest brother is become a parent again, and I am to be godmother of my namesake. My father bade me return home tomorrow, so we can depart for Leeds as early as possible." Relief warred with disappointment in his dark eyes. "I must congratulate you, it seems. However, I regret that you must hurry away. Your friends must be sorry to see you leave so suddenly."

"I feel churlish, leaving this abruptly. It seems a poor return for the kindness I have received." At that moment, the gentleman on her right offered to serve her more fruit. After she accepted with thanks and exchanged pleasantries with him, Anne was relieved to have a moment to take a sip of wine and glance around the table. Seated directly across from her, Grace caught her eye and smiled. Anne remembered their brief conversation before dinner, and vowed silently to write to Grace as soon as she arrived at Matthew's home in Leeds.

Mr Deschevaux spoke to her again. "It has been such a pleasure to spend this time with friends," he said. "I may wish it were for a longer period, but must be grateful for what has been. Do you expect to visit Fanny and her parents in Kent during the autumn months?" Anne shook her head, then said regretfully, "I fear not. I am not certain how long I will be with my brother and his wife, and there are certain commitments this winter in York. I expect to be in London for at least a few weeks after the New Year though." At that moment, Lady FitzMaynard rose, and led the ladies to the drawing room. Anne glanced back at Mr Deschevaux, only to catch his eye as he watched her walk away. Her cheeks burned with embarrassment as she turned her gaze away and hurried to catch up with Grace.

Anne entered the drawing room, where she found Grace already seated at the piano-forte, as she idly turned over some music. "Grace, will you be here over the winter or will you be otherwhere? Mayhap you could visit me at York for a few days. You would be most welcome." The two young women began to discuss possible plans for their next meeting. Fanny joined them after a few minutes, and the conversation turned to general matters. As Lady FitzMaynard steered the party to the ballroom for dancing, Anne slipped quietly away.

She entered her room and shut the door. She wandered restlessly around, her mind in a turmoil, wondering about Fanny and Mr Burrell, looking forward to seeing her niece, and (always in the back of her mind) picturing the look of disappointment in Charles' eyes when she told him of her early departure. She found her night rail, warm robe and slippers carefully laid out on the *chaise*, a blue carriage dress ready for the next morning. All else was packed and ready; only her writing materials, the clothes she wore and her toiletries remained. She sat at the table, pulled out her notes and began to write.

Chapter 18

The moment she entered her brother's house, Anne sensed that all was well. She was ushered immediately to her usual room where she found a delightful fire awaiting her. Appreciatively, she glanced around the comfortable apartment as she flung off her pelisse and hat. She washed her face and hands, smoothed her hair, and changed her half-boots for slippers. A tap on the door occurred and Diana's voice asked, "Anne, are you ready to go down?" The two young women descended the stairs. Matthew, Robert and her father were seated near the fire, in earnest conversation.

As soon as he saw Anne and Diana, Matthew jumped up and embraced his sister warmly, as the other two men rose. "Anne, my dear, it has been too long!" he exclaimed. Matthew turned to Diana and said with a warm smile, "Miss Farleigh, I am delighted to see you again. If you recall, we met over Christmas, two years ago I believe, at a rout-party at Farleigh House. It is a great pleasure to welcome you here." Diana sketched a curtsey and said, "Mr Emmons I appreciate your gracious welcome. I do recall meeting you and your lovely wife."

Anne interrupted with asperity, "Matthew, these pleasantries are all very well, but I burn with impatience. How are Lydia and my namesake?" As Matthew showed the ladies to their seats, he sobered. "Lydia is well. She is recovering quickly, and shows no signs of fever or complications. Little Anne is tiny and we must take every precaution. She made her appearance earlier than expected, so arrangements have been more complicated than we might wish."

Anne laid her hand on his arm and asked again, "How is she, Matthew? I knew she was small; is there something else?" Matthew smiled and patted her hand. "No, no, dear sister. All fingers and toes accounted for, no obvious difficulties. She is a beautiful baby, if I may be so bold. Tiny and still rather delicate. The doctor visits every day to keep both Lydia and the child under his eye, to be sure they both continue to do well." Anne smiled with relief as she turned to Robert and her father.

"No more serious faces and no more business discussions! We've a christening and a wedding to discuss. This is a happy time for our family, so let us enjoy it!" Robert, who was engaged in a low-voiced conversation with his betrothed, returned her smile and agreed whole-heartedly. Matthew looked from Robert to Diana with a rueful smile, and extended his hands to both.

"I should be shot!" he exclaimed, "I completely forgot to extend my congratulations. Welcome to our family! We have waited for Robert to settle for this age, and I can see he has chosen well." Diana blushed furiously, murmured inarticulately and turned to Robert. Robert hugged her impulsively.

"Thank you, brother! She is a prize indeed." Anne agreed enthusiastically. "She is a dear friend, and I am delighted to have her for my sister." Mr Emmons suggested, "Matthew, ring for some champagne so we can toast my new daughter and granddaughter." Just then, the housekeeper entered and curtsied slightly. "Excuse me, sir. Mrs Emmons is awake and has asked for Miss Anne." Anne rose precipitously, and sped from the room. She entered her sister-in-law's room, where Lydia reclined on her *chaise longue* near the fire, a cashmere shawl draped over her legs, and an exquisitely embroidered silk shawl around her shoulders.

Anne paused for a moment, and looked keenly at Lydia; she noted the thinness of her face but also the luminous happiness in her eyes. "Anne, dear one," said Lydia, holding out her hand. "How glad I am to see you." Anne crossed the room, and bent to hug Lydia gently. "How are you, my love?" she asked affectionately. "I understand that you have produced a beautiful little girl." Lydia beamed. "She is lovely, Anne; wait until you see her. Small, of course, but perfect in every way. And amazingly strong, all things considered. When she cries, you can hear her downstairs unless someone gets to her immediately. She is very demanding." Anne laughed.

"Good lungs have ever been an Emmons trait. Who does she look like, Lydia?" Lydia considered and responded, "I find it hard to be sure at this moment but we think she will look like you." She smiled fondly. "When first Matthew saw her, she was asleep. Then, when she opened her eyes, he said, 'Why, it's Anne!' Her eyes are the same shade of violet blue as yours, you see, and her hair is all soft dark curls." Anne flushed with pleasure. "I look forward to making the acquaintance of this niece of mine. In the meantime, how does little Walter? Is he quite jealous?" The conversation continued on a thoroughly domestic note, until Lydia's maid came in, curtsied and said in a most unsubservient manner, "Mrs Emmons must rest for a little, Miss. Doctor's orders."

Several days later, Anne was seated in the drawing room, sipping a cup of coffee gratefully. The weather had deteriorated since their arrival, and they were now into their third day of rain and wind. Diana sat opposite, next to the fire. "Tell me about Lord and Lady FitzMaynard's ball, please. Who was there?" Anne mentioned Lord and Lady Jersey, Lord and Lady Sefton and a few other notables. "Mr Martin Burrell was also there. I believe he is connected to Mr Drummond-Burrell in some way. He is engaged with a politician from Kent, and he and Fanny seemed to enjoy each other's company," said Anne. She proceeded to describe the decorations, especially the chalked floor and the stars on the ceiling.

"It was a truly lovely effect, Diana," she said enthusiastically. Interested, Diana asked several questions about the design and the artist. "But did it not damage your gown or your slippers?" Anne shook her head, and replied, "Lady Kidwell warned us to mind our gowns. Frankly, my silver sandals were worn to rags by the end of the evening. I do not think the chalk made a difference there." Diana looked slightly shocked at Anne's casual indifference to the ruin of an expensive pair of dancing sandal, then recovered as Anne continued, "I had already worn them several times this season. You know how fragile such slippers are; I consider myself fortunate to wear them more than one evening, I can tell you!"

"What about you, Anne? Was there anyone especially interesting to you?" asked Diana. Anne mentioned Lady FitzMaynard's cousin Grace Worthington, a kind young woman and a welcome new acquaintance. Diana arched an eyebrow as she scoffed gently, "A delightful new friend, I am certain. However, you know that is not what I meant." Anne blushed profusely, and then told her Mr Deschevaux had been present, and they had danced together. At that, both Diana's eyebrows rose, but before she could say anything, a maid entered, curtsied slightly and said, "Miss Emmons, Mrs Emmons wondered if you would come and sit with her for a little." Murmuring a hurried farewell, Anne fled the drawing room, as Diana looked after her speculatively.

Anne paused on the landing to catch her breath and calm her thoughts. "It's only natural that Diana would be interested to learn who was present, and which spent time with whom," she thought. Resolutely, she pushed aside the memory of Charles' admission of his feelings for her. "I still can't believe he was serious. Never to have given a sign, then suddenly..." She sighed deeply and gathered her skirts to continue up the stairs.

Lydia held out her hand eagerly and said with a smile, "Come, my dear, meet your new niece!" Anne noticed the swaddled bundled nestled in Lydia's other arm moving slightly. She sat in the chair next to Lydia's couch and squeezed Lydia's hand. "Do let me see her." Lydia loosened the shawl and as the soft white wool fell away, Anne saw the pink cheeks and long dark lashes, the small head crowned with dark curls. Enchanted, Anne glanced at Lydia and asked, "May I hold her, Lydia?"

"Of course, Anne! She is accustomed already to being passed from admirer to admirer." The soft warm bundle was laid carefully in her arms, and, as Anne gently touched one soft cheek, the eyes opened and gazed back at her solemnly. Anne glanced up at Lydia, with misty eyes. "She is lovely, Lydia. Such beautiful skin." Lydia beamed fondly, "We were surprised and pleased, Anne. You may remember little Walter at this age. He was a fine, healthy baby but not a beauty the first month or so. Matthew is quite besotted with his little girl, I do assure you." Little Anne suddenly began to fuss and gnaw on one tiny fist. Lydia blushed and said, "She is hungry. Pray excuse me, dear Anne, while I take care of her."

With some surprise, Anne asked, "Will you not have a wet nurse, as you did with little Walter?" "Because she arrived early, we were caught out, and no one was available. Now, the doctor says that we should not change things at this present." Lydia paused, and blushed again. "I am not sure how it comes about, but I no longer care to have a wet nurse. There is something rather special about this time with her. I should not discuss this with you, as you are unmarried, but I think you may understand. My mother insists that nursing the baby myself is dreadfully common. The whole situation made her very uncomfortable and she returned home shortly before you arrived. I'm so happy to have you here, Anne..." Before she could continue, the baby let out a wail, and Lydia began to undo the ribbons at her throat. Her maid came in, and Anne found herself out the door in a trice.

Anne and Diana strolled on the terrace the next morning after breakfast. Diana looked out over the gently rolling lawn and asked, "What happened at the ball, Anne? You seem uneasy. Does this have aught to do with Mr Deschevaux?" Anne looked at Diana, then away, as she struggled for words. Diana continued, "We have been friends for a long time, and exchanged many confidences. You need not fear to trust me now." The two young women sat on a bench, and Anne told Diana about the ball, and how she felt while dancing with Charles. She also told Diana of how he had so abruptly and unexpectedly disclosed his regard for her.

"I was so surprised. I never dreamt of such a thing, Diana. I felt ... foolish. Then he told me of his business dealing with my father." Anne rose and paced across the terrace. "You are aware my father has always had ambitions for my marriage. Charles Deschevaux is the perfect candidate: impeccable birth, an old established estate, received everywhere. I have been acquainted with him for years, esteemed him as a friend of Fanny's family. Only recently did I begin to contemplate other possibilities. He has been a guest in our home, and I never saw a sign of a business connexion between him and my father. Now I find that he has been my father's client for some years."

She swung around to face Diana. "He has assured me that the debt is repaid, that he never discussed me with my father. But how can I believe that?" She resumed her seat next to Diana and gazed at her toes. "I fear that he has a sense of obligation to my father and that he may see marriage to me as a way to please my father."

Diana said nothing for several moments. "How do you feel about him, Anne? As a person, I mean." Anne said, "I have a great regard for him. We *converse*, Diana. Over the years, seeing him so often in company with Fanny and her family, I have been at ease with him. Only in the last several months, in York and at Lord FitzMaynard's home, have I thought that there...might be something more. He kissed my hand..." Anne blushed fierily and her voice trailed off.

"Is it not possible that he has the same feelings for you? Why are you convinced his emotions could only be gratitude to your father? You are an intelligent young lady, well educated and knowledgeable in the things you need to know to run a home. You are by no means an antidote. Is it so impossible to believe that he has developed feelings for you?" Anne looked up, laughing. "Thank you for the compliment,

Diana! '...by no means an antidote' indeed!" Anne sobered quickly. "When you put it that way, it does seem more possible. Fanny has always told me that I think too much but, over the years, I've been reminded on more than one occasion of our family's connexions with trade and that my father's fortune is a significant factor in my welcome in certain circles."

Diana said drily, "We have never really discussed this matter. Yet I can tell you that a lack of fortune renders many women superfluous, regardless of birth. I may say that I have some experience of that. I can also assure you that your father's fortune has nothing to do with my devotion to your brother." Diana's eyes glowed. "When Robert asked Mr Farleigh for permission to court me, I was amazed. Your brother is such a good man, Anne. Your father has raised his children to be kind and to look beyond the surface in their dealings with others. Robert is intelligent and interesting, unfailingly courteous. He is as great a gentleman as any of my acquaintance. Mr Farleigh did not question Robert's worthiness to court a member of the Farleigh family. Your father's fortune was certainly a factor in that matter. This is the way of our world. Are you willing to miss an opportunity for happiness because of excessive sensibility?"

"If you scratch the surface of many families at the highest level of society, you will find members who have had to make their own way. That is also the way of our world. Some have done it through the military, the church or the law. Others have had to find other means, as Mr Deschevaux has apparently done. Your family's business dealings have been conducted with honour and dignity, so far as I know. You have no reason to feel such doubt. If I am able to perceive your brother's merits and come to admire and love him, why do you find it so difficult to envisage that Mr Deschevaux may perceive your quality and care for you?" Before Anne could reply, her father and brothers came out to the terrace to join them.

The conversation became general. Anne noticed how Robert's eyes turned immediately to Diana, and the warmth of the glance they exchanged. She blushed slightly, as she felt like an intruder and more than slightly envious. The conversation turned to the wedding. Mr Emmons asked Robert what plans he and Diana had made. "Well, sir, I plan to buy a licence. Reverend Markham, the Dean, has already agreed to perform the service. Mr and Mrs Farleigh insist they must provide the wedding breakfast."

Diana broke in, touching Anne's shoulder, "And I hope that you, my dear friend, will attend me that day." Anne hugged Diana and accepted with great pleasure. "But what day have you selected?" asked Mr Emmons, with some impatience. Robert and Diana exchanged glances. "We have not yet determined a date, sir. We await Lydia's recovery, so that she and Matthew can join us. Sometime during the Christmas season may suit." Anne's eyes widened. "Oh, Father, Christmas would be wonderful. Matthew, Lydia and the children could come to us for the holiday festivities. A house party would be such fun, and a wedding would add to it delightfully!" Mr Emmons rubbed the bridge of his nose thoughtfully.

"When you put it like that, I cannot imagine anything better. Well done, my boy, well done!" Matthew said cautiously, "It sounds wonderful. However, let me discuss it with Lydia. I am not sure if she has any plans in mind with her family..." "An excellent idea, Matthew," said Anne warmly. "I do hope she finds this a good idea..." Matthew quitted the room. While he was gone, Diana and Anne discussed the wedding itself. "Small, of course. Robert's family, and my aunt and uncle. I also wish to include Jane Chamberlayne and her parents," mused Diana. "That sounds perfect," said Anne. "What will you wear, do you think?" Diana smiled. "I had thought to wear my best winter gown. It is green velvet trimmed with lace. I have a matching velvet redingote edged with fur." "That sounds perfect for a Christmas wedding," Anne replied.

A few days later, as Anne sat with Lydia and her namesake, Anne broached the subject of Robert's and Diana's wedding. "Do you like the idea of a Christmas wedding, Lydia? Does it fit in with your plans?" "It sounds delightful. My only concern is travelling with Baby. The weather can be extremely cold in December," replied Lydia. "She is doing well, is she not? She seems to have grown in the short time we have been here," said Anne as she reached a gentle finger to touch the baby's soft cheek. Lydia's face lit up. "She is so much bigger and stronger now, Anne. The christening is in three weeks. Her first expedition! We will see how she takes the ride to the church."

Chapter 19

As she swayed in the carriage on the return journey to York, Anne was certain she would never forget little Anne's baptism. Nothing proceeded as planned. The weather did not cooperate; rain fell in sheets and cold winds blew for days before the first date scheduled. Mr Parker, the curate, conducted Lydia's churching at home as the weather was so inclement. "I refuse to take Baby out in such weather. I will not risk her getting wet and chilled," declared Lydia. Matthew dispatched a note to the church, postponing the rite scheduled for the next day. All conceded that it was a wise move, as the rain continued for two more weeks before it finally let up to reveal a clear, clean blue sky as crisp dry air swept in.

Another note was dispatched to the church, proposing another date which was not acceptable as Mr Parker was to hold services at another church that day. Finally a date was settled. While they waited, Mr Emmons dispatched two men and a carriage back to York, to obtain some additional clothing for himself and Anne, and Ellen, Anne's maid.

"Clearly, we will be here longer than expected. Miss Farleigh, if you will write a note to your aunt, I will have my man leave it at Farleigh House. Anything you wish can be collected as my people leave York to return here." Diana acquiesced and a note was composed with instructions to deliver it to the housekeeper. (Diana privately told Anne, "My aunt may not be in residence; in any case, the housekeeper will know better what to pack for me.")

Days passed, clear and bright, as autumn leaves swirled in the cool breezes. Anne, Diana and Lydia found walking in the shrubbery much more pleasant, as the paths were sheltered and warmed by the sun. "I cannot believe how quickly time is passing," said Lydia. "Baby is almost two months old, and so well and strong." Anne agreed. "She is so round and pretty, Lydia. She has certainly made up for her early start." The three entered a walled garden at the end of the shrubbery, intent on cutting some late roses. There were some benches placed along the path around the garden and the ladies sat down to enjoy the beautiful day. Although the recent rains had flattened any full blooms, there were buds a-plenty, some that still showed colour and others already partially opened. The ladies' conversation turned to the wedding.

"My aunt and uncle are so kind. My aunt just wrote to me and insisted that I have a new gown and all the trimmings. She plans to have my gown made by her favourite *modiste* in London. She and my uncle are determined that my wedding clothes shall be everything of the best," Diana said with a smile. Later that afternoon, the party was increased by Matthew's friend who was standing godfather to little Anne, John Warden who was accompanied by his wife. Cheerful and ready to be pleased, Mr and Mrs Warden proved a delightful addition to the group, introducing new subjects for conversation at the dinner table and in the drawing room afterwards.

The morning of the baptism dawned clear and fine. The party walked up the path to the church. As their eyes accustomed themselves to the dim interior, Anne saw Mr Parker lighting candles at the altar and a few local people waiting for the morning service to begin. Mr Parker began the service with the prayers and the gospel reading ordained for baptism, and concluded the thanksgiving. Anne and Diana as godmothers and Mr Warden as godfather were seated together. Robert rose and looked at them with a tender smile and began.

"Dearly beloved, ye have brought this Child here to be baptised..." Anne was transfixed by Robert's warmth and conviction. Lydia placed the baby in Robert's arms, and he turned to the three godparents, saying "Name this Child." Anne said clearly, "Anne Isobel Emmons." The remainder of the baptismal rite proceeded through the Lord's Prayer and the thanksgiving. Then Mr Parker came forward and exhorted the godparents to remember their promises and to ensure little Anne be taught the nature of those vows and the things she needed to learn to lead a Christian life. Anne was deeply moved and struck by a sense of responsibility. She listened to the Morning Prayer service following the baptism with a new awareness.

After the service, the congregation filed out, greeting Mr Parker, then offering Lydia and Matthew their best wishes for the little one. The party turned toward their carriages, to return home to celebrate the baptism over a hearty breakfast. Anne and Diana said little on the short journey, both turning over the leaves of their prayer books as they pondered their new role in little Anne's life. Upon arrival at the house, Anne made her way to her room to bring out a gift she had brought for her little niece to commemorate her baptism. When she descended to the drawing room, she found her brother and sister-in-law seated by the fire.

"Where is everyone?" enquired Anne. "You are not the only one to need a moment," answered Lydia with a smile. "I believe Father Emmons is taking a turn in the shrubbery with Robert and Diana, and Mr and Mrs Warden ascended to their rooms. Randall will ring the bell for breakfast in fifteen minutes or so. Pray be seated, my dear sister." Anne handed Lydia the gift and took the chair opposite. "And where is the guest of honour?" "Ah, yes," replied Matthew with a rueful grin. "She is upstairs being bathed and changed by your amazing Miss Crawford. On the ride back, she narrowly missed soaking her mama and me as well. She will have a nap whilst we enjoy a well deserved meal."

Anne laughed, while Lydia opened the gift. Two items were revealed: one was a small golden cross set with pearls on a delicate chain, the other a prayer book beautifully bound in white with a special book plate inscribed to "Anne Isobel Emmons on the occasion of her Baptism from her Devoted Aunt & Godmother". Lydia pressed Anne's hand and smiled, "She will wear your gift with pleasure when she is a bit older! The prayer book is lovely, something she can use her whole life. Thank you, dear Anne." At that moment, the rest of the party came in and breakfast was announced. As they prepared to go into the dining room, Randall announced Mr Parker and his wife. Lydia invited them in. As everyone was seated, Anne appreciated her place between Robert and Mr Warden. Conversation rose. A few days later, Anne, Diana and her father left for York.

"I will be glad to get home," said Anne. "It has been a delightful visit, but I was not prepared to spend almost two months!" Diana responded, "I as well will be glad. I have many things to see to." "Please call on me if I can be of any help. I will be happy to shop with you, for example!" The two girls laughed, and Mr Emmons looked up from his papers with a sympathetic smile. As the journey wore on, conversation dwindled, and Anne found herself studying at the autumn landscape, thinking over the last several weeks...

As late autumn merged into winter, Anne was preoccupied with her efforts to write, as she spent hours in her sitting room reading and making notes. The weather made it easy for her to do this, as it had deteriorated shortly after she and Mr Emmons returned home. Needing to stretch, she walked over to the window. The cold rain lashed the window as she looked out, and noticed the few leaves that remained looked like wet rags clinging to the tree branches. A letter from Fanny lay unfolded on her desk. Fanny wrote of the autumn in Kent, the mellow weather they had enjoyed, and her anticipation of the winter in town.

"*Mr Burrell's appointment has been renewed, and he will make a report to the House after the New Year. I wish we could be present. I hoped to be in attendance, to lend support, but the gallery is closed to women. As we cannot get in, mayhap he will read it to us. I, of course, assume that you will be in London this winter. Mourning for the death of the poor queen will, of course, result in a quieter winter in town than usual. Please write and tell me your plans.*" Anne was amused to see no mention of the topic of Mr Burrell's speech. As she stood by the window, she mused "Fanny must be most interested in Mr Burrell to even consider sitting through a report in the House of Commons."

She returned to her desk and wrote a return letter to Fanny, telling her of Robert's engagement to Diana and their wedding plans, as well as baby Anne's baptism. "*As you can see, it may be well into January or even later before we will be able to leave. Please tell me when the date for his report is fixed; I will do my best to be there to support you!*" It occurred to her to ask about Charles Deschevaux, and she pondered the matter while the ink dried on her pen. She dipped her pen again, and continued without mentioning his name. She closed her letter affectionately; when the ink dried, she folded it, sealed it with a wafer and wrote Fanny's direction. She walked out of the room, to take her letter downstairs for the post.

As Anne crossed the hall, her father called to her from the library door. "Anne, my dear, would you come talk with me a while? I have an idea for you to consider." Seated in her favourite chair, Anne looked up at her father. "An idea, Father? What are you about?"

"I have some business affairs that will take me to London after the New Year. I know that you usually spend some time there with Fanny and her parents during the Season. My plans are somewhat uncertain, but I expect to be detained in London for several weeks, even some months. What do you say to our taking a house, my dear?" Anne turned a surprised face to him.

"A house? I can't say; I never thought of it. Where do you wish to be, Father?" He paced before the fire. "I had thought of Russell or Bedford Square. Both are respectable neighbourhoods, near the British Museum and convenient locations for meetings with colleagues. I also found a charming house on Upper Brooke Street, quite close to Grosvenor Square. The location is an easy distance to spend time with Lord and Lady Kidwell and Fanny," he smiled down at Anne with mischief in his eyes. "...and also a much better address if we wish to entertain," he added with a wink.

"Entertain, Father?" she echoed. "Yes, certainly, my dear. After all these years, it would be pleasant to repay the kindness you have received. Robert and Diana may wish to receive friends as well." Anne thought about it, and pronounced in favour of the Upper Brooke Street location.

"We can bring some of our own people, of course, who understand our ways, and I can check with the school to see if any of the older students are ready to make a start-it would be excellent experience. I am sure Lady Kidwell will know of a suitable registry where we could hire any additional servants we may need. When do we go?"

"As soon as may be, after the wedding," Mr Emmons said, rubbing his hands together. "Robert and Diana may join us for some time. As far as the house is concerned, I thought you would prefer Upper Brooke Street, so have taken an option on it. If it meets our needs, I will look into purchasing it. There is a rumour that the owner might wish to sell."

"That is an excellent plan. Robert has engaged on some significant redecorating of his house. He has plans for a delightful sitting room fitted up especially for Diana. He asked me about her favourite colours and flowers, what she liked to read and so on. If they accompany us to London for a while, that would allow the work to be completed," said Anne slowly. "I will speak to him about it."

She rose from her seat, kissed her father's cheek and went up to her sitting room, already engrossed with plans. As she passed through the hall, she asked a footman to request Mrs Hubbard to visit her. Seated at her desk, she wrote first to Lady Kidwell to obtain the name of the best registry office and for recommendations for victuallers and other purveyors. She also enquired about dates that might be convenient for entertaining. Although the season would be not be under way, she wanted to select dates that did not conflict with Lady Kidwell's and Fanny's schedules.

Pulling out her household book for reference, she noted down some plans for two events at home for Robert and Diana. She pondered. "A dinner before the wedding would be so pleasant. Mr and Mrs Farleigh, Matthew and Lydia, Mr and Mrs Chamberlayne and Jane, of course, are all well known to Robert and Diana and to each other. The Dean and Mrs Markham must, of course, be present. I must also ask Jane about her young man. An evening party, perhaps the night of the day after the wedding? Card tables in the library, possibly a few couples standing up in the drawing room, and an excellent supper. We could hire a few musicians to provide music whether or not there was to be dancing." Anne considered inviting guests from out of town, but decided to speak to Robert and Diana first.

Just then, a tap at the door caused Anne to raise her head. Mrs Hubbard presented herself, with a small curtsey. "You wished to see me, Miss Emmons," she said. "Yes, indeed, Mrs Hubbard. As you know, we will go to London for a few months after the wedding. Which of the staff do you think should accompany us?"

"Ellen, of course, will accompany you, Miss Emmons, and Mr Emmons' valet, Mr Kyrk, must be included. Do any servants come with the house, ma'am?" "Oh my, I never considered that," said Anne, somewhat mortified at her oversight.

"'Tis easily discovered, Miss Emmons. I will enquire of the master. You will also want to fill places from a registry office." She frowned. "I have not been to London in some years, and do not know if the one used then is still the best. If I may, ma'am, I suggest that you write to Lady Kidwell and ask her advice on the best registry. Some suggestions on purveyors would also be helpful."

"I have already done so, Mrs Hubbard. Now, of course you will be with us..." "Excuse me, Miss Emmons, but I thought Mr Emmons told you. I cannot accompany you and the master to London this time," said Mrs Hubbard in some confusion. In consternation, Anne laid down her pen. "Oh, but Mrs Hubbard, I counted on you. I have never managed completely on my own..."

"I am sorry, ma'am. Mr Emmons mentioned that you would all spend some weeks after Mr Robert's wedding in London, and I ventured to ask about some improvements to the kitchen, and a personal matter as well." She paused. In spite of her consternation, Anne encouraged, "A personal matter, Mrs Hubbard?" "Indeed, ma'am. My niece and her husband are expecting a baby sometime in the winter after the New Year. She is my sister's only child and has begged me to come to her. My sister died some years ago and she has no one else..." She paused again.

"A new closed stove will be installed after the festivities are over, and there will be a great deal of cleaning and rearranging in the kitchens and pantry area. However, I ventured to ask if I might take a few weeks to support my niece after the kitchen is sorted. Mr Somers is agreeable and Mr Emmons saw no difficulty."

"Mrs Hubbard, of course you must attend your niece," said Anne warmly. "Meanwhile, I do appreciate your counsel on how to prepare and proceed." The two ladies laid their heads together and Anne resumed her notes.

Chapter 20

A few days later, Anne visited at Robert's town house. "Do you think Diana will be pleased?" he asked eagerly. The master suite had been transformed. Oh, Robert," breathed Anne as she turned slowly to take in the changes. "This is truly lovely. She will love it, I know." "I have ordered a pair of Argand lamps for this room, one for the writing table, with a single chimney, and a second for the mantle that will have a double chimney. She has told me how much she loves to read and work on her embroidery, and these will give her excellent light, especially during the winter when it grows dark so early." He rubbed his hands together. "The one for the mantle is of silver with crystals and etched glass shades. I am having it engraved for her." "How thoughtful and kind you are, Robert. Diana will be delighted," replied Anne.

They returned to the drawing room and discussed plans for the wedding festivities. Robert liked the idea of a dinner but discouraged the evening party, to Anne's disappointment. "I know you want only to celebrate with us, but you know how retiring Diana is. I believe she would prefer spend time quietly with all of us as a family, getting better acquainted with my father and brother. We will be off to London within a few days, in any case, so there is no need to entertain too extensively before we leave. We will stay with you and Father after the wedding until I must return to York to take up my duties. You will have quite the houseful." Mentally resolved to have a special dinner anyway, Anne acquiesced. "When will Diana see her new rooms?" she asked.

"After we return from London. While we are away, the drawing room will also be refreshed. We discussed some changes there and she has seen those plans. The bedroom, dressing room and her sitting room will be a complete surprise." Anne asked, "Has Matthew written? Will he and Lydia come with the children?"

"Yes, they will be coming. They will arrive a few weeks before Christmas and then, when we depart for London, they will return to Leeds. Lydia simply couldn't bear the thought of travelling that distance in winter with the children. Besides," Robert said confidentially, "Matthew was not enthusiastic about all of us sharing a house for what may be a few months. He is a bit self-conscious in regard to having the children about, and Lydia, of course, will not leave them, especially with the baby so young."

Anne nodded. "I will put them in the guest rooms which overlook the garden, near me. That will allow you and Diana some privacy in the other wing. I know she will stay at Farleigh House until the wedding. However, she may wish to bring some boxes here to make things easier. I will make sure everything is in order for you both." She beamed at Robert affectionately. "I am so looking forward to this winter." Anne then took her leave.

Anne returned home, where she took the opportunity to meet with Mrs Hubbard and the cook to discuss a dinner the evening before the wedding. "Mr Robert loves your pigeon pie, Mrs Clay, and Miss Farleigh has a real taste for wine jelly. Mr Emmons, as you know better than anyone, will not consider it dinner unless there is a roast of beef or a ham. Some escalloped oysters or buttered crab would be a good remove." She thought for a moment, and requested, "Please draw up a bill of fare including these items to present to me tomorrow. I would appreciate your suggestion for a soup. Since this is a very special occasion, it would be lovely to have a grand cake." The three women ended with a discussion of the glass house and what might be available in the way of fruit and vegetables. "It would be wonderful if there is a pineapple," said Mrs Clay wistfully.

Anne made her way up to her suite and seated herself at her desk. She took up some letters that awaited her attention. The first was from Lady Kidwell. She unfolded it, hoping it contained answers to some of her questions. To her relief, it did. *"There is an unexceptionable registry office near the Strand. They even offer rooms to conduct interviews if you prefer not to interview at home. My friend, Mrs Oliphant, was completely satisfied with the dresser she hired from there, and I have heard nothing but good reports of them."* She also offered suggestions for suppliers. *"Tomlin's Jelly House offers truly delectable moulded jellies, and Dawson's Confectioners has delicious rout cakes and macaroons. I have found the best butcher's shop to be Giblet and Son."*

Her letter continued on to discuss her family's health and her schedule for entertainments during the season. *"We do not entertain as frequently as in prior years. Fanny does not seem to care for it as much as before and Lord Kidwell is quite busy at this present, although that may not be the case in the spring. We are so looking forward to your arrival in town."*

Lady Kidwell mentioned that Mr Burrell had called several times, and expressed her relief that nothing further had been heard from Carleton Thomas or his family. They had seen Mr Thomas at the theatre and a distant bow was the only acknowledgement exchanged. She closed affectionately, with a request for Anne to remember the Kidwells to her amiable father.

Anne put Lady Kidwell's letter with her other notes for London housekeeping, then descended to find her father. As usual, he was in his library, intent upon his correspondence. "My dear sir, have you a moment?" she asked affectionately. He looked up, and a smile of welcome lit his face. "Certainly, my dear, you have all of my attention." "Will there be servants in place in the house, Father, or do we need to hire all?" she asked.

"There is a butler, and a housekeeper that the owner has retained, and I understand that there are a few maids and a footman or two. There is also a groom in the stables. We do have the option to hire all of our own, if you prefer. I am glad that the butler and housekeeper are in place, as Mrs Hubbard will not be able to accompany us." Anne was also relieved. "I am so glad that there will be help to start out. Lady Kidwell has referred me to a registry office but it will be much easier to have people on hand while we get settled. Did the owner tell you anything about them? If we get on well with the existing people, we may not need to hire additional, with our own who accompany us."

"My thoughts exactly. The owner indicated that the butler and housekeeper have served his family for some time. It seems they were hired for the London house exclusively and know it extensively. If you wish, I can write to my agent in London to have him hire some additional help. If you care to send some instructions, I will be happy to put him onto it." Anne considered the matter.

"I will suggest to Mrs Clay that she accompany us. She is an excellent cook. She has mastered several French dishes; certainly, I never ate a ragout better than hers at any table. She also knows your favourites and how we like things. Who else can make that cake that you like so well? If she accompanies us, we should be able to make do very well with the current arrangements to start. We can always make changes later if we must." She rose and walked to the door.

Anne paused as she looked over her shoulder. "Father, have you heard from Mr Deschevaux?" "No, my dear, I have not," he said quizzically. "What makes you ask?" Disconcerted, she answered, "No particular reason. I had the thought that, if he happened to be in York during the Christmas season, we should make him welcome. He is known to all of our party and he would be a pleasant addition to our celebration." Anne thanked her father for his time, slipped out of the room and ran up the stairs, not seeing his raised brows and satisfied smile.

Back in the privacy of her library, Anne sat limply down at her desk, shocked at her own forward behaviour. Looking for distraction, she picked up the second letter. Anne was delighted to see that it was from Emily. She spread it open and was thrilled to read of Emily's engagement. *"My aunt and I left Bath to visit Leamington Priors. Poor darling, her digestive disorder combined with an unfortunate outbreak convinced her that the waters at Leamington could do her more good than those anywhere else, especially as it seems there are so many baths. We stayed at the Bedford Hotel, which was most conveniently situated. The day after our arrival, we visited Mrs Rackstrow's library to see if we could find a novel for our evening readings where she met an old acquaintance, Mrs Cheylesmore. The lady invited us to dine the next evening with her and her nephew by marriage.*

Apparently, her late husband's family is an old one from Coventry, and her nephew escorted her to take the waters at Leamington Priors. It seems she does not like to travel any distance, as she is a martyr to illness in a coach. They were staying in the Oxford Hotel, which was no great distance. Mr Richard Rotherham, her nephew, was most kind. Our aunts spent so much time comparing symptoms and discussing the merits of the various baths and wells, we perforce had to converse with each other..."

Anne smiled; it was so obvious that Emily and her intended had found much to say to each other. Her happiness glowed from the pages. Excursions to Warwick Castle and Kenilworth, balls at the Assembly Rooms, walks in the elegant new Priory Gardens, it was clear that Emily and her intended had enjoyed every moment of their time in Leamington Priors under the benevolent eyes of their respective aunts. He had a comfortable home between Leamington Priors and Warwick from which he was able to visit frequently, and Emily's aunt (no doubt espying which way the wind blew) decided to extend their stay several weeks.

"As you are aware, my parents were concerned about my

continued unmarried state. When my aunt wrote to my mother with the news that an acceptable bachelor was paying attention to me, and I <u>allowing</u> it, my parents hastened to join us. (My father's biliousness gave sufficient excuse for wanting to take the waters, I presume.) My parents and his aunt were introduced; she presented Richard to them. Fortunately, all were pleased with the acquaintance. All circumstances conspired to further their happiness.

When Emily's return to her parents' home in London was finally accomplished, it was no surprise to anyone that Mr Rotherham appeared within a few weeks. Their wedding was set for a date in March, *"Mama insisted that I wait until she had time to order my bride clothes. Richard's parents are both deceased, sadly, but he has a sister and a brother, as well as his aunt, who will support him. He has a small house in town, and his sister and Mrs Cheylesmore will accompany him for the winter. They will stay on after the wedding to enjoy what they may of the Season."*

It seems that Mr DeWitt had made inquiries concerning Mr Rotherham's family and was satisfied with what he discovered. Not aristocratic; however, the family was comfortably off and well connected. Although the family fortune had come from trade in the middle part of the last century, the Rotherham family was long established in Coventry and had married into several respectable families in the area, including the Cheylesmore family. Mr Richard Rotherham's grandfather had been well educated and had served as a Member of Parliament for the area. "It seems ideal in every way," mused Anne.

"Richard is a gentleman of respectable birth and fortune so my father was satisfied. It remained only for Richard and me to find ourselves willing to oblige, which we were. My sentiments are not what I expected, Anne. We are <u>comfortable</u> together, enjoy the same sorts of entertainments, and laugh at the same foolish jokes. He is a well-looking man, but I do not consider him the handsomest man of

my acquaintance. Although he seems happy to see me when I walk into the room, I do not believe that he has eyes only for me. I do not feel that heart-pounding, desperate rush of emotion when we dance. (Remember when I thought I was in love with that unsuitable young man in our second season? What WAS his name?)

With Richard, I can relax and enjoy the dance, and know that he is enjoying it as well. I look forward to being his wife and having my own family with him. I had once thought that only a blazing passion would do; instead, I find myself delighted with the warmth of a cosy fire. Somehow I am certain that the warmth and cosiness will grow as we share our lives."

Anne dropped the letter in her lap, lost in thought. A thousand feelings were roused -happiness for Emily, surprise at Emily's frankness, and (to her own surprise) some envy and dissatisfaction with her own situation. She wondered at herself. She was looking forward to her brother's wedding, to having her own house and entertaining in London. Anne caught herself; not her own house, she reminded herself, her father's house. "Will I ever have my own place in life?" she wondered. "What might it be like, to be truly the mistress of a home?" Her thoughts inescapably turned again to Charles. She was still amazed at her own temerity in encouraging her father to invite Charles. (She had no illusion that he would wait to see if Charles happened to be visiting York; she was certain a missive was already on its way.)

Chapter 21

Resolutely, Anne put the future out of her mind, and reviewed her composition. Reading over it, she was content with her work. She was especially pleased with the conclusion and the delicate line drawings contributed by Miss Crawford. She sat upright in her chair as she pondered her next step. Anne knew she could ask her father to have it printed; he would request enough copies for family and friends, tastefully bound. However, she was not satisfied with that. "If I am interested in material like this, surely there are other women who might enjoy it as well. Why should I not share it? If a woman has a talent for writing, why should she not publish?"

After much thought, she decided to consult with Mr Chamberlayne. She would have him read her work. Anne knew he would tell her whether it had merit. She laid her work carefully in its portfolio and tied the ribbons. She set it aside, and then wrote a brief note to Mr Chamberlayne, asking if it she could call on him in the afternoon. After dispatching the note, she worked contentedly on a new project while awaiting a reply.

Later that day, Anne stepped into a chair and gave the address of Chamberlayne's Bookstore. In her nervous state, it seemed but a moment until the chairmen set her down in front of the shop. She stepped out of the chair, paid the two men handsomely and entered the shop, feeling as if she were going to meet her fate. To her relief, only Jane and her father were there.

Anne handed her portfolio to Mr Chamberlayne and explained how her interest in the Romans had been ignited and her desire to share her writing. Mr Chamberlayne took the portfolio, smiled kindly at Anne and said, "My dear Miss Emmons, there are many talented women authors these days. I will be honoured to read your work and I will give you an honest opinion on whether it should be published." Smiling with pleasure, she impulsively hugged Mr Chamberlayne and Jane.

"Thank you a thousand times, dear sir! I look forward to your opinion." She and Jane then entered the shop to browse some new editions and to share each other's news. Jane whispered, "You must know that Hugh will be coming home for Christmas. His mother told me that he has done very well in London, and has been given leave to spend some time with his family." She blushed rosily and smiled.

Anne hugged her friend again, and replied, "I'm delighted for you, my dear. I know how happy to see him you must be." Anne shared her news about the plans for Robert's and Diana's wedding. "You and your parents must, of course, be present at the wedding breakfast," she added affectionately. "And Hugh as well, if you wish to ask him. Diana was most insistent." "Anne, that would be lovely. Thank you so much for including him," Jane dimpled.

"The invitation cards will be sent shortly. The celebration is only a few weeks away. You know they selected the day after Christmas for their wedding." Anne added, "I must get busy." Jane offered to help her write the cards but Anne declined her offer gracefully. "I appreciate your offer of assistance, my dear, but there are not many to write. Addressing the invitations is the only thing Mrs Farleigh will allow me to do; she has the entire breakfast planned. The wedding will be very small, and Robert and Diana have insisted on only family and old friends such as yourselves in attendance at breakfast. Diana is somewhat shy, as you well know."

Anne then turned the subject to the house in London and her father's interest in buying a house there. Impulsively, she added,

"Mayhap, you could come for a visit this year. There are so many places I want to show you, such as the British Museum and the Tower of London. The bookstores and libraries as well. We could have a delightful time." Jane hesitated, "It sounds wonderful but I do not know..." She hesitated. "You are very busy with your society friends, are you not? I understand you are acquainted with some very important people and I fear I would not fit in well. I do not want to appear pushing, or create difficulties for you." Anne was taken aback, and then understood completely.

"My dear Jane, you could not appear pushing if you tried. As to my society friends, you know Fanny very well. The social season does not really begin before spring. Besides, you must know that she and I have rather stepped back from Almack's and other *Ton* affairs. Whilst I enjoy an acquaintance with Lady Jersey and attend a few parties and so forth, I hardly live in a whirl of engagements."

Anne smiled wryly. "I understand your concerns so well. I felt rather like an intruder during my first visits with Fanny and her family in London, especially when Lady Kidwell presented me and I was given vouchers for Almack's. I did feel a fish out of water, I admit, and still do upon occasion. However, as I grew up and realised that I had my own talents and interests, somehow the approval of society, as you put it, became less important. My father and eldest brother may make their livelihoods in business, but they are as well educated and as gentlemanly as any man I met in London. Your circumstances are not so very different to mine, my dear. I would not force you to attend events at which you do not think you will be comfortable. There are so many things to see and do, you will not be bored."

Mischievously, she added, "Who knows, Hugh may find time to escort us to a play or a lecture at the Royal Society. That would not be too oppressive, would it?" Jane shook her head at Anne and conceded that such an outing might not be too much for her. "I will think about it and discuss it with my father. After all, no decision need be made this very moment." With that, Anne had to be satisfied.

Returning home in her chair, Anne resolved to write the cards of invitation that very evening. She arrived home with barely enough time to change her dress for dinner and to join her father in the library before dinner was announced. Her discovery that her father was expecting a business acquaintance to call after dinner gave her a reason to excuse herself to her sitting room after their meal was concluded. Before she picked up her pen and the box of invitation cards, she could not resist peeking at her notes for her novel. As she glanced through them, an idea struck her and she wrote busily for a time, adding several pages to her manuscript. She read through them again, changing a few words here and there, and then set them carefully aside.

Anne then addressed the cards for the wedding breakfast in her neatest script. As she carefully sanded and set aside the last card, she leaned back in her chair, content with her evening's work. Anne glanced twice at the clock, horrified to see how late it was. Ringing for her maid, she crossed to her dressing room to prepare to retire. When Ellen entered, Anne apologised for keeping her so late.

"Just unfasten my gown, and I can disrobe on my own, Ellen. I was lost in my work and did not notice the time." Shocked, Ellen remonstrated, "Miss Emmons, my duty requires me to be available when you require. It's improper to apologise." Anne recognised that Ellen was seriously discomposed by her apology and meekly allowed Ellen to remove her gown and assist her with the various hooks and laces.

Clad in her night rail and dressing gown, Anne sat at her dressing table as Ellen took down her hair and brushed it vigorously. Once Anne's hair was neatly braided, Ellen gathered the discarded gown and some other items of clothing, bobbed a curtsey and said austerely, "Good night, ma'am." "Good night, Ellen," Anne replied.

"Thank you." As the door closed behind the maid, Anne could not help but smile.

"I had no idea that an apology would overset her so much." She gathered her jewellery pieces and put them away. Then she rose and blew out the candles in her dressing room. Entering her bedroom, she was grateful for the turned-down bed and the lamp burning on the table next to her chair. She picked up *Persuasion*, suddenly wanting to lose herself in the romance of another Anne. She put her book on the table, sat down and nestled into the chair, then picked up her book to read.

The next morning, Anne was down early for breakfast. She left the stack of invitation cards on her father's desk for the post and went on to the dining room, experiencing an appetite for heartier fare than usual. She picked up a plate and walked over to the buffet. After she took a small helping each of eggs and cheese, she added a roll and a slice of pound cake to the plate. She seated herself at the table, she poured out a cup of tea. Sipping her tea, she jotted some notes as she enjoyed her breakfast. Engrossed in a possible guest list for the dinner Robert had approved, she was so absorbed that she jumped with surprise when her father kissed her cheek.

"Good morning, my dear! Hard at it, I see," he said with a smile. "Indeed, Father. Time is getting away from me. There is much to do for the wedding, and, of course, our removal to London."

"I am glad you remind me, my dear, as I've received a letter from Jackson, my agent, regarding the house. He has had a complete tour from attics to cellar. The house is in excellent condition and ready for occupancy. The exterior is stone with ironwork, and the interior boasts some impressive plasterwork ceilings and fireplaces. He has described the rooms and there are sufficient rooms for all to be comfortable. There is a large first-floor bed chamber with a stairway to access the library below, which I have ventured to claim for myself."

His eyes crinkled in a warm smile as he continued, "And for you, my dear, there are three rooms on the next floor that I think you will find adequate. The bedroom and dressing room I've chosen for you, as well as the rooms for Robert and Diana are being updated, but I have requested some special alterations to your third room that will, I venture, render it much more comfortable for you."

Smiling in response, Anne asked, "Dare I ask what you plan, sir, or is it to be a surprise?" "Oh, a surprise, of course. I will tell you that the room in question is across the hall from the bedroom, at the back of the house. I thought it would be quieter for you and that's all I will say on the matter."

Mr Emmons paused to fill his plate and take his customary chair at table. "Jackson also writes that a reasonable complement of servants accompanies the house. With our own cook and our personal servants, we should be perfectly comfortable." Anne nodded agreement but privately reserved judgement. Retainers of several years had their own quirks and expectations. She was sure that some adjustments would be required by all. She resolved to get the housekeeper's name and the direction to write to the woman personally. Her father added, "I don't know if I mentioned it, but Jackson asked his lordship about selling. Apparently, he is interested and Jackson has put in the offer."

Later in the day, Anne called at Farleigh House with her lists and notes, so that she and Diana could put their heads together with Diana's Aunt Farleigh. The three ladies sat in Mrs Farleigh's comfortable *boudoir* and enjoyed the early winter sunshine as it poured through the windows. She asked Mrs Farleigh if there were any names to be included on the guest list for the dinner the night before the wedding. "I had hoped that Lord and Lady FitzMaynard would still be in the country but they are away. It seems you have thought of everyone, my dear," she assured Anne. Anne smiled and asked if Mrs Farleigh would suggest a particular dish that Mr Farleigh would enjoy. Mrs Farleigh smiled.

"Oh, my dear, Mr Farleigh is most easy to please. As long as there is a roasted *something*, he will be content. Men in general enjoy a roast. However, he does have a fondness for a salmon pie and (dare I confess?) a fondness for sweets. He is especially fond of a baked carrot pudding or sack pudding. Still, I beg you not to inconvenience your cook." Anne laughed.

"Dear ma'am, it would be no inconvenience at all. Mrs Clay has planned for a number of removes, and would be glad to include a special something to Mr Farleigh's taste. Of course, there will definitely be a roast; she is considering either beef or turkey and may decide to have both." Mrs Farleigh twinkled. "Indeed, then, all of the men should be well served." The ladies then turned to the question of Diana's gown. "The *modiste* brought the gown from London for a final fitting. It is delightful, I think," said Mrs Farleigh. Diana breathed, "Oh, Anne, I never dreamed of a gown so fine. You must see it."

The ladies went up the stairs to Diana's dressing room, where the *modiste* and her seamstress were making the final alterations. Palest gold silk, delicate blonde lace, golden beads and embroidery, the gown was designed to emphasise Diana's warm colouring. A Witchoura mantle of soft brown velvet lined with the pale gold silk and trimmed with sable would keep her warm on the way to and from the church. All the other accessories toned with the gold and brown, and included a topaz set consisting of earrings, a cross on a golden chain and a delicate band for her hair.

Cheeks glowing, Diana confided that the topazes were a gift from Robert. "Oh, my dear, what an elegant *ensemble*! You will look beautiful-Robert will be so proud," enthused Anne. A lovely morning dress in soft fawn and a dressing gown of rich deep green velvet were ready. A walking dress and matching travelling cloak of deepest brown kerseymere trimmed with sable were also completed. "I thought this would be suitable for the journey to London. I would not be disrespectful of the late Queen, even though I have no expectation of attending any important functions for some weeks." Anne replied,

"I do understand. I have a dark grey travelling cloak and bonnet. That with black gloves should be suitable for half-mourning."

Diana asked Anne what she planned to wear to the wedding. "My dear Madame Josette is almost finished with my gown, which is of rose velvet with silver embroidery. I have commissioned a new redingote as well, of silver grey kerseymere lined with grey silk and trimmed at the neck and cuffs with chinchilla. There will also be a pelerine and muff of chinchilla, as well as a velvet bonnet." Her mother's diamond drop earrings would be her only jewellery. Diana, Anne and Mrs Farleigh fell into an animated discussion of the items still awaiting completion for Diana's *trousseau.*

"Do not forget that you will remove to London shortly after the wedding," cautioned Mrs Farleigh. "You will want to look about you there, for there are so many shops and *modistes.* You will enjoy much greater choice than here in York. I will give you a list of some of my favourite purveyors, and I am certain you will find others." Anne and Diana looked at each other and smiled.

"I know that Fanny will be happy to assist as well," said Anne. "She will arrive in London shortly before we do." Diana smiled in agreement. "I already have so much more than I am accustomed. I will enjoy looking, but can't imagine purchasing too much more finery." Anne shrugged. "One never knows. There are shawls, perfumes, fans. Not to mention books..."

Anne returned home and went at once to meet with Mrs Hubbard and Mrs Clay. She told them of her conversation with Mrs Farleigh, and asked Mrs Clay about the dishes planned for the dinner. "Well, ma'am, I could certainly manage a fish pie for a remove. In addition to the list you gave to me, I had planned for oyster soup. I will make an old fashioned marchpane cake, with some decorations. What about a nice sack cream to serve with it?" "That sounds tempting, Mrs Clay." Anne beamed. "Mrs Hubbard, give me your opinion. Will the meal please my father, do you think?"

"Well, Miss Anne, Mr Emmons has always liked fish pie, although it is not his favourite dish. Both he and Mr Robert are very fond of the marchpane cake; the sack cream will be a nice compliment, but will not overwhelm." The three women nodded in agreement, and Anne said, "Well, then, we can consider the courses set as planned. I am certain Robert and Diana will be delighted. Thank you, Mrs Hubbard, Mrs Clay." Anne returned above stairs, and retired to her room.

Chapter 22

Seated at her desk, Anne busily addressed a note. Dispatched by footman to the post, there was ample time for response. She also wrote to Fanny and to Emily to tell them of the change of plans and of her anticipated earlier arrival in Upper Brooke Street. *"I am a bit nervous about the butler and housekeeper. My father tells me they have been in service there for some years. I wrote to the housekeeper, a Mrs Russell, but have received no response as yet. I hope she will be receptive to our presence. I understand that the house has been let occasionally for a few weeks at a time. I believe we will be the first long-term tenants. Father intends to buy the house but I do not know if the offer will be accepted, or how long the transaction will take. The situation is excellent."*

Having sealed and addressed her letters, Anne pulled out her manuscript and made some more notes. After she reviewed her material, she began a first draft. Completely absorbed, she wrote on until the clock struck. Anne checked the time and was surprised at the lateness of the hour. She rose to her feet and rang for Ellen.

She selected the first appropriate gown to hand: a sapphire blue velvet with long sleeves and a low neck edged with a twist of silk and delicate lace. She laid out the golden reliquary locket and a pair of earbobs of gold set with sapphires. Ellen came into the room with a pitcher of warm water for washing.

"Oh, Ellen, bless you. I'm late. Pray, unfasten my gown so I may freshen and change as quickly as possible." It seemed impossible, but, with Ellen's help, Anne descended the stairs sedately as the gong for dinner rang. Ellen had even managed to take her hair down, brush it thoroughly and replait it with sapphire blue silk ribbon. The ribbons and gown, accented by her earbobs, deepened the colour of her eyes to a clear dark blue. Anne felt ready for anything when she entered the drawing room. Until she met the gold-sparked gaze of Charles Deschevaux...

Anne froze in shock. Just then, her father said urbanely, "Anne, love, that was only the first gong. You have time for a glass of ratafia or sherry if you would like." "Thank you, Father, sherry would be lovely," said Anne breathlessly, her gaze locked with that of Mr Deschevaux. He approached and took her hand. "Miss Emmons, it seems a long time since we danced at Littlebrook." He bowed over her hand. She looked at him in bewilderment.

"Mr Deschevaux, I did not realise you were expected. Forgive me..." Her father broke in with unusual heartiness. "Just a surprise for you, my dear. Here is your sherry." She freed her hand from Mr Deschevaux's grasp to take her glass, stepped away from him and took a seat, her thoughts in a whirl. The two gentlemen took up their conversation, a discussion of business matters to which Anne paid no attention.

"Why is he here?" she pondered. "What do I say to him?" In spite of her exchange with her father, she had not expected to see him at this time. Remembering their walk in the gardens at Littlebrook House made her blush. Her memory of her words to her father about including Mr Deschevaux made her feel even more awkward.

The second gong for dinner rang and the three adjourned to the dining room. To her relief, Miss Crawford was just approaching the door, and they all went in together. "I spoke with Mrs Hubbard whilst you were occupied, my dear, and asked for a less formal setting," said Mr Emmons.

Anne looked around the room and saw that most of the leaves

had been removed and the dining table moved to a position before the fire, with the covers laid for four. "Just the thing for such a raw evening," said Miss Crawford. "A cosy dinner *en famille*." As they took their seats, a footman and maid entered to serve the first course. After the bisque of fish was served, the ladies took some slices of roasted turkey and some grand salad with pickles. Her father and Mr Deschevaux accepted the turkey with buttered parsnips and large wedges of oyster pie. Conversation was general, and Mr Deschevaux gave news of their friends in Kent, particularly Lord and Lady Kidwell and Fanny. He mentioned the fact that Martin Burrell had an opportunity for a better government appointment.

"Lord Kidwell and I have both expressed our interest in his candidacy, and the selection will be made within the month. So far, no other candidate has been brought forward, so it appears he has a reasonable chance for success." "And how is Fanny?" asked Anne.

"Quite well, I understand. She and Lady Kidwell have been busy. I believe they plan to remove to London in January." "That's surprising," Anne remarked. "Fanny doesn't usually like to go much before April, for the Season." His eyes twinkling, Mr Deschevaux noted that Parliament, and the government offices, would be meeting.

Mr Emmons asked a question about the new government that had been seated that summer. "As you know, there has been a great deal of turmoil, especially in regard to the Corn Laws," responded Mr Deschevaux. "However, that reminds me of our business..." "Yes, yes, we will get to that after we dine," interjected Mr Emmons. He turned the conversation to the Christmas holiday and Robert's upcoming wedding, and discussed their plans to remove to London shortly afterwards.

"Miss Farleigh has spent little time in London. Anne will have the opportunity to take her about, help her form some acquaintance and shop before the season. I have a deal of business, so plan to be established there for some months." Mr Deschevaux said wistfully, "It sounds delightful, a real family party."

With a jovial smile, Mr Emmons suggested, "You are most welcome to join us. I know Robert and Miss Farleigh would be delighted. The wedding will be quite soon, and you can remove to London when we do. As you have your own quarters in town, you've only to let your people know." Anne kept her eyes fixed on her plate, right hand clenched in her lap while her left pushed salad around her plate with her fork. "Oh, Father?" she thought, dismayed. "You have no idea..."

Fleetingly, Anne thought of Robert and Diana, and wondered if they knew her father was going to invite another guest. In the back of her head, a little voice said, "In your heart, you are glad he is here", but she still felt mortified at her father's words. As Mr Deschevaux responded, she glanced at him in surprise. "If I will not be in the way, I would be honoured to be part of your celebration."

As the servants cleared and served the second course, Miss Crawford interjected, "It's to be hoped that the weather holds. We so wish for fine weather for Christmas and the wedding." Gratefully, Anne added, "It has been cold but clear, and the sky has been that lovely bright blue. Such a day would be perfect." Mr Deschevaux glanced at Anne with a smile.

"We must hope for clear days." He changed the subject and continued, "I just read a most interesting book. It has probably come your way. Have you had the opportunity to look at 'Antiquities of York' by Mr Cave? I brought my copy with me in hopes of visiting some of the places he mentioned, to look for the Roman elements." Anne forgot her embarrassment in enthusiasm.

"Indeed, I have, sir. That book is a favourite of mine, and I find it intriguing to visit the sites he described with it in hand. I have viewed my city with new eyes, I assure you." Mr Emmons interjected, "In fact, I had to purchase a copy for her own, as she held mine for so long." Miss Crawford joined in the conversation, and the four enjoyed a lively discussion of Mr Cave's book and other topics as the second course was served. Mr Emmons offered to take Mr

Deschevaux to visit Chamberlayne's book store and some of the sites mentioned in Mr Cave's book the next morning, which he accepted with alacrity. As Anne observed Mr Deschevaux's easy camaraderie with her father, she could not help but be pleased. She had seldom seen a young man engage her father in such relaxed conversation. As she mused, dinner came to an end.

Miss Crawford cleared her throat gently, and Anne started slightly, then rose. "Tea in the drawing room would be pleasant," she said, and the two ladies moved to the dining room door. "That's right, my dear," said Mr Emmons, "we shall join you in a bit." As she passed through the door, she heard Mr Deschevaux say, "Now, sir, about that business..." In the drawing room, Anne poured out cups of tea for herself and Miss Crawford. "Amelia," she said, "I fear the gentlemen will be longer than 'a bit.' I know Father when he gets caught up in a business discussion."

"My dear Miss Anne, I must agree. I could not help but observe that Mr Deschevaux has been eager to discuss some matter, and Mr Emmons has delayed the conversation. This is the logical moment." Anne's tea grew cold on the table next to her, as she tried to interest herself in a book. Casting the book on the seat beside hers, she rose and walked over to the fire. Miss Crawford glanced up from her needlework with some surprise. "My dear...?"

"I am sorry, Amelia, I just cannot seem to settle this evening." Anne turned to face her, and tried to cover the real cause of her discomfiture. "I was so surprised when Father invited Mr Deschevaux for our Christmas and the wedding celebrations, and to return to London with us. I must send a note to Mrs Farleigh in the morning to make sure that we will not disarrange her numbers for the wedding breakfast." Miss Crawford agreed.

"I was also somewhat taken aback. I will not speculate on his reason. However, it does seem unlike Mr Emmons to issue such an impulsive invitation." Anne walked back. "I wonder what business they are discussing for so long. It must be quite absorbing, for Father to keep Mr Deschevaux so engaged." Anne seated herself at the piano-forte and picked out a tune. Miss Crawford said, drily, "That is the first time I have seen you show an interest in your music in many months." Anne shrugged.

"I never particularly enjoyed it. The piano-forte does have the advantage of occupying the hands and the mind, especially when one is so out of practice." She bent her head as she played a simple melody, one of the first she had learned while still in school. Mr Emmons and Mr Deschevaux entered the drawing room, still conversing earnestly. Anne looked up but did not cease to play, while Miss Crawford said placidly, "There you are, gentlemen. Would you like some tea, or do you prefer some claret? There are a decanter and some glasses on the table there." Breaking off their conversation, both men elected claret, and poured themselves glasses. Mr Emmons seated himself by the fire, across from Miss Crawford, but Mr Deschevaux crossed the room to stand by the piano-forte.

"Miss Emmons, I was not aware that you played." Anne shook her head, and said honestly, "I learned as a child, but never enjoyed it. I have not practiced regularly for a few years now." Mr Deschevaux smiled. "Your music is pleasant, none the less." When she finished the tune, she rose and the two joined the others at the fire.

Chapter 23

C hristmas dawned clear and cold, but not bitter. Anne woke early, before the stars had set, and was glad to see no hint of cloud. She hastened to pull on her dressing gown and slippers, and crossed the room to light a candle and put more coal on the fire. As the room warmed, she thought about events. Matthew, Lydia and the children had arrived without incident a few days ago. Anne smiled; Miss Crawford was engaged in assisting the nursery maid with young Walter and baby Anne. She apparently took the little boy's wilfulness as a personal challenge. Robert and Diana had both come early Christmas Eve, and the entire group decorated the drawing room and hall with evergreens: holly, rosemary, and ivy were twined with red and gold ribbons and draped over doorways and mantelpieces. As the garlands warmed, the fresh scent filled the house. In the centre of the mantelpiece, a thick candle waited to be lit.

Charles Deschevaux had clearly enjoyed the entire event; he seemed to be everywhere at once. That evening, the children abed, everyone sat down to dinner with good appetite, and then gathered in the drawing room. Lydia and Diana had played the piano-forte in turns, both of their repertoires including some old fashioned Christmas songs. After a merry time, Robert escorted Diana back to Farleigh House and made his own way home, while the remaining party retired.

Anne sat at her desk and reviewed her notes for the day. Everyone would be awakened with a hot beverage (coffee for the men, chocolate for the ladies). She had organised the carriages for those who planned to attend the Christmas service at the Cathedral. Upon return, a hearty breakfast would be served. The table was already set, with a gift at each place. Anne had deliberately tried not to cram too many activities into the day, as she wanted it to be a comfortable time for Diana to get acquainted with the family more personally.

Matthew and Lydia would make sure little Walter received his gifts in the early morning before they came down. That evening, Diana and Mr and Mrs Farleigh would join them for Christmas dinner, after which there would be music and a chance to dance. Anne had engaged some musicians so that none of the ladies would be tied to the piano-forte; if anyone wanted to dance, no one would be left out. If the party became lively, she also had some games ready to suggest. Mrs Clay had been brewing and baking for some days in preparation, so Anne had no fear of any difficulties with food or drink. At this moment, Anne happily looked forward to whatever the day might bring. She rang for Ellen to help her dress for the morning. While she waited for Ellen, Anne decided she would wear the deep violet double sarcenet. It was suitable for church and the events after the service as well. Just then, Ellen appeared with her washing water, and Anne began her *toilette*.

Anne checked her reflection to be sure she was ready. The violet gown was one of her favourites this winter. The details of the long sleeves, the double flounce of delicate creamy lace at the throat and cuffs made it very feminine. She was also able to accommodate the obligatory black ribbons for mourning the old queen's death with elegance. Today her eyes seemed to match her gown. Tidying a curl, Anne was confident she looked just right.

"Thank you, Ellen. You always take such good care of me." Crimson-cheeked, Ellen bobbed a curtsey, and hurried from the room with a dress that needed mending. After she donned her redingote and bonnet, Anne made her way to the stairs. In the hall, she met Miss Crawford. "My dear Amelia, happy Christmas," she said with a smile and a hug. "Happy Christmas to you, my dear." As they descended the stairs together, the two discussed the plans for the day.

"I must confess that I am look forward to the service this morning," said Miss Crawford. "I had forgot how boisterous a young child can be. Little Walter is a delightful boy but he is indefatigable." "I am aware, Amelia. I distinctly saw his nursemaid near to exhaustion when we visited for the baby's christening." Miss Crawford chuckled. "I do believe that he may be ready for some lessons. He is exceedingly bright; some occupation may be what he needs." As they walked, they reviewed the arrangements for the day.

"The dining room is ready for breakfast when we return from church," said Anne. She glanced at the clock. "Anyone who wishes to attend should be in the hall shortly." She put on her gloves, gathered up her prayer book and reticule, and entered the hall. To her surprise, only Mr Deschevaux waited. "Your father accompanied Mr Robert Emmons and Miss Farleigh to the church. We will join them as soon as may be." The three hurried out to the carriage, and were on their way.

Upon their return to the Emmons' home, the party discussed the music at the service. "The choir sang amazingly well, I thought," enthused Diana. Anne agreed wholeheartedly. As the party went in to breakfast, everyone agreed that the choir's singing and the organ's accompaniment enhanced the moving service which celebrated the Nativity. Robert added, "I must confess, I find the Christmas collect to be most comforting with its message of renewal." As they took their seats, the packages at each place captured everyone's attention. A chorus of grateful thanks arose as the gifts were opened. Mr Emmons was particularly grateful to receive the gift of *Britannia Romana: The Roman Antiquities of Britain,* which Anne had found.

"Where on earth did you find this, my dear? And in such excellent condition." Anne replied, "Mr Chamberlayne assisted me, sir. He obtained a catalogue of a scholar's library put up for sale, and I offered for it immediately." She added with a twinkle, "I could not resist; subject matter aside, the bindings go so nicely with your other volumes." Mr Emmons laughed, even as he opened the first volume and lost himself in the first page. Anne was delighted with a fragile antique fan of sandalwood with the blades delicately carved in lacy openwork, picked out in gold with a matching gold silk tassel. There was no card. She fluttered it gently, as she enjoyed the faint scent stirred by the motion.

"I must thank my benefactor, but it's very hard to do when he or she is unknown," she said, looking round the table. "Well, my dear sister to be," laughed Diana, "you must possess yourself of patience. Maybe the riddle will solve itself." She held up a fragile crystal bottle. "I, too, have a mysterious benefactor. Is this not lovely? The scent is so subtle." The happy babble continued. Mr Deschevaux opened a small package to discover a slender oblong of ivory, intricately etched and pierced in a geometric design. It was obviously very old. Intrigued, he lifted it to study the design further.

"How very interesting. It is most unusual." Anne leaned forward. "It is a bookmark, once used to keep one's place in the Muslim holy book. The clerk told me it was carved in India." He looked up and smiled. "I must thank you all." He looked from Anne to her father and the rest of the company. "Not only for this gift, but for your hospitality on this festive occasion. I am honoured to be so welcomed." He carefully turned the delicate piece over in his hand to find the pattern continued on the reverse. "I will treasure this." Anne smiled, happy and relieved at his pleasure.

After breakfast, the party dispersed. Mr Emmons carried his treasure off to the library, accompanied by Mr Deschevaux. Anne descended to speak with Mrs Hubbard and Mrs Clay regarding Christmas dinner. Mrs Clay affirmed, "The Christmas pie is in hand, Miss Anne. I have turkey with goose, chicken, pheasant and as delicious a ham as ever was cured already in the case and ready to bake for tonight's dinner. Of course, gentlemen require a roast as well, so there is a fine sirloin of beef to be roasted as well. A dish of buttered carrot and turnip, and some pickles will set it off lovely, with some beet root for colour. I will have some removes, and the marchpane cake with the sack cream is already finished. Never fear, Miss Anne, an extra guest will be no trouble, and I have some green peas put aside that will make a beautiful soup. It will be ready when needed." Anne beamed at the two ladies.

"Mrs Clay, I have no doubt that our Christmas dinner will be most memorable for being perfect in every way." She thanked them both for their efforts, before she made her way abovestairs. She reviewed the guest list for the evening and realised there were ten expected for dinner, so stopped in the dining room to be sure an extra leaf was in the table. She was relieved to see that the table was ready for the evening.

The room was most inviting, from the spicy citrus scent of orange pomanders heaped in a silver bowl on the sideboard, to the freshness of the garland draping the mantelpiece. Spread with immaculate white linen, two silver epergnes were ready for their loads of fruit and nuts, and two silver candelabra were ready with creamy beeswax candles for the evening's illumination. A fire lay ready in the grate. She nodded and made her way to the drawing room. Here too, perfect order reigned. She sighed with pleasure, and ran lightly up the stairs to tap on the sitting room door assigned to Matthew and Lydia.

"Lydia, my love, may I speak to you?" The door opened with alacrity, as Lydia's maid curtsied her into the room. "Of course, dear one. Pray, sit here and we'll have a comfortable coze. Baby has been just been fed, and is about to go off to sleep." Lydia was seated in a comfortable chair next to the fire and waved Anne into the armchair opposite. Nestled in her lap, baby Anne drowsed sweetly, heavy lashes occasionally lifting only to drop again. Anne, of course, was besotted at once.

"My dear sister, she is so beautiful. A few weeks have made such a difference." Lydia smiled fondly. "Indeed, she has all but made up for her early arrival. She can lift her head, and, I swear, she smiles at me. She gets so excited when Matthew or I walk into the nursery. I believe she has dimples in both cheeks."

"And little Walter? Does he like being an older brother?" asked Anne. Lydia considered the question. "He seems to be coming to terms. He was most jealous at first. I was a bit concerned. However, in the few days we have been here, I've seen a change. Your Miss Crawford has been working with him, giving him some simple lessons. She says that he has been bored. He seems calmer, somehow." Anne asked if there were any thing that she or the children needed.

"My dear, I believe you and Miss Crawford have thought of everything. We are most comfortable." Anne rose and continued on her way to her own sitting room. She dropped into the chair by the fire to gaze into the glowing embers. As they left the dining room, Robert had astounded her when he confided that he had invited Mr Deschevaux to attend the wedding. Generally, only immediate family were present at the ceremony itself; friends and other relatives were generally welcomed at the wedding breakfast. She recalled Robert's smile as he said how much he liked Mr Deschevaux.

First her father, now her favourite brother, had succumbed to Charles Deschevaux's charm. For a moment, she was confused. Then she reasoned: the gentlemen had much in common, all well-educated and well-read. Her father had guided Mr Deschevaux's efforts to re-establish his family estates. It was no wonder they were at ease with one another. Anne suddenly recognised that she had seen no sign of the emotion she had glimpsed in his eyes at Littlebrook House. She was unsure if she were glad or sorry...

Chapter 24

Anne woke with a start. She sat up in bed, momentarily forgetting where she was. Unaccustomed noise filtered through the draperies. London... She lay back as she felt a surge of anticipation. As her thoughts drifted, she thought about the wedding, seeing Robert and Diana wrapped in a golden glow of happiness. The wedding breakfast had been a triumph for Mrs Farleigh. The Twelfth Night celebrations had been especially joyous. Then the trip to London-thank goodness the winter had proven milder that the last two. They had made excellent time.

The house was larger than she had expected, and appeared to be in excellent order. Mrs Russell was clearly an efficient manager, even though her manner was off-putting. Mr Emmons had been satisfied with the arrangement of his room and dressing room above the library, and he revelled in the private staircase that allowed him access at will. She smiled as she remembered her first sight of her own rooms. The bedroom and attached dressing room were both lovely and comfortable. The dressing room even connected to a tiny room perfect for Ellen to occupy. However, her sitting room was perfection itself... Across the hall from her bedroom, it was a small room with a large window that looked out over the back.

Unusual for a town house, there was a small garden as well as the mews set within the walls. She hardly noticed the view as she took in her desk. She had never seen anything like it. Made of pale wood inlaid with a design of flowers in contrasting woods, it stood next to the window, where it looked like a table on a stand. Her father put a key in her hand, and indicated the keyhole in the side of the desk. When she inserted the key and opened it, she discovered that a dainty chair with a blue brocade seat slid out; the middle section then pulled out and the two table top sides slid apart to reveal an elegantly formed writing surface lined with red leather, including an elegant pen drawer. Her father demonstrated how the writing surface could be elevated if desired, and showed her the two drawers concealed in the base. When the chair was replaced and the writing surface closed, the top sections closed and the desk locked automatically. Next to it was an elegant Argand lamp on a wall shelf, ready to provide illumination for night-time reading and writing.

At one end of the room was a small fireplace with a white mantle, and two comfortable wing chairs separated by a small table. At either end of the mantel two elegant gilt and crystal girandoles were mounted which illuminated a landscape hanging over the fireplace. The other two walls were occupied with white painted bookcases. Already unpacked were the books she had had sent from home. As a special surprise, there were some new ones on the shelves. A richly patterned carpet covered the floor.

Anne's reverie took a turn. She closed her eyes with a sigh. The afternoon before their departure, Anne received a note requesting her to visit Mr Chamberlayne at the bookshop. She paused only to put on her gloves, bonnet and pelisse and was on her way. "What news, Mr Chamberlayne?" she asked as she entered the shop. "Have you time to step around to the office, my dear Miss Emmons?" he responded. Once settled facing each other across his desk, Mr Chamberlayne placed a parcel before her. "Your manuscript, my dear," he said. "There are letters enclosed." In fact, there were three. In the end, the answers were the same: all three declined to publish her work, despite finding much to praise. "Did you read these, Mr Chamberlayne?"

"I did, Miss Emmons. I was pleased to see how favourably they responded to your efforts." "And yet they all declined to publish," she replied, her eyes downcast. Mr. Chamberlayne leaned back in his chair and paused before responding.

"My dear, an author's first work is seldom accepted immediately. If you will read the letters more closely, there are suggestions to help you make your work more likely to be published. I think you should consider them. First of all, you need to decide in what form you wish to publish. If you want to publish this composition as an article in a periodical, it is too long for a single article and yet too short to publish in installments. If as a pamphlet or even a book, it is too short. I sent a copy to Mr Smith at the British Museum to review, and he had some suggestions for further study, to expand some of your material. If you are serious about this, you will need consider these issues, make some changes and try again. You have made an excellent start, although you may not consider that is so at this moment."

Anne's cheeks burned. Sunk in disappointment, she barely remembered to thank Mr Chamberlayne for his efforts before she stuffed the letters into her reticule and picked up the manuscript. She went straight home and up to her rooms where she thrust the manuscript out of sight in a drawer and sat down heavily before the fire. Finally allowing herself to give way, tears of disappointment trickled down her cheeks. As she glumly gazed into the fire, there was a knock on her door, which she ignored. After a few minutes, the knock was repeated and her father's voice came through.

"Anne, may I speak with you?" She rose and slowly crossed the room to admit her father. Mr Emmons looked at her keenly, as she averted her tear-stained face. "What's this about, my dear?". "I visited Mr Chamberlayne," she muttered before her voice failed.

"Ah, yes. The manuscript. I take it his news was somewhat disappointing." He crossed to the fireplace and sat down; perforce, Anne had to resume her seat as well. "What exactly did he say?"

Anne said despondently, "Mr Chamberlayne was kindness itself, as always. He tried to encourage me, but the letters said it all. No one was willing to publish it. All my work, wasted!"

"May I see the letters, my dear?" Knowing her father would not accept "No" for an answer, she rose and pulled the crumpled missives from her reticule and handed them over. Deliberately, her father smoothed and read each letter in full, making no comment. When finished, he sat back in the chair and looked at her thoughtfully.

"I find these letters most encouraging. I understand you are disappointed. Yet, the letters show these gentlemen found much of value in your work. I know enough about manuscripts to realise that, if a work is truly unacceptable, the letter of refusal is couched in no uncertain terms, assuming a letter is even written. What did you expect?" Anne winced as she observed that her father did not enter into her feelings. "I did not know what to expect. However, I had hoped..." Her voice trailed off. Deliberately, her father rose.

"My dear Anne, do you suppose every business venture in which I engage is successful? Many times, I have had to revise agreements, change terms, formulate new plans, and sometimes failure still results. If you seriously want to write for publication, you must treat your work seriously as well. One's friends and family may applaud a completed project, whether it is a new musical piece performed satisfactorily, a piece of needlework well wrought or, in your case, a finished piece of writing. Writing for publication is not the same. Try to look at this as a business matter, not a hobby. When you are calmer, reread those letters and I think you will see what I have seen." He crossed back to her and kissed her.

"Do not let a disappointment completely overset you, my dear. You have more resolution than that, I hope." He left the room, leaving Anne to her thoughts. She retrieved the manuscript from the drawer, gathered the letters, her original work and notes, and put them all in a beautiful antique box. Closing the box, she sighed, turned back to her desk and sat down to write notes, one to Mr Chamberlayne thanking him again for his efforts, and to the three gentlemen who had reviewed her manuscript, to thank them for their attention and suggestions.

The boxed manuscript had been included with the books Anne had selected to accompany her to London. That box now sat on a shelf in her sitting room. Anne threw back her covers, rose and splashed water on her face. Ellen entered the room, and helped Anne dress for the day. Anne had selected a most becoming day gown, to bolster her confidence before she met with Mrs Russell later that morning. Now that she had been in London a few days and observed the workings of the house, Anne had a few changes she wished to make. However, she wanted to review her notes and the letters from Lady Kidwell beforehand, and have her thoughts organized before she summoned the housekeeper.

A special dinner was scheduled for tomorrow, in honour of Robert's and Diana's marriage. Lord and Lady Kidwell, Fanny, and Mr Burrell had accepted their invitations, as had Charles Deschevaux. She also knew her father had invited a business colleague. The repast consisted of several of Robert's (and her father's) favourite dishes and she wanted something special to suit Diana's tastes. "Ellen, please ask Mrs Russell to attend me in my sitting room," said Anne. Ellen curtseyed briefly, and left the room.

Anne crossed the hall to her sitting room, and unlocked her desk. Pulling out the chair, she slid out the writing surface, and spread out her notes. As she perused her notes, she made a list of purveyors whose specialities she wanted to sample, in the hope that Mrs Russell was familiar with them, or at least was willing to experiment. "I hope those recommended by Lady Kidwell will be acceptable," she thought. Mrs Russell's manner had been icily civil, at best, and Anne hoped to clear the air. She took up her pen and a fresh sheet of paper, then reviewed the fare for the coming dinner, making notes of a few additions. Just then, Ellen admitted Mrs Russell to Anne's sitting room.

"Pray, be seated, Mrs Russell. I want to tell you how satisfied we are with your arrangements in the house." "Thank you, Miss Emmons, but I prefer to stand," replied Mrs Russell without inflection. "I am glad you are pleased. Your instructions were quite clear." Anne looked up, meeting Mrs. Russell's eyes for a moment. "I have reviewed the dishes planned for tomorrow and want to add a few items. My sister is very partial to wine jellies and Tomlin's Jelly House in St James's makes moulded jellies a speciality. Are you familiar with them?" Mrs Russell's lips pursed slightly.

"I am well acquainted with Tomlin's, Miss Emmons. Their jellies are certainly acceptable, especially if a cook does not have the skill required." Anne's eyebrows rose slightly.

"Mrs Clay's skill is not in question. I just thought of a particular jelly that Lady Kidwell served. *Oranges en Ruben,* I believe, was the name. It was luscious, a red wine jelly served with alternating stripes of flummery in the skins of oranges. I prefer to order them, and thought to send a message to Tomlin's today."

"I will attend to that, ma'am. It should be no great difficulty. Was there anything else?" "Yes, there is. The main rooms and my father's and my rooms are lovely. Still, I noticed that some of the other guest rooms and the morning room seem a bit out of date. I want to see all of the rooms looking fresh. Do you still have the fabric samples and so forth?" Mrs Russell raised her head and tightened her lips.

"I am sorry if something is not satisfactory, ma'am. I followed my instructions scrupulously. The rooms you mentioned were satisfactory to his lordship, and, as they were not included specifically in the instructions he passed on, I did not think it appropriate to change them. I will be happy to bring you the pattern books and samples." Anne laid her pen aside.

"As to your instructions, Mrs Russell, I have already expressed my pleasure with the rooms that have been updated. I just want all of the rooms to be freshened, not just a select few. Is this a problem?" "Certainly not, ma'am, I will just write to his lordship to make sure he approves of such wholesale redecorating." Mrs Russell curtsied briefly and turned toward the door. Anne's eyebrows rose as she gazed at the housekeeper in some displeasure. Just as Mrs Russell reached the door, Anne said, "A moment, Mrs Russell."

The woman turned, and Anne said gently, "I will be visiting the shops today; pray give me a list of any necessary purchases." Mrs Russell responded in surprise, "But I normally do the shopping, ma'am."

"Today, I will see to it. If you have preferred merchants, please note them on your list. Since I will be out, I will also look in at Tomlin's and order the jellies." Mrs Russell nodded, and turned back to the door. "Mrs Russell," said Anne quietly. The housekeeper stiffened and turned again.

"Before you write to his lordship, I suggest you confer with Mr Emmons, as he is negotiating the purchase of this house from his lordship, and has placed me in charge of managing the household." Mrs Russell's face flushed and she curtsied again. "You may go." Anne dropped her eyes to her desk and the housekeeper made her escape. Anne was surprised to find herself gripping her pen convulsively. Consciously, she relaxed her fingers and placed the quill in the inkwell.

Clearly, Mrs Russell was not happy with her position in her father's household and, equally clearly, not aware that his lordship intended to sell the property. The woman was a very competent housekeeper and familiar with the house; Anne had had no fault to find with the servants or the organization of the household and Mrs Russell's books appeared to be in excellent order. Mrs Clay had approved of the quality of the supplies in the kitchen, and the manners of the deliverymen she had met. Mrs Russell chose and frequented good quality merchants.

Anne had hoped to retain Mrs Russell, but was uncomfortable with the woman's cold, unbending and abrupt manner. Absently, she gazed out the window. She could replace Mrs Russell, but she hesitated to take such a drastic step; she disliked the thought of putting anyone out of work in winter, especially since the season would begin soon and desirable positions might be scarce. She resolved to try again after she returned from shopping. She would need to give Mrs Russell information regarding any household purchases for the housekeeper's books in any case, and would attempt a *rapprochement*.

Anne made up her own list of purchases she desired to make, then closed and locked her desk. She crossed the hall to her dressing room, where she selected a dark grey kerseymere walking dress and black half-boots, and rang for Ellen. After she changed, she surveyed herself in the mirror. Not one of her favourites, the dress was none the less fashionable and warm. Rather plain with a simple trimming on the cuffs and shoulders of a black and silver braid, the dress had a high collar trimmed with delicate white lace that she fastened with a simple silver brooch. The matching redingote fastened with silver buttons. She put on the grey bonnet, picked up her gloves and reticule. Ellen met her in the entry hall with Mrs Russell's list.

"Mrs Russell's compliments, Miss Emmons. She asked me to give you her list." "Thank you, Ellen. Off we go now." The two young women left the house, got into the carriage and were on their way, after Anne gave the direction for Tomlin's Jelly House. "I thought we would start there, and then proceed. I do want to go to Fortnum and Mason's; I have very specific instructions from Mrs Clay. I also wish to visit a specific merchant for spices. Father gave me the direction for an excellent man who carries a wide selection. I see from Mrs Russell's list that a stop at Twining's in the Strand is also in order." They got down at Tomlin's, and were met by the manager. Anne explained what she wanted, and he beamed as he indicated that there would be no difficulty in meeting her order, and offered her samples.

"A dozen and a half of the *Oranges en Ruben*. An excellent choice if I may say so, Madame. We have another delectable jelly, made of white wine and peach syrup. May I tempt you?" Finding both delightful, Anne smiled, "Certainly you may, sir, and that will be all for now." She reflected that the jellies would complement each other nicely and that Diana would be delighted. She gave the order for delivery the next day and asked for the statement of account so she could pay. The manager stammered, "Indeed, Miss Emmons, we customarily send our invoice at the end of the month. There is no need...."

"I appreciate your kindness, sir, but wish to settle my accounts as I go. My father prefers to settle accounts at the time, and I find his system answers very well." Having made the payment, obtained the receipted invoice and bade the manager good day, Anne, with Ellen beside her, made for the carriage and continued on about their errands. Upon her return, Anne visited the kitchens to speak to Mrs Clay.

"Tomorrow, you will receive delivery of jellies from Tomlin's Jelly House. They are for the dinner. Mrs Robert will be delighted as she is so very fond of wine jellies. Jellies can be somewhat time-consuming to make and I thought it better to order these, as they are a late addition to your plans, and I know you are already busy. I have ordered extra of both kinds, Mrs Clay. You are so good with jellies, and these are unusual and delicious. I should like you to take one of each flavour of the extras, and see if you can come up with a similar contrivance, so we may enjoy them in York as well as here in town. The extras are to be shared by the staff." Mrs Clay beamed.

"Thank you, ma'am. I do appreciate that. Jellies can't be rushed. I must say, I am curious to taste them. I'm sure we can produce something satisfactory. I will have you sample what I make as soon as I can create a good one." "Thank you, Mrs Clay. I knew I could rely on you. Whilst in town, we will, of course, order from Tomlin's as it would not be fair to steal their specialties. However, it would be delightful to serve a similar jelly at home." Turning to go upstairs, Anne turned. "By the way, Mrs Clay, is Mrs Russell in?"

"I believe she is in the housekeeper's office, ma'am." "Thank you very much." Anne returned to the hall and asked the butler, "Turner, please have someone send Mrs Russell to me at her earliest convenience." "Yes, Miss Emmons. I'll certainly do so." "Thank you, Turner." She started towards the stairs, and then paused. Glancing about, she saw no one in the entry but Mr Turner and herself. "Turner, are you happy here?" Taken aback, the butler looked at her. "I beg your pardon, miss?" "Are you satisfied with your employment here?" Anne asked.

"Indeed, I am, Miss Emmons. The terms of service are quite clear, if I may say so, and I have no concerns to speak of," replied Turner. "Is there a problem, Miss Emmons? You have only to say...." "No indeed, Turner. We are pleased with the house and the staff and with your work in particular. My father has been delighted. You are most efficient, and we have no intention of making a change at this time. I just wanted to be sure that you are satisfied." Relieved, the butler responded, "I am delighted to hear that, miss. May I reassure the staff in general on that head?"

"By all means, Turner." Dismissing him, Anne mounted the stairs to her room. She put off her outer wear, and returned to her sitting room. Pulling the receipted invoices from her reticule, she organized them neatly for Mrs Russell. She seated herself at her desk and wrote a note to Lady Kidwell, asking if she would be at home for callers later that day. Then she rang for a maid and requested that her note be delivered immediately. She was standing by the window, gazing out into the little garden, when Mrs Russell arrived.

"Ah, Mrs Russell, thank you for being so prompt," said Anne with a smile. "Pray be seated," gesturing to the small chair she had placed next to her desk purposefully. "I delivered the shopping to Mrs Clay, and wanted to give you the invoices for the household books." Mrs Russell curtsied slightly and sat stiffly on the edge of the seat. "I hope you found everything without difficulty, Miss Emmons," she said coldly. "There was no difficulty, Mrs Russell. I've visited London many times, so had little inconvenience." Anne seated herself at her desk, and decided on a direct approach.

"Mrs Russell, we have been in residence several days. I cannot help but see that you are not satisfied here, and I would like to discuss the matter. Is there a difficulty of some sort? If we are short of staff, we may certainly hire additional people. If there is some other issue, I would appreciate it if you would tell me so it can be resolved." Mrs Russell looked down at her folded hands, and said expressionlessly, "I have no complaints, ma'am." Anne's face flushed with colour.

"Mrs Russell, I do not expect us to become friends. However, I do prefer to live in pleasant conditions. You make it obvious that you are not content with the situation, and I want to resolve the problems. If we cannot come to an understanding, you will want to consider a position elsewhere. What are your thoughts?" Mrs Russell pursed her lips, and looked at Anne with disdain.

"I've served in this house for over twenty years. I was in service elsewhere before that. Never have I worked for a family in trade. His lordship has let the house from time to time but always to families of quality. Had his lordship informed me he intended to let the house, never mind sell it, to persons in trade, I would have given my notice immediately, I can tell you, rather than stay to see the tone of this establishment lowered."

"I see. What exactly do you find unsatisfactory?" She watched Mrs Russell struggle to answer. Finally, she was able to come up with a response. "A female cook! No household of consideration would have such. A male chef is preferred in an establishment of quality."

"You have partaken of Mrs Clay's *cuisine* for almost two weeks now. Can you point to any deficiencies? Any inadequacies of management? The fact that she is not a man, which seems to be your only criticism, is irrelevant to me and to my father. We prefer to consider the quality of her dishes, and her loyalty to our family. I have never had a guest at our table find a dinner prepared by Mrs Clay to be inadequate; in fact, more than one has begged for a receipt. Mrs Clay has been with us many years. She knows my father's tastes and favourite dishes, and is always working to learn new techniques."

Mrs Russell was silent. Anne rose. "I am sorry for your dissatisfaction, Mrs Russell, but can offer no solution to your specific complaint. None of the other servants seem to share your concerns. My father has not yet commented to me about the situation, and I would prefer not to bother him with this. Please consider your options this evening. If you cannot adapt to our occupancy and present a more congenial face, I'm afraid that you will have to leave. Please let me have your decision tomorrow." Mrs Russell, nonplussed, also rose. "Leave? You would have me go?" Anne looked at the woman.

"Mrs Russell, your work is excellent. Unfortunately, you reflect your personal dissatisfaction in a way that is not pleasant for those around you. I am aware that you have been with this house for many years. If you can accept the new ownership of the house, and present a civil front, there is no need for a change. However, if you cannot accept the current status, I see no alternative to your departure. I prefer not to have to find a new housekeeper, but will do so rather than face your icy disapproval every day. I have the name of a highly reputable agency and can start the search when necessary. Please let me know your thoughts tomorrow."

Anne reseated herself at her desk and took up her pen. Mrs Russell stood, irresolute. "Thank you, Mrs Russell," said Anne quietly. "That will be all. I'm sure you have duties awaiting you, and much to consider." Mrs Russell curtsied slightly and departed, angry colour in her cheeks the only sign of her inner turmoil.

Chapter 25

As she sat in Lady Kidwell's drawing room, Anne poured out the details of the situation and her last meeting with Mrs Russell. Lady Kidwell reassured Anne that she had handled it well. Anne thanked her and said, "Just before I left, I gave the receipted invoices to Mrs Russell; I'm sure the fact that they are paid will sink me even lower in her estimation. Lady Kidwell, if I do find myself in need of a housekeeper tomorrow, I hope you will give me the benefit of your wisdom." Lady Kidwell laughed and professed herself ready to be of service if needed. She left Fanny and Anne in the drawing room and went to her dressing room to prepare for her afternoon engagement.

As Anne and Fanny sipped their tea, Fanny said, "Anne, I'm sure you remember my friend Eleanor Wentworth. She happens to be in town at this moment. Kate has come for Emily's wedding, and Eleanor wanted to plan a small party for Kate's friends to celebrate her recovery. I hope you will join us. Eleanor and Kate both think very highly of you. Diana will be welcomed as well if she wishes to join us." Pleased, Anne made haste to agree. "I've not seen Miss Wentworth since that first season and will be glad to meet her again. It will be delightful to see dear Kate. I do hope she is fully recovered."

Fanny sobered. "Alas, she has not. She is still frail but she is in good spirits, and at least is able to go out if she takes care. She will not be in town very long; she will not be parted from the children for any length of time." Anne asked about Kate's little boys. "They are two and three years old now and both underfoot, like puppies. Kate and her husband decided to leave them in the country where the air is so much better." Fanny and Anne decided to do a little shopping, so they put on their bonnets and pelisses.

The first stop was Fortnum and Mason's, where Fanny selected some of her mother's favourite tea, and Anne ordered some jars of pheasant in aspic, some special honey and some cheeses to be delivered to the house. They continued on their way from St. James's to Hatchards bookstore in Piccadilly. Anne and Fanny browsed the shelves. Fanny immediately seized on a slim volume entitled *Beppo*. Anne wandered on and discovered Drake's *Shakespeare and His Times*, in which her father had expressed an interest. She picked up the two volumes and looked for Fanny to see if she were ready to depart.

"Are you finished, Fanny? If we go now, we have time to stop by Madame Jeanette's. You mentioned that you wanted a bonnet to wear with your new walking dress." Fanny looked up. "Oh yes. I will just take this. Some poetry is just what I need. Did you find something?" "I saw nothing for myself but did find something for my father," Anne replied. The two completed their transactions and received their packages. As they made their way to Madame Jeanette's establishment, they engaged in an earnest discussion of Fanny's walking dress and the bonnet she wanted. "Not black and not too big," she said emphatically.

"I want a grey silk with some shirred white lace to frame the face. The ribbons can be black velvet and the ostrich feathers dyed black; they can be changed when the mourning period is over in February, after all." "I am certain Madame Jeanette will have just the thing. She has always found the perfect frame for you," said Anne. "The grey and black with the accent of white will be most becoming to you."

Their shopping completed to their mutual satisfaction, Anne left Fanny at her home and returned to Upper Brooke Street. She thanked the footman who admitted her and handed him the parcel of volumes, instructing him to place it on the desk in her father's library. She turned toward the stairs to go up to her room as she removed her bonnet, when Mr Turner entered the hall and said, "Good afternoon, Miss Emmons. If I might have a moment..." Turning, Anne smiled. "Certainly, Turner." As she looked at him inquiringly, Mr Turner coughed discreetly. "Mrs Russell and I have had occasion to discuss various household matters and, I believe, have clarified some issues. She hoped to have a few words with you when you returned, if convenient."

Anne quailed inside. "I will be happy to speak with Mrs Russell after I have tidied myself. Please have her come to the morning room in about an hour." Mr Turner bowed. "Yes, Miss Emmons. I will make sure she receives those instructions." Anne turned back to the stairs and ascended to her dressing room. She removed her bonnet and pelisse, leaving them on a chair to be put away. She turned to the washstand, poured water into the bowl and washed her face and hands. Anne checked the mirror anxiously and smoothed her hair. "What will she say? Suppose she's decided to give notice?" A thought occurred to her. "Suppose she wants to stay?" Stopping by her library, Anne picked up her memorandum book, a pencil and some paper, and then descended to the morning room.

Wanting to appear calm, Anne took a seat at the table and began to look through her notes, adding current personal expenditures to her daily records. Absorbed in her work, she did not hear the door open. Mrs Russell cleared her throat. "Miss Emmons." Anne started and turned. "Good afternoon, Mrs Russell. I hope you reviewed the invoices for the housekeeping records." "Yes, Miss. Do I understand correctly that you prefer not to place purchases on account?" Anne thought about it. "I do see that it would be more convenient to run accounts for regular household shopping. I think it would be best if an invoice were requested at the time of the purchase, then given to me. Then I can pay it promptly. Do you think that arrangement would work?"

"Yes, Miss. That should be satisfactory for all concerned." Anne gestured at a chair across the table. "Pray, Mrs Russell, be seated. Mr Turner said that you and he had discussed household matters and that you wanted to speak to me." Perched stiffly on the edge of her chair, Mrs Russell folded her hands in her lap. She lowered her eyes as she took a breath. "Miss Emmons, when we spoke earlier, I said more than I should. When Mr Turner understood my thoughts, he was able to ... resolve some concerns for me. I hope you can overlook my rudeness. I have been content in my present position and will do my best to give satisfaction." Surprised, Anne could only look at her for a moment.

"This seems rather sudden. Are you sure you have fully considered?" she asked. Mrs Russell blushed deeply. "I am embarrassed that I was so lost to propriety, ma'am. I was under a misunderstanding which Mr Turner was gracious enough to correct. I hope you are still willing to give me an opportunity to show I can meet your requirements." Anne felt bewildered.

"Well, Mrs Russell, I don't understand your sudden change of heart but we can certainly see what results. I hope you are sure." "You will see, Miss Emmons. You will not regret this." Anne drew a breath. "All right, Mrs Russell, we will consider the matter closed, at least for now." Mrs Russell rose and curtsied, then whisked herself from the room. Alone, Anne sat back in her chair, stunned.

The next morning, Mr Emmons joined Anne at breakfast. "Good morning, my dear." He helped himself at the sideboard and sat opposite Anne. "Good morning, Father. May I pour you some coffee?" "Thank you, yes. By the way, I do appreciate the book. I glanced at the first volume this morning and I believe it will prove to be quite absorbing." Anne smiled with pleasure. Silence fell on the morning room as Mr Emmons looked over some correspondence as he ate.

Anne quietly sipped her tea and mulled over her final arrangements for the evening's dinner. Just then, Mr Emmons spoke.

"I've intended to ask, my dear, are you satisfied with the staff here?" Anne gave the matter some thought and remembered her last meeting with Mrs Russell. Calmly, she replied, "Yes, I am, sir, at this moment. If we are here when the season is at its peak, it will depend on how frequently we entertain. At this present, however, the arrangements are satisfactory. Have you noticed a problem, Father?" "No, indeed. I just wanted to be sure you were content." She twinkled at him and riposted, "After your delightful surprise of my lovely rooms? I could never be so ungrateful! You have entrusted me with the management of the house. If I find a need to make adjustments, I will not disturb you with the business."

Mr Emmons chucked. "I was sure you would get into the way of it. I think our people are settling in well. Kyrk has mentioned no difficulties of any kind." Anne replied, "Mrs Clay is satisfied with the kitchen equipment and the vendors; she said everything was of the best, and I have noticed no problems with our meals. Plans for this evening's dinner are well in hand, and I expect it to be a triumph. Ellen is delighted with the fittings in the dressing room and happy with her room next to it."

"Speaking of tonight's dinner, Lady Jersey has accepted. She was from home when I wrote to her, but is in town now, and said she will be delighted to attend," said Mr Emmons as he handed a note across the table to Anne. Anne read the note, a gratified smile on her face. "It will be a pleasure to see her. I did not know it was Lady Jersey you had invited. When did you receive her reply, Papa?" Mr Emmons frowned.

"I believe it came this morning in the post. The post was given to a footman who gave it to Turner, I think. At any rate, it was on my desk when I returned." She refolded the note, and saw Lord Jersey's signature scrawled in the corner for a frank. Anne nodded to herself;

a missive from one of the highest-ranking members of the *ton* would definitely have raised her employers in the eyes of their housekeeper.

"The table will be nicely balanced and it will be pleasant for Diana to meet Lady Jersey in a less formal setting among old friends. Lady Jersey can be intimidating at a Society event." She rose from the table, walked around to kiss her father, and left the room. Meeting Robert in the hall, Anne asked if Diana were awake. "She is indeed, and you will find my bride in our sitting room, reading a letter from Mrs Farleigh.". Anne thanked Robert with a smile and ran up the stairs to tap at the door.

The two young women entered the carriage a short time later and discussed their plans. Diana conceived a desire to visit Mrs Bell's shop to view some new designs. "I've seen gowns designed by Mrs Bell several times in *Ackermann's* and have yearned to visit her shop." Anne laughed and said she would consent if they would stop at Hookham's before they returned home. Diana, of course, agreed. "A new novel would be a treat." Just then, they stopped in front of Mrs Bell's shop and descended. As they entered, a young woman approached and said enquiringly, "May I help you, ladies? Have you an appointment?"

Anne inclined her head. "We have no appointment but hoped to look at some of Mrs Bell's designs. My sister may be interested in ordering a gown." The young woman absorbed the excellent quality of Anne's and Diana's costumes at a glance and murmured, "Pray, be seated, ladies, I will order some tea for you, and let Mrs Bell know." She left the room. Anne and Diana seated themselves on two chairs. Within a few minutes, a young maid came in with a tray with cups and tea, which she poured out. They sipped their tea as they waited, Anne gazing around the shop.

Some bolts of fabric and trimmings were displayed on one counter and a case with various laces occupied space on the opposite wall. Some hats and bonnets on stands perched on top of the case. She rose and walked over to examine the lace. "Very fine, indeed," she commented. She crossed to the counter and was about to comment on the silk, when a different young woman entered. "Good day, ladies," she said with a smile, "I regret that Mrs Bell is not available. I am Miss Johnson, her first assistant. Perhaps I can help you."

Diana went to stand by Anne. Anne returned Miss Johnson's smile. "Good day. I have recently returned to town with my sister who is wishful to see some of Mrs Bell's current designs. Would that be possible?" Miss Johnson did not bat an eye. "As it happens, she has completed a few for the upcoming season as well as some for this winter." Looking at Diana, she asked, "Did you wish to see something particular, Madame?"

In a fluttered voice, Diana said, "Well, I'm not sure... A walking dress and something for evening would be nice. Of course, a bonnet to compliment the walking dress...." "Very good," Miss Johnson replied briskly. "A moment, ladies." She disappeared to the back, leaving Anne and Diana by the counter. "Look at this silk, Diana. This would look delightfully on you for evening. It would be lovely with black ribbons until the mourning period is over and then you could change them." Anne held up a corner of a rich plum coloured silk. Diana hesitated.

"It's rather dark, is it not? I've never worn so dark a colour." "It is a very rich colour and I think would look most becoming with your warm colouring." Unbeknownst to them, Miss Johnson had returned. She looked at Diana's brown hair and creamy complexion appraisingly and agreed with Anne's statement. "*Damascen* is indeed a deep colour but has a warm undertone that would keep it from overpowering you, Madame. The trimming selected would also make a difference." The three put their heads together over a few drawings.

"I'm really not sure about these," Diana murmured. "I think something simpler..." Anne asked Miss Johnson, "Would it be possible for us to reserve the silk and make an appointment to see Mrs Bell tomorrow?" "I am sorry, Madame, but I do not know her plans for

tomorrow, and that particular silk is one of our most expensive...."
Anne lifted an eyebrow.

"I do understand your dilemma. In that case, I will purchase two dress lengths of the silk and leave my card for Mrs Bell. Will that be satisfactory?" The assistant flushed, "Certainly, Madame. I shall put the silk aside..." Anne smiled. "No indeed, my dear. If you will give me an invoice, I will settle it immediately and we will take it with us now."

Shocked, Miss Johnson wrote out the invoice and handed it to Anne. She glanced at the staggering total, opened her reticule and pulled out the required sum. Handing the notes and her card to Miss Johnson, Anne murmured, "We will wait in the carriage while someone wraps the silk; the footman can bring it out." Anne turned, took Diana's arm and guided her to the door. Miss Johnson glanced at the card, and cried "What shall I tell Mrs Bell, Miss Emmons?" Anne smiled sweetly over her shoulder. "Why, that we hope she has time available for us but, if not, another *modiste* will have the opportunity to work with that lovely silk."

Whisking Diana through the door and into the carriage, Anne paused only to instruct the footman to bring out the package. Diana, shocked, whispered, "How extravagant you are, dearest. That silk was entirely too expensive..." Anne patted her hand and said composedly, "Not at all, Diana. It is my gift to you, and will look charmingly once you have found a design that suits. I feel certain we shall hear from Mrs Bell. Indeed, I suspect she was in fact on the premises but did not want to appear too eager to cater to unknowns. She has a reputation for being rather exclusive. All shall be well. Even if we do not hear from her, there are several others. Lady Kidwell has patronised Mrs Gill for several years; she made some lovely gowns for Fanny and Lady Kidwell, as well as a very elegant walking dress with which I was charmed."

The footman came out with the package, which he placed reverently on the seat opposite Anne and Diana, took his place and the carriage drove on. Stopping at Hookham's, the young ladies spent a delightful hour as they browsed and discussed possible selections. Diana finally selected two novels and Anne purchased the most recent editions of *La Belle Assemblee'* and *Ackermann's*. "We can see if there is anything that appeals to you in the plates." She also picked up Mr Peacock's *Nightmare Abbey*. "This looks interesting." Diana glanced at it and smiled. "May I borrow it when you finish it?" The clerk wrapped their selections, and they were on their way.

Chapter 26

A s the carriage drove through town, Anne gazed idly through the window. Diana cleared her throat. "Anne...., the silk is truly beautiful, but... TWO dress lengths, dearest? That seems too much." "You will see," Anne replied. "Depending on the design, the extra fabric may be needed for other things. I saw one plate of a dress that had an apron; the silk could also be used to make a bonnet or line a cloak. It will not go to waste, I assure you."

Diana looked at Anne speculatively. "I have never seen you so decisive, Anne. You were so firm with Mrs Bell's assistant, and seemed so confident." Anne blushed rosily. "I am trying, Diana. If I am to be in charge of my father's house, if I want to be taken seriously, I have to make decisions and be prepared to stand by them. It is a new endeavour. You do not realise how I quake inside!" Diana sympathised. "I can imagine. I, too, have difficulties with that. I am accustomed to following Aunt Farleigh's lead and considering her preferences. Robert encourages me to make decisions based on my own tastes but, sometimes, I'm not even sure what they are!" They laughed companionably.

They arrived back in Upper Brook Street and Diana requested that the silk be carried up to her sitting room. The young women mounted the stairs and parted to go to their respective dressing rooms. There was time to relax and prepare for the evening ahead. Anne stopped by her sitting room to put her novel on a shelf. As she turned, she noticed some notes on the top surface of her desk. She removed her pelisse and bonnet, crossed to her bedroom and sat down in the chair near the fire. Opening the first note, she was pleased to see it was from Fanny.

"I gave her your direction and she will be writing to invite you and Diana herself. I wanted you to be aware so you could plan. Eleanor is happy you will come and looks forward to meeting Diana." The other note was from Emily, filled with plans for shopping. Smiling, Anne picked up the notes and the key to her desk, and walked back to her sitting room to write her replies.

Later, in the drawing room with her father, she sipped a small glass of sherry as he enjoyed some claret. Her eyes, deepened to violet by the deep amethyst gown she wore, sparkled as she thought of the evening to come. Robert and Diana entered and joined them before the fire. Diana asked for a glass of ratafia and sat near Anne. Anne told her of the party planned by Fanny's friend and her inclusion. "How kind of Miss Wentworth. I look forward to meeting her and your other friends, Miss DeWitt and her sister. Has Miss Wentworth never married?"

"I believe she was engaged to be married. It was the second time I visited London so it must have been about four or five years ago. It was very sad; Fanny told me he contracted a putrid sore throat, and was gravely ill for some months. His family sent him to a doctor in Bath but nothing could be done; he passed away." "How tragic to be so bereft," sympathised Diana. "I know such a death is not uncommon, yet it is always a shock, somehow." A momentary silence fell, and they could hear the conversation between Robert and Mr Emmons.

"You and Matthew must do as you think best, Father. I am quite satisfied as I am. You know my ambitions do not lead me in that direction." Mr Emmons responded gruffly, "I thought so, but wanted to give you the opportunity to make a change or at least express an opinion." Robert smiled with affection, "You have always been the kindest of fathers." Just then, Turner announced Lord and Lady Kidwell, Fanny and Mr Burrell. Fanny and her mother swept over to Diana and Anne, hugging and kissing each, deluging them with greetings and congratulations.

Fanny sat next to Anne and said, "I am so happy to see you! I wanted to call sooner but Mother has had me engulfed in fabric samples and fashion plates. She insists that I need a new wardrobe for this season even though I do not intend to attend many balls." Anne laughed. "Your mother will have her way, Fanny. I suspect you will attend more balls than you plan. Diana is also having some new things made. We bought fabric at Mrs Bell's today and hope to see her again soon. Her assistant did not seem too optimistic but I feel certain Mrs Bell will make time for us." Fanny looked dubious.

"She is very exclusive and I hear she will not accept new customers unless recommended." Anne laughed again. "I hope she will see us but, if not, there are other talented *modistes* in town. Mrs Gill, of course. And my dear Madame Josette at home suggested a young woman in Cheapside who has an eye for colour and what will best become the individual." She told Fanny about the *damascen* silk, and how shocked Mrs Bell's assistant was when they took it away with them. "I suspect Mrs Bell has an exclusive with that silk and she may decide to accept us as customers even without a recommendation. If it is not to be, I'm sure we will find someone else."

Suddenly Anne had a peculiar sensation and glanced around. Just over her shoulder, she saw Charles Deschevaux standing with her father, Robert, Lord Kidwell, and Martin Burrell. He glanced up, caught her eye and smiled. Instinctively, she smiled back and felt suddenly happier. Before she could rise, Lady Jersey was announced and entered the room, already talking as was her wont. "My dear Anne, how wonderful to see you after all these weeks!" Anne hastily stood up and went forward to meet her guest as the other ladies rose.

She curtsied quickly and responded, "Lady Jersey, I am delighted you accepted my father's invitation. I believe you are acquainted with Lady Kidwell and her daughter Fanny. May I present my new sister, Diana Emmons? She is lately married to my brother Robert." Diana blushed furiously as she murmured inaudibly and sank into a deep curtsey. Lady Jersey smiled graciously. "Your new sister? How delightful!" She took Anne's arm and moved toward Mr Emmons and the gentlemen.

As they crossed the room, she said, "I am acquainted with three of these gentlemen, so I must assume the fourth is your brother Robert. Am I correct in thinking his bride is from York, then? What is her family?" Anne replied, "She is a Farleigh, my lady. She lived with her aunt and uncle at Farleigh House. She and I have been dear friends for some years." "Ah, the Farleigh's. I believe I have met them at some time. A good family, as I recall." Anne's father stepped forward and saved Anne from having to respond. Mr Emmons bowed courteously and said, "Lady Jersey, how good of you to come this evening. You honour my home."

Anne moved away as her father introduced Robert and the other guests greeted her ladyship. She turned back to Lady Kidwell, Fanny and Diana and gestured toward the seats. "Ladies, shall we sit down?" Almost immediately, dinner was announced and Anne perforce led the way to the dining room.

Anne looked around her table and was gratified to see smiles and easy conversation taking place. Everyone seemed content after the first course. The collared salmon with oysters and shrimp had been acclaimed, Lady Jersey going so far as to ask for the receipt. As the second course was laid, Anne cast an eye over the table. She knew her father and Lord Kidwell would be pleased with the roast beef with horseradish and pickles, which the *Orange en Ruben* jellies would complement. Some turkey cutlets with mushrooms, a pupton of veal, bisque of fish for soup, and a salmagundi helped fill out the course.

Robert murmured, "Diana seems to enjoy herself this evening. My father has balanced his time chatting with her and Lady Jersey well."

Anne nodded. "Of course, Martin Burrell is an easy conversationalist unless he gets into a political discussion. I am thankful that Lady Jersey is so well placed. Robert, do you know how Lord Kidwell came to sit next to her?" Robert raised his eyebrows.

"I think it was a machination of our father though I am not sure how he managed it." Before Anne could pursue that idea, Charles Deschevaux caught her eye and smiled. "A delightful dinner, Miss Emmons. Dare I assume our friend Mrs Clay is in charge?" Anne laughed and said, "You certainly may. My father would sooner be without his valet than to miss Mrs Clay's cooking." He leaned slightly toward her. "It seems a time since we have met. I hope you have been well?" Her colour rose slightly.

"I am well, thank you, sir. And you?" "Well enough, I suppose. Busy at least." He looked at her intently, "Do you enjoy London, Miss Emmons?" "I've had little opportunity, sir. There has been much to do getting the house settled, and my sister and I have begun some shopping." He smiled again. "In that case, I want to invite you to attend the British Museum with me, with Miss Crawford, of course. They have received some new antiquities which I think you would like to inspect. May I procure tickets?" Eyes alight, Anne said, "That sounds delightful! I must ask my father..."

Charles broke in. "Already done, ma'am. I spoke with him when I arrived. I actually invited you and your father together, but business forced him to decline and he suggested Miss Crawford in his place. Will the day after tomorrow suit?" She faltered, "I believe so, but I must confirm with Miss Crawford. I am not sure which is her day out." Her eyes twinkled. "She is out this evening. An educationist with whom she has corresponded invited her to attend a meeting of the Antiquarian Society, and she accepted with alacrity. I am not sure what the subject of this evening's conversation may be, but hope to hear all about it. She has paper and pencil with her in case she wishes to take notes."

Robert claimed her attention at that moment, and the footmen cleared the table for the last course. They then served an array of custards, preserved fruits, a plate of cheese cakes and, of course, the peach jellies glowing golden in their crystal glasses. Some dishes of dried fruits and nuts rounded out the table.

As the ladies departed the dining room for the drawing room, Anne whispered an excuse to Lady Kidwell and slipped away. She hurried to the kitchens and found Mrs Clay seated before the fire as the kitchen maids did the dishes and cleared the kitchen. "Mrs Clay, the dinner was wonderful. Father, and indeed all the gentlemen, pronounced the roast first rate, and Lady Jersey requested your receipt for the collared salmon. She said the sauce was perfection." Mrs Clay turned pink with pleasure.

"Thank you, ma'am. I'm sure I appreciate your telling me. I will write out the receipt immediately and have a footman bring it up. What about the jellies, Miss Anne? Did they take?"

"Indeed they did, Mrs Clay. The *Oranges en Ruben* were excellent and Mrs Robert enjoyed her portion very much. I must say, the peach jelly was a real success as well. Both the ladies and gentlemen commented on how delicate and fresh the peach flavour was. Have you tasted them yet?"

"I have, ma'am, and I am sure it will be simple to make the peach jelly. In fact, it's given me an idea for a champagne jelly or ice. The oranges will take a bit more time to figure out, but I believe I can come up with something similar. I was thinking of a red wine jelly with a hint of orange juice and finely chopped orange peel layered with the flummery in a jelly glass. It would look lovely on the table, and I think would come close to the flavour. I'm not quite sure yet how to get it properly in the orange shell." Hurriedly, Anne said, "I know you will work it out, Mrs Clay, and it will be delicious. I must go back to our guests." She hurried back to the drawing room and was in time to receive a cup of tea from Lady Kidwell.

The gentlemen entered the drawing room to find the ladies chatting animatedly. Mr Emmons led them to a sideboard where decanters of claret, canary and brandy waited with glasses. "Gentlemen, there is tea by the fire or these other libations as you prefer." Mr Deschevaux walked to the fire and requested a cup of tea. Anne poured a cup and passed it to him with a shy smile. "If I may, I will call tomorrow afternoon to see if the next day will be convenient. I would like to bespeak our tickets."

"I'm sure I will have an opportunity to speak with Miss Crawford by then." Conversation halted for a moment. "Have you made any more interesting finds, Mr Deschevaux?" His eyes lit up and he leaned forward slightly.

"As a matter of fact, an interesting object did surface. My tenants were ploughing a field that had lain fallow for some years. We were discussing trying some winter crops in future, and they decided to prepare the field. There were several odd bits of metal and rock and so forth, which they put in a box and set aside. They just remembered it and gave it to my bailiff. He cleaned the objects in water and most were just broken bits, a few coins. However, there was a piece of carved amber, a delicate head which appears to have been broken off of a miniature statue. It's tiny, about the size of a man's thumb nail. As soon as my bailiff saw what it was, he wrote to me. It is a miracle that such a small item was found. I have not yet seen it, of course." Anne's eyes sparkled in response.

"How thrilling! You must be all anticipation of seeing it." "I am, indeed. One reason I am looking forward to visiting the Museum is to see if any of the new acquisitions are similar to the description I've received and to ask about the use of amber. I am most curious about this object. In fact, I am considering having the piece sent on to me, so I can take it to the Museum to show a librarian." Anne drew in a breath. "How exciting that would be! If you do decide to have it sent, dare I hope for a glimpse?" Before he could answer, Lady Jersey requested more tea and the conversation shifted.

After the guests departed, Mr Emmons escaped to the library. Diana yawned. "It was a lovely evening, Anne. The dinner was delightful, and all the company seemed so comfortable. Lady Jersey was nothing like as terrifying as I had heard. Mr Martin Burrell was amiable and seemed most attentive to Fanny." Anne laughed.

"Indeed, he is, ever since they met at Littlebrook House. Fanny has also acquired a new enthusiasm: politics. Something she never thought twice about before then. Still, neither she nor Lady Kidwell has said anything about a definite interest so I am asking no questions." She stretched her toes to the fire as Diana shot her a mischievous look.

"It was so pleasant to see Mr Deschevaux again. I do not believe we have conversed since we all arrived in town. Robert and I enjoyed his company so much at Christmas and at our wedding; he seems like an old friend, if not a member of the family. Don't you think so, Robert?"

"Absolutely, my dear. He and I are much engaged in the next few weeks," replied Robert, as Anne sat bolt upright, eyes wide with confusion. Murmuring a disjointed excuse, she fled, remembering the warm kiss Charles had pressed on her wrist when he took his leave. In the hall, she asked the footman if Miss Crawford had come in. Receiving an affirmative answer, Anne hurried up the stairs to tap at her mentor's door.

Receiving permission to enter, Anne had the presence of mind to ask Miss Crawford if she had enjoyed the evening's conversation at the meeting of the Antiquarian Society. "Very much, my dear. It was most informative; I have taken a great many notes and have the names of several books to seek. I was content to listen. However, there were one or two other ladies present who did not hesitate to contribute their mite to the discussion. Quite refreshing."

"Mr Deschevaux was here this evening and invited us to visit the British Museum to see some new antiquities. He suggested the day after tomorrow. Will that be convenient for you?" Surprised, Miss Crawford responded, "Of course, Miss Anne. As you well know, I am at your disposal." She smiled. "It does help that this is an excursion after my own heart. How kind of Mr Deschevaux to include me in the invitation."

"He is most kind," Anne murmured. "He will call tomorrow to confirm the day so he can obtain tickets." She proceeded to tell Miss Crawford about the amber carving. Giving Anne a penetrating look, Miss Crawford probed, "You seem to have had quite a conversation with Mr Deschevaux." Anne took a turn about the room.

"Amelia, I find myself at something of a loss. I have been acquainted with Mr Deschevaux for some years as a friend of Lord and Lady Kidwell's. We have danced together many times and I enjoy his conversation. We have interests in common. I have been happy to consider him a friend. And now I am not sure what to think." Anne proceeded to tell Miss Crawford about his revelation at Littlebrook House, her growing awareness of him, his confession of his feelings for her and his business relationship with her father, and her worry that somehow her father had manipulated him into pursuing her.

"I have feelings for him... But I do not want my marriage to be part of a business transaction or debt repayment. My father likes Mr Deschevaux; I have never seen him so relaxed and at ease in conversation with anyone other than Robert, Matthew and Lord Kidwell. I also know that Mr Deschevaux is the pattern-card of the man he wishes me to marry. My father wants me to marry soon and I fear that he may encourage Mr Deschevaux behind my back. On one hand, the excursion to the British Museum is exactly the sort of entertainment I enjoy and Mr Deschevaux is an ideal companion; on the other, I don't want to encourage him to think I am expecting a... a... courtship until I am certain I would welcome it." Miserably, she added, "I do him the justice to believe he feels something for me. I just want to be sure... But how can I?"

Miss Crawford looked at her in astonishment. "My dear girl, your skills at dissimulation have certainly improved. I had no idea that matters had progressed to this degree." She paused. "Anne, has your father ever put you in a situation to your disadvantage? I mean to say, a situation where you would be harmed." "No," Anne replied. "Has your father ever sought anything other than your welfare?" "No, of course not," Anne responded. "Has your father ever given you reason to doubt his love for you?" "No," whispered Anne, "he has not."

Miss Crawford paused. "My dear Anne, in all of my years with your family, I have observed your father to be a kind, considerate and caring person, devoted to you and your brothers. Whilst he has made no secret of his desire to see his children advance in status, I have seen no indication he would push any of you into a situation that might cause unhappiness. You must decide if you trust your father. By the same token, you must also look honestly at Mr Deschevaux. You indicate that he told you his debt was repaid in full. Do you have reason to distrust him?" Anne looked down. "No, I have no reason to doubt his word." Miss Crawford nodded.

"If that is the case, and there is no debt, your father has no means to compel Mr Deschevaux to pursue you. Therefore, it only seems reasonable to assume that Mr Deschevaux is serious in his intentions." She looked at Anne rather severely. "You must apply rational thought to determine your own feelings, and what you want. It is unfair to use your father as a barrier to hide behind. If you feel the need to confirm Mr Deschevaux's statements, you have only to ask your father. However, that raises the question of trust." Putting her arm around Anne's shoulders, she guided her erstwhile pupil to the door.

"The excursion to the museum will be an opportunity to look at Mr Deschevaux and the situation clearly. I know he has declared himself but he has not raised the matter again. Consider your feelings calmly and decide if you want Mr Deschevaux as a suitor. Unfortunately, you are the only one who can answer that question." Opening the door, Miss Crawford said, "Good night, my dear. I suggest you put the matter aside until tomorrow. Sometimes, the light of day can make all manner of things more clear." Speechless, Anne embraced her old friend, and fled to her own room.

Chapter 27

In the sanctuary of her room, Anne sank into the chair by the fire. When had she turned her father into such a tyrant? Her father had never tried to compel her into marriage; he had never discussed a particular person. He did have ambition for her to marry well, but she knew he would never push her into a distasteful situation. She had refused multiple offers, and he had never so much as commented. Come to that, it had never occurred to her that her father might use influence on a suitor until she became aware of Charles Deschevaux as a man. There was nothing to prevent her father and Charles from being friends and associates whether she married him or not. Why was she so overly suspicious?

As she gazed into the dancing flames, she remembered her conversation with Miss Crawford years ago, after the party given for Louisa Dixon. "I am not ashamed of my father. He is handsome, educated, genuinely kind and scrupulously honest in his business dealings. He is an honourable man. I have known Charles Deschevaux for several years. Lord Kidwell has known him his whole life, and has nothing but good to say of him, particularly how he saved his family estate after his father and brother did their best to waste it. Why am I so worried that my father will somehow try to coerce Charles, or that Charles will see marriage to me primarily as a means to a financial advantage?"

She jumped to her feet to pace her bedchamber and then crossed the hall to her sitting room. She removed the box with her manuscript materials from the shelf, set it on her locked desk and stared at it. "Amelia said to consider how I feel about my own value. I have never done that; I have set that question aside as I have this manuscript. Perhaps the real problem is that I am afraid to be found wanting, unworthy of regard." She remembered the mean comments made by Louisa and others at that party, sneering at the work that generated her family's wealth. She thought about her lack of traditional feminine accomplishments. "I don't paint, can't sing, and don't enjoy playing an instrument. I dislike embroidery. Certainly, I will not be put on display." She smiled wryly as she considered her expensive education which some might consider to have been wasted.

"I can dance well. I read and can write a coherent, polished document, whether a letter or something else. I also have a head for accounts. I am interested in many things and can converse intelligently. My talents seem to be of the practical sort which is no bad thing for someone responsible for the smooth functioning of a household." She found that thought to be obscurely cheering. She rose, returned to her bedroom, and prepared for bed.

Awakened by the scent of chocolate, Anne sat up, astonished to realise that she had slept deeply all night. "I truly thought I would be awake, agonising over things." She smiled and threw back the covers. She put on her dressing gown and took her chocolate over to drink by the fire. She sipped her chocolate and considered her plans for the day. "If no word comes from Mrs Bell today, I will send a message to Mrs Gill to arrange a visit to her shop. I also must reply to Emily's note. And of course, Mr Deschevaux will call today." She pondered that. Surprisingly, all she felt was anticipation; she looked forward to seeing him and to the excursion to the museum tomorrow. She smiled to herself.

"I am not a belle like Fanny and I cannot trace all of my ancestors back to a king or conqueror. However, I can carry on an intelligent conversation, order a good dinner, deal with a difficult household

matter, and play a tune if I must. Not a mean bit, at any rate."
She finished her chocolate and rose to go to her dressing room.
Anne decided to wear a walking dress in slate blue kerseymere. It
was a warm and becoming gown. Even though the colour was not
specifically a mourning shade, she considered it suitably decorous
and the black trim made it acceptable. The high collar finished with
black velvet ribbon and soft creamy lace framed her face becomingly.
She was especially partial to the pleated flounce finishing the skirt,
and the matching spencer with its epaulettes of black cording with
little tassels and the pleated trimming at the waist. She laid the dress
ready and put the spencer with the bonnet, convenient for when she
was ready to leave the house. She rang for Ellen, and sat down before
her mirror to brush her hair.

Once she had completed her *toilette*, Anne went to her sitting
room to write to Emily. "A shopping expedition with Diana and
Emily would be just the thing. I am sure they will enjoy each other's
company. It will be so pleasant to spend time with both of them. If
Mrs Bell has time for us, we can go there; otherwise, there are Mrs
Gill and several others who will be glad of our custom. I shall find out
if either has any special shopping to do. I wonder if Fanny would care
to join us...." Musing happily on her shopping excursion, she glanced
out the window. Grey clouds, heavy with rain loomed.

"Oh dear, gloomy and rainy. I wonder how cold it is." She made
a mental note to be sure to wear the black wool mantle if she went
out, and to take her umbrella. On her desk, Ellen had left a few notes
delivered earlier for her. The top one was of an unfamiliar hand and,
upon opening it, she glanced at the signature first. A response from
Mrs Bell. Smiling, Anne read the brief missive. As she had expected,
Mrs Bell would be glad to make time for her and Diana, and asked
Anne to send a message appointing a convenient time. Anne laid the
note aside; she would confer with Diana and her friends regarding a
shopping expedition first. It would do no harm for Mrs Bell to wait
a little for a reply.

She read a brief note from the headmistress of the Grey Coat School, thanking her for the books, and giving her new information regarding a few of the older students with whom Anne was acquainted. She indicated that a few young women were ready to be placed in employment, and that one in particular had the makings of a good lady's maid.

"Her sewing is excellent; she can not only darn exquisitely, she can cut out and sew. She was briefly apprenticed to Mrs Greyson, and was assigned to wait on her daughter. She displayed a good eye for colour and style-I must say I never saw the Greyson chit look so becoming. The family left on an extended journey after a few months. The girl had experience with dressing hair, so only wants more practice and exposure to new styles. She reads, and writes a clear hand."

Anne thought of Diana immediately. Diana had not yet acquired a maid to her liking and was kind and patient. Since she needed to speak to Diana regarding their shopping expedition, she resolved to go to Diana without delay. Finding Diana in the drawing room, Anne showed her Mrs Bell's response.

"As you see, sister, Mrs Bell has accepted us as clients. I was considering a visit to her shop for Monday. What do you think? Shall we share our visit with Emily and Fanny?" Diana thought about it, and concurred. "I would enjoy it of all things, and the addition of Emily and Fanny will be delightful." She smiled mischievously. "With four of us, I should be able to take my time and not make a hasty selection. When I went shopping with Aunt Farleigh, sometimes she and the dressmaker talked about me as if I were not there. Occasionally I accepted their choices just to be agreeable. Do you remember that celestial blue walking dress I had a few years ago? The colour did nothing for me and the style was dreadfully unbecoming."

Diana blushed. "I do not mean to seem ungrateful to my aunt. However, I find it so much more enjoyable to go shopping with my friends and not as an object of charity." Anne patted her hand. "I can only imagine. It is difficult to stand against the particular desire of one who means nothing but kindness. I will write to Emily and Fanny immediately; if they are agreeable, I will send Mrs Bell a note. I thought I would also send a note to Mrs Gill." She paused for a moment. "Diana, are you satisfied with the maid assigned to you at present? I have a particular reason for asking but, if you are pleased, there is no more to be said."

Diana shrugged. "Well, she is trying very hard and it does take time to get to know one another... Sometimes, I have the feeling she is uncomfortable with the position." Anne smiled and said, "If you are interested in making a change, I have received a note regarding a young woman named Eliza Hall, who is about to leave the Grey Coat School and is in need of a place. She wants very much to be a lady's maid." Handing Diana the note to read for herself, Anne continued, "I thought of you immediately. If you are willing to train a very new maid, this girl may be ideal. I met her briefly and her manners are excellent."

Diana considered and assented. "It seems a good plan. The note indicates the headmistress and her assistant are planning to come to London; mayhap they could bring her with them." "I will send an Express to the school with your suggestion that they bring Eliza to us. It should answer very well. I'll also send notes to Fanny and Emily regarding our shopping expedition." Diana said, "Excellent. I will talk to Becky about the change and see if she will tell me what she would like to do." The two walked upstairs to their respective tasks.

Two hours later, Anne's notes had been dispatched via a footman, and she and Miss Crawford were sitting in the drawing room with Mr Deschevaux. Anne's cheeks were still glowing from his greeting. After bowing courteously to Miss Crawford, he waited until she turned away and then took Anne's hand. He bowed lower, deliberately turned it over and pressed a swift kiss on her wrist. Looking up at her, he smiled and straightened. She was sure he had felt her racing pulse. Belatedly paying attention to the conversation, Anne realised

Miss Crawford had asked her a question. "I'm sorry, Amelia, I was wool-gathering." Patiently, Miss Crawford repeated, "Will one o'clock tomorrow suit you our excursion, my dear?"

"Indeed, yes. That will be perfectly convenient," she replied, aware she had made no plans in anticipation of this event. They chatted about the treat in store, exhibits they had seen before and new exhibits they looked forward to visiting. Mr Deschevaux shared information from a manuscript over which neither Anne nor Miss Crawford had lingered.

"How very interesting, sir!" exclaimed Miss Crawford. "Do you think we may see that particular document tomorrow, Mr Deschevaux?" Anne managed to keep up with the conversation, even to comment from time to time, but, in the back of her mind, she relived that kiss on her wrist again and again. That smile... "How could he be so bold?" she wondered. She was even more amazed at her own response; she still felt the tingle of his kiss. Finally, Mr Deschevaux took his leave, indicating he would call for them the next day.

Anne made her way upstairs to her sitting room and stood by the window gazing out, uncertain what to do next. She needed to do something, anything, to wrest her mind (and body) from the liberty taken by Charles Deschevaux. Suddenly, she craved fresh air but did not know where to go. Glancing at her desk, she picked up a note she saw lying there. Anne recognised Fanny's handwriting, tore it open and read it. *"Shopping Monday sounds delightful. I have a slight cold, so will stay in today. If you are not afraid of contagion, I would love to see you."*

Anne breathed a sigh of relief-she could walk to Grosvenor Square and have a comfortable chat with Fanny. She summoned Ellen and sat down to change her slippers to black half-boots. Ellen hurried in and helped Anne into the spencer and bonnet, found the black kidskin gloves, and laid the warm black mantle on Anne's shoulders. "Here are your reticule and umbrella, Miss Emmons.

Shall I accompany you, or would you prefer to take a footman?" Anne thought about it.

"I don't plan to do any shopping, so shan't need assistance with parcels. I would like you to come with me. Just a quick walk there and back. Wrap warmly and bring the other umbrella, then we can be off." Ellen vanished, while Anne made her way downstairs to the entrance. Within a few moments, Ellen was there, in a hooded cloak, clutching a second umbrella.

"Hopefully, we shan't need them!" exclaimed Anne as they headed east towards Grosvenor Square. Turning south, they reached the house. Situated on the corner, it was smaller than several they had passed, but the knocker was on the door and the brass gleamed a welcome. They mounted the steps and knocked just as the first icy rain drops fell. Thankfully, the door opened and Anne and her maid stepped into the entry. Giving her card to the butler, Anne asked for Fanny.

"I will see if Miss Kidwell is in, Miss Emmons. Pray wait here." He bowed her into the small reception room, then departed. Within minutes, Fanny entered. "Anne, my dear, I'm so glad to see you!" Turning back to the butler, Fanny instructed, "Please take Miss Emmons' maid to the housekeeper for a cup of tea. We will ring when Miss Emmons is ready to leave." Fanny took Anne up to her sitting room. Removing her bonnet, mantle and gloves, Anne hugged Fanny gently.

"You look remarkably well for someone with an epidemic cold, dear. How are you feeling, Fanny?" "All the better for seeing you! I was surprised that you walked on such a dreary day. Raining, too, I see," Fanny remarked with a smile. "We can discuss our shopping expedition. I am so looking forward to it, and am determined to be completely well." They put their heads together and, after considering the appointment with Miss Bell and the visit to Mrs Gill, they also determined to visit Soho Square Bazaar.

"I've never visited the bazaar, and it is a bit out of the way, but

I long to see it. There are stalls for linen drapers, lace and other goods. Also, they have several book stalls," enthused Anne. "It sounds delightful!" replied Fanny. "Do you want to go to Soho Square before our visits to the *modistes,* or after?" Anne pondered. "Let's go beforehand. If we find fabrics or trimmings we like, we can take them with us. We can go in the morning, if you'd like. Will you come to breakfast early, perhaps at 8:30? After we eat, we could go to the bazaar, get back in time for a nuncheon, and go on to the dressmakers' establishments."

"An excellent plan," Fanny said, "and now you can tell me what sent you here on foot, in such haste." Wide-eyed, Anne gazed at Fanny, her mind a blank. As Fanny looked at her quizzically, Anne paled, and then flushed a deep, burning red that seemed to rise from her toes. She stared down, half expecting to see smoke rising from her slippers. She lifted her head and gathered the shreds of her poise. "I need advice, Fanny. I am unsure of myself and do not know what to think."

"Ah, this concerns Charles Deschevaux, I take it. Has he spoken?" Anne paced the floor. "No, he has not, not since our time at Littlebrook House. He asked then if there was hope, and I said there was. Since then, he and I have been in company frequently. He spent the Christmas holiday at our home and has become fast friends with my father and with Robert. With me, he is as he has always been – kind and courteous. However, now and then, he looks at me ... differently. And he has kissed my hand as if he were more than a friend." Anne blushed again. "Yet he says nothing. I don't know what to think or what to say to him." Fanny sighed.

"What do you want him to say?" Anne burst into tears. "I don't know! I am so confused. I like him very much as a person. We enjoy many of the same things. We are going to the museum tomorrow. My father, my brother, even Miss Crawford, all find him congenial. I miss him when he is not present. When he kisses my hand in *that* way...." Anne pressed her hands to her burning cheeks.

"Is that enough, Fanny?" She paced again. "Sometimes, I think I could happily live out my life unmarried, occupied with my writing projects. Then I think how wonderful it might be to marry and have children, with the right man. How do you know, Fanny if the feeling is right? If he is the right man, how does a woman encourage him?" Fanny sighed.

"I am not sure how to answer you, dearest. Consider my engagement to Carleton. At the time, I thought Carleton *was* the right man for me. He was so handsome; we danced together like a dream, enjoyed the same entertainments. Looking back, I realise now that I was besotted by his handsome face and the pleasure of dancing with him. I never knew him. We spoke of nothing but Carleton, his hopes, his plans. We shared very little. I know he thought I was pretty, and he was glad to be connected to a family of rank." She smiled wryly.

"He was extremely appreciative of my portion and of my future inheritance, as Father's estate is not entailed. I do not believe he thought of marriage to me as anything more than a good business arrangement. Our engagement ended so abruptly, in such a... *cowardly* manner. And he replaced me so easily. It was a long time before I could accept the truth, which is that Carleton felt nothing for me and the Carleton I thought I loved did not exist. As you see, I am not the best person to advise you."

Rising, Fanny embraced Anne. "Let us put on our wraps and walk out to the gardens for a little while. Maybe fresh air will clear our heads. As they put on bonnets and mantles, Fanny looked at Anne enquiringly. "You mentioned the way he kissed your hand. Anne, what did he do?" Anne whispered, "He took my hand and turned it over. One time, he kissed my palm. The last time, he pressed his lips to my wrist." She turned her face away. "Fanny, it was like an... electric shock. I felt it *everywhere*. Then he..he *smiled* at me. I did not know where to look. Then, without a word, he turned away like nothing happened." The two left the house and crossed to the gardens in the square.

They walked in silence for several moments. Fanny turned to Anne. "As I am sure you are aware, Mr Burrell and I have become very close. He has not spoken of marriage to me, or, as far as I know, to my father. I do not know what may come. I will tell you that I respect him as a person in ways I never even considered with Carleton. He is dedicated to his work. He talks to me about matters of substance and listens to my opinions. He has shown me that he considers me a sensible adult, not a pretty child to be indulged. From what you have said, it seems that you and Charles Deschevaux may be forming a similar friendship. I think you will know what is right when you feel it. There is no hurry, after all. One of the mistakes I made with Carleton is allowing myself to be swept along too quickly, when I was too young to understand what was really important." She smiled suddenly.

"And Mr Burrell dances very well indeed." They glanced at each other and laughed. Anne pressed Fanny's hand. "Thank you, Fanny. I do feel better. You are my dearest friend, and I knew you would be honest with me." They engaged in desultory conversation as they strolled back to the house. Anne collected her maid and her umbrella and returned home, much relieved.

Chapter 28

⬩

Anne dispatched a note, inviting Emily to breakfast early on Monday. She looked for Diana to discuss their Monday expedition with her, but Diana was out with Robert. Anne left a note on her dressing table. Returning to her sitting room, she found the bills of fare for the next week on top of her desk. Unlocking and opening her desk, she sat down and reviewed them quickly.

Noting that they were in Mrs Russell's neat script, Anne was pleased to see that the lists included several of Mrs Clay's specialities, including curd tarts, ham in a case and a pheasant pie. She added buttered parsnips and spinach to the dinners and suggested a special breakfast to be served early Monday morning. She ordered tea and chocolate, toasted bread, some of Mrs Clay's especial preserved cherries, sliced cheeses and cake, to be served at eight thirty in the morning room.

"That way, it won't interfere with Father and Robert having their breakfast later." Laying the bills of fare aside, she wrote Fanny a note confirming the time for breakfast on Monday. She also noticed the pattern book and fabric samples on a table by the door. She glanced at them and found samples that appealed to her for the morning room. A primrose and white striped wall covering for the fireplace wall with coordinating pale primrose paint for the other walls.

"Warm and sunny, completely right for a 'morning' room." A gold-rimmed mirror for over the mantle and delicate china ornaments would keep the room light and feminine. Suddenly she remembered a carpet that had been in a room redecorated at home last year. It was a soft blue woven with a central medallion in yellow with bouquets of flowers in the corners in pinks, pale blue and lighter yellows.

"Perfect! I will write to Somers and have it sent here. No sense in having it rolled up in the attic in York when it will suit this room." She also thought of a pair of Sevres vases in a similar shade of blue with gold trim and ornamented with birds, which had been stored in a trunk for many years. "I will request the vases as well. That room will be a breath of summer!"

Pulling out pen, ink and paper, she wrote to Mr Fraser who had furnished the samples, asking him to call. She also wrote her note to Somers regarding the carpet and the vases. Feeling satisfied with her morning's domestic efforts, Anne closed and locked her desk, picked up the notes, and went downstairs. She gave the notes to Turner for dispatch, and asked him to have Mrs Russell join her in the morning room.

As she entered the room, she eyed the furnishings critically. The small rosewood sofa with the curved arms and woven back would suit; she would have the seat reupholstered in blue velvet, and have some loose cushions made for added comfort. She surveyed the two chairs flanking the fireplace; they had the advantage of being comfortable with their low arms, curved backs and tufted upholstery. She was pondering leaving them as they were, covered in worn tan morocco, or having them recovered as well, when Mrs Russell entered the room. Anne turned and smiled.

"Mrs Russell, thank you for being so prompt. I've reviewed the meals you and Mrs. Clay have planned, and find them very suitable. As you see, I've added a few dishes. I'd like to add something more substantial for breakfast when we have returned from Grosvenor Chapel Sunday morning and there is a special breakfast for Monday morning. I am having an early breakfast for Mrs Robert and two friends before we embark on our errands."

Handing them to Mrs Russell for her review, she turned back to the room. The rest of the furnishings were acceptable, she thought. Mrs Russell asked, "At what time did you want the ladies' breakfast served on Monday morning, ma'am?" "For the ladies, I thought eight thirty would be suitable. Mr Emmons and Mr Robert may have their regular breakfast at ten o'clock as always. Does that seem reasonable, Mrs Russell?" The housekeeper nodded.

"Indeed, Miss Emmons. There should be no difficulty." "Excellent. I would appreciate it if you would review these with Mrs Clay as soon as possible. If anything is needed for later in the week, I can look for it as we shop on Monday so please be sure that I receive any lists from you or Mrs Clay before Monday." Turning back to the room, she added, "I intend to have this room redecorated, Mrs Russell. I have written to the gentleman who provided the samples to request him to call at his earliest convenience." Mrs Russell nodded and replied, "Yes, ma'am. Will that be all, Miss Emmons?" Anne released her to her duties and returned to her dressing room to prepare for the outing to the museum.

Mr Deschevaux was punctual to the minute and handed both ladies into his carriage. At the museum, he had arranged for a private tour with a librarian. As Miss Crawford and the librarian discussed the various displays, Mr Deschevaux courteously escorted Anne. After viewing the Greek and Roman antiquities in the gallery, they walked on to view a new exhibit of gold objects donated by Mr Bowdich. "Two gold disc pendants and some gold beads, from the Asante in Africa," said Mr Deschevaux.

"How intriguing. I know nothing about that country," replied Anne. "I know little myself, other than the Asante trade in gold, ivory and slaves. I understand Mr Bowdich is writing a book on his experiences there. I look forward to reading it," commented Mr Deschevaux. Anne was shocked. "I thought the slave trade was illegal." "Sadly, ownership is not. Traders manage to find a way, in spite of the penalties if caught." They found that their views on this subject coincided. As they rejoined Miss Crawford and the librarian, Mr Deschevaux pulled a small box out of his pocket. Opening it, he showed Anne the little amber piece he previously mentioned.

"However did you get it so quickly? How lovely! It is so delicate and beautifully carved. The amber looks like honey." He smiled. "I sent a man on horseback after our first conversation about it. I knew you would enjoy seeing it. I brought it today hoping that the museum can provide information." The librarian examined it with interest. "I have never seen anything quite like this but Roman carving is not a subject I have studied extensively. However, one of the others may have some information. May I take this with me?" Mr Deschevaux rescued the piece.

"I prefer to keep it by me for now, sir. By all means, see if someone is available to talk to us. We can enjoy the exhibits while we wait." Anne bit her lip as the librarian took his leave, obviously somewhat miffed. "I believe you may have offended him, sir," she whispered. "I am sorry if that is the case. Still, I prefer not to let the piece out of my sight at this moment," Mr Deschevaux replied. "I understand. I, too, would be reluctant to let him make off with my mosaic," she smiled.

Just then, the librarian returned. To Anne's surprise, an old acquaintance, Mr. Smith, accompanied him. Recognising her and Miss Crawford, he shook hands with them both, and let Anne introduce Mr Deschevaux. "I understand you have a piece for me to see. Where was it found?" Mr Deschevaux told him the story and gingerly placed the amber head into his hand. Turning it over and examining it carefully, Mr Smith smiled.

"A lovely piece and ancient; it may well be Roman or even Etruscan work. It must have been a family treasure. There is a piercing in the headdress. This may have been a pendant. Very fine quality amber and very clean. I do not think we have anything like this in our collection. Found in a field, was it? Amazing that it was even noticed." Mr Deschevaux smiled and concurred.

"We have found other artefacts occasionally so my people know to watch carefully." "Other artefacts?" queried Mr Smith. Anne recognised the same level of excitement generated by her mosaic and smiled. After a series of questions, Mr Smith made a note of the location of Mr Deschevaux's estate and asked if he could visit in the coming summer months.

"I would certainly like to see your other finds and look at the area, if you would not object." The conversation concluded with mutual compliments and a tentative plan for Mr Smith to visit in the summer. As the two librarians departed, Mr Deschevaux turned to the ladies and suggested a stop at Gunter's before returning home.

That evening, only Anne, her father and Miss Crawford were at dinner. Miss Crawford told Mr Emmons about the manuscripts at the museum with great enthusiasm, leaving Anne to her thoughts. She reflected on the day, not noticing that Miss Crawford and her father were finished. "My dear," coughed Miss Crawford. With a start, Anne looked up. "I have requested tea in the drawing room, if you are finished," said Miss Crawford. "I hope that suits?" "Indeed yes, Amelia. I am so sorry; I was wool-gathering," Anne replied gratefully. The ladies rose, and left Mr Emmons to his brandy. Anne did not notice her father's satisfied smile.

Robert and Diana came in as they crossed to the drawing room. Robert joined his father, and Diana proceeded to the drawing room with Anne and Miss Crawford for tea. "We had a delightful evening," enthused Diana. "We dined with an old school friend of Robert's and his wife. A charming couple." Miss Crawford replied, "How pleasant. It is always diverting to meet up with old friends. I'm sure Mr Robert was in his element." Diana smiled. "Indeed he was. His friend is also in orders, so they had much to discuss." Anne was lost in her own thoughts when Diana said affectionately, "I hope you had an enjoyable day, dearest." Anne looked up with a start.

"Oh, yes, I certainly did. Mr Deschevaux escorted Amelia and me to the British Museum. We saw some very interesting exhibits, and stopped for refreshments at Gunter's. Most entertaining." Diana twinkled. "For you, indeed. I know how much you enjoy the museum. I think Gunter's would have been more to my taste. Did you have ices?"

"No, tea and cakes were more appropriate for the weather. It was too chilly for ices, to my mind." To change the subject, Anne told Diana and Miss Crawford about her plans for the morning room. Diana was very interested in the colour scheme. "The pale yellow with the touches of blue sounds lovely. I think the morocco covering those arm chairs may be wrong for the room, though. May we look at it together tomorrow?" Anne agreed, glad that Diana was interested. The conversation continued in a desultory manner, when they were joined by the gentlemen.

The conversation shifted to family matters, as Mr Emmons had received a letter from Matthew. "He writes that Lydia is completely recovered, and the baby is fat and healthy. Apparently, she has made up for her early arrival and is doing well. Little Walter is also much improved; the daily lessons he receives are keeping him busy and interested. Matthew is considering taking a run to town. There are business matters he wants to discuss with me, and a bit of shopping to be done for Lydia. She does not want to leave the children just now." He smiled. "Apparently, they are both doing so well she wants to enjoy them." Anne smiled sympathetically.

"I can imagine that she does. She had a trying few months, dealing with her own recovery and with the worry about little Anne's health and then Walter's jealousy and bad behaviour. Does Matthew plan to stay with us, sir?" Mr. Emmons glanced at the letter.

"He does not mention specific plans. I thought to write to invite him." "Please do so. I will have rooms prepared and he can come at his own convenience," replied Anne, already thinking of an acceptable suite. Turning to Diana, she asked, "Have you had an opportunity to talk to Becky?" Diana smiled.

"Indeed I have. She actually dislikes being a lady's maid, even though the pay is better. She came to this house several years ago.

A previous tenant had a French chef who insisted on having an assistant. Mrs Russell hired her, thinking Becky would wait on the chef. In fact, he had trained her to shop, to grow fresh herbs and on how to use the various kitchen implements. By the time, the tenant and the chef departed, she had progressed to preparing vegetables, certain sauces and some puddings. Becky showed me a collection of receipts she wrote up based on the chef's instructions, and some are quite detailed. Her great desire is to become a cook. Because she is a good worker and cleans thoroughly, Mrs Russell kept her on as a maid. Whenever Becky has some free moments, she goes to visit Mrs Clay."

Impressed, Anne said, "So she can read and write. I will confer with Mrs Clay. If we entertain more, an extra pair of hands will be very useful in the kitchen." Diana urged her to do so. "Becky would be grateful for the opportunity to return to the kitchens. She is still maintaining the herbs in a little cold frame and expressed great admiration for Mrs Clay." Anne resolved to speak to Mrs Clay in the morning.

Later that evening, she sat beside the fire in her bedroom, cosy in her rose velvet dressing gown, with her book lying closed in her lap. She gazed drowsily into the flames, lost in thought. She had no doubt that a situation would be found for Becky, as she was certain Mrs Clay would be delighted to have an assistant. It also meant an opportunity for Eliza from the Grey Coat School. As she mused, thoughts of Charles Deschevaux drifted through her mind. She had missed him at dinner and afterwards. "I would have enjoyed hearing his thoughts on the exhibits today. I wonder what he did this evening. If only I had dared invite him to dine with us..."

Chapter 29

The next few days passed like magic. As expected, Mrs Clay was delighted with the idea of an assistant and willing to work with Becky. "She's a good worker, I must say, and those receipts she wrote out are very neatly done. She understands herbs as well. We will see how we go on," she said when Anne spoke to her about the matter. Anne received a response to her Express to the Grey Coat School and looked forward to Eliza's arrival within a week or so; Becky would continue to act as Diana's maid until Eliza's arrival.

The early breakfast was served without a flaw; Emily and Fanny were punctual, and Mrs Clay's breakfast included buttered eggs, which the four young ladies devoured along with the cheese, toasted bread and preserved cherries. Diana and Anne led the way to the carriage, and they were off to the Soho Square Bazaar. They were impressed with the variety of booths, and the fact that the bazaar was intended to give work to veterans of the late war, their wives and widows.

At the linen draper's counter, Anne found the white flannel requested by Lydia and purchased the requested lengths; Emily purchased several lengths of muslin and cambric. They proceeded to the booksellers, where all four ladies made purchases. After a couple of hours, Diana and Emily were ready to proceed to Mrs Bell's shop.

Diana and the modiste soon had their heads together over designs for the *damascene* silk. Diana had her way with a higher neckline, fuller sleeves and simpler trimming. Instead of the double row shown in the design, Diana preferred a single row of tassels in the *damascene* colour to trim the lower portion of the skirt and to edge the sleeves. Mrs. Bell also had some delicate lace in the same shade to further veil the neckline. Mrs Bell suggested a sleeveless black lace half-dress and ribbons to wear until the mourning period was over. "As you can see the black won't be near the face, and will satisfy conventions. What jewels will you wear?" Diana hesitated. "I have not yet decided. What would you recommend?" The two conferred further and Anne wandered over to see what Emily and Fanny were examining under Miss Johnson's attentive eye. She herself needed nothing at the moment, so was entertained by her friends' discussion.

After concluding Diana's business with Mrs Bell, the foursome drove on to Mrs Gill's and then to Miss Harris's establishment in Cheapside. Despite herself, Anne was impressed by Miss Harris's designs and bespoke a walking dress and pelisse in a rich blue *sicilienne* woven of silk and cashmere. After leaving, the ladies decided to return to the Emmons's house in Upper Brooke Street for refreshments. Anne chuckled to herself as she recalled the look on the footman's face when he saw the number of parcels procured by the four young ladies.

Emily's wedding preparations were almost completed and she was looking forward to marrying Mr Rotherham and returning to his home. Emily and Diana were well on the way to becoming fast friends, as Anne had hoped. Anne foresaw a merry time ahead this season for the four friends. Diana was looking forward to the *damascene* gown, planning to wear it at the Kidwell's ball in a few weeks' time. Anne rose from her dressing table to put on her warmest bonnet and mantle. She was due at St. George's to speak to Mr Hodgson about the charity schools overseen by the parish. She was especially interested in the newer primary school which taught boys and girls. The weather had worsened and, even with a hot brick for her feet in the carriage, the short journey was bound to be chilly.

Upon arrival at St. George's, Mr Hodgson turned her over to one of the governors who escorted her around the premises. She was impressed with the number of children served but was discouraged by the rigid curriculum. "You say the school trains boys to be tailors while teaching girls to be bonnet makers and such? What if a child shows a particular talent or interest?"

To her secret dismay, she discovered that the school had been founded with very practical goals, designed to teach poor children a basic skill and the ability to read their catechism. There were no "extras," such as history or languages, and nothing to foster a desire to read and learn beyond the limited education and the skills offered.

"We are more concerned with them being able to support themselves in their place in life. As a charitable work, we are serving the greatest number we can by providing training suited to their needs and position in society. We have neither the funds nor the staff for additional studies. Besides, these children have had no opportunity to consider talents or interests."

Silenced, Anne finished the tour, left a donation and returned home. After going to her dressing room to remove her mantle and bonnet, she visited the library in search of her father. Mr Emmons rose to his feet and came around the desk to kiss her cheek. "I see you've been out, my dear; your cheeks are blooming, as is your nose," he said with a smile. She smiled back. "Indeed I have, Father. I've been to the St. George's school. It was rather discouraging." "How so?"

She described the curriculum. "It seemed so limiting and impersonal." Brows raised, he agreed, "To be sure, it seems so. However, consider the number of children in the school; I'm sure the instructors do the best they can for them. Another thing to remember is where they are located. It is likely many of their donors are from the highest level of society. Many of the aristocracy are not comfortable with the idea of those from the lower classes advancing; these charity schools must walk a fine line between helping their students and being seen as a hotbed of radical ideas. Besides, your Grey Coat School also has a limited curriculum, does it not?"

Stung, Anne said, "Father! I have selected the prize books myself...!" "Yes, yes, my dear, but the school itself provides the girls with a basic education and domestic skills suitable for going into service, does it not? You've selected prize books that fit within that area. As I recall, the last ones were Bibles and household management books, not poetry or history books. How many girls in the school have expressed a desire to do other than domestic work?"

Anne bit back an angry retort and considered his question. "You are right, Father. The vast number is fitted for domestic service. I think a few girls may have helped in the school with younger students, but I am not sure if any have gone further as educationists. Yet it seems so unfair to limit children's opportunity to learn like this. And so many do not receive even this much education." Mr Emmons patted her hand.

"I encourage you to stay involved. Look at the positions you have established for the young woman from York with Diana and the maid here with Mrs Clay: two young women who are cultivating certain skills, with the desire to rise. Talk to the instructors at St. George's; if there are signs of a particular ability, the teachers will know. You may get a chance to help individual students privately. You have been involved with the Grey Coat School for some time now, so you have made the acquaintance needed to do this. You will need to start from the beginning at St. George's school, and it will take time. I think you will find it rewarding." Anne nodded.

"I understand what you are saying, Father. I will consider what you've said. I will also write to Miss Collison at the Grey Coat School to see if any of the students have used or shown interest in the scholarship to the school in Leeds. I am ashamed to think I have not pursued that, to be sure the scholarship is useful." She rose to leave, only pausing as he said, "I am very proud of you, my dear." She pinkened, and blinked sudden tears away. "Thank you, Papa," she murmured, and left the room.

The next morning, Anne awoke to a dark, cold morning. She shivered into her dressing gown and slippers before going to the window. Looking out, she saw the trees bent over in the wind, lashed by sleet. According to the reply she had received from Mr Fraser, he would visit that afternoon regarding the morning room decoration. "That will be pleasant," she thought. "At least we'll have the illusion of sunshine."

Returning to her bed, she kicked off her slippers and crawled back under her quilts, dressing gown and all, to sip her chocolate. As she finished her chocolate, she tugged the bell pull for Ellen, and got out of bed again. Sliding her feet into her slippers, she passed into her dressing room to get ready for the day.

Surveying her wardrobe, Anne chose a new walking dress, made by Madame Josette and delivered just before they left York. Made of rich dark bottle green Circassian cloth, there were three rows of black velvet ribbon at the hem and on the cuffs. Black velvet ribbon also caught the puff of the sleeves at the top of the arm. Ivory lace frills decorated the high neck and edged the sleeves. A black velvet belt emphasised the high waist. It had a matching pelisse, lined in black silk and edged with sable, and a bonnet with a high crown and deep brim in bottle green velvet and trimmed with a cockade of black velvet ribbons, which she did not expect to wear today.

"This dress should be warm enough." Soft black leather slippers on, and she was prepared for the day. Crossing the hall to her sitting room, she was thankful to see the fire blazing and the lamp over her desk lit, ready for her. Picking up a small pile of correspondence waiting for her attention, Anne unlocked the desk, pulled out the chair and sat down.

She had written several notes, when she was interrupted by a discreet cough. When she looked up, a footman said, "Pray excuse the interruption, Miss Emmons. Mr Turner wanted me to advise you of a caller. Mr Deschevaux is in the drawing room. Are you at home, ma'am?" Anne paused, surprised, and then replied, "Yes, of course. Pray show Mr Deschevaux to the drawing room and tell him I will be with him shortly. Oh, and have tea brought in."

Rising, she closed her desk and crossed to her dressing room. She checked to be sure her hair and dress were tidy, then ran lightly down the stairs. Anne entered the drawing room and saw Charles standing before the hearth warming his hands before the fire.

"Mr Deschevaux, this is a surprise. I thought no one would be brave the weather today." He turned and smiled, and walked towards her with his hand out. "Indeed, the weather is unpleasant, but it is worth braving it to find delightful company." He took her hand and kissed it. Anne withdrew her hand hastily. "Pray, be seated, sir." She turned to take a seat by the fire but was arrested by his hand on her arm. "Not yet, Miss Emmons. Not until I have said what I have to say." He took a step away and then turned.

"Miss Emmons, I told you months ago of my regard for you. You were not ready to entertain a discussion of the matter. I have not spoken of it since then. However, this situation cannot continue. I have tried to be content as your friend but that is not enough." He paused and looked at Anne for a long moment. "Will you marry me, Anne?" She stood looking at him, eyes huge in a suddenly pale face, taken completely by surprise. "Before you answer, I would have you know these things. Firstly, I have discussed my intentions with your father and he approves. I accept that you may not appreciate that but I admire and respect your father too much to ignore his position in this matter. Secondly, please believe I am in earnest."

Anne moved mechanically to her favourite chair by the fire and sat down. At that moment, the maid and footman entered with tea. The footman positioned the tea table before her and the maid set the tray down, then they both left the room discreetly. Anne looked up at Charles and gestured at the chair across from her. "Pray be seated sir, so we can discuss this." As he took his seat, she poured a cup of tea, added the milk she had observed to be his preference and handed him the cup. She looked up from her own cup to see him gazing at her with a faint smile. "Taking the wind out of my sails, ma'am? It is hard to maintain that level of earnestness over a tea tray." She smiled back.

"In truth, sir, I ordered the tray before I came down. Had I known the reason for your visit, I might have thought otherwise." After a pause, where both took a few sips of tea, Anne looked at him. "I remember everything you said at Littlebrook House, Mr Deschevaux. You must understand, I was completely unprepared for your declaration. I have appreciated your kindness and friendship since then, but wondered how you could conceal such feelings before and after that occasion. There were so few signs of your continuing regard. And now you ask me to marry you? Indeed, I think you must explain why you wish to marry me, sir." Carefully, he set his cup down.

"Very well then. I want to marry you because I love you." He looked at her calmly. "There it is. That is all." It was Anne's turn to put down her cup. "But...why? I'm so very ordinary." Impetuously, Charles rose.

"Why? How do I know? I do not know *why*, any more than I can determine the moment it happened. I have planned to marry once I knew the estate was safe. When in London, I attended parties, balls and entertainments, and I met many charming young ladies. For a variety of reasons, I felt no inclination. Then I met you at Fanny's betrothal ball. You were so very young; I thought you a charming child. However, each time I came into company with you, I was struck by something about you. Although you seemed to enjoy parties and dancing and fashion, like the other young ladies of my acquaintance, you also had other interests. You looked at other people differently. Months might go by, and yet, when I would see you again, it was as if you had always been there. We *talk*, Anne, we converse; we don't just exchange inane social remarks. I love that intent look you get in your beautiful eyes when you are thinking about something. I cannot explain it more clearly than that, I'm afraid. I just love you. That is all."

Anne couldn't take her eyes away from Charles' face. She saw that he was serious. The simplicity of his "I love you. That is all" caught at her heart as nothing else could have and put to rest many of the doubts and questions that had so troubled her. "You truly love me?" She gazed into his eyes. "Yes, I truly do," he replied huskily. She rose from her seat and walked away from the fire. "I must tell you, I have wondered and agonised for weeks over what you might feel for me, and I for you. So many doubts have crowded into my mind. I did not realise that it was so simple, so beautifully simple." She turned back to him and smiled.

"I love you, too, you see. I would be happy to marry you, Charles." "You will?" He crossed to her in a few strides and took her face between his hands. "Anne, my darling Anne. You have made me the happiest of men." Solemnly, he kissed her forehead and her cheeks. He looked intently into her eye. "I will do my best to ensure that you will not regret this decision nor have cause to doubt again." Then he lowered his head and kissed her lips. Warm, soft... Her hands found his shoulders and clung. He raised his head and held her gently for a moment, then led her back to the fire. Placing her on a small settee, he seated himself next to her and took her hand. Reaching into his pocket, he pulled out a small leather box.

"In my family, we have a custom. The man gives his *fiancée* a betrothal ring when she accepts his suit. This has been in my family for many years and seems to belong with you. I hope it pleases you." Opening the box, he held it out. She disengaged her hand from his and took the box. The box contained a heavy gold band of filigree work showing stylized flowers and leaves, set with a single cabochon sapphire that glowed in the firelight.

"Oh, my dear Charles, this ring is truly exquisite." Removing it from the box, she slipped it on her finger, only to find it fitted well. He took the hand wearing his ring and kissed it. "A happy portent for our future." She felt again that tingling, and she knew from the smile in his eyes when he looked at her that he was fully aware of it.

Chapter 30

Anne and Charles sat before the fire, talking quietly. Just then, the footman entered. "Miss Emmons, a Mr Fraser has called. He says you are expecting him. At his request, I took him to the morning room." Flustered, Anne rose precipitously. "I completely forgot! The morning room decoration! Oh, Charles, I am so sorry but I must see him, if only to apologise." Charles smiled.

"I understand. Is your father in his library? I would like to speak to him and can do so while you discuss your business with Mr Fraser." Waiting only for an assent from Anne, Charles vanished from the room.

Anne strode swiftly to the morning room. She apologised for keeping him waiting and showed him the samples she had selected. He gazed around the small room and nodded. He said firmly that the tan chairs must be recovered. Anne told him of the carpet and the Sevres vases she had requested from York. Although he was reluctant to approve without having seen them, he did agree that her description made them seem appropriate for the room.

"Once we have our scheme, we can begin the process. I will order the velvet for the sofa, and bring samples that may suit the chairs next week. A straw-coloured satin, perhaps... We can remove the current carpeting and at least begin with the furnishings. I am certain I can put my hand on a Sevres urn that would look well on a column between the windows and compliment the vases on the mantle. Hopefully, the carpet and vases will have arrived when next we meet. Have you considered coverings for the window?"

Shocked to find she had not considered them, Mr Fraser assured her he would bring some drawings and fabric samples for those as well. Firmly instructing her to notify him as soon as the carpet and vases arrived from York so he could look them over for his final design, he left after bowing over her hand. She smiled as she returned to the drawing room.

Sitting before the fire, Anne emptied her now-cold tea into the slop bowl and refilled her cup. She gazed at the ring on her finger, admiring the radiance of the sapphire and the gleam of the gold filigree in the light of the candles and firelight. Somehow, she just could not take it in; Charles loved her! She realised that she had cared for him longer than she knew; witness her concern, nay, her jealousy when he danced twice with Fanny at the ball in York. Just then, Diana entered the room.

"What is this I hear, Anne? Robert and I were greeted with the news that you are betrothed, and to Charles Deschevaux! When did this happen, dearest?" Anne looked up, distracted, and then leaped to her feet to hug Diana. "Just now. Look!" She held out her hand for Diana to see the betrothal ring. Diana admired the ring and looked keenly into Anne's face.

"Are you happy, dear one? Do you love him?" Anne glowed. "Yes, I do love him, and he loves me. I never thought to be so happy. He asked me to marry him and I asked him why he wanted me." She walked towards her seat by the fire and then looked back at Diana. "You know my fears, my doubts. He answered my question by saying he loved me, and that was all. I was so struck, Diana. He resolved all my worries." She laughed. "I feel so foolish now." Diana laughed with her. "I am so glad for you. I hoped for this moment. You and Charles are perfect for each other in so many ways." They sat together on the settee, and talked about Anne's betrothal and ideas for the wedding.

Anne laughed again. "We have not discussed it. While Charles was proposing, Mr Fraser came to see me about the morning room decorations. I was so mortified; I had forgotten all about him. Fortunately, Charles wanted to speak to Father, and my business with Mr Fraser did not take long. I had hoped he would come back to me soon but I daresay that he, Father and Robert are discussing things in the library." Diana jumped up. "Why not join them?" Anne rose, and they proceeded to the library.

The door to the library stood ajar and they heard masculine laughter as they approached. Pushing the door open, Anne and Diana peeked in. Mr Emmons, Charles and Robert stood by the fire, glasses in hand, Robert saying, "I am delighted with your news, Charles! You and Anne should deal extremely." Diana chuckled and the three looked around. "There she is," said Mr Emmons. "We are overjoyed for you and Charles, my dear." Anne ran to him and he hugged her warmly. "Of course you are," she scoffed, "You have been angling for this moment for months now." Mr Emmons laughed again. Anne turned to Charles and smiled as he held out his hand to her.

The two couples and Mr Emmons seated themselves. Charles squeezed her hand, and, under the cover of general conversation, "I am very happy, you know." She whispered back, "As am I." Just then, Robert said, "We must celebrate! Let us have some champagne." Mr Emmons rang for Turner and requested champagne. "The best glasses, you know, Turner." The butler bowed and hurried away.

"My dear sister, you and Charles should discuss the marriage arrangements soon. I know the church discourages weddings in Lent, but we should be able to get permission. It is not that uncommon. I can talk to Reverend Hodgson, if you like." Charles broke in. "Anne should choose the day when she has had time to think about it. Let us enjoy the moment. We can consider the details another day." Anne smiled at him gratefully.

Just then, Turner entered with the champagne, followed by a footman with a tray of crystal glasses. The bottle was opened, the frothing wine poured into the glasses, and toasts were made. Mr

Emmons looked at Anne tenderly. "You remind me very much of your mother, my dear. I think she would be happy today." Anne blinked back tears as they raised their glasses to salute the late Mrs Emmons.

Just then, Turner announced Lord and Lady Kidwell, with Miss Fanny Kidwell and Mr Martin Burrell. "Show them in, by all means" said Mr Emmons. As the company exchange greetings, Anne whispered to Fanny, "Do you all have plans this evening, Fanny?" Fanny replied, "As it happens, we do not." Anne beamed, "Excellent! You must stay to dine. Please tell your mother and Martin." She slipped away and, upon reaching the drawing room, summoned Mrs Russell.

"Mrs Russell, I must ask you to confer with Mrs Clay. We are increasing our covers for dinner this evening to include Mr Deschevaux, Lord and Lady Kidwell, Miss Kidwell and Mr Burrell. Mrs Clay will have to do her best, as the dinner we planned for this evening will require adjustment. Please let Turner know we will require more champagne and four more glasses." "Very good, ma'am," responded Mrs Russell calmly. "At what time should dinner be served?"

"Shall we say at five thirty Mrs Russell? That hour is unfashionably early, but Mr Emmons and Mr Robert will both be hungry as they did not have their usual nuncheon earlier in the afternoon." "A good idea, Miss Emmons," agreed Mrs Russell. She returned to the library in time to hear Diana suggest that the ladies retreat to the drawing room. "We will be much more comfortable," she said as she turned toward the door. "A good idea," agreed Anne as she linked arms with Fanny. Leaving a brief instruction with the footman for the champagne, the ladies passed through the door.

Seated cosily before the drawing room fire, Fanny turned to Anne and said, with a laugh in her voice, "I believe you have news for us?" Anne laughed aloud. "Indeed I do. My dears, I am betrothed! And I hope you will stay for dinner, as I have give instructions for places. We must celebrate." Lady Kidwell indicated that they had planned to dine at home. "A note to the housekeeper, and we are yours!" Leading Lady Kidwell to the writing table in the morning room, Anne returned to the drawing room.

Fanny and Diana pulled her down on the sofa between them." "Have you decided where you will have the wedding?" they asked in unison. Anne laughed. "Dear ones, we have not discussed it at all. We have had no time to consider anything." Lady Kidwell sailed back into the room, smiling at the three heads together near the fire. Seating herself in a chair across from the sofa, she said, "Anne, my dear, you must be guided by me. Decide *nothing* in a rush. There is no need to hurry things, after all. We are in Lent, and mourning for the Queen shall end soon. Besides, is not dear Emily getting married shortly? You may wish to consider a date in April after Easter."

Anne smiled affectionately. "You are all kindness, ma'am. I will certainly consult with you on this." The footman came in with champagne, accompanied by a maid with a tray of delicate crystal glasses. The ladies waited as the wine was poured, the glasses passed, and the servants bowed themselves out. Fanny spoke first, "Well, dearest, whatever details must wait, it is not too early to think about your gown. Surely you have some ideas about that." Anne laughed, "Oh, Fanny, how like you! Yes, I have thoughts on that."

Sipping her champagne, she said, "The gown I wore to the ball at Littlebrook House... I have it here. It is very special to me, and I am thinking of taking it to Mrs Gill for modification to wear as a wedding dress. The train and so forth, you know." Fanny gazed at her in surprise. "Instead of a new gown? The gown is indeed lovely and most becoming, but still..."

Diana interjected, "I have not seen you wear it, sister, but I believe I know the gown. The lavender blue is a perfect colour for you, but it seems a shame to alter it as you will soon be able to wear it again." Anne shrugged. "We will see. I want to discuss it with Mrs Gill. Trimming is different now, and it may not be possible to alter it well." Lady Kidwell remarked, "I remember at the ball, thinking how well it became you when you danced with Charles." Lady Kidwell was surprised to see Anne flush a deep rose while a secret smile played over her lips.

Lady Kidwell's eyes sharpened. "I see nothing wrong with the plan. You girls have plenty of new gowns after all. There will be time for something to be made if needed." The conversation turned to fashion in general until Anne had a thought. "Lady Kidwell, what can you tell me of Charles's home? Although I visited you in Kent many times, I do not recall ever seeing it, even in passing." Lady Kidwell frowned. "My dear, you are correct. Charles was frequently away with his horses or else up to his eyes in estate business. Our households got out of the way of making calls after his dear mother died." She pondered the question.

"His family really did come over with the Conqueror, you know. Mount Place... The house is brick and very old. The main part is Jacobean but his great-grandfather made some additions. It is interesting; the house and several out buildings are built around a square courtyard. Inside, there is a magnificent stairway, as I recall. A great deal of French influence, especially as several of Charles's ancestors sought French brides. His grandmother was French." Anne nodded. "I remember years ago Fanny told me about his family, but I thought it was an exaggeration. He has told me about the orchards and gardens but not the house itself. It sounds very grand." Lady Kidwell shrugged.

"I believe it was at one time. Sadly, Charles's mother died when he was only a boy. His father rather lost his head and began gambling and drinking heavily. The older son took to those activities as well. Between them, a great deal of money was diverted from the estate and lost. Fortunately many of the family treasures were entailed with the house but maintenance was not, shall we say, consistent. Charles has had much to do to restore the house, indeed the whole estate, to order. However, there is a deal of work left to do." She smiled.

"Frankly, I do not think Charles has a taste for grandeur. There is even a title, but he has yet to use it." Anne took comfort from that comment. She felt a surge of interest in the house. Perhaps Charles would let her assist with bringing the house to life; it would be a way to make it feel her own, too.

The door opened and the gentlemen walked in. Charles' eyes went straight to Anne's face; she promptly blushed and looked down at her hands. Then she looked up and smiled. Robert walked behind the sofa to put his hands on his wife's and sister's shoulders. "Another wedding in the family!" Lady Kidwell laughed. "Indeed, sir, Fanny and Diana have been asking Anne when she wishes the ceremony to be." Charles interjected quietly, "Anne will have all the time she needs. There is no hurry, after all." Anne looked at him with gratitude. "Thank you, sir. I am not accustomed to being the centre of attention like this. It is a bit disconcerting."

Mr Emmons boomed jovially, "Well, this is a happy day, none the less. Plenty of time to settle the business later. I will only say, I am delighted with this event." Just then, Turner announced that dinner was served. The party rose and adjourned to the dining room. As the company took their place, Anne saw at a glance that Mrs Clay had outdone herself. The simpler repast previously planned had been augmented; buttered crab and spinach stewed in cream as well as a second soup also graced the board. Lord Kidwell, seated on her right, spoke, "My very best wishes for your happiness, my dear Anne. I am delighted for you and Charles." She pinkened and said, "Thank you, sir. You have always been very kind to me."

"I look forward to having you in the neighbourhood, you see. Charles has kept bachelor quarters at the old house long enough." Anne laughed. "A feminine touch needed, my dear sir?" She glanced around to see that everyone was served and tasted her soup. Mrs Clay's oyster soup! Always a favourite of hers. She closed her eyes as the rich creaminess slipped down her throat. Conversation became sporadic as everyone concentrated on their plates. As the first course was cleared, conversation became general once again. When the second course was laid, Anne was glad to see that lemon cheesecakes and some custards had been added to supplement the prawns, duckling and apple fritters and other dishes previously planned for the evening.

As the meal progressed, old friendship allowed the conversation to flow across and around the table, not restricted by formality. Finally, the table was cleared and the footman brought in nuts, candied fruits and the decanters, including more champagne. As the wine was poured, Mr Emmons rose. "Before the ladies withdraw, I would like to say again how happy I am to announce the engagement of my beloved daughter Anne to Charles Deschevaux. I am even more delighted to share this moment with dear friends. I ask you to join me in drinking to the health and happiness of Anne and Charles."

Glasses were raised amidst smiles. Anne and Charles exchanged glances, then Charles rose. "Mr Emmons, of all the reasons I have to be grateful to you, and there are many, I am most appreciative for your approval of my suit for your daughter's hand. I will do everything I can to make her happy. Thank you." The glasses rose again as Anne, with tears in her eyes, blushed deeply.

Once the glasses were empty, Anne rose and the ladies followed her back to the drawing room. The tea tray was already waiting for them. Once she had poured out, Anne excused herself briefly. Drying her eyes, she hurried from the room, making for the kitchens. Mrs Russell and Mrs Clay were conferring as she entered the room.

"Mrs Russell, Mrs Clay, you were superb. The dinner was perfect. Mrs Clay, Lady Kidwell praised the turbot pie and the creamed spinach, and Mr Deschevaux ate three of the lemon cheesecakes. Everything was delightful. I am only sorry for the short notice. It must have been very awkward." Mrs Russell and Mrs Clay looked at each other and smiled.

Mrs Clay answered prosaically, "Well, ma'am, it was a bit of a challenge but, once we decided on the additions, it wasn't too bad. That Becky, ma'am, was an enormous help. She made the Soup a La

Julienne and the spinach in cream, and they both came out a treat, I will say. And as the dishes were finished, she put them in the serving vessels, ready for the table. Very neat-fingered she is. A good day's work when she came to my kitchen, ma'am." Mrs Russell added, "An excellent team, if I may say so." Anne smiled gratefully at the two, glad to see their *rapprochement*.

"It was wonderful. Pray accept my compliments and extend them to Becky as well." She returned to the drawing room and slipped into a chair near the fire, as Lady Kidwell, Fanny and Diana chatted. Diana poured Anne a cup of tea and passed it to her. "Is everything all right?" she asked. Anne nodded and said, "Indeed it is. I just needed a moment, and I wanted to congratulate Mrs Russell and Mrs Clay. It seems your Becky has proven herself a treasure!"

Diana smiled, and Lady Kidwell interjected. "Mrs Russell? Ah, it seems things have resolved themselves." Anne laughed. "It appears so. I will just be glad when Eliza arrives so Becky can spend all her time with Mrs Clay. I could see that Mrs Clay has great plans." The ladies laughed and chatted, enjoying the relaxed companionship. When the gentlemen joined them, the camaraderie continued even as the conversation expanded.

Chapter 31

A few days later, Anne was reading in her library when Mrs Russell came to the door. "Miss Emmons, the waggon from York has come. The foodstuffs have been sent to the kitchen, and there are some packing cases and a large bundle from the house. Where would you like the packing cases placed? Anne stood up quickly, laying her book down on the table.

"Have the packing cases and bundle taken to the morning room and opened, Mrs Russell. Carefully, please, as I hope there will be two porcelain vases in at least one. I will be down in a moment." Anne retired to her room to wash her hands then ran lightly down the stairs. She was a bit taken aback when she entered the morning room.

Quickly realising that the "bundle" was the carpet which had been rolled and wrapped, she bade the maids to untie the ropes and unroll it part of the way. "It is perfect," breathed Anne. The deep blue border emphasised the colours of the flowers in the centre medallion and the corners. Delving in the crates, she discovered the Sevres vases. Much to her delight, she also found a pair of porcelain figures, an elegantly dressed lady and gentleman. "Are they not lovely? I do not remember these." Mrs Russell handed her a folded message.

"A letter from Mr Somers was in one of the crates, Miss Emmons." Anne took the message and sat down in one of the chairs to read it. "Ah, I see. Mr Somers writes that the figurines were packed up at the same time as the vases so he ventured to include them. He also writes that the rug was thoroughly cleaned before it was wrapped up to send. That is excellent. They are charming. I may not use them in the morning room but will definitely want them somewhere. I must thank Mr Somers for his diligence." She looked up at Mrs Russell.

"Mrs Russell, please inform Mr Fraser that the carpet and vases have arrived so we can proceed with the decoration of this room. I would like to complete this scheme as soon as possible." Mrs Russell curtsied slightly and replied, "A note will be dispatched immediately, ma'am."

Anne put the vases on either end of the mantelpiece for safe keeping and directed the maids and footman to move the rolled carpet to the wall. She was contemplating the small figures when Mr Emmons walked in. "Ah, my dear, I see you are hard at work. What have you there?" She showed the figures to her father. For a moment, he contemplated them in silence.

"I remember those. They were in your mother's room. She treasured them a great deal. I am glad you have them now." He glanced at the vases. "Those vases were also hers. When I had that carpet installed in one of the bedrooms, I had the vases and figures put in there as they looked so well together. I am glad they will be used again." "My mother's, sir? I had no idea. I cannot remember her room."

"No, my dear, I would be much surprised if you remembered her at all. You were so very young." He kissed Anne's cheek and left the room. Thoughtfully, Anne set the figurines on a side table, then seated herself at the marquetry writing table by the window. Pulling out a sheet of paper and a pen, she sketched an arrangement of the furniture and mantle piece, intending to show Mr Fraser. She sat there idly, gazing out the window. She shivered as she watched the wind blow the rain against the glass and pulled her shawl more closely around her shoulders. Definitely not a day to go out. She returned upstairs to her library as it was much cosier.

Once settled in the chair next to the fire, Anne took up her book again. She sat for a moment, gazing into the dancing flames. "Hard at work..." her father had said. But she hadn't been "at work". She had directed the maids and footman, had placed a few pieces of porcelain, had even sketched a plan but had done no real "work". Glancing around her library shelves, her eye fell on the antique box. She got up, unlocked and opened her desk, and retrieved the box.

Anne had not opened the box, had not even thought about the manuscript it contained, for weeks now. She drew a breath; then she removed her manuscript, notes and the three letters Mr Chamberlayne had given her. After re-reading the letters, she carefully folded two of them together and laid them aside. The third, she read again. Mr Rudolf Ackermann's secretary had written regarding the opinions of Mr Ackermann's editor. Mulling over the comments in that letter and the opinions expressed by Mr Chamberlayne, Anne had an idea for a new approach.

Anne stood up and walked to the shelf on which she had placed the recent editions of Ackermann's *Repository of Arts*. Bringing them back to the desk, Anne reviewed several of the articles in each edition. Then she picked up her manuscript and read it through, slowly. Getting out pen and paper, she began to write out a new outline based on her manuscript. She wrote for some time, absorbed in her task. Pausing, she stood up and stretched, walking to the window. Still grey and gloomy, rain falling sideways in sheets. Returning to her desk, she read through the new outline and added some notes. Satisfied, she set it aside. The downstairs maid entered.

"Mr Turner asked me to bring you your correspondence, ma'am." Anne took the messages, thanking the maid and dismissing her. Opening the first, Anne found a letter from Jane Chamberlayne. Jane and Hugh were married!

"He finished his studies and his training in London. He came home and has been accepted to work as a solicitor with Mr Jenkinson, the attorney. As you know, Hugh's father had left him

a competence (to make up for leaving the business in Leeds to his brother George, I suspect), so we had nothing to wait for. We will be living with my mother and father for the time being. It will be comfortable enough, as they have plenty of room.

We have rooms on the third floor and there is a small room near them in which Hugh has set up an office. (I am delighted, as you may imagine, as his law books and notes take up a great deal of room!) There is a tiny room off the dressing room which I have claimed as my closet, my own private retreat. I will continue to help in the shop at least for a while and we are hoping to build up a savings. Hugh procured a licence and we were married at St. Mary's very quietly. I missed you very much, my dear friend."

Anne looked up, feeling torn. On one hand, she was delighted for Jane. Jane and Hugh Heron had been promised since they were very young. Hugh's schooling had taken him away from home for several years except for brief visits, and letters had been no substitute for his presence. They had waited a long time. However, Anne was sad and a bit hurt that she had missed the wedding. "I will not dwell on that. I know Jane had no thought of marriage when I left for London. I would wager that Hugh simply swept her off her feet." Suddenly amused at the thought of the earnest Hugh sweeping practical Jane into a whirlwind marriage, her spirit lightened and she felt only pleasure for her friend's sake.

She set the letter to one side. The next note was from Mr Fraser, expressing pleasure at her news and promising to call within a few days' time armed with samples of fabrics and workmen to take away the sofa and chairs for recovering. Paint and wall covering could be done quickly when those pieces were out of the way. Picking up the letter from Jane, she ran downstairs to see if her father was in the library.

Finding him seated next to the fire, perusing a book, Anne sat across from her father and waited for him to look up. Mr Emmons met her gaze with an enquiring lift of an eyebrow. "Yes, my dear? Do you want something? Anne smiled at her father. "No, I just wanted to give you some news. Jane Chamberlayne has married Mr Heron. Such a surprise. Apparently he arrived home and whisked her straight into wedlock with a licence." Mr Emmons laughed. "Well he might. They were betrothed for years and there is really nothing for them to wait for, is there?" Taken aback, Anne thought about it.

"Well, if her family and his brother were agreeable, I suppose not. It makes sense in many ways. Jane has been working on her wedding clothes for the last year or more. I have seen some of her linens. Her embroidery is exquisite." "Well, then, my dear, you will want to pick out a suitable wedding present." Anne nodded.

"I believe I will write to Mrs Chamberlayne. I have ideas but want to be sure... I know Jane's taste so it will not be difficult, once I decide." Her father laughed. Anne said thoughtfully, "I had hoped Jane would come to stay for a few weeks but I assume this will be a busy time, with her and Hugh setting up their rooms in her parents' house and Hugh taking up his new position. Should I extend an invitation to them both, Father?"

"A question for Mrs Chamberlayne, my dear. As far as I am concerned, Mr and Mrs Heron are always welcome in my home. You know that Hugh's brother George is a good friend to Matthew in Leeds. I have met him several times in the course of business and found him to be sound. Through George, I have followed young Hugh's career with interest. However, between his new position and your plans, this may not be a good time. Mrs Chamberlayne will know, I'm sure." Anne returned to her library, and picked up her pen to write to Jane, expressing her congratulation on Jane's marriage to Hugh and best wishes for their happiness, and telling Jane about her own engagement.

"I wish you and Hugh very happy, dear Jane. You have waited so long! I would be remiss if I did not share some news of my own. Charles Deschevaux has asked me to marry him and I have accepted. We have no specific plans at this present, but no one

seems to think a long engagement would be necessary. I will write again as soon as the details are decided." Jotting a quick note to Mrs Chamberlayne about a wedding gift for Jane, she took both letters downstairs and laid them ready for the post.

A few days later, Anne and Fanny were at Gunter's enjoying tea with Emily. "How do your wedding plans go, Emily?" asked Anne. Emily grimaced. "My mother and I see things very differently, I'm afraid. She envisions a grand wedding at St. George's, such as Kate had, while I would prefer something quiet with just my family and a few close friends. At least, my wedding clothes are ready." Anne asked, "What gown will you wear?"

Emily's face lit up. "At least my mother and I were able to agree on that. With my hair, I have to be very cautious with colour. I found a pale peach *sicilienne* for the gown with a darker shade of velvet for the pelisse and the ribbon trim. Mother, of course, was rhapsodising over a pink silk that would have suited Kate; somehow, we came to agreement. She had some lovely *blonde* lace put aside for me which is perfect. We also selected a quantity of chemises and other linens. I already had a quantity of new clothes from my travels with my aunt so I really have all the clothes I require. Richard's house is well stocked, so very little is needed for the household."

Emily sighed. "Frankly, I think Mother is trying relive shopping for Kate's wedding. Kate is not doing well and we are all worried about her. Her husband will take her back to the country as soon as I am married. Mother and Kate have always been so very close..." Fanny and Anne drew closer. Anne took Emily's hand and Fanny said, "Oh, Emily. I am so sorry. I thought she was improving."

"She was. I am convinced this cold, wet London winter, with all the sooty smoke, has aggravated her condition. Her husband considers that, if he can just get her back to the country, she will regain her strength. She insists on staying for my wedding. Richard has purchased a special licence and we want to have the wedding at home, so Kate can see it. If we can but convince my mother."

Fanny suggested, "Have Kate talk to her. If your mother understands that this is your wish and has Kate's endorsement, she may see an earlier date is for the best. Then Kate could go back to the country and you and Richard could go your own way." Emily brightened. "I believe that might succeed. I have been trying to keep this problem from Kate but she may be the key to solving the dilemma." Looking at Anne and Fanny, she asked, "Do you think you could come to me at a moment's notice? We have been through several seasons together and I want you both to be present." Anne responded without hesitation.

"Just send a message; I will be there." Fanny agreed heartily. Emily beamed. "Excellent! My dear friends, it may not be the most fashionable wedding of this year but it will be blessed by friendship and happiness." Anne refilled everyone's cups, and the conversation turned to the all important subject of the wedding breakfast. During a lull in the conversation, Fanny asked, with an arch look, "Have you told Emily your news, Anne?" Emily looked inquiringly at Anne, while Anne blushed furiously.

"Nothing has been announced as yet, but...I am engaged to be married." "Really?" gasped Emily. "I never... To whom?" "Charles Deschevaux," replied Anne. "Oh, Anne, I am so happy for you!" exclaimed Emily. Fanny put in, "He is an old friend of my family and a great favourite with Anne's father and mine. It is in every way an excellent match." Emily looked at Anne for a moment.

"Are you happy, my dear?" Anne patted her hand. "Indeed I am. We are sincerely attached and have much in common." Even as she spoke, she squirmed at the blandness of her statement. "Sincerely attached? How bland it sounds," she thought, feeling the inadequacy of her own words. "So sensible. Such a rational attachment." Turning the conversation back to Emily's coming nuptials, the three chattered on.

A few days later, Anne received a letter from Mrs Chamberlayne. "*My dear Miss Emmons, I was so delighted to hear from you. As you know, Jane and Hugh are living with us for the time being, so they are not in need of many furnishings at this present. Jane and I have completed her linens and other wedding clothes, which are lovely, if I say so myself. Jane was sorry that you were from home and could not be here for the wedding and the breakfast. However, holding the wedding so quietly was a sensible decision. Dear Jane can be so very practical. Hugh is busy setting up his room. He already has one or two clients."*

Anne smiled as she read that comment. At that moment, an idea for the perfect wedding gift for Jane struck her. While out shopping, she had seen a beautiful rosewood sewing box lined with silk that would be perfect for a newly-married matron. At the same shop, she had seen a writing box, also in rosewood, in a similar style. The writing box came with a stand so could be used at home like a writing table, or the box alone could be taken with Jane while travelling. Both were inlaid with a delicate design in brass on the outside and had silver fittings inside. The pair would suit practical Jane perfectly.

Chapter 32

Mr Emmons sat across a small table from Lord Kidwell, where they were enjoying some late afternoon refreshment at Arthur's. "I was not aware you were a member here," said Lord Kidwell. "I am fortunate that several acquaintances of mine are on the committee," replied Mr Emmons modestly. "It is a quiet place for the most part. I am not often in London and find it convenient to have a place to hold a private conversation with a friend." Both men sipped their wine.

"You indicated you had something to discuss," reminded Lord Kidwell. "Yes, yes. I have been meeting with my man, Deschevaux and his solicitor regarding the settlements," sighed Mr Emmons. "Finicky business, that. Rather distressing to have to contemplate one's own death and the possible death of one's child." Lord Kidwell nodded. "I understand. I remember going into all of that when Fanny was engaged to young Thomas."

"The difficulty is, I am baffled by the pair of them. Anne will not discuss it at all. She knows that there will be thirty thousand pounds in trust for her upon her marriage which her husband cannot touch. However, she is not aware (and neither has anyone else been up to this point) that that is not the end of the matter. When her brothers reached their majority, I settled sixty thousand pounds and a property on each of them. I have every intention of doing the same with Anne upon her marriage. This leaves an additional

247

thirty thousand pounds to go into her husband's hands under normal circumstances, and the matter of a property to resolve. She refused to discuss it, told me to handle it as I thought best. I never thought to see her so missish!"

He paused to refresh himself. "Now young Deschevaux is content to have Anne's entire dowry tied up in trust. It will not do! So I settled it with Deschevaux's solicitor myself. The trust will be administered by myself, Matthew and my man of business, as is already established. I want to add one more trustee and thought to ask if you might oblige. After all, Deschevaux's main property is in your area and you will have a better idea of how they are going on. What do you think, sir? Are you willing?"

Lord Kidwell was surprised by this turn of events. "Of course, I am willing to serve as a trustee. Anne is like a member of my family and I will be honoured to assist." Mr Emmons leaned forward. "As established in the settlement agreement, Anne will receive the income from the trust for her use at her own discretion. The remaining thirty thousand pounds will be transferred to Deschevaux. As far as property is concerned, since neither will voice a preference, I am leaving her the use of the London house for her lifetime with ownership to go upon my death to her children. Hopefully, before that event occurs, one or both of them will see sense and allow a more reasonable property arrangement. Young Deschevaux has agreed to pin money and a jointure for Anne and the Deschevaux estate is to go to their oldest son. Anne's trust will provide dowries for their daughters. Young Deschevaux signed without reading it closely."

Mr Emmons snorted. "Fortunately, his solicitor is a sharp fellow with his client's interests at heart." Lord Kidwell nodded, rather dumfounded by the unexpected confidence, not to mention the amounts in question. "Will Anne have access to her principal?" he asked. Mr Emmons nodded. "When she reaches thirty years of age, she can request withdrawals which must be approved by her trustees. Depending on how she and Deschevaux deal together, I am contemplating a removal of the requirement for approval. I want to wait, to see how they go on. The trust arrangements permits the trustees make such a change if warranted." A wry smile lit his face. "One good thing is that neither of them has anything to do with my will. None of my children or grandchildren will suffer, of that you can be sure."

Lord Kidwell smiled back and raised his glass to his friend. "It must be a source of great satisfaction to you. My Fanny will be all right. Fortunately, the estate is not entailed and there are no other relatives with a claim. I like your idea of a trust, to ensure she has means regardless of circumstance. I will consider that and discuss it with my man of business." Mr Emmons relaxed in his chair. "And how does Miss Fanny, sir? She is blooming as always, but seems quieter somehow. Is she enjoying London?" Lord Kidwell frowned. "Not as in past years. She does not seem interested in the balls and assemblies this year. Somehow, though, she appears more...content."

"Ah," nodded Mr Emmons. "A young man in view, perhaps? Mr Burrell seems pleasant enough." Lord Kidwell nodded consciously. "She does seem to be comfortable with him. It has been a long time since that disaster with Mr Thomas. I own, I would like to see her well settled." "I understand exactly how you feel," rejoined Mr Emmons. The two frustrated fathers nodded over their glasses.

"Well, Kidwell," said Mr Emmons, "I appreciate your patience listening to this. There are few people with whom I can discuss this kind of personal dilemma." He set down his glass. Glasses were refilled and the gentlemen settled down for a discussion about meeting for dinner at Lord Kidwell's club the following week.

Whilst her father was out, Anne was in her library, trying to write but could not focus her mind. Why did her father worry so about settlements? With her funds tied up in trust, she was as well protected as possible. She stared into space as she recalled the brief interview. Just then, a tap sounded on her door, and Miss Crawford entered. Pausing as she entered, she directed a searching look at Anne. "My dear Miss Anne, what is to do? You seem distinctly ruffled." Anne sighed.

"I am and I feel very foolish. My father wanted to discuss the marriage settlements with me. Apparently he and Mr Deschevaux and their representatives are meeting to determine how to arrange the business. I did not want to consider the matter. It just did not seem that significant today. He was annoyed with me and I did not know how to explain my feelings to him." Miss Crawford looked at her sternly.

"Miss Anne, you should feel foolish indeed. You are fortunate that your father wishes you to be aware of these matters. The settlements are for your protection and for your children's benefit, and are part of the marriage transaction. Without them, everything would transfer directly to your husband's hands, leaving him in control of any funds, properties or other assets. By offering to discuss this with you, your father was giving you an opportunity to tell him if you had a preference." She shook her head as she sat opposite Anne. Shocked, Anne looked at her.

"Oh, dear, such a thing did not occur to me. I know I have a dowry set up in trust with the income to come to me. It did not enter my mind that there might be something else." "Are you aware of the arrangements made when your brothers came of age?" asked Miss Crawford. "No, I'm not, Amelia. I was away at school when Matthew reached his majority and in London when Robert came of age. No one mentioned such matters to me. I know Matthew's estate and Robert's townhouse were settled on them at those times but never considered that anything else might be involved." Miss Crawford nodded.

"Of course, I do not know all of the details, but I do know that in addition to property, a sizeable sum was transferred to each of them. I am certain your father intended to make equal arrangements for you upon your marriage or a specific time. There are also issues such as your mother's jewellery and personal possessions."

Anne was taken aback. "Property? You mean a house? But Charles has his estate in Kent and property in Devonshire. I cannot imagine..." Miss Crawford looked at her with a touch of impatience.

"My dear young woman, you have a good mind. I pray you to use it! In addition to his home in York and his business interests, your father owns several properties in Yorkshire and the London house. Such a property could guarantee you a home for your lifetime, especially in the event of your husband's death. It could also provide an estate for a younger son or for a daughter. If a time arose where funds were needed, property is an asset that can be rented or even sold out right. Please remember, these matters affect any children you may have as well as yourself."

"You are absolutely right, Amelia. I have been foolish indeed. When my father comes in, I will beg his pardon and ask him to explain what arrangements have been made. At least I can make it a point to understand what provisions are in place. It does seem, no matter how one feels, everything comes down to business," Anne replied, with a sigh. Gently, Miss Crawford patted her hand.

"My dear, nothing is ever as simple as one could wish. Living IS a business. You already understand household management; what is that if not business? You are paying wages, purchasing goods, negotiating for services. Wherever you live, those matters must be addressed. Thousands of women end up poor and living hand to mouth. The marriage settlements will provide you a measure of independence and security, which are blessings indeed. They take nothing away from the fact that you and Mr Deschevaux care for each other."

Anne acknowledged, "I have taken my situation for granted. I have much for which to be grateful, not least my father's care." Miss Crawford rose. "I am glad you are taking our discussion to heart, my dear. Now I must write some letters unless you have need of me."

Anne turned back to her desk, only to be interrupted by a maid. "Miss Emmons, you have a caller." "Indeed? Who is it?" The maid replied, "It is Miss Kidwell, ma'am." Anne nodded. "Show her into the morning room, please, and ask Mrs Clay for some tea. I will be right down." She ran lightly down the stairs. She entered the morning room to see Fanny gazing around. "My dear, the room looks lovely! I thought you had decided on stripes." Anne smiled.

"It is pretty, is it not? I had thought the primrose stripe paper would suit, but he brought additional samples and I could not resist this pale yellow silk. It may seem a trifle outdated to some but the room just seems to glow with sunshine. I had intended to have the chairs recovered in fabric but he found enough of the tapestry work to do them both and the flowers go so well with the rug. I am satisfied." Fanny nodded as she gazed around. "The plain draperies at the windows are most elegant and balance the rest of the room very well indeed. It is so much brighter and more cheerful." Anne gestured Fanny to be seated on the sofa.

"What brings you out at this time of day, Fanny? Normally you would be changing for dinner." Fanny shrugged. "I felt the need of a walk and thought we could visit awhile. Has a date been set for your marriage?" Anne shook her head. "Not yet. I am thinking of a date in April, after Easter, as your mother suggested. With Jane newly married and Emily's wedding hopefully so soon, I thought it better to delay a bit. Why do you ask?" Fanny smiled, "I was just thinking. Such a number of weddings!" Anne laughed. "I understand. At least I found the perfect gift for Jane."

Fanny laughed. "Well done, Anne! What about Emily?" Anne shook her head. "Nothing as yet. I am considering a dinner set. I have seen a Spode I like, but wanted to look at the Wedgewood display before I make a decision. Have you selected anything yet?"

"Kate and I have put our heads together. You know Kate cannot get out and her mother frets Kate's nerves so frequently, hovering. I can go about and bring back ideas and we talk about them. I have been told that she and her husband likes the idea of a wine cooler and I told her about several I have seen. I have settled on a silver tureen. It is prettily engraved, with a lid and a stand. Rundell and Bridge has it, and I do think it will be perfect. Emily has talked to Kate about the wedding. Kate will speak to her mother and ask that Emily's wedding be brought forward." Fanny sobered.

"Kate truly wants to go back to the country as soon as possible to spend time with the children. I think it will be the best place for her and so does her husband. It is just that her mother clings so." Anne asked, "Why does she not accompany Kate back to the country? It seems a reasonable plan and she may be of help to Kate." Fanny shrugged.

"She feels Kate should be in London to consult with the doctors. She cannot accept that there is little a physician can actually do for Kate. Dr. Knighton has told Kate she would be better in the country with clean air. He is sure her health could improve significantly. Her mother cannot believe there is no simple cure, insists on pressing tonics and nostrums on Kate, and will not just let her rest. She and Kate have terrible arguments which upsets Kate's husband. He wants Kate to have peace, quiet, clean air and good food, and thinks she will be better off if her mother is otherwhere. To be honest, I sympathise with him. However, this leaves poor Emily in the middle."

Anne nodded. "Hopefully, Emily will soon be married and on her way to her own home." Fanny agreed. "I pin my hopes on Kate."

A few days later, Anne received a note from Emily, the messenger waiting to take her reply. *"My dear friend, the wedding is for tomorrow. Pray come to St. James's tomorrow morning at 10:00. It is all arranged. Kate prevailed upon Mama to consent to an early marriage, and, once she agreed, Papa and Richard made haste to make the arrangement. It will be very quiet. There will be a breakfast at home immediately after. Do tell your father and Mr Deschevaux that we are expecting them and apologise for the short notice."* She entered the breakfast room to find her father just finishing his coffee.

"Papa, Emily writes that her wedding is set for tomorrow morning and asks me to attend. She did tell me to be sure to tell you that you and Charles are expected for breakfast at the DeWitt house immediately afterwards. Will you come, sir?" "I am so sorry, my dear, but I have a meeting scheduled and cannot fail. I am just leaving this moment. If you hurry, I will be happy stop at your intended's rooms to see if he might be available. He can escort you and Fanny home. I am passing his direction." Gratefully, Anne said, "Thank you, sir. I will give Emily your regrets." Pausing only to kiss his daughter's cheek, Mr Emmons strode out. Going quickly to the morning room, she dashed off a quick note to Emily, and gave it to the boy to take back. She returned to the dining room and helped herself to tea and toast.

Chapter 33

With a sigh of pure satisfaction, Anne put down her pen. Standing up and stretching, she picked up a few books from her desk and returned them to the shelves. Walking over to the window, she gazed out at yet another grey, rainy morning. "At least, the final copy is complete," she thought with pleasure. She had taken portions of her manuscript and woven them into a readable, pleasing composition. She turned back again to pick up and reread the letter from Mr Ackermann's secretary regarding her manuscript.

"I will send this new work to Mr Chamberlayne and ask him to review it with this letter, to see what he thinks. I think it will make a suitable submission for an edition of *Ackermann's Repository*. I can do more revision on the manuscript itself." She put the letter she had written in response to the letter from Mr Ackermann's secretary, and the fair copy of her final composition, folded them together and laid them aside. Moving to the fireplace, she sat next to the fire and stared into the glowing coals.

Scenes from Emily's wedding and the breakfast following floated to her mind. Most of all, she enjoyed the picture of Emily, radiant in her peach gown, gazing up at her Richard. Unalloyed happiness. She remembered the small group, lost at the altar in St. James's during the ceremony, followed by the signing of the register. Kate had been present, gaunt but happy, leaning on her husband's arm. Fanny and Anne had stood together, beaming at Emily throughout the service.

The company at the breakfast included Lord and Lady Kidwell, Mr Deschevaux and, to Anne's surprise, Mr Burrell.

The feast was served with charming informality, allowing Anne and Mr Deschevaux, Lord and Lady Kidwell, and Fanny and Mr Burrell to gravitate to each other. Emily and Richard Rotherham had eyes only for each other as they drifted from group to group to receive congratulations. Anne noted how little either of them ate. Emily and Richard left early in the afternoon to begin their journey to Warwickshire, leaving his aunt and sister to be entertained in London. Kate and her husband returned to the country a few days later.

Anne picked up her letter and composition, and walked down the stairs to the library. Much to her relief, her father sat at his desk, occupied with correspondence. Looking up at her over the gold rim of the spectacles he had recently begun to use. He rose with his hand out. "Anne, my dear! Pray come in and sit down." Removing the spectacles, he rubbed the bridge of his nose ruefully. "I hope I become accustomed to these soon. They make it easier to read but pinch a bit." Anne smiled sympathetically.

"I want to show you something, Father." Handing the letter and her composition to him, she continued. "I have revised my work and have it ready to send Mr Chamberlayne to review, before sending it to Ackermann's. Would you mind reviewing it and my letter to the secretary there?" Mr Emmons looked at her in surprise.

"Of course, my dear. I would be delighted. Leave it with me, please, and I will read it when I have finished this letter." Anne rose, went round the desk and kissed his cheek. "Thank you, Father. Please tell me what you think." She returned to her dressing room and rang for Ellen. When Ellen appeared, Anne said, "It is rather chilly, and I want my rose Norwich silk shawl; it is warm and cheerful. I cannot seem to find it." Ellen curtsied. "I took it downstairs to clean, Miss Emmons. You may not recall but there were some dirt streaks where it brushed against something. I will fetch it immediately." Anne smiled.

"Thank you, Ellen." As she waited, she browsed through her gowns; pulling out the sapphire blue velvet, she thought, "I have not worn this since we left York. I will wear it tonight for dinner. So warm and becoming." She laid it across the chair, put the sapphire earrings in the drawer of her dressing table, and laid out the sapphire blue ribbons for her hair. She also laid out an embroidered silk shawl. A new acquisition, it was of a soft light blue embroidered with lilies in sapphire blue, white and pale pink and deeply fringed. Just then, Ellen walked in with the shawl Anne desired.

"Thank you, Ellen. As you see, I have chosen what I will wear this evening. The blue slippers, I think. We dine at home this evening, so I will be up to change accordingly." "Everything will be ready, Miss." Throwing the rose shawl about her shoulders, Anne picked up her book and went down to the morning room.

Seating herself before the fire, Anne opened her book. She glanced around the room, enjoying the warm tones of the walls and the cheerful hues of the flowers in the carpet and porcelains. Her rose gown and the flowered shawl added to the warmth and brightness. Time flew by, then Turner's voice suddenly startled her. "Pardon me, Miss Emmons. You have a delivery." Bewildered, Anne rose.

"A delivery, Turner? I am not expecting anything." "The container is rather large, ma'am. Shall I have it brought in?" Flustered, she said, "Oh, yes...yes, indeed." The two footmen came in carrying a large crate. Turner handed her an envelope. "This accompanied the object and may explain, Miss Emmons." "Thank you, Turner." As the footmen uncrated the object, Anne read the note.

"Dearest Anne, This note accompanies something I have long wished to give you. The corbeille de mariage *is the groom's gift to his bride, and another tradition in my family. I hope you enjoy what it contains as much as I delighted in assembling it for you. I will tell*

you more about it when next I see you. Pray remember me to your father, your brother and all. I am, as always, yours. Charles"

Folding the note with shaking hands, she laid it on the writing table and turned just as the object was revealed. A rosewood casket on short curved legs and polished to a glow, it had a delicate porcelain plaque of a basket of flowers set in a gilded frame on the hinged top. Smaller plaques ornamented the front and sides of the casket and the carved legs were delicately gilded. Lifting the lid, Anne gasped. Inside were several wrapped packages. Lengths of antique lace, an inlaid handkerchief box filled with daintily embroidered handkerchiefs, a silk bag containing a fan with ivory sticks that were delicately pierced and gilded and the leaf painted with a courting couple in a flower-filled garden were the first things she saw.

Then she lifted out a leather box. Opening it, she saw a sapphire necklace, a simple chain of graduated stones set in gold with the largest centre stone designed to nestle at the base of the throat. "Oh, my," she said, stunned. More packages remained. A cashmere shawl and a long lace scarf next appeared. A prayer book, bound in soft green morocco with a gilded design and her initials. Her hands caressed the smooth leather as she laid it carefully on the writing table. Finally, at the bottom, another box, this one bound in rubbed and faded red velvet. She sat down, holding it carefully.

"My dear Miss Anne, what is all this?" asked Miss Crawford, who had entered the room quietly. Anne glanced up at her. "A gift from Mr Deschevaux. The groom's gift to the bride..." Miss Crawford's sharp eyes took in the laces, the fan, and the sapphire necklace. "Goodness me," she said faintly. "I have never seen anything like this," whispered Anne. Looking at the box in her hand, she gently opened the lid. This time, deep green emeralds glowed: a gold cross set with emeralds on an intricate chain, emerald earbobs and a matching bracelet.

"It is...it is too much. Can it be right for me to accept this?" Anne questioned. Miss Crawford rose. "Let us consult with Mr

Emmons." She left the room, leaving Anne in a daze, contemplating her gifts. "The casket alone is exquisite," she thought, "and very old. How extravagant of him!" Picking up the prayer book, it fell open to a ribbon, marking the marriage service. Faintly underlined were the words "...*as Isaac and Rebecca lived faithfully together, so these persons may surely perform and keep the vow and covenant betwixt them made, (whereof this Ring given and received is a token and pledge,) and may ever remain in perfect love and peace together....*" She reread the section, her eyes filling with tears.

Gently closing the book, she laid it again on the writing table. "A love token indeed," she thought. For the first time, she realised the depth of feeling the Mr Deschevaux concealed beneath his pleasant manner. Just then, her father accompanied by Miss Crawford came into the morning room. Miss Crawford took a seat near the fireplace, while Mr Emmons laid his hand on Anne's shoulder. "What's to do, daughter? Miss Crawford said that you desired to consult me." "Look at this, Papa, all gifts from Charles. They came in this beautiful casket. He called it a...", she consulted the note, "'*corbeille de mariage*' and is the groom's gift to the bride. I have never seen anything like it. We have not yet even set a date. Is it proper for me to accept such an extravagant gift?" Mr Emmons patted her cheek.

"You must have been surprised. You so seldom call me 'Papa'!" Pulling a chair over to sit near her, he looked at the laces, the jewellery, and so forth. Taking her hand, he said, "Well, my dear, he explained this tradition to me and told me what he planned to include in the *corbeille*. The marriage settlements have been signed so your betrothal is official. As your affianced husband, in the tradition of his family, he is expected to give such a gift, symbolising your transition to wife. I had heard of such things. He discussed giving this gift to you when we signed the settlements. I see no reason for you not to accept the *corbeille* and its contents."

"But, sir, is it advisable for me to accept jewellery of this nature?" queried Anne, anxiously. "I do not want to do anything improper."

Miss Crawford added, "The situation is a bit singular, sir, I must confess." Looking thoughtful, Mr Emmons rubbed his chin. "I can understand your concern. However, Anne is betrothed to Mr Deschevaux. He may give gifts to her as he pleases. Most of these are unexceptionable. I grant you the jewellery is an unusually valuable gift; however, I see no reason to question the propriety of such a gift. If you are uncomfortable, you do not have to wear it publically until after your marriage, after all."

"That is so. I will talk to Charles about it. I can save the jewellery for when we are married if I still have doubts." Mr Emmons rose. "That is an excellent plan, as he will be joining us for dinner. You will have an opportunity to speak with him then." Leaving the morning room, he shut the door behind him. Anne turned to Miss Crawford. "Would it be imprudent, do you think, to wear a piece of the jewellery tonight? If Charles is going to dine here quietly with us, he may like to see how much I appreciate his kindness and generosity." Miss Crawford laughed.

"If you are that eager to wear it, do so, my dear. You have your father's permission to accept the gift, after all." Anne carefully repacked the shawls, laces, handkerchief box and prayer book in the casket. Picking up the two boxes containing the jewellery, she summoned the footmen to take the *corbeille* to her dressing room. She and Miss Crawford climbed the stairs to her rooms.

Standing before her mirror later, Anne studied her reflection. The sapphire necklace was a perfect complement to her *ensemble*. She lifted her chin. The largest stone rested just below the hollow of her throat. "Thank you, Ellen," she murmured. Downstairs, her father, Robert and Diana, and Mr Deschevaux were waiting in the drawing room. She joined them just in time for Mr Emmons to place a glass of sherry in her hands. Charles approached, eyes on the sapphires glowing at her throat. "Thank you for wearing that," he said quietly. "It looks beautiful on you, as I knew it would." Anne impulsively touched his cheek. "Charles, such an extravagant gift, and everything perfect. I am overwhelmed." He smiled.

"I have plotted that surprise for so long. It is a tradition in our family, as I mentioned in my note. I am delighted that you were pleased." He grasped her hand, gazing into her eyes. "Your eyes look as blue as the sapphires themselves tonight, my love." Anne blushed deeply, unable to look away. Just then, Turner announced dinner. Charles smiled, drawing her hand through his arm. She took a hasty sip of sherry, then they crossed to the dining room. Drawing out her chair, he seated her carefully. Then he took the chair next to her, grinning mischievously as he sat. Leaning towards her, he whispered, "I am reluctant to share your attention tonight. At last I will be able to speak to you."

Robert and Diana sat directly across from Anne and Charles, with Mr. Emmons at the head of the table. Anne could not say what was served. Glancing across the table, she caught Robert's teasing eyes looking from her to Charles and back again. He lifted his glass in a silent toast as Anne went scarlet. Just as suddenly, her embarrassment lifted and she joined in the laughter and conversation that flowed easily around the table. When Charles grasped her hand, she turned hers over and clasped his warmly.

As Robert and Mr. Emmons joked back and forth, Anne said softly, "I hope your family would have approved our marriage. I understand it is an ancient line..." Charles looked at her, and grinned. "Oh yes, it is certainly old enough. Please do not let that intimidate you," he said with a chuckle. She looked a question.

"Ancient, but certainly not grand. Legend has it that the ancestor who came over with the Conqueror was a stable boy, who spent most of his time keeping the horses fed and cleaning up after them. His claim to fame was providing a fresh mount to a fallen knight on the battlefield, but no one knew which knight it might have been. After William was crowned, somehow the fellow ended up with a farm and a few horses that survived the battle. He made up the name. And that is how it all began."

Anne's eyes widened as he chuckled again, and she smiled. "You are making fun of me." He looked at her warmly. "I am sure I shall, but not at this moment. My family built up their property and their wealth by marrying neighbours' daughters, farming and breeding horses. They did acquire a certain status and even some honours; there was a barony. However, my ancestors also had a habit of having a foot in more than one camp. In Cromwell's time, the head of the family went to France to serve the surviving Royal family; he died there, childless.

Meanwhile, his younger brother stayed in England and kept busy on the estate. When the restoration came, the younger brother was confirmed in the ownership of the property but the barony went into abeyance when the older brother died. It took some doing for the heir to get it restored. My grandfather and my father were very proud of the ancient name and title and the fact that we still held the estate. However, what was accumulated was the result of hard work and careful management."

He sobered and looked down, as his fork pushed some food around his plate. "My father and brother wasted a good deal of what several generations had nurtured. I am more ashamed of their carelessness than of my family's humble beginnings. I still do not use the title. To me, 'the baron' is my father." Anne nodded. "Now I understand why it was so important to you to clear the debts and restore what you could." Just then, Diana asked Anne a question, and the conversation was diverted.

Chapter 34

Sitting in a small parlour at Arthur's, Mr. Emmons took a sip from his glass of port. Lord Kidwell and Charles Deschevaux looked at him expectantly. He said slowly, "I have been corresponding with a relation of mine, who is with the East India Company. I cannot go into detail, but, suffice to say, there is a move to establish a port in the east, on an island called Singapura. It will allow the British Navy to have an outpost, to defend trading vessels from pirates, and will also allow an expansion of trade. I have sent three trusted employees with him, to see about establishing a trading station, with a view to forming a possible banking accommodation. They should arrive at Singapura very soon, weather permitting. It will be a rather delicate matter, so I may wish to go myself at some point. I tell you this, as this may be an excellent investment opportunity if all goes as I hope." He smiled faintly.

"Anne does not know, of course, as she was very young and then away in school, but I was used to travel extensively. I have missed it and would not object to making this journey." He looked at Charles. "I rely on you to convince my daughter to marry sooner rather than later. I would see her wed and secure before I may have to depart. I intend to discuss my plans with her, but require your support in this. My sons are both aware; indeed, Matthew and I have corresponded extensively about this matter." He glanced at Lord Kidwell.

"And you, my friend, I hope you will continue to stand as Anne's

263

kind support, just as you have done these many years now. If she is safely married, she will want for nothing, but I count on you to ease her concerns." Taking another sip of port, Mr. Emmons contemplated the fire for a moment. "If I must go, I will correspond with you both to the best of my ability. The journey takes three to four months, assuming good weather, and this expedition will take several months. I am fortunate, as I will have connexions there already."

Lord Kidwell looked at him in some shock, "I had no idea you were contemplating such a drastic move. Are you sure you need to go yourself? Is there not someone else......?" "No," said Mr. Emmons decisively. "If an additional presence is needed, I am the one best suited for this task." He smiled. "In all honesty, I would welcome the opportunity." Charles asked, "Have you spoken to Anne about this at all, sir?"

"I have never discussed business with her in any depth in the past. Indeed, I have never encouraged her to ask questions about any of these matters. She knows Matthew has things well in hand, and that I take a turn if something interests me or if Matthew requests my participation. She knows that our family income is derived from banking, business and trade matters. That has been sufficient. My longest periods away from England occurred before I married. Anne's mother had no wish to travel, and I had no wish to leave her, so confined my excursions to London and Edinburgh. Then, the war with France made travel difficult for many years. Still, when Matthew and Robert were away and Anne in school, I did manage to make a few journeys. This, however, could turn into a lengthy matter, so Anne must know enough about it to understand what is happening, where I may go and why. I will discuss this with her at the first opportunity. I just want you both to be aware, and you, Charles, to try to convince her to marry soon. If I must go, I will be off on the first available ship."

Charles nodded. "Please send word when you have spoken with her on this matter. I do not want to speak prematurely."

Meanwhile, as Anne was attending to correspondence at her desk, Ellen interrupted her. "Miss Emmons, I have something to show you. Indeed, I do not know how it happened..." Anne looked up, surprised. "Whatever is the matter, Ellen? Is something wrong?" "No, Miss, not *wrong*, just a bit confusing." Rising, Anne accompanied Ellen to her dressing room. "You see, Miss, I was straightening the wardrobe, looking out any gowns that needed any attention. I found two bandboxes on top of the wardrobe that had been pushed to the back. They contain two of the new gowns commissioned from Madame Jeanette and delivered the day we left York." Anne looked at the two bandboxes in amazement.

"Indeed, I had forgotten all about them. I wonder which gowns they are?" She looked at Ellen and smiled. "It is as if I were receiving an unexpected gift." Opening the first, she saw a rich bronze green satin, with velvet ribbons. "Oh yes, I remember this. This will be perfect for this evening." Setting it aside, Anne opened the next bandbox. Shimmering silk of a soft clear blue tone and fragile lace appeared. Anne stood entranced with the gown in her hands. "This is perfect," she whispered. The soft blue silk had a velvet belt of a darker tone under the breast embroidered with flowers in glittering crystal beads in blue, violet, rose and diamond-like clusters. A narrow band of similar embroidery with ruched velvet ribbon above and below it decorated the hem. The lace at the neckline matched that which edged the puffed sleeves. She looked up at Ellen with tears in her eyes.

"I ordered this in the autumn. Madame Jeanette had warned me that it would take longer, because of this special embroidery and the lace. She was very particular about the lace. This will be my wedding dress." Ellen took the dress reverently. "I will take care of it, ma'am. It will be safe until you are ready to wear it." Wiping the tears from her eyes, Anne nodded. "It is exactly what I wanted. It is similar and yet very different to the ball gown I wore at Littlebrook House. To think I have had this here all these weeks and did not know it!"

Ellen flushed vividly. "My fault, ma'am. I should have remembered the delivery..." Anne said soothingly, "No harm has been done, Ellen. Indeed, I believe it has been for the best. I have a lovely new gown to wear this evening, and my dilemma regarding a gown for my wedding has been solved. Please do not be upset. Please put the blue gown safely away, and press out the bronze green for this evening." Ellen bobbed a curtsey and made her escape. Anne returned to her correspondence. Once she finished with the last note and put it in the stack to go out, she sat idly, lost in thought. Just then, a maid interrupted her reverie. "If you please, ma'am, Lady Kidwell and Miss Kidwell have called." Anne rose.

"Please show them to the morning room, and request a tea tray. I will be down in a moment." She tidied herself, then ran lightly down the stairs. Entering the morning room, she exclaimed, "Lady Kidwell, Fanny, how glad I am to see you both! What brings you here this afternoon?" Anne embraced each, and sat on the sofa next to Fanny.

"Well, my dear," began Lady Kidwell. "We have been shopping, and I took it into my head to stop in to see how you are. The weather has been so gloomy and we have seen little of you the last few days." Just then, the footman entered with the tea tray. Once he had deposited the tray and left the room, Anne poured out and replied, "I know. I have had little desire to go out, with the ice and the wind such as it has been. I have been trying to make plans and reading."

Fanny smiled. "I can see you, curled in a chair by the fire in your library upstairs, engrossed in a book." Anne smiled back. "Indeed, I was. I know that is too lazy for you, however. Did you have a successful shopping excursion?" Fanny enthused, "We certainly did. Mother has decided to redecorate her little sitting room, and we found a delightful chair and table at that cabinetmaker's shop where you bought your wedding gift for Jane. I was wondering if you could give me the name of the gentleman who refreshed your morning room. It is so bright and cheerful." Anne smiled again, "Ah, that would be Mr. Fraser. I will be happy to give you his direction. He was most efficient." She went to the writing table, took out a sheet of paper and a pencil, and wrote quickly.

"Here you are, Lady Kidwell. I think you will find him agreeable. If you have favourite items you wish to keep or to bring in from elsewhere, he is amenable. If you prefer a new scheme, I am sure he will be able to please." Lady Kidwell took the paper. "Thank you, my dear. That is most helpful. We will certainly speak with him. I have been thinking about your situation as well. Have you taken your gown to Mrs. Gill? What does she suggest for it?" Anne shook her head.

"No, and I do not need to do so. I have had the perfect gown all along. Two band boxes were put away and forgotten. So, dear ma'am, I will not have to have the ball gown altered. Poor Ellen was afraid I would be angry. Instead, I feel that I have received the most delightful surprise."

Curious, Fanny asked, "And what was in the other bandbox, Anne?" Anne laughed. "A lovely bronze green satin that I will wear this evening. You will see it when Father and I come to dine this evening, before we go to the opera house."

Anne turned to Lady Kidwell. "I have a novel for you, ma'am. I finished *The Heart of Midlothian* a few days ago. I believe you will find it quite enjoyable. It is by Walter Scott and is extremely well written. I had it laid by to bring to you this evening but you can take it with you now." Excusing herself, she ran lightly from the room. Returning momentarily with a neatly-wrapped package, she beamed at her old friend.

"I had it ready in the hall so I could not forget it." Lady Kidwell exclaimed, "Thank you, my dear! This is just what is wanted for these cold, wet days. I have been looking forward to reading this. I know

Fanny enjoys his poetry greatly, but I find his novels to be more pleasurable." Fanny nodded.

"Alas, it is too true. I have much more taste for poetry than for novels in general. I know Mr. Scott's novels are well received, bur I vastly prefer his poems. I have *Harold the Dauntless* awaiting my attention at home, and Mr. Burrell has lent me a volume of poems by Mr. Leigh Hunt." Anne said affectionately, "It has ever been thus, Fanny. I believe I am too prosaic to enjoy poetry the way you do." The ladies laughed. "Have you received any word of how Kate does since she returned home? I realise it is a short time, but I have been most concerned." Fanny nodded.

"They arrived home safely. Her husband was most solicitous, and they took the journey in easy stages. There was a surprising event. You may recall that Emily worried that her mother would insist on accompanying Kate if she could not influence Kate to stay in town. Well, Mrs DeWitt stayed in town to entertain Mr Rotherham's aunt and sister. A very happy turn of affairs! They seldom come to town, so Mrs DeWitt will be of great benefit to them. She is invited everywhere, after all."

Anne clapped her hands. "That is excellent! Dear Kate will have peace and quiet to recover, and her mother will feel that she is doing something useful. Who thought of that solution, Fanny?" Fanny replied, "I am not sure who originated the plan but, after Emily and Richard's wedding breakfast, Richard confided his concerns that his aunt and his sister would have a difficult time in London to Mrs DeWitt and asked if she could recommend someone to assist them with the intricacies of London society. It seems Mrs Cheylesmore is rather well connected herself, so it is no hardship for Mrs DeWitt to provide some guidance. Making plans with Mrs Cheylesmore and Miss Rotherham distracted her, and she hardly noticed when Kate and her husband slipped away."

Lady Kidwell interjected, "I myself have entertained Mrs

Cheylesmore and her niece. Miss Rotherham is a delightful young woman with elegant manners." Anne and Fanny exchanged glances.

"We should call on her. I will check with Diana, and the three of us can make a morning call, make her feel welcome," suggested Anne. "An excellent idea, dear," said Fanny. "I expect that she is fairly close to our age. If she stays for any part of the season, she may wish to do some shopping. We could certain offer to accompany her, or at least suggest some shops to visit."

Lady Kidwell said approvingly, "A kind plan, my dears. As it happens, I have their direction. They are staying in Mr. Rotherham's townhouse near Cavendish Square, a perfectly respectable area. By the way, I received a note from Lady FitzMaynard. She will bring her cousin Grace to town for at least a part of the season. They are expected within the next few weeks, as Grace will require some gowns." Anne was pleased.

"How delightful! I liked Grace so much. I am glad Lady FitzMaynard is bringing her early; she is so very shy. She will find it easier to begin with small parties, where she has acquaintance with at least a few people. As soon as I know when to expect them, I will plan a dinner. Does Lord FitzMaynard accompany them?" Lady Kidwell nodded. "Indeed. I believe there is an issue in Parliament in which he takes an interest." Anne replied, "Excellent! I will make a quick list, so I can plan what to serve. Then I will schedule a date." Lady Kidwell caught Fanny's eye, nodded slightly, and they both rose.

"Well my dear, I believe we shall leave you to it. We look forward to seeing you, your family and, of course, dear Charles this evening." Anne rose as well. "It was so good of you both to call. I will not say goodbye, just good afternoon. We will be with you before too long." Fanny and Lady Kidwell both hugged Anne and took their leave.

Anne ran up the stairs to her library. She opened her desk, seated herself, took paper and pen, and made her list. "Lord and Lady F, Grace, Lord and Lady K, Fanny, Mr Burrell, Charles, Robert and

Diana, Father, myself, and Miss Crawford-that is thirteen, an odd number. I will speak to Father. Fourteen is a comfortable number, and Grace will know most of them. I think that will be perfect. Now for a suitable dinner..."

She gazed absently out the window. She would have to ask Mrs. Clay what fish was available; a fish pie or buttered lobsters? Definitely a roast of beef with a fricassee of parsnips, a dish of buttered sprouts and a brown soup, accompanied by stewed mushrooms and truffles. For a second course, a Salmagundi, crayfish soup, roasted pigeons with a claret sauce? Charles was very fond of lemon cheese cakes, and custard with preserved fruit always went well. She wrote busily, and made a note to meet with Mrs Russell and Mrs Clay as soon as she had a date.

Setting her notes aside for future consideration, she turned to her correspondence. Reaching to take up her pen again, the sound of a soft tap on the glass startled her. Rising, she went to the window, pulled the drapery aside and saw the sleet had begun again. Leaning her head against the window, she gazed out dreamily, watching the icy water pool on the path below.

Chapter 35

A maid opened the door to her library, startling Anne. "Pardon, ma'am," murmured the girl as she bobbed a quick curtsey. "You have a visitor downstairs." Stepping forward, she proffered a small tray bearing a card. "Thank you," said Anne mechanically as she picked up the card. "Charles!" Running to her dressing room, she tidied herself hastily. She hurried down the stairs to the drawing room. Charles turned as she entered and caught her in his arms.

"Such haste!" he chided as he hugged her gently, then kissed her hand. They exchanged greetings as they stood hand in hand. "I am so happy to see you," she stammered. "I keep thinking about...." Drawing her to a chair before the fire, he seated her and then sat down himself. "I, too, keep thinking about our future." Leaning forward, he took her hand.

"Anne dearest, have you thought about a date?" he asked. Anne blushed and looked down. "I have. At first, I was considering waiting until after Easter, but now... I do not know. That seems such a long time." He squeezed her hand, and replied, "I am glad to hear you say that. I would prefer an earlier date, I must confess. We are well suited, your father and our friends are satisfied; why should we wait?" Anne blushed more deeply. "I, too, would like to marry soon. But what must we do?" Charles smiled.

"We could have the bans declared, but that would take three weeks. An alternative would be a licence, or even a special licence."

Anne frowned. "A special licence? Are those not very expensive and rather difficult to obtain?" Charles nodded. "They are more expensive than regular marriage licences, and the Archbishop of Canterbury must issue them. However, they allow a man and woman to marry when and where they wish."

"'Where they wish'? What would that mean?" asked Anne, a bit confused. Charles explained, "If someone wished to marry at home, or in a different parish than where he normally lived, a special licence would allow that. There would be no bans, and no requirement to marry in a particular jurisdiction. With so many of your family and friends in the North, I thought you might like to have a choice...."

"How thoughtful you are! I confess, I have been torn. Matthew has written that he plans to come to London, but then his letters are so full of Lydia and the children and he postpones. I hardly expect to see him before the spring, if then. And, of course, Jane is busy with her husband and new life. Yet many of my family and friends are here in London at this present. I can hardly expect everyone to be present regardless of where we marry." Charles hesitated, and then took her hand.

"There is another reason that we may wish to marry sooner rather than later." Brows raised, Anne looked at him questioningly. "Your father is waiting to hear from some business colleagues about a certain venture in the east. He may have to travel there himself to put matters in order, and said that he would like to see us marry before he must depart." To his surprise, Anne smiled.

"The port in the east? I heard him speak of it with Matthew when we were present for little Anne's christening. I do not believe they noticed I was in the room. I do not pretend to understand the matter, but I could see that Father was quite engrossed with the entire business. I am not surprised he considers going there himself. When I was small, Matthew and Robert used to tell me exciting tales of Father's travels as a young man." Her calm reception of his news disconcerted Charles.

"Does the prospect of his taking such a journey not worry you?" Anne replied simply, "Worry? Of course. But what can I do? He will do as he thinks best. For some years, he has limited his travel, partly because of the wars but also to be with us after our mother died. We are all adults now and England is not at war so he is at liberty to make such a journey if he chooses. I hope it does not become necessary."

"And his desire to see us marry as soon as possible?" Anne did not speak for several minutes. "He has looked forward to my marriage since I reached my eighteenth year. I understand that he would be reluctant to depart on such a journey if I remained a spinster. However, if I were uncertain or unwilling, I would not hesitate to request a delay." She suddenly smiled mischievously.

"Fortunately for his peace of mind, I am not unwilling if it satisfies you to wed so hurriedly. I would not have you pushed into a hasty marriage, especially knowing that he may not be required to make this journey. After all, it will be a few months before he can reasonably expect to receive any news."

Charles held her hand to his cheek and said, "I would marry you tomorrow if that were possible." Anne chuckled, then sobered. "Do you have a place for our marriage in mind? There is Grosvenor Chapel, of course. I have attended services there since we moved into this house. Or we could marry here. What are your thoughts?" "You shall choose the place, dearest. What I have been considering is what we will do after the wedding. I hope that, after our wedding, we can drive into Kent, so you can see the house. You may wish to change some things, have your rooms decorated differently. If this is practicable, I would have your father and, of course, Miss Crawford accompany us as the neighbourhood would be thin of company and I would like your father to see your home before he embarks on his travels. What think you of this plan?"

Eyes shining, Anne declared, "It seems perfect to me. But the weather.... It is so cold. Would that make the journey difficult?"

Charles shrugged. "It could create some difficulties. However, it is late in the month, and I hope that, by the time we have the licence, the weather will have turned more favourably. After all, it is not so cold as in December, and the journey is not terribly long; we should be able to accomplish it in two or three days." Anne thought. "What must we do to procure the licence, Charles?" He smiled.

"Your brother Robert and your father have already considered that. None of us being personally acquainted with the Archbishop of Canterbury, Robert thought to have the dean of the Cathedral write a letter attesting to your being of good standing in your parish in York. Once he has received that letter, Robert, your father and Lord Kidwell will accompany me to the Archbishop's office in Doctor's Commons to make the formal application, if you are agreeable, dearest." She smiled softly.

"It sounds perfect, my dear." She made a decision. "I believe we should be married here at home by Reverend Glen. I have attended Grosvenor Chapel regularly since we came to this house, and I am acquainted with him as he has delivered the services there occasionally. We can have our wedding breakfast immediately after the wedding. Does that sound agreeable?" Charles kissed her hand. "My love, I believe we have a plan."

Reluctantly, Charles rose to go. Anne walked him to the door. "Will I see you later?" she asked wistfully. "Yes, indeed. I will take dinner at Lord Kidwell's this evening, so will see you there. It is getting late, and I must go." He kissed her hand, then her cheek. She caught a glimpse of the clock as she turned away, and ran upstairs with a shriek. Fortunately, Ellen was ready for her. The bronze-green gown and all of its accompaniments lay ready, wash water steamed gently in the pitcher, and Ellen curtsied as Anne rushed into the room. "It is all right, Miss Emmons. You will be ready in no time." Anne stood as her maid unlaced, unhooked and helped her out of her clothes to wash, and helped her to slip into her petticoats. Anne donned a dressing gown, then seated herself at the dressing table.

Ellen took down her hair to give it a good brushing. Anne was lost in thought.

"I wonder when Robert wrote to the Dean and how long it will take to receive a reply. When will Lord and Lady FitzMaynard arrive with Grace? Would Mr. Hodgson object to the curate performing the wedding service? He is the vicar after all." She glanced up just as Ellen finished with her hair. Dressed with soft curls around her face and forehead, the rest was twisted high on the crown of her head with gold and bronze-green silk ribbons entwined. Behind the knot, Ellen had carefully placed a golden comb.

"Thank you, Ellen, that is perfect. The dress now." Turning to the mirror, Anne was very pleased with the glowing colour of the new gown, trimmed with the same gold and bronze-green ribbons as in her hair. She slipped the emerald earrings into her ears and clasped the chain with the emerald cross about her neck. Ellen smiled. "Miss, you look lovely." Anne blushed and thanked her. Once her *toilette* was complete, she put on her gloves, then gathered up her evening cloak and reticule, and ran lightly down the stairs to meet her father, brother and sister-in-law.

Once assembled at the Kidwell house, the laughing and chattering group took their seats around the table. Seating was informal, and Anne was pleased to find herself between Charles and Robert, with Fanny directly across from her seated next to Martin Burrell. The conversation flowed easily. Anne could not resist peeking at Charles out of the corner of her eye. He caught her glance, smiled, and then dropped his napkin. As he bent to pick it up, he grasped her hand under the table, squeezing gently. As he straightened, he let her go and winked. She was still looking at Charles, when Robert elbowed her inelegantly on her other side.

"My sweet sister, you could at least say 'Good evening', you know," he whispered with a grin. Aloud, he said, "Anne, my dear, how charming you look! I hope you've had a pleasant day." For a split second, she glared at her brother, and then had to laugh. "Good evening, Robert," she replied with exaggerated courtesy. "I thank you for the compliment. I had a lovely day, thank you. And you?" Robert was in a teasing humour and, with Diana on his other side, alternated his quizzing remarks to the two young women. Fanny smiled across the table. The conversation halted briefly as the footman poured wine, and Lord Kidwell rose to his feet. He beamed around the table.

"My dear friends! It is my great pleasure to see your faces at my table. Although intended as a quiet family dinner, this evening we celebrate. Not only are my young friends, Anne and Charles, soon to be married, we have another announcement to make. I am delighted to announce the engagement of my daughter Fanny to Mr. Martin Burrell. I give you a toast: to both of the happy couples!" Anne's cheeks flooded with colour as she clutched Charles's sleeve.

Her eyes went to Fanny's face across the table. Silver eyes aglow and cheeks blazing, Fanny looked at Martin as if he were the source of all joy. "When did this happen?" she asked. Fanny looked at her with a smiling face, and answered, "Today, dearest. Martin asked me this afternoon, and went straight to Father. It was after we returned home, so there was no time to tell you before. We decided that this would be the best way to let everyone hear our news. We can celebrate together." Robert and Diana broke in with their congratulations, and for a few moments everyone talked at once.

In the drawing room, Fanny and Anne sat together on a sofa, as they had done so often before. Fanny asked, "When do you and Charles plan to marry, Anne?" "Soon," she replied. "Charles will apply for a special licence, and then we will be married at home." She paused thoughtfully. "I think in the morning room. That room is so fresh and cheerful; then we can go straight to the wedding breakfast in the dining room. What about you and Martin, Fanny? Although I was not surprised that you and Martin wanted to marry – you *have* smelt of April and May for weeks now," she teased, "I did not know he was going to ask you so soon." Fanny sobered.

"It will be a while, I am afraid. Martin and Father discussed the settlements, and there are matters still to be resolved. Also Martin wants to be more certain of his position. His finances are comfortable, but he has no desire to be thought a fortune-hunter. So we are considering a summer wedding, at home in Kent." She squeezed Anne's hand. "You will be a near neighbour, dearest. You can help Mother and me plan the arrangements." She laughed.

"Father is delighted, of course. He likes Martin very much, and respects him, too. He says Martin feels just as he ought." The two put their heads together to discuss these interesting plans further, whilst Lady Kidwell drew Diana out across the room. When the gentlemen joined them, another toast was offered, and more laughter and conversation rang out.

Chapter 36

The next day, Anne received a letter from Grace Worthington saying that she would accompany Lord and Lady FitzMaynard to their Berkley Square home, and they expected to arrive the next week. *"The trip is likely to take several days, as the weather has been so cold and there was rain which has turned to ice. Lord FitzMaynard has planned our journey carefully for our comfort. The coach with servants and luggage left this morning, and we leave tomorrow if the weather is tolerable. We are in York at this present, as my cousin had a final fitting, and some last shopping to do. We should be there within a sennight if the weather is tolerable, from what he tells me."* Consulting her calendar and the date of Grace's letter, Anne tentatively selected a Friday ten days after Grace's expected arrival date for a dinner party.

"I want to allow them time to arrive, get settled and rested. Travel at this time of year is not particularly pleasant." Gathering Grace's letter, the notes she had made for her party and the calendar, she went to her father's library. To her surprise, Robert was with him, and they were both looking at a letter. "Ah, just whom we want. Anne, the letter from the dean has come. He sent it Express, so it arrived sooner than I expected." Errand forgotten, Anne was startled. She swallowed and whispered, "What did he say?" Robert came around the desk, letter in hand.

"It covers everything we wished. He indicates you are a member of the Church of England, known to him and, most importantly, free to marry. An excellent introduction to the Archbishop of Canterbury." Anne smiled. "So this means the application for the licence can go forward?" Mr. Emmons leaned forward. "Indeed, it can, my dear. I will confer with Charles and Lord Kidwell to establish the earliest convenient time to visit the Archbishop's offices in Doctor's Commons. And what of you, my dear? You've dropped some papers; did you have something you wished to discuss?"

Anne stooped and gathered her notes and the letter. "Yes, Father. Grace writes that she and Lord and Lady FitzMaynard are on their way to London, assuming they left when they intended. I thought to schedule the dinner party for a Friday about two or three weeks from now. Do you have a preference?" Mr. Emmons looked at her in some astonishment. "Two or three weeks? Will that not complicate your plans?" Anne was puzzled for a moment.

"Plans? Oh, you mean for our wedding? No indeed, Father. I have already planned the dinner; it needs only a date, and it is not to be a formal affair. I thought to have our wedding quietly here at home on a Saturday morning, depending on Reverend Glen's schedule. We can have the wedding breakfast here, immediately after. We do not yet have the licence, nor has Charles spoken to Mr. Glen. I thought to have the dinner for Grace before Charles and I marry. I would like to hold it before her first visit to Almack's. Lady Jersey has promised vouchers for her, and assured me that Fanny and I will also receive vouchers so we can be present." She smiled reassuringly.

"Mrs. Russell and Mrs. Clay will manage beautifully, you may be certain." Anne handed her father her guest list for the dinner. "As you see, Father, it will be a manageable party. I have thirteen guests here; do either of you," looking from her father to Robert, "have a suggestion? Even numbers do balance well." Mr. Emmons suggested, "Why not discuss this with Miss Crawford?" Anne was a bit surprised but, after a moment's thought, concurred. "What an excellent idea." Leaving the room, she saw Mr. Turner crossing the hall with measured tread. "Mr. Turner, is Miss Crawford in?" He turned. "Yes, Miss Emmons, I believe she is in her chamber." Anne nodded. "Thank you."

She ran lightly up the stairs and down the hall. Tapping lightly, she said, "Amelia? Are you there?" She heard Miss Crawford's "Come in," and entered. Miss Crawford was seated by the window, perusing a letter. She folded it, and rose. "My dear Miss Anne, pray come in. Won't you be seated?" gesturing to the chair opposite. "Thank you. It seems an age since we've had talked." Miss Crawford smiled. "My dear, you have been very busy." Anne patted her hand affectionately. "You have been quite occupied yourself."

Miss Crawford nodded. "Very true. As you may know, I have gone to several meetings of the Antiquarian Society with Mrs. Smythers. She and I were at school together, and both became educationists. Whereas I went into it young, Mrs. Smythers became a teacher as a widow. A distant cousin inherited the bulk of her husband's estate, leaving her a house in a respectable neighbourhood here in London, and a small sum of money. Being reluctant to hang on a stranger's sleeve, she decided to open a school for girls." Intrigued, Anne leaned forward.

"A school? How ambitious! Who are her pupils?" Pleased at her interest, Miss Crawford continued. "The house is quite large, fortunately. She has ten girls, daughters of well-to-do merchants who want their daughters to know how to behave as ladies, yet to be well enough educated to have practical abilities as well. Several are from industrial cities. They all live in, so she also has a significant staff. It is quite an establishment; she has four teachers and an assistant living in, as well as instructors and masters who come in. She has been successful in her venture."

"How does she select her pupils?" Miss Crawford smiled. "She began with advertisements in certain newspapers. Now she relies on word of mouth." Anne asked, "But how do you two manage to attend meetings? Isn't the Antiquarian Society a club for men?" Miss

Crawford rose to adjust the drapery. "Indeed, the members are men; however, women are allowed as guests. Mrs. Smythers is distantly connected to a fellow, who has been kind enough to sponsor us. But you had something to discuss with me, did you not?"

Anne nodded. "Indeed. I am planning a dinner for Miss Worthington, to be held in a week or so. At this present, I have thirteen of us at table. Do you think Mrs. Smythers, would care to join us?" Surprised, Miss Crawford replied, "Why...I have no idea, but I can certainly enquire." Anne was pleased. "Please do so. I will let you know the exact date as soon as possible. Amelia, I was thinking of visiting the British Museum tomorrow afternoon. I hope the weather is more pleasant. If you would care to join me, it would be splendid. It is much more enjoyable with someone who shares one's interest."

"My dear Miss Anne, I am always at your disposal." The two women sat quietly for a moment, comfortably at ease. Looking up, Anne asked, "Amelia, after the wedding, Charles wants to take me to Mount Place in Kent for a few weeks. He has suggested that you accompany us, and I do hope you will." She glanced at Miss Crawford fleetingly. "My father will accompany us as well, if his business permits, but I would be more comfortable with a female companion. I know that such would generally be one's mother or sister; you have always filled that place in my life." She rose to gaze out the window. "I know many things will change after my marriage, but I would like to retain your company, if possible." She turned.

"I am aware you have resources and you may have made other plans. However, I hope you will consider what I have said." Miss Crawford rose, eyes glistening with unaccustomed tears. "My dear girl, I am deeply touched. I confess I have been giving the inevitable changes some thought. I will be delighted to visit your new home with you." Impulsively, Anne embraced her former governess.

"Thank you so very much, Amelia! Your support will make it less... less... *daunting*. I will be taking on new responsibilities amongst strangers. Whilst I am confident I can learn Robert's tastes and the management of the household, having a friend at my back will make it a bit easier." She turned to the door. "I will go down. I must have a word with Father." She went to her own sitting room, to leave her notes on the desk, then headed down to the library once more.

"Father," she began as she opened the door, "I've invited Amelia and her friend Miss Smythers to join us, which still leaves us with an awkward mix. Both of them are guests at the Antiquarian Club from time to time, and I know you also attend there with Mr. Dent. Perhaps you could invite an acquaintance from the Club? It would make for some interesting conversation, and perhaps keep the focus slightly off of Grace at least initially." Her father laughed. "And what are Miss Worthington's interests, my dear?" Anne puckered her forehead.

"She enjoys gardens, music, and reading. A group of us met to discuss some new novels and women writers. She plays the pianoforte beautifully." Her father nodded. "Excellent. I can see that this will be a lively evening." Anne laughed and closed the door. She glanced at the tall clock on her way to the drawing room. Plenty of time, there was over an hour before it would be time to change. She directed a passing maid to bring tea to the drawing room, and breathed a sigh of pleasure when she saw the bright fire burning. Taking her favourite chair, she gazed at the leaping flames. The maid brought the tea and set it on the table at hand. "Thank you." The maid slipped from the room. As the door drifted closed, she could hear the sound of the knocker.

Anne poured out a cup of tea. Just as she reached out for her book, Turner opened the door. Bowing slightly, he presented her with a card on his silver tray. Brows slightly raised, she met his eyes as she took the card. "Who is it, Turner?" she enquired. "I am not expecting anyone."

"No, miss. She gave her name as Mrs. Ware." Glancing at the

card, she saw the full name "*Mrs. Reuben Ware*" in a rather elaborate script. Rather mystified, she turned it over to see a pencilled note, "Louisa Ware, from Selby". Recalling the small village south of York, she said, "Show her in, Turner, and please have an extra cup brought in." He bowed slightly, and said, "Yes, Miss Emmons."

A few minutes later, a tall, slender woman entered the room. Anne rose; as the woman curtsied, Anne recognised her. To her shock and dismay, she discovered her visitor to be none other than the former Louisa Dixon, now Mrs. Reuben Ware. Anne stood rooted in surprise, as Mrs. Ware approached. Holding out her hand, Mrs. Ware said, "Miss Emmons, it is good of you to receive me." Anne drew a breath.

"Mrs. Ware. What a surprise. Won't you please be seated?" The maid slipped in with the cup and set it neatly near the teapot. Gratefully, Anne lifted the teapot. "Won't you have some tea?" Mrs. Ware nodded. "Thank you very much. I would love some. It is bitter cold today." Anne poured, and passed the cup, then picked up her own. An awkward silence grew as the two ladies sipped. Finally, Anne placed her cup on the table and said formally, "I must congratulate you on your marriage, Mrs. Ware. I hope you are very happy." Mrs. Ware flushed an unbecoming scarlet.

"You are generous, ma'am. As I recall, I was ... somewhat less than gracious when last we met." Anne lowered her eyes and said nothing. With difficulty, Mrs. Ware continued, "I was jealous, you see. I realise that is no excuse, and I do not expect you to forgive me. When my sister returned from Littlebrook House and told me what had happened, I was mortified. My thoughtless words and poor behaviour caused her to disgrace herself. She will spend the rest of the winter and spring with me in York, as my aunt has decided to delay her season."

Anne looked up. "Your sister chose to say those things, Mrs. Ware. She was old enough to know better." Desperately uncomfortable, Anne leaned back in her chair. "Mrs. Ware, let us be direct. You have called here today to see me. May I know why?" Mrs. Ware shifted in her seat.

"As you may know, my husband and I live in Selby. He has business interests in York and in Leeds." Now scarlet with embarrassment, she looked raptly at the hands she had folded in her lap. "I did not realise, when I married my husband, that he had business connexions in those cities." "Ah," Anne thought, "now I understand." Mrs. Ware rose and stood by the fire; she gazed into the flames for a moment, then turned to face Anne. "I do not wish my, and my sister's, poor conduct to jeopardise his business. I wanted to approach you myself, to apologise." Anne rose.

"My father does not discuss business matters with me, and I have no influence with him regarding those matters. If you are asking me if I told him about our past ... unfriendliness, I have not. However, other people heard you, and your sister, say unkind things to me and about me. Fanny and Lady Kidwell know about the tensions between us; Mr. Deschevaux told me he had heard you say malicious things about others. I cannot say whether my father knew at the time, or what he may know today. However, it is long ago and unimportant now. I do not intend to discuss our conversation today with my father, and would have no reason to bring up the past. You need not fear me." She turned to the door, opened it, and turned back to Mrs. Ware.

"I thank you for calling, and wish you well in your marriage, Mrs. Ware." Left with no choice, Mrs. Ware gathered her things and turned to leave. "Thank you for receiving me, Miss Emmons. Dare I hope I will see you in York one day?" Looking at Mrs. Ware coolly, Anne replied, "It is, of course, possible. However, I am soon to be married and will spend most of my time elsewhere." Mrs. Ware nodded. Both ladies bowed slightly, and the footman escorted Mrs. Ware to the door. Anne leaned on the door, and breathed deeply. After a few moments, she made her escape for her dressing room.

Soaking a cloth in water, Anne pressed it to her face. Louisa

Dixon, calling on her after all this time, was a complete surprise. Anne sat down and considered the brief interview. To her surprise, she felt nothing but a slight pity for Louisa. "I know my father would never be so unjust as to blame Mr. Ware for the childish malice of Louisa and her sister. If he asks me about it, I will make little of it, especially since we will be distantly connected by marriage. Poor Louisa, on tenterhooks regarding her husband, and having to take a disappointed and disgraced Maria in tow. It will be a difficult time for them both. Apparently news of my engagement to Charles has not reached her. Mrs. Eastland must be displeased with her and her sister." Unable to prevent a slight smile, she smoothed her hair and nodded to herself.

She returned downstairs to recover her book, and left instructions to have her dinner on a tray in her sitting room that night. "Robert and Diana are dining out again, and Father is meeting someone at his club. I will wear my new quilted satin dressing gown and slippers, relax by the fire, and read."

Chapter 37

The next several days flew past. Lord and Lady FitzMaynard, with Grace in tow, arrived at their house in Berkley Square without incident. The dinner in Grace's honour was delicious, as expected, and surprisingly lively. Mr. Dent, whose wife was still in the country, was delighted to accept and brought with him an unexceptionable young man named John Grant whose uncle was a fellow member in the Roxburghe Club.

Conversation focused on books and reading at dinner; afterwards, Grace entertained the company in the drawing room with her superb playing. Mr. Grant's father not only collected books but music, and young John Grant keenly appreciated Grace's skill on the pianoforte. The evening went very late indeed as the two played and sang, sometimes singly and sometimes in duet.

Anne had no opportunity to chat privately with Grace but, as the guests departed, Grace pressed her hand. "Thank you a thousand times! It was a delightful evening, and everyone so kind. It was thoughtful of you to plan this for me." "I am happy it was agreeable. I have always found a private gathering of friends to be much more comfortable." Hastily making plans to see each other soon, Grace departed with her aunt and uncle. Fanny and Mr. Burrell with Lord and Lady Kidwell were the next to make their departures. Miss Crawford and her friend Mrs. Smythers were engaged in conversation near the drawing room fire, leaving Diana and Anne free to chat.

"It was a splendid dinner, Anne. Mrs. Clay truly exceeded herself tonight."

"Indeed she did. Everything was delightful. Grace seemed to enjoy herself as much as I had hoped. Renewing her acquaintance with Fanny and her parents and with me, and meeting additional pleasant companions will give her a small base of support. That is important, I think. One's friends and connexions can be a...a bulwark when out in society." Diana's brows lifted. "A bulwark?" Anne nodded.

"When one is new, it can be difficult. Some may be envious of appearance or money; others resent a newcomer claiming a place in what is a rather closed society. Such people can be unkind or even actively malicious. Having friends to support one gives a great deal of comfort, and helps one to build a little confidence."

"If that is so, you have given Grace a good start," responded Diana. Just then, Robert, Charles and Mr. Emmons entered with Mr. Dent and Mr. Grant in tow.

"Dent and Grant are taking their leave, but wanted to pay their respects first," Mr. Emmons announced. Anne and Diana rose, and the two gentlemen bowed. "Miss Emmons, thank you for a lovely evening. I cannot remember a more congenial party." She gave her hand to both gentlemen. "Thank you, Mr. Dent. We were delighted you could come."

She turned to Mr. Grant and said, "I am so pleased we had this opportunity to meet you, Mr. Grant. Thank you for coming." He bowed slightly, face flushed. "It was an honour to be included, Miss Emmons. I am most grateful."

As the gentlemen left the room, Anne and Diana resumed their seats. Mrs. Smythers rose. "A most elegant evening. Excellent conversation and Miss Worthington is an exceptionally talented musician. She will put some noses out of joint this season, I'll warrant." Miss Crawford stood beside her. Mrs. Smythers turned to her. "I must take my leave, my dear. I asked the carriage to return for me, and I have kept them waiting long enough." She curtsied slightly to Anne and Diana who curtsied back.

"I thank you for inviting me this evening, Miss Emmons. It was most kind in you." Anne smiled. "It is I who must thank you, Mrs. Smythers. We enjoyed having you with us very much, and hope you will join us again." On a wave of pleasantries, Mrs. Smythers made her departure. Mr. Emmons, with Robert and Charles, returned to the drawing room. Miss Crawford murmured her good night and slipped quietly from the room.

Charles seated himself next to Anne, while Robert leaned over the back of Diana's chair. Mr. Emmons stood on the hearthrug, Looking at Anne, he said, "Well, my dear, an excellent evening. Well done!" Anne smiled and blushed. "I am glad you are pleased, sir." Charles squeezed Anne's hand and said, "I see I shall acquire a charming hostess and skilled housewife, when we marry."

"Speaking of marriage, have you given Anne the news?" asked Robert. "News?" Anne looked at Charles enquiringly. "Yes, my dear. We have our licence. We can now make our plans in earnest." "Oh, Charles!" Anne threw her arms around his neck, then retreated, crimson with embarrassment. "No need to colour up, my dear," her father said indulgently. "Do you have a day in mind?" Anne thought. "Today is Thursday. Wednesday next is when Grace will make her first appearance at Almack's. Would the Saturday following be too soon?" she asked.

"Not for me," replied Charles ardently. Diana remonstrated, "Anne, are you sure you can be ready so soon?" Anne laughed. "My dear, I have been making lists since Charles asked me to marry him. I have my gown, the morning room has been decorated and will be perfect for the wedding. I have planned what to serve, and a list of guests to invite to the wedding breakfast." She looked at the group around her.

"I hope a small and intimate gathering will be agreeable, as I would like to share this with my dearest friends and family."

She looked at Robert, and said, "The only thing remaining is the celebrant. Is this sufficient time to ask Mr. Glen? Do you think such short notice will offend him?" Robert smiled. "As it happens, I took the liberty of speaking to the rector and to Mr. Glen. The rector is agreeable, and Mr. Glen has expressed his willingness. It remains only to confirm the day, which I will be happy to do tomorrow."

Mr. Emmons had listened intently. "What a well-organised family I have. It seems all is arranged, and with little fuss." He rubbed his hands together. "I must say, my dear, I am looking forward to this, and will take care of planning the journey into Kent. Let us say, we set our departure for the Monday following the wedding. How does that sound?" Anne looked at her father, her brother and her *fiancé*. All were smiling at her benevolently.

She began to laugh. "Well-organised, indeed, Father. Somehow I feel sure you have already made all the plans necessary, and were just waiting for a date to put them forward. I do know your ways, sir." She looked around. "Diana, what do you think?"

Composedly, Diana responded, "I think it makes perfect sense. You have your gown, and plenty of clothes. Until you see your new home, there is no sense to try to procure goods or furnishings. Many of your friends are in town, so will be able to share your joy. I see no reason to delay further."

Anne sobered. "I shall miss Jane, as well as Kate and Emily. I think, however, it would be impossible to set a date that would be convenient for everyone." Mr. Emmons took over. "It is agreed then. Saturday next at, say, half past ten o'clock in the morning." He then called for some champagne, and a toast was drunk to celebrate.

The next morning, Mr. Emmons sent for Anne to see him in the library. "And ask her to bring her lists. She'll know what I mean." A short time later, Anne presented herself, lists in hand. "I am sorry to keep you waiting, sir, but I was not yet dressed. You wanted to see me?" "Yes, my dear. With your wedding so near, I wanted to know your plans." Anne consulted her list. "Of course, Father. Charles told me he had asked an old friend, a Mr. Waycott, from Devonshire to support him. I am torn between asking Fanny and asking Diana." Mr. Emmons sat back in his chair.

"I understand your dilemma. You have been friends with both for many years. However, in this instance, I think you may safely ask whichever you wish. Your friends both hold you in great affection and would not hold such a decision against you. You may also recall that Diana has the greatest dislike of being brought forward in company."

With some relief, Anne said, "That is true. I will ask Fanny today, and I will let Diana know personally. For the wedding itself, I want to keep it very intimate. Diana and Robert, Miss Crawford, Lord and Lady Kidwell. I had thought about asking Lady Jersey, but will not presume. I asked Charles if he had anyone else he would like to invite in addition to Mr. Waycott but he does not. He has a sort of cousin, who lives in Canterbury, but they have never been close, and he has little communication with him. His godmother, who left him the property in Devon, died many years ago. It is rather sad, I think." She looked at her father.

"I think you, Miss Crawford, Robert and Diana, Lord and Lady Kidwell, Fanny and Mr. Burrell, Charles and me would be perfect. Do you agree?" He nodded. "Indeed, my dear, I don't think it could be better. What about the breakfast afterwards?" She pulled out her lists again.

"I thought to invite more friends to join us at half past eleven. I have planned a meal I think will suit. I wish to ask Grace, Lord and Lady FitzMaynard, Lady Jersey and Lord Jersey if he cares to come. Diana's aunt and uncle are on their way to London, expected any day, so I planned to send a card-Diana knows where they will be staying. Lady Kidwell's friend Mrs. Eastland and her husband are in town and she asked me to include them. Since they are Charles' connexions as well, I see no difficulty. Robert also wanted me to invite Mr. Taylor and his wife. Can you think of anyone else, sir?" He nodded.

"My friend Dent is at something of a loose end at this present, as is his young friend Mr. Grant. I know Mr. Grant is a stranger among us, but Dent and I have been acquainted for some years. He is also well known to Lady Jersey. It would be a kindness to include them." Anne nodded slowly, remembering Grace at the piano looking up at Mr. Grant. "Do you know anything about Mr. Grant, Father?" He shrugged.

"He is from Preston, in Lancashire. A well-connected family, from what I understand. He has a small estate just outside the town. His father made money investing in shipping and cloth mills. They are comfortably well off. His father was never one for coming to London, but the family is approved in the area, and in Lancaster. Young Grant went to university in Edinburgh, and did quite well there according to Dent. His interests in history and music brought him to London, of course." Anne thought, then said, "Certainly, Father, we will include them. I will send cards today."

"Breakfast for twenty-four," thought Anne. She pulled out the list she had prepared. "Baked eggs, a ham, sliced cheeses, bread, chocolate, tea and coffee are a good start. I hope Mrs. Clay still has a few jars of apricot marmalade put by; hers is so delicious. Some stewed pears, I think. Mrs. Clay's spiced buns are very nice. I believe I will order Tomlin's *Oranges en Ruben* jellies; they are so beautiful. Maybe some lemon cheesecakes for Charles. A curd tart and a cake will round it out nicely. I'm sure Mrs. Clay will have some suggestions." She picked up her notes, and went down the stairs.

As she crossed the hall, she changed course and went into the dining room. She was pleased with the look of the room. With its pale blue walls and deep blue velvet draperies, it was elegantly appointed. She surveyed the mahogany table appraisingly. With all of its leaves in, it could seat sixteen people. Her eyes fell on the two small tables at either end of the dining room. If the long table were moved, the two smaller tables could be placed as well, seating eight comfortably. She mused, "If all of those invited accept, Robert and Diana, Fanny and Mr. Burrell, Lord and Lady Kidwell, and Charles and I can sit there. Everyone else can be seated at the main table."

She made a note to discuss the possibility of removing a sideboard to clear more space with Mrs. Russell. She passed on to the kitchen where she found Mrs. Clay perusing the next day's bills of fare. Glancing up, she stood hastily to her feet. "Bless me, Miss Anne. You should have sent for me. No need to come all this way down to the kitchen." Anne smiled affectionately.

"I wanted to talk to you about our wedding breakfast. Mr. Deschevaux and I are marrying here at home on Saturday week and will have our breakfast here." Handing over her list, she watched Mrs. Clay settle her spectacles on her nose. Nodding as she went, Mrs. Clay commented, "This is nicely planned, Miss Anne. There is one thing, though. The cake." Anne said, "The marchpane cake? You know how fond Father and Robert are...."

Mrs. Clay interrupted, "I do, and none better. But this celebration is a wedding and a proper wedding cake is what you should have. I baked the layers as soon as I heard that Mr. Deschevaux was courting you, and they have been mellowing ever since. I know your tastes, Miss Anne, and I made sure to leave out the fruits you don't much like, and put in extra of the fruits you do. Instead of a marchpane cake, you will have a bride cake and that is that." She nodded emphatically. Anne nodded meekly and smiled. "Thank you, Mrs. Clay, I know it will be delicious. So I will consider the bill of fare for this breakfast settled."

That matter resolved, she went up to her sitting room and sat down at her desk. She wrote her cards of invitation quickly, addressed each except for the one destined for Mr. and Mrs. Farleigh, and took the stack downstairs. Beckoning to Mr. Turner, she said, "Turner, please have a footman deliver these this afternoon." Blushing, she added, "They are invitations to my wedding breakfast, so it is important that he deliver them as promptly as possible."

Turner bowed and said indulgently, "I will attend to it immediately, ma'am." Anne returned upstairs and wrote notes to Fanny, Lord and Lady Kidwell, and Mr. Burrell, and went back downstairs with them. After a moment's indecision, she went to the morning room. As always, its cheerful colours brightened her spirits. She found Diana sitting by the fire, reading.

"Sister!" she exclaimed. "I did not expect to find you here, and I am so glad to see you." Diana looked up and said with a smile, "I do love this room. It feels so warm and sunny. I am glad you are being married here." Anne sat down opposite Diana. "I have wanted to speak with you about the wedding." Diana nodded. Looking directly at Anne, she asked, "Who do you wish to attend you, Anne?" She was taken aback by Diana's forthright question. "It is difficult...."

Before she could continue, Diana interjected, "You and I have been friends for some years. We have shared interests, and I have the honour to be married to your brother. You and Fanny, however, have been intimate friends since you were little more than children. You have shared so many things. It would not hurt my feelings or offend me, should you choose Fanny to attend you on your wedding day. My dear sister, you must choose to please yourself. It is your day, after all."

Anne looked at Diana searchingly, and said, "My dear, you are all that is generous and good. Thank you for being so gracious, and so open with me." They smiled at each other, and soon were deep into a discussion of the plans for the wedding breakfast and the journey to Kent the next week.

Chapter 38

The week flew by. Mrs. Russell indulged in a flurry of rearranging the dining room and the morning room to be sure each room had sufficient seats for the events to come. Fanny was delighted to be Anne's attendant (and that Anne had invited Mr. Burrell). To Anne's secret surprise, all the invitations to the wedding breakfast were accepted, even by Lord and Lady Jersey. Anne continued to write her novel, but made little real progress with all of the distractions resulting from her up-coming wedding. One afternoon, she encountered her father in the entry, just returning from a meeting. "Father, may I speak to you for a moment?" He looked surprised.

"Of course, my dear. I am at your disposal. Come to the library where we can be comfortable." Seated across from him at his desk, Anne asked, "Father, I just realised that you have never returned my article or the letter I wrote to Mr. Ackermann. Have you not had time to read it?" He nodded.

"Indeed I have, daughter. I thought the article was excellent. I was pleased that you had made several of the changes suggested. I am proud you could accept such guidance." Surprised, Anne asked, "If you have read it, why have you not returned it? I would like to send it for Mr. Chamberlayne's consideration...." Mr. Emmons leaned back in his chair, clearly pleased with himself.

"No need to concern yourself, dear child. I took it to Ackermann myself, and we discussed it. He was quite impressed with it. However, he felt it would appear to better advantage as a pamphlet. I showed it to Mr. Smith at the British Museum, and he also felt that the article would make an excellent pamphlet. So I wrote to Chamberlayne. He has arranged for the printing, and they will be placed on the shelf in his shop, near Mr. Cave's book. A similar arrangement is being made in here in London, with Mr. Smith's input." Anne sat still, lips parted, all colour fled from her cheeks. "You...took it to Ackermann's? Without a word to me?" she whispered. "Why, yes, my dear. I thought that was what you wanted."

She stared at him in shock. "Father, I wanted to you read the article and the letter, and give me your opinion. I had not yet decided...." He smiled. "And that is why I took it to Mr. Ackermann myself. I am glad to have had the chance to meet him. A most interesting man." Looking at her closely, he said in concern, "My dear, are you all right? You are quite pale." Anne controlled herself, nails digging into her palms.

"Father, I appreciate your desire to help me. I wanted to decide for myself what would happen to my work. To have it taken out of my hands like this, with no discussion...." She rose and walked to the door. Looking back, she asked him, "Will you at least tell me if my name is to appear on the pamphlet?" Mr. Emmons, puzzled, responded, "No, my dear, you had indicated that you would not wish it. However, your initials will appear. It will say 'by A.E.'" She pulled open the door.

"Pray, excuse me, Father. I must go to my room. I have some work waiting for me." She had almost made her escape, when her father said, "My dear, you seem upset. Is there something wrong?" She turned slowly. "Something wrong? I am unhappy and feel somewhat betrayed that you took my work, without my knowledge or consent, and made such arrangements. I am not a child, Father. I cannot help but feel you would not have taken these steps if Matthew or Robert had asked for your opinion on such a matter. I realise a lady seldom conducts business for herself; she should, however, be consulted and informed. I appreciate your desire to protect me and to give me your guidance. I am sure the arrangements you have made are excellent. I just wish I had been included in the decision."

Turning away, she closed the door behind her and went quietly up the stairs. Sitting in her chair at her desk, she pulled out the notes for her novel but was too disquieted to concentrate. "I suppose I should be grateful. My writing is, or will be, printed and placed where people may read it. My father and Mr. Ackermann seem to consider it worthy of being published, and Mr. Chamberlayne is the person I would have chosen for such an endeavour. Yet I feel as if they stole something from me. I should have been consulted. Am I wrong to feel as I do? Am I being childish?" She rose and walked to the window. She gazed out, absently noting the gathering clouds.

"It is out of my hands so there is no point in being unhappy. I must endeavour to put this behind me, work on my novel, and prepare for the wedding." Resolving that any decision made on her future works would be hers alone, she turned back to her chair and picked up her notes. She read through them, making some changes. She was writing busily, when she heard her father at the door. "May I speak to you, Anne?" Reluctantly, she put down her pen and rose. "Of course, Father. Please come in."

They sat before the fire silently for several moments. Abruptly, Mr. Emmons said, "I have considered what you said. I must acknowledge that it did not occur to me to discuss the matter with you." He smiled slightly. "I still think of you as my little girl, you see. Even though you will soon be married, in my mind you are still a timid school girl, needing my direction. I meant it for the best." Anne smiled back reluctantly. "I realise that, Father. I know you meant to be helpful." He winced.

"That stings. Does it help matters if I say I will not make that mistake again? Even though you may show your future efforts to your husband first, I hope you will still come to me. I am very proud of you, you know. You remind me very much of your mother."

She looked at him curiously. "In what way, sir? I know I resemble her somewhat, but remember nothing about her. Neither you nor my brothers speak of her; sadly, I have no memories of her." Mr. Emmons nodded.

"I am aware. Your brothers and I were much grieved, and, by the time you were of an age to understand, I was reluctant to talk about your mother; the memories were still painful. Your brothers were away much of the time, and, when home, were too busy to discuss the past. I do not know if they ever talked to each other about her." He paused, gazing into the fire. "Your mother loved to read, and she also liked to write. She wrote stories for the boys, as well as poetry. She also wrote essays about anything that interested her." He looked at Anne with a teasing light in his eyes.

"Like you, she was not very inclined to music. She enjoyed listening to music and she loved to dance, but disliked having to practice. She had had lessons on the harp and the fortepiano, but seldom played after we married." Mr. Emmons paused and took a sip of tea. "I took everything I could find of her writing and had volumes printed. I wanted you and your brothers share them with your children. I regret did not give them to your Aunt Janet, or to Miss Crawford, to read to you; I was afraid you would ask questions that I would find too painful." He smiled slightly.

"You did not seem to need them; you made up your own stories. I gave your brothers their copies when they married; I believe Lydia reads the stories to little Walter now. Your love of reading and your talent for writing remind me very much of your mother, as does your diffidence and preference for old friends to new society." He studied his cup for a moment.

"It was for your mother's pleasure that I began to accumulate a significant library. I believe it was the only thing she missed from her family's home. She was happiest at home with her children, managing the household and able to indulge in her reading and writing to her heart's content. During the marriage negotiation, her father warned mine about her 'bookish' tendencies as if they were a defect. When we were first married, she made me promise that, if we had a daughter, she would be as well educated as a son. I should have engaged masters to teach you Latin and Greek, as well as sending you to school. I may have failed her in that." He sighed.

"You inherited your colouring and your facial features from her. However, when you look up from a book because you are considering an idea or a phrase, there is a look in your eyes.... That is when I see her the most." Anne did not know whether to smile or weep. She had missed so much. However, the idea of having a volume of her mother's writings....

"Dear sir, pray do not distress yourself. I could wish that your or someone had read my mother's stories to me as a child. But to read her writings now...that is a gift I did not expect. I look forward to receiving them, Father. I am sorry to bring you pain, but I have often wondered about her, and why you never spoke of her. I will be so pleased to have a copy of her work."

Mr. Emmons patted her hand. "It was selfish of me. I have not spoken of my dear Caroline for many years." He suddenly looked in her eyes. "It pleases me that you and Charles have developed an affection for each other. You always feared that I meant to arrange a marriage for you, regardless of attachment. It is true I hoped you would marry someone of status in the world. However, I never desired you to marry someone for whom you had no regard." Mr. Emmons paused.

"Our marriage was arranged by our fathers. Her family was one of an impoverished branch of a notable family in Durham. My father and hers struck a acceptable settlement—money in exchange for a daughter of suitable pedigree. Caroline and I were introduced two weeks before the marriage. I thought her ... resigned, as I was. I had no attachment, and thought she would do as well as any young lady. I did not know until our wedding night that she was frightened and angry. It made the first weeks of our marriage very difficult indeed." He sighed.

"I like to think that, had I known her feelings, I would have pressed for a delay in our marriage, so we could get to know each other. It took time, but we managed to develop a friendship that grew into a deep devotion. I believe she would be pleased with your betrothal, as you have known Charles for some time, have much in common, and enjoy each other's company."

Mr. Emmons rose. "Forgive me, my dear. I have some letters to write." He smiled. "I sent for some of your mother's things, which I had stored for you some years ago. Her writings are included, and I believe you will enjoy some of the other objects as well." Anne also rose, and stood on tiptoe to kiss his cheek. "Thank you, Father." She watched him leave the room. Turning back, she resumed her seat at her desk. She picked up her pen, but sat gazing into space, pondering what her father had told her.

"I wonder what she wrote. He mentioned other things. Perhaps some of her favourite books.... One can tell a great deal about a person considering his or her choice of books". She glanced at her pen and realised the ink had dried. Dipping it again, she turned her attention to her notes. Absorbed, she wrote on, until the clock struck. Startled, she looked up and was astonished at the time. A discreet sound at the door alerted her that Ellen was waiting for her. She put down her pen and rose. Ellen came into the room with several notes in her hand.

"These have been delivered for you, ma'am. I thought you would wish to see them immediately." "Thank you, Ellen. That was very thoughtful of you." She sat down again, and began to glance through them. A note from Fanny asking her to call the next day; acceptances to the wedding breakfast from Lord and Lady Jersey and Lord and Lady FitzMaynard and Grace; affectionate congratulations from Emily and Jane. She penned a hasty reply to Fanny, and put the others aside. "Please give this to Mr. Turner so it can be delivered this evening. Is it time for me to dress for dinner? I believe we dine early this evening."

"Yes, ma'am. Mrs. Russell asked me to remind you that dinner is at six o'clock tonight, as the Master has an evening appointment. I believe Mr. and Mrs. Robert are dining in this evening." Ellen shot a glance at Anne. "Will Mr. Deschevaux be dining this evening?" Anne smiled. "Yes, indeed. He, Miss Kidwell and Mr. Burrell, and Miss Crawford, of course, will join us at table."

Chapter 39

$\mathcal{A}$nne woke very early. It was not yet dawn; the darkness was lighter and the room shadowed. She rose to look out of her window. There were a few stars still visible and the sky appeared clear. She breathed a sigh of relief, as she so hoped the day would be clear for her wedding. She crossed to the fireplace and, after she stirred the embers, put a small piece of wood on the smouldering remnants.

Curling up in the chair near the fire, she mused about the day ahead. "I am fortunate," she thought. "I love him. I *like* him and enjoy his company. My family has a real regard for him. I never thought to be so deeply content. I will miss my father, my brothers and my friends, but we will visit them and they will visit us."

The room gradually lightened as the sun rose. She crossed to her dressing room, sat down before the mirror and began to brush her hair. "I have never lived in the country. Will Charles mind that I do not ride? I will learn if he wishes. I wonder if he has a pinery or succession house. I look forward to seeing his home. Will he allow me make changes?" Thinking of Mrs. Russell, she pondered, "I hope I get on with any servants in place. Thank goodness Amelia goes with me!" She heard Ellen's voice, and laid down her brush.

Ellen entered with maids bearing the bathing tub and buckets of hot water. Startled, Ellen dropped a quick curtsey. "Good morning, miss. I did not expect you to be awake yet. I thought to have your bath ready before the fire in here." She bustled to the fireplace and added an extra log while the maids set the tub in place and filled it. Just then, another maid entered with Anne's chocolate. She took a sip of the hot, sweet beverage as she pondered the morning's events.

It seemed like no time at all had passed when Anne found herself bathed, clad in new undergarments and stockings with a dressing gown flung round her shoulders, when another maid appeared with a tray. Although she knew she should eat something, she felt unable to face it. "Thank you, but I am not hungry. Please take that back to the kitchen." Miss Crawford appeared at the door. "My dear, you should eat a bite or two." Anne sighed.

"Amelia, in just a few hours, we will sit down to an enormous breakfast. I am too...discomposed to eat anything now." Miss Crawford smiled. "A perfectly normal state for a bride. However, you know your father has laid on champagne, and it would not do to go into the day on an empty stomach." Anne sighed again, and reached for a slice of toast. "I will try." Miss Crawford briskly came further into the room. "I did not come to bully you into eating," she said with a lurking twinkle in her eyes. "Miss Kidwell is come. She wanted to see if you needed assistance with dressing."

"Fanny, here? It is not yet eight o'clock." Miss Crawford's eyes twinkled even more. "Indeed. She told me she had thought of sending a note, but did not wish to disturb you if you were still sleeping." Anne rose from her chair, tied her dressing gown, and told the maid, "Please take the tray to my bedroom next to the fire, and fetch covers for Miss Kidwell and Miss Crawford, please."

"By all means, have Fanny come up and the three of us shall enjoy a morning gossip." She arranged the seating and a tea table comfortably, and sat down. She had not long to wait. Fanny bustled into the room. "I hope you do not mind, my love, but I could not keep away. After all, we have been friends for so long, we are nearly sisters." Anne laughed, and gestured at the loveseat next to her. "Please sit, dear. Will you have tea or chocolate, or would you prefer coffee?" Fanny asked for chocolate. "My mother told me I should not bother you so early, or to at least send a note first, but I did not care a rush for that. This is such a special day, and I am so happy for you!"

Diana entered, with her maid Eliza (who had proven quite satisfactory), saying, "We have come to help you dress, my dear sister." Diana seated herself near Miss Crawford. The three reminisced as Miss Crawford busied herself with some embroidery and Ellen quietly prepared Anne's *ensemble*. When all was ready, Anne rose.

"Please sit there comfortably. I can listen and talk from behind the screen." Ellen efficiently helped Anne into her petticoats, and then eased the gown over all. Anne stepped from behind the screen and took her seat at her dressing table. As Ellen brushed her hair, Anne's friends watched. Anne met Fanny's eyes in the glass and couldn't repress a smile.

"Come, you two. I sense a plot. What mischief have you planned?" Fanny laughed. "You know me too well. What gave it away?" Anne's eyes danced. "You have never been an early riser, my friend. Here before eight o'clock? And not in distress? You must be up to some kind of roguery!" Fanny and Diana exchanged glances. "Caught! I suppose we must share it now." Diana laughed and nodded, then went to the door. Eliza reappeared with a large bandbox, accompanied by a footman carrying a crate. Anne looked from Fanny to Diana. "What on earth....?"

Fanny had the footman prise off the lid of the crate. Anne knelt down and gently pulled away the packing. "Ohhhh," she breathed. Gently, she lifted out a cup. Creamy white china, gilt trim and delicately painted flowers. "How lovely!" she cried. Carefully replacing the cup, she rose to embrace Diana and Fanny. "A breakfast set, dearest. The colours seemed perfect for you, and the shape is not in just the common way." "I love it, and am so grateful you thought of me," said Anne. Fanny added, "There are sufficient covers for guests in the breakfast room, and *un petit déjeuner pour deux* to enjoy in private. We found the pattern at the Spode showroom, and thought it just the thing. You must open the bandbox now."

Anne seated herself, and Eliza carefully set the bandbox before her. Within, she found a collection of snowy table linens. With tears in her eyes, Anne lifted out napkins, delicately embroidered in white, an elegant damask cloth, suitable for a long table full of guests, and other linen cloths of various sizes. "It is too much," she stammered. "These are exquisite. How did you do it?" Diana clasped her hand. "Fanny's mother suggested a small warehouse in Cheapside. The merchant had just received a shipment of beautiful linens from Ireland. We had a wonderful time choosing for you, I assure you!"

Anne rose and hugged them both. "It will be delightful to have these beautiful things around me when Charles and I are in Kent. I look forward to your visits so we can enjoy them together. I am so very fortunate in my friends and my family. Thank you both." Just then, Ellen entered the room and said, "Miss Emmons, we must finish quickly. Time is passing." Anne turned to Fanny and Diana. "My dears, if you will wait for me downstairs, Ellen can finish me off and I will join you." As they left, Anne seated herself again at the dressing table.

Ellen pulled Anne's hair up into a high knot, and set in a gold comb set with pearls. She then picked out some soft tendrils around Anne's temples and ears. "That's very nice, Ellen. Thank you." Anne hooked a pair of dainty pearl earrings into her ears, and clasped a pearl necklace around her throat. Ellen said, "You look lovely, Miss." Impulsively, Anne turned to Ellen and said, "I do appreciate your help, Ellen. I am so glad you are going with me to Kent." The maid blushed. "I'm pleased you asked me, Miss. It will be an adventure." She thought a bit. "Miss, if you don't mind me asking, are you nervous, going to a house you've not seen?"

"As you said, it will be an adventure, Ellen, just as it was when we came to this house in London." Inwardly, she quaked as she thought of taking over the management of a new household amid strangers.

Unexpectedly, she heard her father's voice at her door. Surely it wasn't time yet! Her eyes flew to the clock as she called, "Come in, Father!" Eliza curtsied and withdrew as Mr. Emmons crossed the room. Patting her shoulder, he smiled down at Anne

"All right, my dear? Not nervous, I hope." She smiled and answered honestly, "I am a bit nervous, Father." He glanced at the clock. "We have a short time before we must go down. I just wanted to have a few moments, while you are still my daughter, before you become a man's wife." He hugged her briefly. "You look lovely, my dear. I am very proud of you today, and I know your mother would be as well." He handed her a small box and a book.

"Your mother's things were delivered today. I am sure you will want to go through them tomorrow, but I wanted you to have these objects today." The book was bound in crimson leather, with "Writings by Caroline Emmons" tooled in gold on the spine. Anne caressed the soft leather, as if it were her mother's hand.

"Oh, Father, how beautiful it is. I am sure she would be pleased. I will treasure it. It will accompany me on our journey." She opened the small box to see a simple gold cross, set with sapphires, on a chain. She glanced up at her father. "Your mother wore this on our wedding day. I have been saving it for this occasion."

Without a word, she removed the string of pearls and, lifting the chain from the box, she handed it to her father and turned her back so he could clasp it around her neck. Turning back to her mirror, she said softly, "Thank you, Father. It is perfect, and I am happy to wear something of hers on this special day."

They sat before the fire, sharing memories of Anne's childhood and his recollections of her mother's life. All too soon, there was a soft knock at the door. It really was time to go down. They rose, Anne placed her hand on her father's arm and they walked out the door and down the stairs.

They walked into the morning room in sunshine. Anne saw her dearest friends, her brother and, most importantly, Charles, waiting for her. Suddenly, her nervousness was gone, and she was filled with happiness and anticipation. Afterwards, she had no clear recollection of the ceremony. She knew that she and Charles spoke their responses clearly and confidently.

The signing of the register was a matter of moments, and she received her marriage lines with aplomb. Charles and Anne beamed as their friends hugged and congratulated; then the party moved from the morning room to the drawing room to greet the guests arriving for the breakfast.

As they exited, Anne pulled Charles aside. "A moment, my love," she said softly. He looked down at her in surprise. "Is something wrong, dearest?" She smiled. "No. I just wanted to tell you how much I love you. With you, I have found love and friendship, desire and companionship. I never expected such happiness." He held her close. "Nor did I, dearest. I have waited a very long time to hear you say that." He kissed her lightly and set her slightly away from him.

"I will have to save the rest for later, my heart." He smiled wickedly and continued, "A proper response to your statement requires more time than we have at this moment. We must join our friends." She blushed, as he put her hand on his arm. They entered the drawing room together. As Turner served them each a glass of champagne, Anne's father lifted his glass and said, "A toast to my daughter and my new son. Long life, health and happiness to you!"

Later that afternoon, after the breakfast ended and their guests had departed, Anne and Charles sat before the fire in her sitting room. "Your father has tickets for the opera tonight. Would it please you to attend?" Anne looked at him with a smile lurking in her eyes. "What is the opera?" she asked. "*The Marriage of Figaro,*" he replied. "Miss Stephens is singing." Anne laughed. "I think it would be delightful. Would you enjoy it?" He smiled back at her. "Well, it will be more pleasant than watching the clock, waiting for a suitable time to retire."

Anne blushed and laughed again, and he continued, "In all

seriousness, I believe he arranged this as a surprise for us, and has asked Lord and Lady Kidwell, with Fanny, Miss Crawford and Martin Burrell to join us. They will join us for dinner, then we will go to the theatre from here. I will insist, however, that you and I go on our own carriage. He mentioned going somewhere for supper afterwards, and I do not think my patience will stretch that far."

Anne reached for his hand and squeezed it. "Thank you, my love. My father loves to give one delightful surprises, but doesn't always realise that one might prefer to make one's own arrangements." He agreed feelingly.

Charles relaxed in his chair, gazing at her countenance. "It is wonderful being here alone with you. Our friends were most kind and supportive, but I am glad for a peaceful moment just now." She rose and walked to a table holding some decanters and two glasses. "May I pour you a restorative glass of sherry, my love? If you prefer, I can offer you some brandy or a glass of wine." He leaned his head back.

"Thank you, dearest. I would greatly appreciate a glass of wine." She poured a glass of burgundy for Charles and a small glass of sherry for herself. After giving him his glass, she resumed her seat and took a sip of sherry.

"Is your room satisfactory? At least, we have some privacy in this corridor. Did you need anything else?" Charles looked at her warmly. "I believe you and your father have thought of everything. My valet has unpacked what I will need for the next few nights, and is settled himself. When your father arranged these rooms for you, it was as if he had a plan." Anne nodded.

"I believe you are right. I would not say this to him, but I am delighted. He has worried about a marriage for me since I had my eighteenth birthday. I was so afraid he would push me into an arrangement based on an exchange of money for status. I should have known better. However, I cannot deny that he had his hopes, and I am sure the possibility was in his mind when he planned these rooms for my use. I did not think of it before today, but I am so happy now." Charles looked at her seriously.

"If you have any doubts about my feelings for you, or my reason for marrying you, I hope you will be honest with me, Anne. Tell me if you still have doubts." She looked at him thoughtfully.

"I have no doubts at all, Charles. You answered my question before, when I asked you why you wanted to marry me. Your reply was so beautifully simple and direct. I knew I loved you, but could not help but wonder, and you resolved my doubts completely. We are fortunate, Charles, to love and to know that love is returned. I did not expect to be so fortunate as to find a husband who combines the lover with the friend."

He put his arm around her. "There can be only one response to that statement." He pulled her close, and kissed her.

The evening flew by. Dinner was a masterpiece by Mrs. Clay, relished by all. The opera was delightful. Once seated in their rented box, Mr. Emmons announced that he had taken a private room at the Crown and Anchor in the Strand where he had ordered an elegant repast to enjoy afterwards. Charles stood firm in his decision to have a separate carriage for Anne and himself.

Over a chorus of objections, he and Anne drove back to Upper Brooke Street, while the rest of the party went on to have supper. Upon arriving upstairs, Charles escorted Anne to her sitting room. There, waiting for them, was a tray with several covered dishes, on the tea table with two chairs drawn up before the fire. Anne looked at Charles, and said, "You ordered supper for us." He nodded.

"I thought it would be pleasant to have our first supper as a married couple in private." She laughed and seated herself. Lifting lids, she discovered a delicate clear soup, her favourite fish pie, a dish of mushrooms, and a delicate peach jelly. Nestled in ice was a bottle of champagne. "My dear, how elegant!" she exclaimed. He opened the champagne. "After that breakfast and Mrs. Clay's lovely dinner, I did not want too much. I did not want to risk your falling asleep too soon." Anne blushed deeply as he put a glass of champagne in her hand.

Lifting his glass, he held her eyes with an intense gaze. "To you, my wife. This is a moment I have long wished for, and feared would never come." Her throat constricted and her eyes filled with tears. "To you, my husband," she whispered in response. Tearing her eyes away, she busied herself with serving the soup and cutting the pie. "There, my dear. Let us dine while it is still hot."

Conversation was desultory as they ate and sipped champagne. They had just finished when a maid came in to clear away the dishes and tray. When the door closed, Charles extended his hand to Anne to help her rise. "Shall we retire, my love?" he asked in a husky voice. She coloured but met his eyes frankly. "I will call Ellen...." He smiled. "You will not need a maid tonight, dearest."

Epilogue

Three Years Later...

Anne sat comfortably on a chair in the garden with her writing box on a table in front of her. She glanced up from her notes to glance around her. A beautiful morning in early June, the sun was warm and she appreciated the shade provided by the trees. Lily of the Valley and mint scented the air. She sniffed appreciatively. "His grandmother was right; it is a heavenly combination." She turned her attention back to her notes and wrote on, contentedly. As she pondered a new paragraph, she heard her name called.

"Anne!" called Fanny again. Anne rose and went forward to greet her friend. "Fanny, my dear, how wonderful to see you. Is Martin with you?" Fanny hugged Anne and said, "Yes, indeed, although not at this moment. He has business in Faversham. We are both home from London, and will be with my parents, of course, for the next several weeks at least." Anne looked at Fanny searchingly. "Are you well, dearest? I know your mother was anxious about leaving you in town. She must be delighted to have you safely in the country." Fanny laughed.

"My dear, I feel wonderful. The first few months were uncomfortable, but I am quite well, and full of energy." Relieved, Anne asked, "When is the baby expected to arrive?" Fanny laughed again. "It depends on who you ask. My mother is convinced that he or she won't arrive until September. My doctor in London is sure the event will occur in August or even July. It's hard to be certain, but the baby will arrive in its own good time."

Anne eyed her nervously. "Have you seen a doctor here?" Fanny nodded. "We arrived a few days ago, and my mother invited Doctor Doddington from Faversham to visit. He says I am fine and recommended a midwife to attend me. I must say, I prefer the idea of a woman assisting me with the business." Anne nodded. "How is Martin handling all of this?" Fanny shook her head. "He is excited, of course. He is convinced all will be well, and my mother's fussing worries him. He is very patient with her, but I was delighted that he had a reason to be from home today." Anne nodded.

"I understand that. My father was here last year, and it was a serious strain on poor Charles. You know how Father likes to take charge of a situation, and there was really nothing for him to do. And, it must be said that little Charlie was a bit... spotty, although he is delightful now. I was no end pleased when urgent business called Father back to London, and then home to York. He will come for a long visit later this summer, and I know he will enjoy it. Charles is almost looking forward to seeing him again." Fanny agreed. "One would never know about the spots now. Charlie is so round and smiles all of the time, I think. I am sure Charles will be recovered by now. Was Mr. Emmons called back to York concerning the Singapura business?" Anne nodded.

"Indeed. I do not know all the details. Father never discusses business with me, but Lydia mentioned some bits of information she got from Matthew. I think Father regrets not making the trip two years ago, but his representatives have handled things well. I believe there have been some excellent trade ventures, but they decided not to establish a banking office there, at least at this present. It seems to be still rather unsettled."

Fanny mulled it over. "Father was very interested in that business. I know he invested with Mr. Emmons, and he has been very pleased

311

with the results. Martin has also benefited from these opportunities. He is much less concerned about the disparities in our fortunes."

Anne squeezed her hand. "I am so glad. I know his disquietude worried you. At one time, I thought it might be years before you married!" Fanny laughed. "I know. It was hard, but I could not help but honour him. Do you remember Charles's scruples about approaching you, even after he cleared his debt to your father? They are similar in many ways, Charles and Martin. Both very scrupulous in their all of their dealings. We are fortunate." Anne nodded.

"Let us go up to the house, Fanny. I am sure that you would enjoy some refreshment, and an opportunity to put your feet up." The two young matrons strolled to the house, chatting all the while. As they entered through a glass door to the morning room, Fanny gazed around.

"How much brighter it looks, Anne! What a lovely room! It has a feeling of the morning room in London." Anne glanced around. "It only needed a little attention. The lighter walls help, and I ordered new cushions and upholstery. A good cleaning and polishing made an enormous difference. His mother and grandmother had lovely taste. There are beautiful things here; one just could not see them." Lowering her voice, she went on.

"A few changes in staff were needed, and I am afraid one was the housekeeper. She had grown accustomed to checking only on the rooms used by the gentlemen of the family; the morning room and drawing room had gotten into a sorry state. Fortunately, she decided to retire, and her daughter has taken over the household, and is doing wonderfully well. She has an eye for detail that Mrs. Hubbard would approve."

She gestured Fanny to the *chaise longue*, set her writing box on a table, and seated herself in a comfortable chair near the open door after ringing the bell. "I will order some refreshments. Would you prefer tea or some lemonade? It is rather warm today." Fanny put her feet up with a sigh of relief. "Lemonade would be lovely."

A maid came in and curtseyed. "Some lemonade and some of those little cakes Mrs. Andrews made this morning, please, Mary." She turned back to Fanny. "Is there any new gossip in town, Fanny?" Fanny shook her head. "Not at this present, fortunately. It is quiet now, as so many people have left. Martin has been so busy lately and I have been more at home." Sobering, she continued.

"Martin is much concerned over political matters. He sees more and more need for reform. We speak of it at home between ourselves, but it is hard to have a rational conversation in public." Anne asked, "How does Lord Kidwell stand?" Fanny rose with some difficulty and placed her glass on the table.

"He has been loyal to the party, but sees that change must and will come. Many fear a revolt, like that in France. Martin and my father both believe that reform will prevent that. There is great concern about the possibility of violence." Anne nodded. "My father has indicated his concern as well. Some of his clients are manufactory owners. However, Father also sees the needs of workers and their families. It is one reason he supports my efforts with schools. It is a very difficult time for so many." Fanny shivered.

"I am glad to be away from town just now, I confess. Let us talk of something more cheerful. How are Robert and Diana?" Anne brightened. "They are very well indeed. Little Caroline is thriving and baby Amabel is in leading strings. You know Robert has accepted a living." Fanny, surprised, replied, "No. When did that happen?" Anne smiled.

"I have been remiss. It happened about a year ago. Several years ago, an estate came into my father's possession, which included the advowson of a living. There was an incumbent in the church so Father felt no need to do anything about it at the time. He let the previous owner's widow continue to live in the manor for a token rent until her death. The house had been leased until last year, and tenant farmers are working the estate lands. The last tenant for the house moved out. Recently, the incumbent expressed a desire to retire due to poor health, and Father asked Robert if he knew of anyone who would be interested. It seems Robert had been thinking about making a change since little Anne's christening. He and Robert went to see the Dean, who spoke to the Archbishop, and Robert was allowed to accept the living. He and Diana have moved into the manor house on the estate. They seem to be very happy there."

She took another sip of lemonade, and refilled Fanny's and her own glass. "They are close to York, so they can spend time with Father and with Diana's aunt and uncle." Fanny smiled. "It sounds quite perfect. But do they enjoy living in the country?" Anne nodded. "I asked Diana that question myself. Apparently the village is an easy walk from the manor, and she is getting to know the people there. The former rector is still there in the rectory. He and his wife have no family and nowhere to go, and a small income. Robert and Diana do not need the house, and Robert has consulted him on numerous matters. It seems to benefit all." The two went on to chat of other matters. Charles entered unexpectedly.

"Anne, my dear, have you seen....?" He stopped. "Fanny! How delightful to see you. When did you arrive? I do hope Martin accompanies you." Fanny laughed. "Indeed, he does. We arrived yesterday. He is in Faversham on business today, but will stop here to collect me. We are to dine with my mother and father, of course." Charles smiled. "You must all come to us very soon. It has been too long since we have enjoyed your company." He turned to Anne,

"Dear heart, I was going to ask you if you knew where I put some papers, but it has come to me." Dropping a quick kiss on her lips, he murmured, "I really came in search of just that." and departed. Anne and Fanny continued their conversation, enjoying the cool lemonade. After a short time, Fanny rose to take a turn about the room.

"I don't know how it is, but I can't seem to be comfortable for long in any position." Anne nodded sympathetically. "I do understand. By the time I was in the last few weeks with Charlie, I felt as though I could hardly breathe. Would you like to stroll in the shrubbery for a bit? It is shady and cooler at this time of day." The two were walking to the door, when the sounds of arrival became audible.

Anne lifted a finger. "I do believe we have a caller." Martin appeared before them, smiling. He sketched a bow to Anne. "No need to ask how you are, my dear Anne. You are blooming!" He looked at Fanny with concern.

"And how are you, dearest?" Fanny grimaced slightly. "It is hard to be comfortable, as you already know, my love." He smiled sympathetically. "Would you like to go home, dearest?" Fanny sighed. "I think it would be best, Martin." She turned to Anne and said, "I am sorry, my dear, but I think I should go now. Pray, forgive me. I hope you can come for tea soon. I will have Mama write to let you know when for you all to come and dine."

Anne hugged her. "No apology is necessary, dear. I understand completely." She murmured, "I suggest you change into *dishabille* immediately you arrive. Removing those stays will help." Fanny burst into giggles.

Anne was strolling in the shrubbery a short time later, when Charles came to find her. Drawing her hand through his arm, he said, "Here you are, love! I have been looking for you." Anne gave his arm a squeeze. "Martin came and took Fanny home. She was feeling fatigued, and will be more comfortable at home." Sobering, Charles asked, "Did she mention Kate at all?" Anne shook her head.

"No, and I did not bring up the subject. She knows that Kate has died, but I do not know if she knows the circumstances. Poor Kate never fully recovered her strength, and this last miscarriage was just too much. Fanny should not dwell on those matters now while she is in the last stages of her own pregnancy. I am sure that she wrote to Kate's mother and father to express her sympathies. Time enough later for her to find out the particulars. Fanny's mother is adamant about Fanny being kept as cheerful as possible; that is why she is so happy that Fanny has left London and come home. Lady

Kidwell was on tenterhooks lest Fanny discover all." Charles nodded his agreement.

"Have you heard from Emily?" Anne smiled. "Indeed, just yesterday, I received a long letter. She is quite content with her Richard. She said that he has been a tower of strength. After Kate's sad end, Richard arranged for Mrs. DeWitt to visit Leamington Priory. He took a house for her, and she is still there with a companion and a nurse. She takes the waters every day, and finally can sleep without resorting to laudanum. Mr. DeWitt is staying with Emily and Richard and visits his wife every few days. Emily limits her calls, as her mother finds her presence rather disturbing."

Charles frowned. "How very sad. What about Kate's husband and children?" Anne sighed. "After Kate's death, Mrs. DeWitt blamed him for everything. Before Emily and Mr. DeWitt took Mrs. DeWitt away, she and Kate's husband had a dreadful row. At this present, he will not allow her near the children, although Emily, Richard and Mr. DeWitt are welcome to see them. Emily hopes that this stay at Leamington Priory will help restore the tone of her mother's mind so she can try to repair her relationship with her son-in-law." Charles shook his head.

"A bad business. How is Emily herself, and Richard?" As they sauntered down the path, she said, "Apart from her sorrow for Kate, and the difficulties with her mother, Emily is very happy indeed. She and her Richard are both well, as is their little girl. Although she finds Coventry rather unattractive, she enjoys the pageants held there very much, especially the Godiva pageant, and they have attended the balls at the Drapers Hall. They live outside the town, but near enough to take part in the various entertainments there. You remember the beautiful clock that she and Richard sent for our wedding gift? That was made by a clock and watchmaker there in the town. They go to his London house periodically, usually to visit Mr. and Mrs. DeWitt. Her mother does not care to visit Emily in Coventry, although Mr. DeWitt manages to spend time with her and Richard as often as possible." Charles sighed. "It is sad that her family has fallen into such unhappy times."

Changing the subject, Charles said, "I heard from your brother Matthew today. He wrote that Lydia and the children are all well, and he has hopes they will manage a visit this summer. He also mentioned your friend's husband, Hugh Heron. It seems he has done very well for your father's business, and his practice is growing."

Anne nodded. "Jane is so pleased. He has taken offices near Emmons & Son, which gives them more space in the house. She misses York and her parents, but now feels at home in Leeds." Charles suggested, "Mayhap we could invite Mr. and Mrs. Heron to come to us when your brother and his wife will be here? Would that be a pleasant party?"

Anne considered. "I know I would find it so. The real issue is whether Lydia will find an acceptable date for such a journey." She smiled slightly. "You may recall, dearest, the number of times they were expected, only to have Matthew cry off because Lydia could not undertake it for one reason or another. She is very sweet and has been an excellent wife to Matthew, but it is very difficult to pry her away from her home."

Charles laughed. "I do remember." He thought for a moment. "Little Walter will be eight years old this year, will he not? Do they have plans to send him to school?" Anne chuckled.

"Father and Matthew have been discussing it. I believe Matthew would like to send him, as he thinks the boy would benefit from the discipline. However, Lydia won't hear of it. I will say, Amelia helped them find a tutor who has been working with young Walter for a year now, and he has made great strides with the boy's studies and behaviour. I do not believe it will hurt to wait a year or two before sending him away to school." Charles smiled sympathetically. Continuing their discussion of family, they traced their steps back to the house.

Anne and Charles dined cosily at one end of the long table in the dining room. As there was no company, dinner was served in one course. "Asparagus soup!" exclaimed Charles. "I have not had that in some time. It has long been my favourite." Anne smiled. They chatted lightly as the rest of the meal was served. Anne was toying with some peach jelly (from Mrs. Clay's receipts) while Charles enjoyed his third lemon cheesecake when he said, "I am sorry, my dearest, but I must go over some papers after dinner. It may take some time, as they include some financial records." Anne nodded.

"I understand, my love. I believe I will go straight up to my sitting room. I have some work that requires attention." She finished her jelly, and rose. Dropping a kiss on the top of his head, she left the room. Anne chuckled to herself over Charles's delight in the asparagus soup; she had advised the cook weeks ago of Charles's preference and requested that the soup be served at the earliest opportunity. She picked up her writing box, and then went upstairs. She stopped at the nursery to say good night to little Charlie. He was fresh from his bath when she took him from his nurse and sat down in a chair near the fire.

She hummed songs from her own childhood as she cuddled him close. When he finally slept, she put him down in his cradle and smoothed his shining dark hair. Smiling at the nurse, she went on her way to her sitting room. Opening the door, she paused to gaze around the room. Leaving the door ajar, she entered and walked slowly across the room. She loved every inch of it, from the palest blue silk-hung walls to the white painted woodwork surrounding her.

She went to her desk, smoothed the polished mahogany desk top and put her writing box down carefully. When Charles had first brought her home, the walls and the white painted shelves were waiting for her. Charles gave her *carte blanche* to select furnishings from the house, or to order new. She roamed the house for days, learning her way around and finding forgotten treasures. Everything she needed was there.

She found a beautiful carpet in a deep blue, with medallions of flowers in lighter shades of blue, lavender and rose. The small settee was recovered in rose damask, and two armchairs now flanking the fireplace were carefully cleaned as the tapestry covers toned beautifully with the carpet, walls and settee. She found the desk in a small forgotten room on the third floor. The wood was dull and the gilded trim tarnished, but a thorough cleaning and polishing had brought it back to life. The painting her father sent hung over the mantle.

Anne browsed the bookshelves, noticing how well her books from York fitted the shelves. Her display cases rested on a table in front of a window. Recently ordered volumes were bound in similar blue leather with her new initials on the binding. She smiled as she caressed the soft leather. She carried the selected volume over to the desk and sat down. Lying on the desk were several letters. She selected the first, and opened it.

Mr. Chamberlayne wrote that her novel had had a modest success in London and was doing well in Bath and in York. They had recouped all expenses and, if sales continued, they may need a second printing. He mentioned that her pamphlet had continued to sell also. He then enquired about the progress on her second novel. The rest of his letter consisted of family news and enquiries after her health and happiness. Smiling again, she laid it aside to answer later.

She picked up a note from Lady Jersey. Apparently, Lady Jersey was feeling better, although still nervous about the upcoming birth of her next child. The four boys were all well, as was Lord Jersey. She hoped to be fully recovered in time for the season, and expected to see Anne in London then. She laid Lady Jersey's note aside with Mr. Chamberlayne's letter.

Anne opened her writing box and pulled out her notes. Reading through them, she found her place, picked up her pencil and began to write. Anne had added another chapter and had jotted down some notes for the next, when she heard Charles in the hall. She raised her head as he pushed open the door. He came across the room, pulled her up from her chair into his arms. He kissed her slowly and thoroughly.

Holding her close, he sighed and said, "I needed that, my heart. There is nothing so tiresome as going through ledgers and searching out documents to support the figures. I am finally caught up, and refuse to think about business matters any further tonight." She pulled away slightly, and caressed his cheek.

"Come sit down, my love, and I will pour you a glass of wine." He sat by the fire in one of the tapestry arm chairs, whilst she walked to a table holding a couple of decanters. After pouring claret for Charles, she poured sherry for herself, carried both glasses back and handed Charles his. Seating herself across from him, she smiled and raised her glass in a little salute. "I am glad you have things in order; I know how you dislike it when your ledgers and records are not current." He sipped his claret and asked, "And your business, my dear?"

She said, "I spent some time in the nursery with Charlie, then read some letters. I have a few invoices, which I will pay tomorrow. Lady Jersey is feeling more the thing and begins to look a bit forward, even though she is still very nervous. I believe, after four boys, she hopes for a girl. Mr. Chamberlayne is very pleased as the novel is still selling, and mentioned a possible second printing. He wanted to know how the next one is progressing,"

Charles rested his head against the back of the chair and queried, "And how is it progressing?" Seriously, she replied. "You must know, my love, that I am a rather slow and deliberate writer. However, I am pleased so far. Today, I wrote another chapter, and made a quantity of notes for the next. I believe this one may run to three volumes." He drained his glass.

"It appears that we have both had a measure of success today, dearest." She smiled, and sipped the last of her sherry. "Indeed we have, my husband." He rose to his feet and went to the door. Looking back at her with a glint in his eyes, he said, "I can think of a very ... satisfying way to conclude a successful day, my heart." Holding his gaze, Anne rose, put down her glass, and crossed the room to join him. Hand in hand, they closed the door behind them.

THE END

PGXL3520USA